Julie Anne Li... ...o was ...ce torn betwe... ...enres: ...e-curling roma... Now ...e gets to write... ...When ...he's not creatin... Julie can be found ...arpooling her thr... ...ids around northeastern Ohio and ...lotting with her shamelessly enabling friends. Winner ...f the Daphne du Maurier Award for Excellence in ...ystery/Suspense, Julie is a member of International ...hriller Writers, Romance Writers of America and ...sters in Crime. Learn more about Julie and her books ...julieannelindsey.com

...ustine Davis lives on Puget Sound in Washington State, ...atching big ships and the occasional submarine go by ...d sharing the neighbourhood with assorted wildlife, ...cluding a pair of bald eagles, deer, a bear or two, and a ...illess raccoon. In the few hours when she's not ...anning, plotting or writing her next book, her favourite ...ings are photography, knitting her way through a huge ...arn stash and driving her restored 1967 Corvette ...oadster—top down, of course. Connect with Justine on her ...ebsite, justinedavis.com, at Twitter.com/justine_d_davis ...r on Facebook at Facebook.com/justinedaredavis.

ACCIDENTAL WITNESS

JULIE ANNE LINDSEY

COLTON'S DANGEROUS REUNION

JUSTINE DAVIS

MIX
Paper from
responsible sources
FSC
FSC C007454

This book is produced from independently certified FSC™
paper to ensure responsible forest management

For more information visit www.harpercollins.co.uk/green

MILLS & BOON

First Published in Great Britain 2022
by Mills & Boon, an imprint of HarperCollins*Publishers* Ltd
1 London Bridge Street, London, SE1 9GF

www.harpercollins.co.uk

HarperCollins*Publishers*
1st Floor, Watermarque Building,
Ringsend Road, Dublin 4, Ireland

Accidental Witness © 2022 Julie Anne Lindsey
Colton's Dangerous Reunion © 2022 Harlequin Books S.A.

Special thanks and acknowledgement are given to Justine Davis for her contribution to the *The Coltons of Colorado* series.

ISBN: 978-0-263-30335-3

ACCIDENTAL WITNESS

JULIE ANNE LINDSEY

For Jen Jen

Chapter One

Jen Jordan adjusted her six-month-old son, D.J., in the baby sling across her chest, as she moved through the Crestwood Kentucky Community Center. Her days as a swim coach had transitioned to evenings as a swim instructor when Dylan Jr. was born, but she didn't miss the coaching, not when she had a perfect cherub-faced little swimmer of her own to care for. She and D.J. had just wrapped another eight-week set of Water Babies lessons, a small mommy-and-me-style class designed to help parents and their up-to-two-years-old children relax and bond. And Jen was ready to celebrate.

Her phone exploded with the pops and dings of waiting messages, texts and notifications as she exited the old stone building, populating with news of everything she'd missed while in the pool and locker room.

She dialed her roommate, Madison, on her way through the lobby. Madison hadn't answered Jen's calls before class, but their shared location-tracking app had suggested she was at the park, a place she often went to think. She supposed Madison had gotten lost in a good book, or an enthralling run, but the sun was setting now, and Madison should be home. With a little luck, she hadn't already eaten, because Jen planned to treat tonight.

"What should we get for dinner?" she asked D.J. as she waited for the call to connect.

D.J. cooed and blew spit bubbles, clearly happy with whatever the adults decided. He'd be as thrilled with tonight's bottle as every one before it. His chubby arms and dimpled fists pumped cheerfully as she tousled his curly brown hair.

Her call to Madison went to voice mail.

Maybe she was in the shower.

Jen unlocked her car and strapped her son safely into his rear-facing car seat, enjoying the warm summer breeze across her cheek and in her still-damp hair. "If Auntie Maddie doesn't answer soon, Mommy's choosing pad Thai," she told him, then dropped a flurry of kisses over his cheeks, nose and forehead until he laughed.

She slipped into the driver's seat and locked the doors, then checked her phone once more. She and Madison had downloaded a tracking app for friends months ago, when Jen was still pregnant and constantly feared something might happen to her or her baby. She'd worried daily that some bizarre, unforeseen tragedy would strike while she was out somewhere alone. The app had made her feel as if, whatever happened, Madison could find her. The heightened paranoia was, no doubt, a side effect of losing her fiancé, Dylan, and Madison's husband, Bob, only months prior. The men had been victims of a roadside bomb shortly after leaving their military base in Afghanistan. Both soldiers had been due home, permanently, this summer. If things had gone differently, Jen and Dylan would've been planning their wedding right now, and Madison would be celebrating her fifth anniversary with Bob. But life had a way of turning everything upside down. Dylan Jr. was proof of that. She hadn't even realized she was pregnant until after the funeral. So she'd spent most of her unexpected pregnancy afraid of when the next tragedy would strike, and certain she couldn't withstand another loss.

Thankfully, Madison had been a good sport about the app, and they'd used it frequently for fun things, like impromptu outings, meals and meetups.

Jen frowned at the phone, then stared through her windshield at the twilight settling over the town. According to the app, Madison was still at the park, but why? Madison was the first person to lecture Jen about the dangers of being out alone after dark, even knowing Jen could take care of herself. She was right, of course, because basic self-defense had its limits. Especially if an attacker was armed, or erratic, and thanks to a new street drug in the community, crime was on the rise.

If Madison was ten years younger, and not grieving the loss of her husband, Jen might've suspected she'd met someone and didn't want to say goodbye. But that wasn't the case, and when Jen returned her gaze to her phone, the little avatar representing Madison disappeared.

She tapped the screen, then closed and reopened the app, but nothing changed. Either Madison had uninstalled the app, or her phone was powered off. Neither seemed reasonable. Though it was possible, Jen supposed, that her friend's phone battery had died.

An odd bolt of intuition and fear stilled her breaths and limbs, then her heart began to race. She dialed Madison again, set the phone in her car's cup holder, then shifted into Drive. The park wasn't far from the community center. She could be there in ten minutes or less, if traffic cooperated.

This time the call went directly to voice mail. As it would if the phone's battery was dead. She blew out a long breath and tried to loosen her grip on the wheel, but it was too late. The possibility Madison was in danger, no matter how unlikely, was more than Jen could stand. She'd relax when she knew her friend was safe, and not a moment sooner.

She raced across town at five miles above the posted speed limit, careful to avoid lanes with turning cars and slow drivers. She redialed Madison at every red light and stop sign along the way. Each with the same result. Voice mail.

Wherever Madison was, if her phone was dead, she still hadn't plugged it in.

Jen hit the turn signal and piloted her little sedan through the park's entrance only eight minutes after leaving work. The lot was empty, the lawns, playgrounds and ball fields devoid of people. Her nerves were strung impossibly tight. She'd told herself not to panic, that the emotions she felt were a result of residual grief and trauma, nothing more. But instinct clawed at her.

No, she told herself. She and Madison didn't live in a war zone. There weren't any roadside bombs or looming enemies. There were museums and parks. Libraries and restaurants. Recent drug-related incidents aside, Crestwood was a great place to live.

She lowered the volume on the radio as she drove through the small rectangular parking area, thankful Madison's car wasn't abandoned in one of the spaces.

Another tally in her mental column of reasons *not* to suspect she'd been abducted.

Unless Madison had walked or jogged to the park. If so, it wouldn't have been the first time, even this week.

Jen powered her window down and scanned the silent area, unwilling to park or get out at night with D.J. When no one came into view, she drove on, navigating the long narrow access road to an old carousel where Madison liked to sit and read.

Her senses stayed on high alert as gravel crunched, impossibly loud, beneath her tires. The sliver of cloud-covered moon in a bruised indigo sky did nothing to help her search.

The carousel creaked and rattled with a heavy gust of July wind when she drew near. The attraction was historic and normally busy until ten o'clock on summer weekends, but a stalled restoration project had put an end to that for now. And at the moment, the usually whimsical ride, with its bridled horses and mirrored accents, seemed more like something from a nightmare than a fairy tale. Even the park itself seemed to have taken on a sinister vibe. Funny how something so beautiful by day could seem so entirely foreboding at nightfall.

Jen nudged the gas pedal and concentrated on projecting her voice, without alarming anyone who might be nearby. "Madison?"

The world was eerily silent, filled with the reaching limbs and creeping shadows of ancient leafy trees. An erratic security light flickered and buzzed overhead, raising the fine hairs on the back of her neck and arms to attention. The shape of a dark sedan was barely visible beyond the light, obscured so effectively by shadow she wasn't completely sure what she saw. Who would park back here at this hour and why? Teens making out? Something stolen and abandoned? She swallowed hard and hoped the reason wasn't anything more heinous.

"Madison?" she tried again, feeling the sudden lightning bolt of certainty that something was truly wrong. She strained her eyes against the suffocating night, willing her friend to appear, then dialed her number once more before finally turning the car around. The call, again, went to voice mail.

She idled another moment, accessing the texts and messages she'd missed while in the community center's cement dungeon of a pool and locker room. She'd thought to do so earlier, before Madison's avatar had disappeared and redirected her thoughts. No voice mails. A ton of spam emails. And a single missed text.

Madison: Don't go home. Wait for my call.

The text had been sent nearly two hours ago.

The sharp crack of breaking twigs pulled her attention to the space beyond the carousel, where a figure had stepped into view. For one brief moment, she imagined it was Madison, and in the next she understood it was not. A large dark silhouette moved in her direction, too broad and tall to be her friend.

The long determined strides of the stranger made it clear he was coming for Jen, not simply headed her way. And as he passed beneath the flickering security light, his balaclava became perfectly visible. As did his gun.

She jerked the shifter into Reverse and pressed the gas pedal with purpose, putting space between her car, her baby and the figure.

Her heart cried out for Madison's safety, knowing this couldn't be a coincidence. The app had said Madison was here, and now she was gone, a masked gun-man in her place.

He stilled in the flickering light as she piloted her little car away.

Chapter Two

Jefferson County Deputy Sheriff, Knox Winchester, fell onto his desk chair with a low growl. Frustrated, exhausted and hungry, he'd already worked an hour beyond his shift, and thanks to the new street drug, MX-10, which had been wreaking havoc on his town, he still had paperwork to complete.

He glared at his watch, then forced himself to sit taller and get started. The sooner he finished, the sooner he could leave. And a week of vacation awaited him on the other side of the sheriff's department door. He was well beyond due for that break and damn ready.

Knox rolled his shoulders, trying and failing to alleviate the knots of tension in the bunched muscles of his neck and back. He needed to go for a run or hit the gym, anything to shed the weight he'd carried away from his last stop of the day. A death scene more tragic than most, and one that was sure to haunt him the rest of his days.

He dutifully began to write as images of MX-10's most recent victim returned to him. Today, the casualty had been a young mother of three small children. She was barely twenty, and living in a small run-down apartment, when she'd overdosed. Her sons, a three-, two-and one-year-old, had been left without care for days before a neighbor finally responded to the crying. The older woman found the body and called the sheriff's department.

The home was a wreck. The kids were filthy and hungry. The preschooler had been feeding his siblings peanut butter and water, waiting for Mommy to wake up. It was a wonder the children had survived. Knox couldn't imagine what those few days would do to the oldest boy as he grew. The other two were unlikely to remember the specifics, though Knox suspected the experience would linger somewhere inside them as they aged. And he didn't dare think of what their lives had been like leading up to Mom's final dose.

Knox groaned, angry and heartsick, pushing the images from his mind, demanding himself to finish the job and claim his hard-earned time off.

An hour later, he felt the weight of the burden lift. He stretched onto his feet, finished with the day and his work, then headed into the hallway. He bypassed the door to the gym, only interested in getting home, taking off his uniform and hitting the shower. At twenty-seven and single on a Friday night, he had the wild plans of a man twice his age, and he was utterly eager to get started. Tonight, there would be steak, cooked and enjoyed on his rear deck beneath the stars. Perfectly scored, thanks to the new gas grill he'd splurged on last spring. Nature. Solitude. Steak. A perfect trifecta.

He slung his duffel bag onto one shoulder and took a deep breath as he headed out, feeling the weight of exhaustion on his mood and limbs. He unbuttoned his uniform shirt at the collar and quickened his pace. A moment later, the lobby came into view, and he raised his hand in goodbye to the intake desk, where Deputy Riley spoke to a beautiful but thoroughly upset woman with a baby.

Knox turned away quickly and kept his eyes on the sliver of moonlight outside the glass double doors. People had problems all the time. Even pretty people with babies. And he would be back to help in nine days.

Right now, he was twenty feet from freedom.

"I need to see Knox Winchester," the woman said, pulling Knox up short.

He slowed to take another look at the woman.

Her cheeks were red and tearstained. Her breaths came in frantic bursts.

Her baby kicked merrily from his position in a sling around her torso.

"I'm sorry," Riley replied, sliding his gaze quickly to Knox, then back. "Deputy Winchester's shift ended hours ago, but I can get someone else to help you."

The woman's shoulders sagged and she nodded. "I called emergency dispatch on my way here. I asked them to look for my friend and a man with a gun at Carousel Park. Can you tell me if they found them?"

Riley's brows rose slightly. "There's a man with a gun in the park?"

Knox released a defeated sigh, turned on his heels and headed back across the lobby, away from his vacation. "I can take it from here," he told the other deputy, offering a tired but appreciative smile. Riley had tried to let him escape, but what else could be done now?

And Knox was more than a little intrigued by the idea this woman somehow knew him. Or had at least been instructed to ask for him.

The woman's mouth opened, then closed, clearly

stunned to see him, despite the fact she'd requested him by name.

He extended a hand in her direction and their gazes met. "I'm—" The words lodged in his throat as a strange familiarity zinged in his tired mind.

"I know," she said, ignoring his offered hand. "You probably don't remember me."

"I remember you," he said, the words nearly landing on top of hers. The flash of images and emotions that hit next were so intense they might've doubled him over if he wasn't suddenly frozen. The fresh swell of grief stole his breath. Memories of the day they'd met took him right back to the moment. She'd worn a black dress and blank expression. She'd been sullen and silent. He'd wanted to introduce himself and tell her he'd loved Dylan too, but she'd kept vanishing, like a ghost in the crowd. Then he'd stepped outside at Dylan's mother's house during the wake, overwrought when Dylan's dad had broken down in tears. And she'd been there.

Knox had stolen a bottle of whiskey from the make-shift bar near the kitchen, then wandered onto the porch. Jen was sitting on the back steps, staring at nothing and drinking red wine from the bottle. The instant camaraderie had anchored him. And when she'd smiled at something he'd said, he was certain they would get through their loss. If a smile was still possible, on a day like that, then he supposed anything was.

How long ago had that been, exactly? *A year now*, he thought. Maybe a month or two more.

His gaze dropped to the baby, and he recalled her with the wine. Had she been pregnant that day? She'd been sick. He'd had to convince her to eat something when she'd started to look peaked and green. They'd assumed the nausea was a result of the awful day, and alcohol on an empty stomach, but the boy's brown curls and dark round eyes told another story. Jen hadn't gotten pregnant after Dylan's death. That was Dylan's child in her arms.

Dylan Stark had been Knox's bunkmate for two years while he'd finished his time in the US army. Dylan had been fairly new. They'd been like brothers. Then Knox had returned to civilian life and become a deputy. Three years later, Dylan had died senselessly during a routine outing with Bob Cramer in the seat Knox had once occupied.

"It's been a while," he said, controlling his tone and emotion, as well as watching his words. She was clearly spooked, and had said something about a gunman.

She wet her lips, and her eyes glistened with unshed tears. "Fourteen months. This is D.J."

"Dylan Jr.?" he asked, rhetorically, the answer blatantly obvious.

She nodded again, and a tear swiveled over her cheek. "Please help me."

"Of course. Tell me everything." He dropped his duffel, crossed his arms and widened his stance, offering 100 percent of his attention.

Her thin fingers curled protectively around the baby tucked against her chest. "There was a man with a gun at the park. I called emergency services on my way here because my roommate isn't answering her phone, and according to an app we share, she was at the carousel only a few minutes before I saw him. Two hours before that, she sent me a text, telling me not to go home, but I didn't get that message until I'd seen the gunman."

"Any signs of her at the park?" he asked.

"No."

Knox looked to Riley, who returned the desk phone's handset to its receiver. "Any word?"

"I just spoke to Deputy Lee," Riley said. "They swept the park near the carousel. No signs of a gunman or the woman."

"Thanks," Knox said. He tipped his head toward the long hallway he'd just walked. Then led Jen to his desk and offered her a bottle of water. He listened carefully as she set out the facts for him. Bob's wife, Madison, was her missing roommate. Knox hadn't known Bob, but his friendship with Dylan spoke volumes about his character. Dylan had had high expectations and inflexible moral standards for himself and the people around him.

"All right," he said, as comfortingly as he could manage, after her official report was made. "How about I follow you home. We'll see if it looks like anyone's been there and decide what to do next."

Jen's eyes were distant as she stroked her baby's chubby arm and dimpled hand. When she dragged her attention back to him, resolve had formed there. "Okay."

Twenty minutes later, Knox parked his truck beside Jen's sedan outside a row of newly developed apartments a few blocks from downtown. There hadn't been any signs of Madison or a shooter at the park, and Knox could only hope that was good news. Perhaps the man with a gun had been a random criminal looking for an easy target this time of evening, and Madison's phone had simply died. Maybe the man hadn't had a gun at all. It was dark, and Jen had been frightened when she saw him. Maybe the fear and shadows had given a completely normal situation an ominous tilt.

He re-buttoned his uniform shirt and abandoned his dreams of relaxation and steak, then put his deputy sheriff hat back on, figuratively and literally. "Here we go," he told himself, climbing out of his truck. Hopefully, Madison was in better shape than the last woman whose home he'd visited.

He rounded the hood in Jen's direction, shoulders back and jaw set. "Which one is yours?"

Jen's cheeks were ruddy once more as she locked her car and met him on the sidewalk with her son. "Two A."

Knox led the way, easily navigating the unfamiliar building. He stopped several feet before their destination, when her apartment came into view. The door was partially open, and a visible mess waited inside.

Chapter Three

Jen's breath caught. Her heart raced and ears rang. The apartment door was open, and from what she could see, hiding behind Knox in the hallway, her home had been ransacked. Thoughts of the masked gunman collided with memories of Madison's text. Panic twisted in her core as she imagined what might've happened inside. An endless stream of ugly and terrifying possibilities weakened her knees.

Knox bent his elbow and raised one fist, silently indicating she should stay where she was. Then he removed the gun from his holster and entered her apartment with the stealth and confidence of a man who'd done this before.

Jen bounced gently, rocking her son and attempting to burn off the energy produced by misplaced adrenaline. She counted silently to measure the passage of time, and sent up endless, fervent pleas that Madison was inside. Safe and alive.

The hope seemed almost childish. Definitely illogical and unreasonable. If Madison were inside, she would've called the sheriff's department herself when an intruder came to the door. If she were okay, the door wouldn't be standing partly open. And if she were home, why had the app said she was at the park?

Had the home already been ransacked when Madison sent the text in warning? Or did she have a reason to suspect it might be?

Jen shook the thought away. How could anyone know in advance their home would be broken into? And if she'd known, why hadn't she called the sheriff's department?

Distant shuffling sounds turned her attention back to the open door. Knox had been inside too long, and she didn't want to be alone in the hallway anymore. She stepped carefully forward, crossing the threshold, prepared to deal with whatever awaited on the other side.

From her new position, she could see across the expanse of her open-concept home. A change from carpet to tile separated the dinette from the living room. Beyond that, an island delineated the dinette from the kitchen. Jen's old desk stood against one wall in the living room and acted as a communal work space. Jen had moved her desk months ago to make room for D.J.'s crib. Madison had another small desk in her room. A hall along the wall with the front door led to the bedrooms and a shared bath.

Knox's voice carried to her ears, speaking quickly on what seemed to be a phone call, presumably to the sheriff's department.

D.J. fussed, and her arms curled tenderly over him. She kissed his head and whispered sweetly, attempting to mask the anxiety and fear pouring off her.

Knox appeared in the hall outside her bedroom a moment later, missing a beat before continuing back to her side. "You aren't where I left you," he said, his gun safely back in its holster.

Jen's shoulders crept upward, towed by tension. "Any signs of Madison?"

"No, but someone's clearly been here."

Around her, the apartment's condition began to take focus. Papers from her desk were scattered over the floor, but her new monitor was still in place. The couch had been taken apart, cushions tossed, along with her grandmother's afghan, yet the television remained. Her kitchen drawers and cabinets stood open. The pantry contents had been thoroughly toppled, but Madison's phone dock, portable speaker and wireless earbuds were untouched on the countertop. "I don't think anything's missing," she said, the words creaking from her throat.

Nothing, except Madison.

"There aren't any signs of forced entry, and it doesn't seem like a robbery," he agreed, eyes skimming the scene. "No distinctive signs of a struggle," he said, setting broad palms over narrow hips. "My best guess is that someone was looking for something."

"What could anyone possibly want from us?" She nearly laughed at the thought. Everything she and Madison had of value was either still in sight or at the bank, not that either of their accounts were especially impressive. "Could the intruder have been looking for cash or credit cards?"

"Maybe," Knox said, turning sharp green eyes back on her. "I called the station. I'm officially on vacation, so other deputies will make the report and handle the crime scene. I won't leave unless you ask me. Meanwhile, I'd like to talk to your neighbors, see if anyone saw or heard anything."

D.J. squirmed against Jen's chest, and she willed herself to remain calm.

"Okay." She moved to the kitchen and sat at the small table, unloading the bottle and formula from D.J.'s diaper bag. It was time to feed her baby, but she didn't dare touch anything unnecessarily until she was told it wouldn't interfere with whatever the deputies needed to do. If there was a clue in the apartment that would lead them to Madison's location, she wanted to be sure Knox or the other deputies would find it.

He moved toward the door. "Will you be okay here, if I step out for a few?"

She nodded. "I'll try calling her phone again."

"Good." He looked down the hall in each direction, then back to Jen. "Do you have a building manager? Someone who overlooks the property?"

She poured premeasured formula into a bottle already filled with water, then gave D.J.'s next meal a shake. "Mrs. Hancock is on our floor," she said, forcing her tone to sound stronger than she felt. "Apartment 2K at the end of the hall."

Knox walked out, pulling the door shut behind him, and her shoulders slumped in response.

She lifted D.J. from the sling and kissed his head, then rested him in the crook of her arm and offered the bottle. His dark brows furrowed as he watched her, sensing her tension, even as he eagerly accepted the meal. "It's okay," she whispered, more to herself than him. "Aunt Maddie will be okay."

Jen needed that to be true more than she'd needed anything in a long time. Madison had been through too much already. It wasn't fair for her to have to endure this too. Whatever this was.

She set her phone on the table and dialed her friend once more.

Voice mail.

Knox returned a few moments later, speaking her name as he knocked, probably so she wouldn't jump out of her skin. She rose on wooden legs to let him in.

"No one answered at the manager's place," he said, bypassing a traditional, though wholly unnecessary, greeting. "A set of deputies are pulling into the parking lot now." He glanced at his phone, then cast his attention to the steps. "I'll brief them before bringing them inside."

Jen carried D.J. back to the kitchen, unsure what to say or how to feel about more deputies in her apartment, then reclaimed her seat.

Knox stood in the open doorway, stealing curious looks in her direction while she stared unapologetically back.

He was tall and lean. His posture screamed authority, and a muscle in his jaw clenched and released repeatedly, betraying his exterior calm. She'd only met Knox twice, but it was easy to see he was made for the uniform and not the other way around. Even years after leaving the military, the soldier he'd been was visible just below the surface. In the way he moved. The way he carried himself. And the almost-over-the-top composure.

She wondered if the evident self-control was present in everything he did, on and off the clock. Then she hated herself for the shockingly inappropriate thought.

Clearly, unlike Knox, Jen was not built to sustain emotional pressure. She was already starting to crack.

He widened his stance and joined his hands behind

his back. The soldier pressed himself against the surface once more.

Jen admired the look. There was something profound about the men and women who pledged their lives to the protection of others. She respected them in ways she could never quite articulate. Until she'd become a mother, it had been hard to understand how one person could put themselves in harm's way for another, because she'd never felt the need to protect anyone at all costs like that. It was easier now, knowing there weren't limits to what she would do for D.J. Still, she wasn't as selfless when it came to the public at large. Because if she let something happen to her, who would care for her baby? And ultimately, D.J.'s safety was all that truly mattered.

The soft sounds of footfalls on carpet reached her ears, and Knox lifted his chin.

A man and woman wearing uniforms identical to Knox's appeared. The trio spoke quietly before Knox led them inside.

"This is Jen Jordan and her son, D.J.," he told the newcomers. "Jen, this is Deputy Van and Deputy Wence. They're going to take over from here."

The pair nodded, then went to work. The woman, Deputy Wence, crouched and unpacked a duffel with the sheriff's department logo, apparently preparing to dust the front door for fingerprints. The man, Deputy Van, headed down the hall.

Knox joined Jen and D.J. in the kitchen. "Can I get you a glass of water?"

Her instinct was to decline. Manners dictated that she should be serving him. He was the guest, which made her the host. Except that explanation for their current roles didn't work. Knox wasn't a guest, not in the traditional sense, and it didn't matter anyway, because when she opened her mouth, the words didn't come.

The situation was too surreal to be true.

Knox checked the refrigerator, then used the pitcher he found there to fill a glass with cold water. He set it on the table, then took a beat to close all the open cupboards. "Why don't we make a list of Madison's local friends and family while the other deputies work," he suggested. "Places she liked to frequent. Coworkers she spent time with. And anyone else she might've been in touch with this afternoon or evening."

"Thank you," Jen said, lifting the glass. She was suddenly parched at the sight of it and drank deeply.

The list he wanted would be simple and short.

"Madison's family lives in Missouri," she said. "She moved here about nine months ago, when my pregnancy became high-risk. Everything is still new to her. She texts to ask for directions to things that are only a few blocks away. It doesn't make any sense that she would be targeted by someone."

Deputy Wence finished dusting for prints, then removed a camera from her black supply bag and began photographing the mess. When she moved on from the living room, Knox began to reassemble the couch.

"Have you noticed anything different about Madison lately?" he asked. "Was she jumpy? Withdrawn?"

"Not really." Jen shifted D.J. against her chest, rubbing his back gently after setting his drained bottle aside. She tried to remember the last conversation she'd had with her roommate, but the days had gone fuzzy since she'd returned to work at the community center. After twelve weeks off with a newborn, adjusting to any sort of schedule D.J. didn't personally set was tough. And Jen often taught evening classes, while Madison worked days. "I'm not sure," she amended. "Our schedules don't always line up."

Knox crouched to collect the papers scattered on the floor, then sifted through them as he made a tidy pile. "Was she seeing anyone?"

A humorless laugh bubbled up from Jen's chest. "Definitely not."

"You sure? Dating seems like a great way to make connections in a new town."

"I'm positive," she said. And if Knox knew Madison at all, he'd have understood how absurd the concept actually was. "Madison is still grieving Bob's death."

Knox stood, then straightened the contents of her desk before making his way through the living room, cleaning as he went. When he finished there, he returned to the kitchen. "I see."

He righted fallen formula cans and prepackaged staples in the pantry. "This is a pretty serious mess," he said. "Given Madison's text, warning you not to come home, it's safe to say the intrusion wasn't random." He turned to face her, resting his backside against the countertop. "Something is going on here. We just have to figure out what that is. She goes off-grid on the night you see a man with a gun, at the place she was last known to be. Then the apartment you share with her is ransacked on the same night. You say she doesn't date or know anyone other than you in Crestwood, so you're going to have to dig deep and come up with something we can use to find her."

"I don't know anything," Jen said, the words erupting with a frustrated snap.

Knox lowered himself onto the seat across from her, scanning her features with practiced eyes. Likely seeing the barely tamped panic she didn't want to show. "Let's try something else. Why don't you tell me about Madison? Start anywhere you'd like."

"She and Bob were married five years," Jen said, the thought popping instantly into mind. "They were from the same small town in Missouri. They practically grew up together, and they had the perfect relationship. When I first met her, I was sure she was the happiest person I'd ever known. We stayed in touch, online and by phone, for about two years before..."

The muscle in Knox's jaw tightened and released again. "How's she been since Bob's death?"

"Not the same." The weight of the words settled over her, and she took a long beat before pressing on. Jen had never told anyone about the impact Bob's death had had on Madison. And despite all that was happening, it felt a little like betrayal to say it now.

Knox waited. Serious eyes searching, and his disposition as patient as ever.

Jen finished the glass of water, then attempted to breathe in his enviable calm. "I think part of Madison died with Bob that day. I didn't realize until weeks later. I'd been so busy getting through my loss, then the unexpected news that D.J. was on the way, that I hadn't called. By the time I realized she wasn't posting on her social media and hadn't emailed or texted me since the funerals, the depression had already pulled her under. She lost a lot of weight, wasn't eating, couldn't get out of bed or go to work. It was bad. I thought I might lose her too, and I demanded she not do that to me. When I told her my pregnancy was flagged as high-risk, that

I was scared and unsure how I was supposed to get through it on my own, she put her house on the market and moved to Crestwood. She's been coming back to herself here. A little bit, day by day. It was as if she completely shifted her energy from absorbing the overwhelming grief to being whatever D.J. and I needed. When my maternity leave ended, and it was time for me to go back to work, she did too."

"But your work schedules are different," Knox said, repeating the fact Jen had offered earlier. "So, it's possible she got a new friend or found a hobby she hadn't told you about yet."

"I guess," Jen admitted, "but that would've had to be recent. I'm sure I would've noticed otherwise, and Madison is an excellent judge of character. She has a sixth sense about people. She'd never intentionally entangle herself with someone capable of this." She dragged her gaze over the recently destroyed apartment.

Knox rested his clasped hands on the table between them. "Is it possible she was slipping back into depression and just hadn't told you? Or can you think of anything else that would explain why she stopped answering her phone?"

Jen searched her memories for some kind of warning signs that Madison's life had taken a negative turn. Had she been so sleep-deprived and baby-obsessed that she hadn't noticed? Madison had spent more time in her room than usual, but Jen assumed adjusting to full-time work after nearly a year off was exhausting. Plus, Madison worked days. She went to bed early so she could get up early. She still helped with D.J. anytime Jen needed.

But what if something had been wrong, and Jen had missed it?

"Sometimes people who've been through a major loss like hers will act out," Knox said. "They can behave recklessly, in rebellion to the fact life is short and incredibly fragile. And people who struggle with depression often find it a vicious cycle, rarely letting go for very long."

Jen stared, suddenly seeing Knox for the deputy sheriff he was, and not simply the friend she'd met at Dylan's funeral, then run to for help. Knox was going through the motions, treating Madison like any other missing person and asking a standard list of canned questions. Too many of which implied Madison might've had something to do with whatever was going on.

Jen leaned forward, feathers thoroughly ruffled as she cuddled D.J. against her. "Madison is in trouble," she bit out. "She's a victim. And we need to help her. She didn't suddenly break bad and get involved with criminals."

Deputy Wence returned, interrupting Jen's rant and drawing Knox's attention. She presented her hand, a plastic baggie of white pills caught between two fingertips. "This was inside the bathroom cabinet, taped to the underside of the sink."

Chapter Four

Knox slid a measured gaze from the pills in Deputy Wence's hand to Jen, willing himself to remain composed, while recognizing the little white devils for what they were. MX-10. "Are those yours?" he asked Jen, gently scanning her stunned face.

"No." The word was breathless, and her eyes wide. "I don't understand." She dragged her attention, reluctantly, from the baggie to Knox.

He lifted a hand, dismissing the other deputy, who easily walked away, taking the evidence with her. "If the drugs aren't yours…" he said, leaving the sentence unfinished for a long beat "…there's only one other person they can belong to."

"Madison doesn't do drugs," she said. "Maybe the pills were left behind by the previous tenant."

Knox shook his head as she spoke, and her expression turned to a frown. "I don't think so."

"Why not?" she asked. "How can you possibly know for sure? It's not as if I've ever checked underneath my sink's basin for contraband. That bag might've been there for years."

"It hasn't," Knox said confidently. "In fact, I doubt

it's been there more than a few weeks. A month or two at the very most, and even that's highly unlikely."

Jen's eyes narrowed in frustration and disbelief. "And I suppose you can be sure of all that after one fleeting look at a baggie of random pills, from two feet away? Is that some kind of special gift? Like the man who can guess my weight at the fair?"

Knox eyeballed her, almost certain she weighed about one hundred and fifty pounds, but didn't dare test his skill. He'd learned long ago never to mention a woman's weight, because no matter what the number truly was, she wasn't happy with it. "They weren't random," he said. "And yes, I can identify MX-10 from much farther away. I've seen enough of it in the last month to make me an expert in everything except its personal use and the location of manufacturing. I have no intention to ever gain firsthand experience about the former, and I would give anything for details on the latter," he fumed, the sight of the drug in Jen's home raising his hackles. He hated that MX-10 had reached her world, even peripherally. "That trash is killing this city, and it's spreading to other towns within my county and jurisdiction. Surely, you've seen the news."

Jen's expression turned distant, and he thought she might be recalling one of the many recent reports about a spike in local crime and overdoses related to this new street drug. "I have," she said. "But that doesn't make any sense. Madison wouldn't do drugs," she reaffirmed. "And even if she did, which she wouldn't, I know she'd never bring them into our home. Not with D.J. here."

"Look," he said, carefully tucking his remaining ruffled feathers out of view. "I've got hidden MX-10 at the apartment of a missing woman who's new to town, has a history of depression and has recently disappeared. The facts are painting a different story than you want to hear, and I'm sure that's tough, but we'll figure it out."

She covered her mouth with one hand, astonished and confused.

"MX-10 reached our county about six weeks ago," Knox said. "How long have you been in this apartment?"

Jen looked at the baby in her arms. "A year. Madison's been here nine months."

"Maybe we can make a list of anyone who's visited in the past month or two," he suggested.

Her chest rose and fell in slow measured breaths. "We don't get company."

"Never?" he asked, trying to sound as disbelieving as he felt. He was lucky to go twenty-four hours without a visit from his auntie, brother or at least one cousin.

"I'm in mommy-survival mode right now," she said. "I work and raise D.J. There isn't much time for anything else. Madison is the same. She works and helps me. It's just us here."

Knox pushed back on his chair, stretching his legs beneath the table, and weighing the possibility Jen had been blind to her roommate's troubles. It seemed unlikely. In fact, Jen seemed like the kind of person who missed very little, though she might not always comment.

Deputies Van and Wence returned to the kitchen, having apparently finished their work. They paused at the door to collect the duffels and pack their equipment.

Knox excused himself and went to see them out.

The deputies promised to keep him in the loop as

Madison's case unfolded, and he locked the door behind them with a bit of relief.

Jen watched him from her seat at the table. The lost look in her eyes tugged at something deep in his core.

"Have you eaten?" he asked, clasping his palms, then giving them a little rub for friction. "I've officially missed dinner, and it seems like some brain food might help us figure out what we're missing."

She rolled her glossy eyes up to meet his gaze, then blinked back a round of unshed tears. "I could eat."

"Good." He rocked back on his heels and worked up his best smile. "How about I order us something good, then stick around and help with the rest of this cleanup?"

A little voice in his mind begged her to agree. Another piece of him worried he wanted an affirmative answer for all the wrong reasons. His attraction to Jen was natural. She was strong, beautiful and kind. And Knox was only human. But she'd been in love with his best friend once. She'd be a married woman today had things turned out differently.

She nodded, and for a fleeting moment, he thought she was agreeing with his train of thought. That he shouldn't be thinking about the ways he wanted to comfort her. *A warm embrace. A caress of her cheek.* When her face flushed suddenly, he realized he'd been staring.

"How about burgers?" she asked, breaking the awkward silence and turning to search through a scattered pile of take-out menus on the island. "Do you like The Bistro?"

"Yep." Knox took her order, then made the call, and thirty minutes later, he and Jen sat at her table for dinner.

D.J. was fast asleep in his crib, and the apartment was silent and still.

They'd cleaned while they'd waited for the meal to arrive, vacuuming carpets and wiping surfaces. Jen had understandably seemed to put her heart and soul into the efforts. Likely attempting to release the pent-up anxiety while erasing all traces of the intruder from her home.

She ferried two fresh glasses of water to the table, while Knox unpacked their meals.

She'd swept her straight brown hair into a messy knot at the top of her head, and a number of errant tendrils had worked their way loose.

He tracked the strands with his gaze as they fluttered against the curve of her neck when she took the seat across from him.

"Thank you," she said softly, looking as exhausted as she likely felt.

His heart went out to her yet again. She'd been through so much already. Did she have to experience the disappearance of her friend too?

"I've been hanging around here all evening," he said, unwrapping his burger and arranging his fries on the open paper. "The least I can do is buy you dinner."

She gave a soft laugh, then lifted the glass of iced water to her lips. "I'm glad you're here," she said, setting the glass aside after a long careful sip. "But I'm sorry I ruined your vacation."

Knox quirked his brow. How had she remembered Riley mentioning that at the sheriff's department? She'd been so upset at the time, Knox wouldn't have blamed her if the entire encounter had been a blur.

"I know you don't have to be here. It means a lot to me that you are. You certainly didn't have to help me clean the house or buy me dinner."

He wiped the corners of his mouth with a paper

napkin and smiled. "I think my auntie would disagree. What kind of person would leave you here alone, upset and with a mess?" His gaze traveled to the door, recalling the most important step that had yet to be taken. "I'm going to make sure your building manager has the locks changed tomorrow. How do you feel about an overnight guest until then? I'd sleep on the couch, of course. Just in case whoever was here earlier gets any ideas about coming back."

Jen's ivory skin paled, and she set her burger aside. "You would do that?"

"I'd like to, yeah," he said. "If you'll have me."

A strange pink hue rose over her cheeks, and she lowered her eyes to the food before her. "Okay."

They ate for several more moments in companionable, if oddly charged, silence. Eventually, Knox decided to unpack the elephant in the room.

"I can't believe you live this close and I didn't know," he said. "I should've come by to check on you at some point." She'd been grieving, alone and pregnant. Madison had sold her home and moved to another state to be with her, but Knox had never even considered looking her up.

"We only met once," she said. "You didn't have any reason to show up."

"True, but I knew you were hurting," he said.

Jen's lips lifted into a gentle smile. "So were you. For what it's worth, I never thought about looking you up to see if you were okay."

Knox's throat tightened uncomfortably, and he took a minute to wipe his mouth and breathe. The unpredictable waves of grief had an uncanny way of always catching him off guard. "He was my best friend."

"He was my fiancé," she said. "We both loved him, but that didn't make you any more responsible for me than I was for you. I'm just glad you're here now. It's nice to have a friend who knows about these things." She lifted another fry, then waved it between them, as if to indicate the previous break-in and everything that went along with it. "I don't know what I'd do if you weren't here."

Knox accepted her words, knowing she'd have been just fine without him tonight, the way she had been for the past year. She'd proven herself smart and strong. The app she and Madison shared was a sensible move for two young single women. Remaining calm enough to call emergency services, while heading to the police department, after facing an armed man, was levelheaded and brave. Jen had been poised and patient at every turn, and a misplaced bubble of pride rose in him.

She watched him as she helped herself to another fry. "Tell me about the pills the deputy found," she said. "Help me understand the possible reasons they were hidden here and what could be happening."

He considered her questions, and all the possible answers, none of which she would like.

When he didn't answer quickly, she set the uneaten fry aside and leaned forward, eyes flashing with barely tamped emotion. "I don't know how to sit here and be helpless. Not when Madison is out there in trouble."

"You aren't just sitting here," he said, the contradiction coming easily. "You've done all you can do, and because of that, authorities are looking for your friend far sooner than they would've been otherwise. You were able to track her and report the presence of a shooter. Those are things that will help us locate Madison. Beyond all that, you're protecting and caring for your son. There's no more important job."

Jen slumped in her chair, but nodded.

"To answer your earlier questions," he added, "I can only speculate about what's happening and the pills' involvement. I've seen more MX-10 in the past few weeks than any other drug in my years on the force combined. Our community is flooded with it, and it's deadly. I have no idea why people are still buying and taking it. It's like Russian roulette." He scrubbed a hand over his hair, then clutched the back of his neck, pushing images of a young deceased mother and her small orphaned children from his mind. "A missing person hiding an addictive substance usually adds up to a user who's strung out. Normally, I'd say the person in question is high and her phone is dead. That she'll be home when she comes back down. The overturned apartment makes me think she could be in debt to her dealer, and is being punished or pursued for that."

"Madison wouldn't use drugs," Jen said, repeating her earlier opinion. "What does all this mean to you, if she isn't an addict?"

Knox offered a noncommittal shake of his head. He didn't know Madison, but the facts he had didn't make her look good.

"Do you think it's possible the gunman wasn't at the park for her?" Jen asked. "Could the timing of all this be coincidence?"

He released a long slow breath, hating the plea in her expression. Jen needed hope, but she was asking for truth, and he couldn't give her both. "I don't believe in coincidence, but anything is possible."

She chewed her lip, considering his words. "Do you think we'll find her?" she asked.

"Yes." He sat straighter, glad to offer at least that bit of good news. "Typically, a person identified this quickly as missing will turn up."

As time went on, however, Madison's odds would change for the worse.

"Do you think she's okay?" Jen asked. "Wherever she is?"

"I suppose that depends on what's going on," he said, avoiding the hard truth Jen didn't need right now. Whether Madison had been abducted or was just on the run, she was anything but okay. "It will help if she's in the right headspace, quick-witted and resourceful."

Jen's blue eyes widened, and an expression of hope brightened her face. "Madison is a survivor, and she's very smart."

Knox hated to disagree, but if Madison was using, or involved with MX-10 in any capacity, she was definitely not smart, and he could only hope she was a survivor.

Chapter Five

Jen awoke to the first determined shafts of sunlight through her bedroom curtain. She'd barely slept, and the light was all it had taken to rouse her once more. The sounds and scents of her quietly chugging coffee maker quickened her heart. The previous day and night rushed back to her like a slap, removing the haze of her fitful sleep.

Madison was missing.

And Knox Winchester had slept over.

The thoughts drove her upward in bed. She peeked at her still-sleeping baby, snuggled in the crib a few feet away, then released a grateful sigh. She needed the extra moment to compose herself before diving into mommy mode.

Her cheeks and core heated at the memories of her unexpected and troublesome dreams. She'd fallen asleep afraid for her friend's safety and thankful for Knox's presence. The reassurance he'd offered, and natural way he'd interacted with her and D.J., had clearly confused her exhausted mind, inciting illicit fantasies. Knox was exactly the kind of man she'd always been drawn to, and his unreasonable good looks only fueled the nonsensical fire she'd felt since setting eyes on him at the sheriff's department.

Her dream had begun as a nightmare. She'd been searching the dark park for Madison alone. The gunman had found her, but Knox had saved her. He'd comforted her, hugged her. Then he'd lowered his mouth to taste her lips. The embrace had felt so real, the kiss so sensual, she'd urged him desperately on. She'd woken in a sweat, excited and ashamed. Madison was missing, but her mind was on kissing Knox instead?

Clearly, the situation was more than she could handle, and her brain had gone on the fritz.

She raked a hand through her ratty hair, and swung her feet over the bed's edge, shaking the remaining dirty thoughts from her mind. A large mug of the brewing coffee would put her back in the right headspace. Finding Madison was all that mattered right now.

She grabbed her phone from the nightstand and checked for missed messages. As she'd feared, Madison hadn't reached out.

D.J.'s eyes opened, and Jen sighed. Her moment of solitude had passed, but it was impossible to begrudge the time she now got to spend with her baby. He yawned and stretched chubby, dimpled arms over his head, flashing her a wide gummy smile.

Her heart gave a heavy kick, and she went to him instantly, feeling the smile split her face in the process. "Well, hello, handsome," she said, lifting him into her arms. "Mommy missed you while you were sleeping. Did you have nice dreams?" She snuggled him close and pressed soft kisses against his warm cheeks and soft downy hair.

D.J. giggled in response.

"How about a fresh diaper and a little breakfast?" she suggested.

Jen changed him quickly, then dressed him in black denim overalls and a white T-shirt with red stars. She tugged matching socks onto his tiny feet and smiled. "So perfect."

He made a cranky face, and she gathered him to her chest once more. Time to make good on her promise of food.

She looked longingly at the blue hoodie crumpled on her floor, considering how fast she could slip it over her tank top and sleep shorts. Putting D.J. down to get the job done seemed unwise as he squirmed in her grip, and she decided it was best to feed him before making any additional delays.

Knox came into view a moment later, leaning casually against her open pantry, a steaming mug in his hand.

The dream she'd just pushed from her mind returned instantly to steal her breath. The strength of his imagined embrace and tenderness of his perfect touch sent a fog of lust and longing across her tired mind.

"Hey," she said, slipping past him to grab the baby formula.

"Good morning," he returned.

His voice was low and rough with fatigue. She might've even been the first person he'd spoken to this morning, and the intimacy in that possibility made her stomach flutter.

"I hope you were able to get a little sleep," she said, focusing tightly on the preparation of D.J.'s bottle. "I can't imagine you were very comfortable." The living room furniture was old and worn. And Knox was at least a foot longer than the couch.

He smiled warmly at D.J., then dragged his cool green eyes back to her. "I did just fine. I hope I didn't wake you."

"Not at all," she said. "I had trouble staying asleep, and this guy likes to rise with the sun." She kissed her son once more, then put the restless night behind her. It was a new day, and that meant a new chance to find her friend. "Have you gotten any news?" she asked, tipping the bottle to her baby's mouth and leaning him back in her arms. "Something about Madison or the gunman? Fingerprints on my door?"

"Not yet," Knox said. He sipped gingerly from his cup, then cast his attention back to the open pantry.

"Hungry?" she asked, wondering if food would make him more agreeable to the set of requests circling in her mind. "I can make something if you want."

Knox shook his head. "I was thinking about making French toast. If you don't mind loaning me your kitchen."

She nearly laughed. Would a stressed-out, sleep-deprived mom mind if a handsome, single lawman made her breakfast? "Knock yourself out," she said. She was tired, not crazy.

He went to work, and she wondered if there was anything he didn't do. He'd appeared as comfortable with a rag and cleanser last night as he did with his badge and gun.

Her heart swelled in appreciation as she moved D.J. to his high chair, then went to pour a mug of coffee. "Did you go home last night?" she asked, realizing he'd somehow managed to change his clothes. "Or do you travel with a change of clothes?"

As much as she'd liked him in his uniform, she could certainly appreciate the view before her as well. A heather-gray T-shirt clung to his chest and biceps, showcasing the lean planes and muscles. Dark wash jeans hugged his narrow hips. He was barefoot in her kitchen, cooking. And she was pretty sure this was how most of her fantasies began. Though the man in her dreams hadn't had a name or face in more than a year, until last night.

Knox arranged ingredients on her countertop, glancing briefly at his clothes. "I keep a go bag in the truck. I'm out overnight unexpectedly more often than you'd think."

She rolled her eyes and sipped from her cup.

"On business," he said, cracking an egg into a bowl. A moment later he added, "Mostly."

Jen shook her head, but managed to keep her thoughts on that topic to herself.

"Vanilla?" he asked, brows raised. "Cinnamon?"

She fished the extract and powder from her baking cabinet, then set both beside his bowl. The caffeine had taken hold, and she was eager to make her request before she chickened out. "I've been thinking," she said, pulling his gaze to hers. "Since there hasn't been any news on Madison, maybe we should come up with a plan."

"A plan?" he echoed, beating the eggs with a fork. "I'm going to need more information."

"Well, you're a cop with time off," she said. "I thought we could work together to figure out what happened to Madison. For starters, we can try to use the app to retrace her steps and figure out what she was up to when things went south."

D.J. began to fuss, empty bottle discarded, and she went to him.

Knox didn't speak, so she continued, "The way I see it, the more people who work this case, the more likely we are to find her," she said. "And I know time is everything. The longer she's gone, the harder it will be to locate her, and the more likely she'll be significantly hurt, or worse, when we do." Jen swallowed the sudden painful lump in her throat, determined to be useful instead of idle. "I'm off work for the weekend, and you're on vacation. We can help."

Knox dropped the first slice of egg-dipped bread onto the heated skillet with a disbelieving laugh. "I had something similar to talk to you about," he said.

She grinned. "Go on."

Knox glanced at her, looking suddenly cautious. "I think you should take D.J. to stay with family or friends for a few days. At least until we figure out what's going on with Madison and the MX-10. That drug isn't something to mess around with, and neither are the people who deal it. We don't even know who the suppliers are, though I've been working on that for months." Frustration raced over his expression, quickly tamped, then replaced with compassion. "There are too many unknowns, and everything that is known spells danger. I appreciate your willingness to help, but you'll both be safer somewhere else." He emphasized the word *both* and tipped his head toward the baby in her arms.

Jen frowned and her stomach knotted. She didn't have friends or family to hide out with. Surely, she'd told him that. It seemed obvious, given that he knew Madison had moved to a new state to help her.

When she didn't respond, Knox pressed on. "Before you argue, remember a gunman saw your car at the park last night, and probably got a good look at you as well. Plus, whoever broke in here would've seen your photos. The intruder had access to personal details while they snooped around. Your place of employment and stores you frequent based on shopping bags, pay stubs and bills. The calendar on your desk tracks your work schedule. It's not safe to stay."

Jen took a seat at the table, hugging her son more tightly and feeling the cutting thread of fear wind painfully in her core. "We don't have anywhere to go," she said, her mouth and throat suddenly dry. "My folks are halfway across the country, and I don't have friends to stay with. I'm not that close to anyone, and bringing a baby is a huge request. Not to mention you think I might be the next target of a gunman. Who can I ask to take us in with that kind of danger in tow?"

"You can fly to your parents," he said. "I'm sure they'd be glad to see you."

She shook her head. "I don't have the money for that, and I won't ask them for it. They kept me financially afloat when I was on bed rest and too stubborn to move to Florida so they could care for me. Plus, my dad isn't well, and I feel as if I've been a source of added stress to them for a year already. It's just complicated."

Knox frowned, the confusion of a man who'd probably never been a burden to anyone visible on his brow.

"Besides," she said, squaring her shoulders, "I want to be here when Madison is found, and I think I can help that process along."

Knox transferred two pieces of French toast to a plate, then delivered them to her at the table, along with a fork, napkin and syrup. He gave her a close inspection before returning to the stove. "You're alone in town?"

"Not alone," she said, kissing D.J. "But yeah."

Knox carried a second plate to the table, then took the seat across from her, digging immediately into his meal. "Do you have somewhere you can spend a day safely? I can come back tonight, if you want." He paused to look at her, then continued cutting his breakfast with a knife and fork. "I'd like to take a look at the carousel. Things might look different by the light of day, and when a car was dispatched last night, the deputy was searching for a gunman, or Madison. They could've missed something."

"Like what?" she asked, a number of awful possibilities rising to the forefront of her mind.

"I'm not sure without looking," he admitted. "That area has a small homeless population, and I typically swing by the park with food and drinks every weekend. Today, I thought I could ask a few questions, see if anyone noticed anything out of the ordinary last night."

She mentally added genuine kindness to her knowledge about Knox. His generosity and selflessness extended beyond what she'd ever imagined. He cared about more than upholding the law and protecting people in danger. Knox cared about his community. All of them, not just the taxpayers. And she warmed impossibly further to him.

"After the park, I thought I'd stop at her place of employment, see if anyone there knows anything about what she's been up to the last few days or weeks. Meanwhile, tech support is trying to locate Madison's phone,"

Knox added. "If the device is powered on at any point, they'll find it."

"I can go with you," Jen said, setting her fork atop an empty plate. "I helped her find this job as a medical records clerk, and I tagged along for the interview. D.J. and I waited in a café across the street. We can do that today, if you want. We won't be any trouble, and I'd rather stay with you."

Knox sipped his water, considering her. His gaze dropped to her plate. "Can I make you a little more?"

"I'm trying to lose the baby weight, not put it back on." She grinned. "But breakfast was delicious. Thank you."

Knox furrowed his brow once more. "It's none of my business, but for what it's worth, I don't see the weight you think there is to lose."

She rolled her eyes, unwilling to unleash those particular frustrations on him. She really was trying to get back into her old jeans, but so far her body had resisted the efforts. She'd gained forty-five pounds, and only thirty had come off. The remainder had reshaped her body in ways her old wardrobe wasn't prepared to handle. Now, even her formerly most comfortable clothes clung to an abundance of curves. She didn't always hate the look, but it was one more thing in a long line of circumstances she couldn't control. And lack of control was something she despised.

Knox rose with his plate, then added hers to it. "You'd be welcome at my aunt and uncle's home in West Liberty. My uncle Hank is former military, and carried a badge for twenty years. His property is secure, and he's trained to protect you, not that there's any reason to think it would come to that. I can take you anywhere you want, but I can't take you with me."

Jen nodded, then stood and pulled D.J. into her arms. "I'm going to get dressed," she said. "You should take this time to get used to the fact we're coming with you. And not to your aunt and uncle's home."

With that, she turned and strutted back down the hall, determined to be useful in finding Madison and not left behind with members of his extended family, whom she'd never met.

KNOX FINISHED CLEANING up breakfast, still smiling at Jen's assertiveness, while she went to change.

His phone dinged repeatedly on the countertop beside the sink, alerting him to the mass of incoming texts from his auntie and cousins.

He'd missed family dinner last night and forgotten to call. Definite cause for alarm in the Winchester family, and apparently punishable by endless texts and voice messages. Friday night dinners were an unspoken necessity to anyone not on duty, and when he'd played hooky in the past, he'd always called to let his auntie down gently. He'd dropped the ball this time, and had some explaining to do as a result. Especially since everyone knew he was on vacation.

He opened a group text to save time, then sent a series of short messages relaying the gist of his situation. There was a moment of silence, presumably while they processed his answer. Then the dings began anew.

Announcing he'd stayed at Jen's house for her protection had incited a fresh round of questions about Jen from his aunt Rosa and his cousins' new wives. His brother and cousins, a private investigator and several lawmen, offered their assistance if he needed it.

He considered suggesting the men in his family take away their wives' phones, then recalled Jen announcing she was coming with him, after he'd told her she couldn't, and decided to concentrate on the problem at hand.

When Jen reappeared in a fitted T-shirt and stretchy pants that emphasized all his favorite aspects of a woman's body, he had to remind himself not to stare. And she wanted to lose weight? Was she nuts?

She slipped a baby sling around her torso and positioned D.J. inside. "We should ask the building manager about my new locks on our way out," she said.

Then she opened the door and was gone.

Knox rubbed his forehead with one heavy palm, while his phone continued dinging.

Jen would fit right in with the little female army his family had recently accumulated, if he ever introduced her. And the women would surely try to recruit her if he did.

Chapter Six

Knox unlocked the doors to his truck and watched as Jen transferred D.J.'s car seat from her sedan to the back of his extended cab. The baby bounced contentedly in his sling against her chest. According to her building manager, the locksmith was on his way, and there would be a new set of keys in Jen's mailbox when she returned.

"I think we should have a cover story while we look for clues about Madison's disappearance," she said, fastening the complicated harness over her son. "We don't want to scare anyone who might know what happened to her by announcing you're the law. I don't know any criminals, but I'm positive they won't talk to you if you lead with that."

Knox smirked. She was explaining things to him as if this was what she did and he was along for the ride. "Is that right?"

"Yes. So, we should try to look like two friends who are out enjoying a day together," she said, closing the rear door and climbing onto the passenger seat. "When we question people, we'll tell them I'm her roommate and worried because she didn't come home."

He shot her a flat look across the cab. "I'm not a deputy sheriff today."

"Exactly."

"Wrong," he said. "I'm the law every day."

She turned her head to face him, unimpressed. "You're on vacation."

And what a vacation it is so far, he thought dryly. Then reversed out of the parking space without retort.

"Do you still have the power to arrest someone while on vacation?" she asked.

Knox rubbed his forehead, then stole a glance at her baby in his rearview mirror. That child wasn't going to get away with anything. His mother was too fond of calling the shots.

"Well?" she asked, forcing Knox to give what seemed like an obvious answer.

"Yes, I can still make arrests on vacation."

"There," she said. "We're all set."

He eased onto the road, unsure whether to laugh or sigh.

They rode in silence for several minutes, slowing as traffic increased near downtown.

Jen twisted at her waist, dramatically examining the scene around them. "What are you doing? The park is on the other end of town."

He rounded the next corner, then slid his truck into an empty spot outside a coffee shop. "True, but I usually take sandwiches with me to the park. Today, I'll have to pick them up from the deli. If we're making that pit stop before the park, we might as well take a look at the café Madison visited every morning while we're here."

Jen craned her neck for a look at the place on her right. "Coffee Cat?" She stared through each window, apparently trying to orient herself. "How do you know she came here?"

"Yep." He climbed out and rounded the tailgate.

Jen appeared on the sidewalk when he reached her door. She secured D.J. into her baby sling, then turned a determined look on Knox. "How do you know she came here every morning?" she asked again.

"Receipts in her bedroom trash." Knox held the door for Jen to enter the coffee shop. A blast of deliciously scented air washed over him as he crossed the threshold. "They were in the report Deputy Wence wrote up last night."

Jen furrowed her brow, then marched on, crossing large black-and-white-tiled flooring. She stopped at a counter near the back wall. The remainder of the small space was peppered by a dozen wooden table sets.

"Welcome to Coffee Cat," the guy behind the counter greeted. He was tall and lean, probably in his early twenties, with small blue eyes and an unfortunate nose. Knox hoped it was naturally crooked and not the result of one too many landed punches. His name tag said Ted. "What can I get you?"

Jen paused to look at the menu, then smiled warmly at Ted. "I'm not sure I can decide," she told him, tipping her head slightly to one side. "What would you recommend?"

Knox grimaced. Was she…flirting? With Ted? He gave the unremarkable barista another look and felt his frown deepen.

Ted smiled and made several complicated suggestions with words like *vanilla*, *macchiato* and *soy* in the titles. Jen moved along the counter with him once she'd made a decision, watching as he worked.

"My friend recommended this place," she said. "She

comes here all the time. Says it's the best. Maybe you know her. Do you work a lot of mornings?"

"Five days a week," he said proudly, beaming as he foamed up her drink. "I don't usually have time to talk though. It can be really busy on weekdays."

Jen nodded, thoughtfully. "My friend's name is Madison. She's tall and thin, really pretty, with long black hair I'd kill for. She probably wears scrubs when she comes in. She works at a clinic downtown."

Ted passed her the coffee, then rang up the order. "The place on Market Street?"

"That's the one. Do you remember a woman like the one I described coming in here a lot?" Jen pressed, digging for her wallet. She stretched and shifted, reaching around the baby attached to her middle.

"Not really," Ted said. "Why?"

Knox groaned inwardly, then met them at the register, unable to watch any longer. "Hey, can I get a plain black coffee?" he asked. "Put hers on my bill." He looked at Jen, his wallet already in hand. "I've got this." He passed Ted some cash, then fixed his most authoritative stare on the man with kitty whiskers embroidered across his apron. "We need to know about the woman, so think hard. She's missing."

Ted blinked. "What?"

"Missing," Knox repeated, turning his cell phone to face the younger man. A photo of Madison centered the screen. Knox had pulled it from her social media the night before and saved it for this purpose.

Ted frowned, dragging his eyes from the image. "Who are you? How do I know you aren't looking for her with nefarious intent?"

Knox snorted. *Nefarious intent.* Who was this kid?

"I'll give you twenty bucks to tell me what you know about her. Answer now, or I'll offer the cash to someone else who works here instead."

Jen gasped, and he slid her a sideways look in warning.

She'd been right to suggest he not announce himself as a lawman to everyone they met. People got tight-lipped when they knew a deputy sheriff was involved, and this kid looked exactly like one of those people.

Not surprisingly, Ted took the money. "I know her," he said. "She always ordered herbal tea or a bottle of water. Sometimes a fruit-and-yogurt parfait or a bagel. She sat at the same table every time." He pointed to an empty two-seater near the window.

Knox nodded. "Was she always alone?"

Ted passed him a plain coffee. "Yeah, but I haven't seen her for a couple days. Is she really missing?"

"Yes," Jen said, her voice going painfully soft. "Thank you for the information."

Ted opened the register to make change, but Knox waved him off, then led the way to the table in question. It felt good to be back in charge.

Jen watched him as they sat. "What now? We already knew she came here."

He cast his gaze through the tinted glass. "She always sat at the window. We didn't know that, and the next logical question is, why? To people watch? Anyone specific? If so, who was she watching and why?"

Jen pulled D.J. from the sling and arranged him on her lap, so he could take in the views. "You're frowning again," she said. "What are you thinking?"

Knox worked his jaw, trying and failing to change his expression. "Madison ordered caffeine-free tea and bottled water on a daily basis. That doesn't strike me as befitting the profile of someone seeking comfort outside themselves. Those are healthy, non-indulgent choices."

"Not exactly hallmarks of an illegal drug user, you mean?"

"No, and something else is bugging me," he said. "Madison worked full-time. How many days a week was that? A standard Monday through Friday, or weekends too?"

Jen puzzled a moment, turning her mug slowly on the table. "Monday through Friday. Why?"

"The receipts in her trash say she was here every day this week and last. This place isn't in your neighborhood, and the coffee isn't that good," he said, making a face at the brew he'd barely sipped. "So, why go all the way downtown if she didn't have to?"

"To sit alone in front of this window," Jen said, turning her attention back to the glass. She lifted the mug and shifted on her seat, struggling to enjoy her foamy drink without lifting it directly over her baby.

Knox smiled. "Mind if I hold him so you can finish that eight-dollar monstrosity?"

She cocked a curious brow, before relief swept over her face. "Sure." She handed her baby carefully to Knox. "I would've paid for my own drink," she said. "I didn't mean to stick you with the bill, and for the record, I don't normally get something with so many bells and whistles. I was trying to get the barista to like me so he'd answer my questions."

Knox snorted a quiet laugh, curling D.J. against his chest. "You raised that poor kid's self-esteem to new heights."

She laughed, then sipped her drink with a sigh. "He

didn't tell me anything until you butted in and intimidated him. Thank you for that, by the way, and for the coffee."

"Don't mention it." Knox made a few faces at D.J., and the kid gave a wide toothless grin. Knox chuckled. Kids were funny, and his family was adding new ones to the roster left and right.

The little man in his arms looked a lot like Jen. The set of his lips and shape of his eyes were all hers, but the rest... The color of his tawny skin, dark hair and brown eyes were all Dylan. Knox could see his friend in the angle of D.J.'s jaw and the mischief in his stare. If he was anything like his father in personality, Jen would have her work cut out for her during the teenage years. Though he was sure she'd manage just fine.

"You're good with him," she said, crossing her legs beneath the table and bumping her foot against his. "Planning on having one of your own someday? Or are you too single to think about that just yet?"

He grinned. "I'd like to have a few, eventually. My brother, Cruz, and I were raised to be friends, not just brothers, and when we lost our mama back in high school, it was the bond she'd created that got us through it. I'd like to pass that gift on to kids of my own. I think family is everything. It's pretty great to know someone always has your back."

Something tilted in Jen's expression, sending a tug of sadness through Knox's heart. He'd nearly forgotten her folks were in Florida and her dad was ill.

"How's your dad?" he asked. "You mentioned he isn't well."

She shrugged. "He had a heart attack a few years back. Hasn't been the same since, but he's still with us, so I'm thankful for that. I'm sorry about your mama," she added. "I didn't know."

Knox's throat tightened the way it always did when someone voiced those words. "Thanks."

An older woman in business-casual attire appeared from the back of the café and made her way around the tables, greeting patrons and making chitchat. Her lack of apron gave the impression of authority. Her genuine interest and obvious familiarity with the guests made Knox suspect she was the owner. The shop's logo was emblazoned on her chest, but she wasn't wearing a name tag.

"Is that the manager?" Jen asked, noticing the same woman who'd caught Knox's eye.

He smiled and lifted a hand when she headed to their table. "One way to find out," he whispered.

"Good morning," she said brightly upon approach. "What a lovely family. And who is this?" she asked the baby in his arms.

"This is D.J.," Knox answered, "and Jen." He tipped his head to the blushing woman seated across from him. "I'm Knox. It's nice to meet you," he said, not bothering to correct her misinterpretation of their group status. "This is our first time here. It's nice."

"Thank you," she said. "I'm Cat."

Knox frowned. "Coffee Cat."

"That's me." She pointed to the logo on her shirt.

Jen laughed, and the bubbly sound warmed him. "Do you come in every morning?" she asked.

"Almost," Cat said.

Knox flipped his phone over on the table, quickly selecting Madison's picture once more. "This is our friend," he said, lifting the device in Cat's direction.

"She's missing. We know she came here a lot and sat at this table, but we're hoping you can tell us more."

"We're retracing her steps," Jen added. "She's my best friend, and she vanished last night."

Cat's expression fell. "I know Madison. Have you called the police?"

Knox nodded. "They're looking for her too."

The older woman covered her mouth with one hand. "Wow. Okay. Let me think. I've spoken to her many times, but never about anything substantial. She always had a notebook and pencil. She sat at this table and doodled." She bit her bottom lip, eyes roaming as she thought. "She took pictures sometimes."

Jen wrinkled her nose. "Selfies?"

"No, through the window. People watching, I guess." Cat motioned to the road outside. "I assumed she did that so she could finish the drawings after she left."

Knox stared at the parking lot and buildings across the street. The clinic where Madison worked was on the next block, and probably accessible from a visible alley. He rocked onto his hip, adjusting D.J. in his arms as he freed his wallet. He flipped the leather bifold open and produced a business card for Cat. "If you think of anything else, or if anyone comes in here asking about Madison. Or us," he added belatedly, as the thought occurred. They were seated before a giant window, after all. "Give me a call."

Cat's lips parted as she read the card. She nodded, eyes filled with concern as she tucked the little rectangle into the pocket of her khaki pants and moved on to the next table.

Jen released a deep breath. "How much do you want

to bet Madison was watching the alleyway, and that it leads to the clinic?"

"Yep." Knox put his wallet away, prepared to ask Jen if she was ready to go, but she was already on her feet, waiting for him.

Chapter Seven

Jen followed Knox across the street, exhausted by the weight of the day. It was still early, but they'd already accomplished so much. Normally, she'd still be in her pajamas, playing on the floor with D.J. Today, however, she'd confirmed the locksmith, traveled downtown, learned new things about Madison's days prior to her disappearance and she was now on her way to talk to Madison's coworkers. Was this what Knox's life was like every day?

She peeked at the handsome protector beside her, wondering how he usually spent his time. She had so many questions about his life. None of the answers were any of her business, but she appreciated how easily he answered everything she was brave enough to ask. Knox Winchester was inarguably gorgeous, but he was a lot more than a pretty face. He was protective, compassionate and kind. Plus, he wasn't afraid to cook or clean. Definite bonus points for those. Unlike so many men she'd known, Knox was capable, and he didn't wait for someone else to do something he could do himself.

She tried not to think about how much she liked all the new things she'd learned about him. Or how refreshing it was to hear him talk about his family. He obviously loved his aunt, uncle, brother and cousins. And he wanted children of his own one day. Her heart fluttered nonsensically at the thought, and her gaze drifted back to her son in his arms.

Knox held D.J. so confidently. He looked natural with a baby against his chest. Maybe there were a lot of kids in his family. She tucked that question away for later, along with all the other things she wanted to know about him, but wasn't sure how or when it was appropriate to ask.

Madison's disappearance loomed heavily in Jen's heart and mind. Each time she thought too long or hard about her budding attachment to Knox, the reminder of why their paths had crossed again hit like a sledge. And she felt like the worst kind of friend.

He turned to her as shame and guilt coiled in her gut, causing her steps to stutter. For a moment, she wondered if he could read her mind. "Ready?" he asked, pausing on the corner.

She nodded, and Knox offered his hand.

"Coffee Cat assumed we were a family," he said. "Maybe that's our cover story. Seems like a good one to me."

Jen gaped at his hand. Her heart kicked into overdrive at the rush of unbidden images from her dream. Those big hands in her hair, cupping her cheeks and drawing her close.

She was an absolutely terrible friend. How could she be thinking of this when Madison was missing?

Knox's smile fell. "You suggested we come up with a cover this morning." Knox lowered his hand, concern wrinkling his brow. "Sorry. I didn't mean to suggest…"

His words trailed off, and his sharp green eyes turned to D.J. in his arms. "I wasn't trying to… No one will ever take Dylan's place," he said finally.

"I know," she said, slipping her hand into his. "My thoughts are all over the place, but I wasn't thinking anything like that." Her cheeks heated as their palms aligned, and the roughness of his calloused skin scraped deliciously against hers. She hadn't held a man's hand in more than a year, and the act felt so incredibly personal, so intimate, it sent little lightning bolts down her spine. *Get a hold of yourself*, she scolded internally, closing her eyes briefly against the intensity.

"You okay?" he asked, the low tenor and attentive tone of his voice nearly buckling her knees.

She wasn't even close to okay. The weight of the last year, of Dylan's sudden death before that and the complete emotional fatigue of being a single mother felt like a thousand-pound weight on her shoulders. Madison's disappearance might be the thing that pushed Jen's precarious state over the edge.

Except she couldn't let that happen. Not for her sake, but for her son's.

"Jen?" Knox pressed, his cool green eyes appraising her in the sunlight.

"I'm fine," she said. Certain he could see straight through her thinly veiled bravado, she added, "Nervous."

He tugged her more closely to his side, then winked down at her.

D.J. smiled and cooed.

"You've got this," Knox promised. "And I've got you."

Warmth spread through her at his simple, comforting words. She squeezed his fingers in thanks, drawing on his cool confidence and reminding herself she wasn't alone.

Knox smiled and made small talk as they moved swiftly toward their destination. Though she didn't think the smile quite reached his eyes. Instead, he seemed to be taking in the details around them, likely registering dozens of things that would never reveal themselves to her.

She did her best to seem as unhurried and casual as he did, especially when they passed others on the sidewalk, or coming and going from storefronts and shops.

When they reached the clinic, he released her hand, then opened and held the door for her.

Their bodies brushed in the narrow space as she passed. The heady scent of him, coupled with his nearness, fogged up her brain as she stepped inside.

The clinic was small but busy. Its pale blue walls were lined in commercial seating, and every chair was occupied. A sign on the door had identified the general practitioners as Michael Martz and Robert Abel.

Jen led the way to a welcome desk on the far wall, positioned beside a closed door leading to offices and exam rooms. A blonde woman in maroon scrubs greeted her with a smile. According to the rectangular badge on her chest, her name was Katie.

Katie set a clipboard on the counter between them and tapped one finger to the empty line at the bottom. With her free hand, she motioned to her headset, indicating she was on a call.

If Jen had been there as a patient, she would've written

her name, time of arrival and appointment on the line. Instead, she shook her head slightly and smiled back.

Eventually, the receptionist finished her call and offered an apologetic grin. "Sorry to keep you waiting. It's been a busy morning." Her gaze traveled from Jen to Knox and D.J. The look turned blatantly appreciative as she took in the tall drink of water on Jen's right. "Who are we seeing today?"

Jen refused to roll her eyes, so she closed them in a long blink before refocusing. She was willing to bet he got those looks everywhere he went, and given the cluelessness on his face at the moment, he probably didn't even know he was being ogled. "We don't have an appointment," Jen said. "We're hoping to ask you a couple questions. My roommate, Madison, works here."

Katie's expression turned quizzical, then thrilled as she pulled her gaze back to Jen. "So you're Jen!" She beamed. "It's so nice to meet you. I'm Katie. This must be D.J."

Jen cast a proud look at her son, content and drowsy in Knox's arms. "The one and only." Her heart simultaneously swelled and broke with the knowledge Madison had spoken frequently enough about them that Katie would recall their names.

"I hear so much about you both," Katie said. "I feel as if I know you already. How can I help?"

"We're actually looking for Madison," Jen said, her throat tightening on the words.

Katie gave a sad smile. "She's not on the schedule today. She almost never works weekends. You didn't know?"

"I do," Jen said. "But she's not home, and I don't

know where she is. I'd hoped you could shed some light. She never came home last night."

The other woman blanched. "Madison is missing?" Her eyes widened, and her mouth formed a tight line. She turned her face away, looking at something beyond Jen's sight, hidden by the wall that separated them.

"When was the last time you saw her?" Jen asked, pulling the other woman's attention back to her.

"Earlier this week." Katie wet her lips, then leaned forward slightly, tipping over the counter. "She didn't come in for her scheduled shift yesterday. I left her a voice mail, but she didn't return it. I thought she'd just overslept or forgotten."

Jen's heart pounded as the news registered. She'd thought Madison had only been missing since the previous evening. Was it possible she'd been missing all day?

Knox moved in closer, angling himself against the counter and sweeping his gaze over the waiting room behind them. "How did she seem to you the last time you saw her?" he asked.

Katie chewed her lip, looking away from them once more. He tracked something Jen couldn't see. "I don't know," Katie said. "She was fine. Quiet and busy. She handled the files and paperwork, so we didn't get to talk much." She turned forward and straightened, no longer their coconspirator. "I'm sure she'll turn up. Probably just needed a day off."

Knox rested a hand on the small of Jen's back, silently comforting her once more. "Maybe," he told Katie. "Any chance we can speak with one of the doctors? Maybe they have some insight. Or perhaps another one of your coworkers. We're open to any information that can help us find her. We don't want to leave any stone unturned."

Jen looked up at him, sensing the subtle authority he'd added to his words.

Katie looked away again, eyes darting and expression turning troubled. "Not today. Drs. Martz and Abel are swamped, and to be honest, Madison was incredibly private. She barely talked to anyone."

"But she told you about me and D.J.," Jen said. "You might know more than you realize. Did she say anything recently that struck you as odd or out of character? Did she seem more distracted or less talkative?"

Katie shook her head while Jen spoke. "No. I'm sorry. I can't help you. You can make an appointment with Dr. Martz or Dr. Abel if you'd like, but I really need to get back to work." Her tone was congenial, but forced, and the ease with which she'd greeted them had thoroughly dissolved.

Knox removed his wallet again, jostling D.J. while he freed a business card and passed it to Katie. "If you think of anything, let me know."

A little gasp escaped her lips as she read the card, then moved it quickly to her pocket.

Knox used his massive palm on Jen's back to guide her away.

She didn't speak until they were on the sidewalk. "That was it?" she asked, shocked and astounded. "Why didn't you ask her more questions? And if you were going to let her know you were a deputy, why didn't you insist she talk? Or at least demand an interview with the rest of the staff? She was clearly hiding something. Even I could see that, and I don't have any of the training you've had."

Knox nudged her forward, not answering her questions. He steered her to the end of the block, then across the street when the signal changed. "I'm on vacation," he said, motioning her to a bench at the edge of a tree-lined park one hundred yards or so from the clinic. "The sheriff's department will do all the official legwork. I'm just nudging a few fence posts to see if a gate opens."

Jen sat, though she wanted to pace, or return to the clinic and ask more questions. "I don't know what that means," she said, reaching for D.J. as Knox lowered his tall frame onto the seat at her side.

"It means I'm just nosing around, putting out feelers and testing the waters. If anything seems amiss, I'll report it to the deputies on this case. If not, we'll keep looking." He relaxed one long arm across the wooden slat behind her shoulders, assuming a casual position, when all she wanted to do was scream in frustration.

"That receptionist knew something," she said. "Did you see how nervous she got? And what was she looking at on the other side of the wall?"

"Agreed," Knox said, "and I'm not sure."

"Did you see her face when she read your card?"

He nodded, eyes fixed on something in the distance.

Jen tracked his gaze to the small parking lot outside the clinic. The lot butted up to an alley, barely visible from her position. There were eight cars divided neatly in two rows. Two high-end sedans, and six cars people could generally afford.

Before Jen could ask Knox what he was looking at, specifically, a figure appeared in the lot.

"Looks like something shook loose," Knox said.

Jen watched in awe as Katie darted to a small red hatchback, dropped behind the wheel, then zoomed away.

Chapter Eight

Jen watched as Knox navigated to the clinic's website on his phone, then searched for a listing of the staff. It only took a moment to find the group photo on the practice's About page, alongside a description of how the doctors met and why they chose to be one of the first new businesses in the revitalized downtown. According to the site, they wanted to be *conveniently located for the people of their community, with better accessibility and extended office hours*. They further claimed to pride themselves on hiring locals and seeking graduates of area schools.

"Madison's not in the photo," Jen said. "She hasn't worked there long, that's probably why, but I think that's Katie." She pointed to a slightly heavier woman than the one they'd met, with longer, blonder hair, but it was definitely the receptionist.

Knox swiped the page away and switched to his texting app. He curved forward over the device, creating shade on the screen, then began to tap a message.

"What are you doing?" Jen asked.

"Reaching out to the sheriff's department."

She'd assumed as much, but had hoped for a more thorough explanation. She chewed her lip as she processed what she'd just seen. "Why do you think Katie ran off like that? The waiting room was packed. She even mentioned how busy they were. Do you think we scared her?" Jen rewound the conversation, weighing all the things that might've triggered Katie's change in demeanor and led to her leaving work so quickly. A new and hopeful thought burst into mind. She inhaled deeply at the possibility. "What if she knows where Madison is? We should follow her." Jen looked in the direction the little red hatchback had gone, but it was lost to a sea of taillights. Her newly gained hope plummeted. There was no chance of catching her now. Knox's truck was still parked outside Coffee Cat, a full block away.

Knox stood and offered her his hand. "I requested an address on Katie. We should have it by the time we get to my truck."

"We're going to her house?" Jen asked, adrenaline rising, then colliding with a discouraging possibility. "What if she didn't go home?" What if she knew where Madison was and was on her way there? And Jen had missed her chance to follow.

"There's only one way to find out," Knox said, wiggling his still-waiting fingers.

She accepted his hand, and they headed back to his pickup at double the pace they'd left it.

Twenty minutes later, they arrived outside an older home in a working-class neighborhood. The hatchback was in the driveway.

Knox led the way to the door, and Jen tried to keep her cool as the hope of seeing Madison again welled in her.

She kissed D.J.'s hair, inhaled the scent of him and played with his chubby, dimpled fingers, working to keep her heart rate calm, despite the number of questions stampeding through her mind. And she prayed she wasn't carrying her baby into a dangerous situation.

Knox rang the bell, and the curtain moved in the window beside the door. When no one answered, he knocked.

Jen counted silently, both to calm her nerves and to gauge the passing time. Thankfully, Knox didn't make a move to leave, because Jen would've stubbornly stood there all night if it meant gaining information about Madison's disappearance. The passing seconds felt like hours as they waited. The frightening truth was that Katie could easily deny them another conversation. And there wasn't anything Jen could do about that.

Four seconds later, the sound of a sliding chain lock was followed by the turn of a deadbolt. The front door sucked open before them, and Katie appeared. She released a heavy breath, then stepped away, offering them entrance.

She closed the door quickly once they were inside, then reengaged the locks. "What are you doing here?" she asked, looking through the front window before turning a deep frown on them.

Knox offered a kind smile, his keen eyes seeming to take inventory of their surroundings. "We saw you leave the clinic in a hurry, and wondered if you were okay," he said.

Jen bit the insides of her cheeks, thankful he'd taken the lead. She wasn't sure what to say. They'd already frightened Katie once, and Knox was probably used to interrogating suspects.

Jen gave the home a careful scan, following Knox's

example and hoping to see something to indicate Madison was nearby.

Katie crossed her arms and shook her head. "You're stalking me now? That's illegal. You should know." She fixed Knox with an angry stare.

He lifted his palms in response. "I'm not here as a lawman. We're here as friends because we think Madison is in trouble."

"We were at the park when you left work," Jen offered. She kissed her baby's head, hoping to convey the idea that maybe they'd been there innocently, getting a little fresh air for her son. "We saw you racing away and worried that we'd upset you. Or that maybe you're in trouble too."

Katie's gaze jumped erratically from Jen to Knox. She wrapped her arms around her middle and stepped back, unsure. "I had a headache, and I came home to rest."

Knox nodded. "The clinic was really busy. That must've been a terrible headache."

"It was," she said.

Jen took a few steps, rocking gently to soothe her baby. She gave the room another long look, desperate for something to stand out. The furnishings were sparse. The space was in need of some general repairs, but everything was clean and cared for. It was the home of a working woman just getting by. Jen's gaze landed on a set of photos across Katie's mantel. All were images of her and a small boy. "You have a son?" she asked. From the photos, Jen would guess the child was probably eight or nine.

Katie nodded, tightening her hold on herself. "His father has custody, but he stays here on the weekends and during extended school breaks. I was in some trouble when I had him, and it was the right decision at the time."

Jen's heart ached at the thought of only seeing D.J. on weekends. She hated the humility and shame in Katie's voice as she explained the situation. Everyone made mistakes, and the woman before them was clearly working to right hers, whatever they'd been.

"I've got a good life now," Katie said. "And a good job. I can't afford any trouble."

Knox's eyes narrowed. "What sort of trouble do you think we're going to connect you to?"

Her skin paled, and her mouth opened. She looked to Jen again, maybe for help, but as much as Jen could empathize with another young mother, Madison was missing, and she needed to be found.

"I don't know w-what you're talking about," Katie said.

"Look," Jen interrupted, voice pleading as she moved forward, trading a sideways glance with Knox. "We don't know what's going on, but something is obviously wrong. I thought I was Madison's only local friend, but clearly she talks to you too. And it seems like you know something about where she is, or what's happening with her. If you do, then we need to know that too. I love her, and I'm scared. I don't want to lose her."

Katie took another step back. "Madison and I weren't friends. We didn't talk, and I don't know anything."

"Anything about what?" Jen asked, the words dragging out in desperation. "What is happening? And why won't you tell me? Madison could be hurt or scared. Or worse," she added, her throat going dry at the memory of how quickly a human life could end. "Did you know

Madison lost her husband last year?" she asked. "She's been through so much already, and I just want to find her and bring her home."

Katie shook her head slowly, eyes glistening with unshed tears. "I'm sorry." Her gaze flickered to the photos of her son on the mantel. "I can't help you."

"We found drugs in the apartment," Jen blurted.

Knox stiffened at her side and reached for her wrist, giving it a warning squeeze.

Katie's eyes widened.

"If she had a problem," Jen said, pivoting her interrogation, "I can get her help. She doesn't have to go through it alone."

"What kind of drugs?" Katie asked, her arms falling limply to her sides.

"MX-10," Knox answered, taking over at the mention of the drug. "It's become an epidemic in this area, and with Madison's history of depression, we understand she's a prime candidate for use. Like I said before, we're here as friends, and we're worried."

Katie blinked slowly, her eyes suddenly distant and unfocused. "I can't help you," she said, her voice flat and defeated. For the first time since their arrival, she looked truly ill. "I'm sorry, but you have to go. I need to lie down."

Knox towed Jen back to the front door by her wrist. "I hope you feel better soon," he said. "We're sorry to have bothered you."

Jen cast a final pleading look at the other woman, hoping Katie would say something more, anything more.

But she only closed the door behind them.

KNOX WALKED JEN and D.J. back to his truck and helped them inside. Then he powered the windows down and started the engine. There were fewer than a dozen cars visible on the street. Driveways were empty, as they often were at this hour in neighborhoods like these. The homes were old and in need of repair, but the lawns, porches and sidewalks were neat as a pin. These were the places where people worked for what they had, and they took care of the things in their charge. Most of the vehicles in sight seemed appropriate for the area. The newest of older-model cars was parked nearly a block away, dark and motionless, with a paper thirty-day tag in the rear window.

Katie and her home fit the area's profile. If he had to guess by the scars on her arms, she'd been a drug user at one time, and that was likely the reason she didn't have custody of her son. Knox could only hope she wasn't using anymore.

When they were safely inside, Knox buckled up and started the engine, then drove around the block and cut back to where they'd started, using an alley between homes across the street from Katie's place. He shifted into Park, this time with an excellent view of the entire block.

Jen didn't ask any questions when he'd driven away, or when he settled the engine once more. Instead, she mixed a small bottle and passed it to her baby. Then offered Knox a granola bar.

He smiled. "You keep snacks in your purse? My grandmama used to do that. Are there tissues in your bra too?"

"Wouldn't you like to know," she answered, pulling a pack of peanuts from her bag next.

It was unsettling how much he'd like to know what was in her bra, but he kept that to himself. Instead, he marveled at her preparedness.

She caught him staring and frowned. "You're still thinking about what's in my bra. Aren't you?"

"I was thinking you're like a cross between Mary Poppins and a Scout. With your bag of necessities, always ready to troubleshoot." He grinned. It was fun to see Jen in action, unafraid and wholly determined. Despite the difficult circumstances, she was headstrong and steadfast. He was sure plenty of people would've cracked, quit or had a breakdown under the pressure, but not her.

Unexpected admiration tugged at him.

She tore the peanut package open and shook a few nuts into her hand. "I'm a single mom. The superhero of our day. It's a heavy cape, but someone has to wear it." She lifted her chin and smiled. "And planning ahead is a top-notch life hack. You should try it."

"I plan ahead," he said. "I keep a go bag in the truck, or I'd be wearing yesterday's clothes right now."

She flicked her blue gaze to him. "Where are your snacks?"

He laughed, then opened his granola bar. It was nice that she thought of everything, but part of him hated that she had to. She shouldn't have to be so wholly self-reliant. Everyone needed someone. Didn't they? The idea of being that person for her popped into his mind, and it felt nicer than it should.

Katie's front door opened, pulling his thoughts back to the moment.

"She's leaving," Jen said, pointing through the windshield, in case Knox had somehow missed it.

Katie hurried down the porch steps and to her car, struggling to manage several overnight bags.

"Looks like her head feels better," he said.

"Looks like she's going somewhere," Jen said. "Is she leaving town? That definitely means we were right. She knows something."

"Probably," he said, already tapping the update into a text for dispatch. Preferably a uniform who was on duty, unlike himself, and not hauling a civilian and a baby around. "I'm letting another deputy know."

"What?" Jen gasped. "We're already here. We have to follow her. What if she's on her way to Madison? What if she knows where she is?"

"Another deputy will—"

"Follow her," Jen said, gripping his arm. "Let another deputy take over when they catch up, but don't lose her."

Unable to argue the reasonable suggestion, Knox shifted into Drive and eased onto the road behind Katie's fast-disappearing car.

Chapter Nine

Knox hurried along the residential streets, monitoring the rearview mirror, sidewalks and scene around him, while keeping an eye on the little hatchback. He mentally tallied the traffic violations as he kept his distance, trying not to alert her to the tail. So far, she was blatantly speeding, had rolled through two stop signs at intersections and had come unnervingly close to leaving her lane a number of times. If she was using her phone while driving, she needed to pull over before she caused an accident, but he was too far back to know for sure.

He radioed their new location each time she changed direction, maintaining communication with the deputy assigned to intervene. Jen would be unhappy if backup didn't arrive soon, because Knox drew the line at putting her and D.J. in danger to follow Katie any farther than absolutely necessary. And he had no plans to run a red light or make any sort of illegal turns in the name of following Katie.

"Something scared her," Jen said, breaking his reverie. Her voice was calm, apparently unfazed by Katie's erratic driving.

"Yeah," he said. "Us." Knox slowed as they reached the main roads through town, putting two more cars between them. "We confronted her at work, then followed her home and insinuated we knew she had information on a missing woman who was in possession of MX-10." It was too late now, but he wished Jen had left the drug detail out of Katie's questioning.

Jen pursed her lips. "She could've just talked. You gave her your card. She knows you're a deputy and you could've helped her."

"People who've had trouble with the law in the past are extremely slow to warm up to the possibility we won't arrest them again," he said. "Even if they aren't doing anything wrong. And she's got a lot on the line with her son's custody situation."

Jen seemed to consider that. "We don't know her previous trouble was with the law."

Not yet, Knox thought, *but we soon will*. Katie was receiving a thorough background check while they kept tabs on her in traffic.

Jen twisted to peek into the back seat. "Out like a light," she said, facing forward with a smile. "The old bottle-and-a-car-ride combination never fails."

Knox couldn't stop his smile, despite his agitation with Katie's driving. "You're an old pro at motherhood already. That must feel good."

"It doesn't feel bad," she said, as she gripped the dashboard on their next turn.

Katie took her next left turn in front of oncoming traffic. Horns honked and drivers hollered.

Knox moved carefully into the turn lane, positioning himself to follow her, when it was safe.

"I want to go through Madison's things when we get home," Jen said, completely at ease beside him. "I thought about it last night, but I didn't want to invade her privacy more than the deputies already had. I don't care about any of that right now. I think she's in serious trouble, and if we find her and bring her home safely, she won't complain about how we get it done. She'll just be glad to be home."

"Agreed," Knox said, thankful she'd chosen an activity that would keep her and D.J. someplace confined and safe. "You know her best, so there's a chance you'll notice something Wence and Van didn't."

"I'm curious about the notebook and pencil Coffee Cat mentioned," she said. "I've never known Madison to draw or doodle. I think it's more likely she was making notes. She's detailed to a fault."

"Another good idea," Knox said, silently cursing the deputy who hadn't caught up with them yet. "I'd like to compare Madison's work schedule with the receipts from the coffee shop. See if there's a pattern in the dates that stands out."

Ahead of them, the little red hatchback accelerated through another intersection as the light turned red. The more cautious drivers in front of Knox stopped, as did he.

A cruiser appeared in oncoming traffic, and Knox radioed the information on Katie's turn.

The cruiser's lights went on.

"Better late than never," Knox muttered.

"Only if he catches her," Jen said.

Knox hit his turn signal as the cruiser headed in the direction Katie had gone. When the light was green for him again, Knox rerouted the truck toward Jen's apartment.

"Wait. Don't go home yet," Jen said, a note of alarm in her tone. "We still have to visit the park."

Knox nearly hung his head. He'd forgotten about that, and he preferred the idea of getting Jen and D.J. back into their building. "We never stopped at the deli," he said, offering a flimsy excuse to skip the outing. "I usually bring sandwiches."

"Good thing everyone likes Burger Haven," she said, pulling a set of gift cards from her magic bag.

THEY CRUISED INTO the park's parking lot several minutes later, armed with five of everything on the fast-food restaurant's dollar menu.

Jen slipped a sleeping D.J. into her sling, then shut the truck door softly, careful not to wake him. She inhaled the warm summer air and sent up another prayer for Madison's sake. Her heart ached at the thought of how this search might end, and she feared for Katie too. Something was wrong, and it seemed as if Madison and Katie were in on it.

Why hadn't Madison let Jen in on it?

A soft snore rose from the baby at her chest, and Jen knew the answer to her question. Madison would never do anything to endanger D.J., so she must've known what she was doing was wrong. Yet, Madison wasn't the kind of woman who did things she knew were wrong. It simply wasn't who she was. Which only made the last two days seem more impossibly surreal. It was as if Jen and D.J. had left the community center after swim class and walked into a completely different world.

Knox strode confidently ahead of her, two handled shopping bags full of food in his massive grip.

Jen hung back, not wanting to make the group Knox planned to speak with uncomfortable. It seemed to her that most people were guarded when being asked uncomfortable questions. Like, if they'd witnessed a gunman in the park last night, for example. A park where many of them might live. A thread of fear weaved through her at the thought. If any of them had seen something awful happen, and was brave enough to talk about it, would they be in danger for snitching? If the shooter somehow found out, where could the witnesses hide?

She offered a warm smile as she put some distance between Knox and her, and moved toward the carousel Madison loved.

She approached slowly, keeping watch on the people in her periphery and making sure not to leave Knox's line of sight. A series of metal blockade fences about four feet tall surrounded the antique ride. She crouched to look beneath the metal carousel floor. It was dark, and she used her cell phone's flashlight to aid her eyes, but only found rocks and dirt.

Next, she examined the horses, but there wasn't anything amiss there either.

Eventually, she reached the far side of the carousel, where four-by-eight-foot sections of plywood had been erected and signs announcing the restoration project and timeline were posted. She trailed her fingers along the makeshift wall, thinking it seemed like a good place to hide in the dark. Even with the security lights on, the barrier would've created long shadows, like the one around the tree where the gunman had appeared.

Jen shivered at the memory, her gaze falling briefly and catching on a thin silvery line. She crouched for a closer look and found pencil marks on the makeshift wall. The marks were hasty and scrawled, but she recognized them as words. As names. And Madison's name was underlined. Below that was a single word.

Abel.

That was also the name of one of the doctors from the clinic. Dr. Michael Martz and Dr. Robert Abel.

"Knox!" The word burst from her lips, causing D.J. to flinch. "Shh," she cooed in apology. She stroked his back comfortingly as she rushed in her protector's direction.

Knox's eyes were on hers, his body moving toward her before she'd taken more than a few steps of her own. "What's wrong?"

"Look." She led him back to the compressed wood, then crouched and pointed to the list. She accessed her phone's camera and took several photos for later.

Knox did the same, then texted his pictures to the sheriff's department. When he stood once more, he caught her with a compassionate look. "We need to tread lightly from here. This could be a crime scene."

Jen froze, her limbs stiff with panic as she nodded.

Knox walked the immediate area slowly, carefully, scrutinizing the area between the list and the gravel access road. He lowered into a squat several feet away.

Jen's heart hammered as he raised his phone once more, this time to his ear.

He announced himself, then added, "I need a deputy at Carousel Park. We've got drag marks, and signs of a struggle."

Jen drifted in his direction, pulled by the tethers of fear and heartbreak. Flashes of unspeakable scenarios blinked into her mind like a fun house strobe light. A faceless attacker. Madison's terror. Her useless fight.

Her abduction.

The world began to shimmer in Jen's periphery, and the air seemed suddenly too thin.

Knox cursed as he stepped carefully into a patch of tall grass along the road's edge. He pulled a set of blue gloves from his back pocket and snapped them on before retrieving something for inspection.

The ground tilted beneath her as the item came clearly into view.

Madison's cell phone.

Chapter Ten

Jen stared at the phone in Knox's gloved hand. Her gaze traveled to the drag marks in the soft earth, then to the list written on the plywood beside her. The names were invisible from only a few feet away, even in the sunlight. Madison had had her pencil with her, but there wasn't any sign of her notebook. Would they find that here somewhere too?

"Looks like it," Knox said, still speaking on the phone, and drawing her eyes back to him.

He stood at the base of a utility pole, head tipped back and eyes skyward. His free hand shielded the sun. "They might be owned by the construction company in charge of the renovations, but there's definitely a security camera, and it's pointed directly at the carousel."

She followed his gaze up the pole to the object in question.

"How soon can you get out here?" he asked. "All right. We'll wait."

Knox disconnected and tucked the phone into his pocket. He turned to Jen with his hands on his hips. "You okay?"

"No." Her roommate was missing, apparently dragged away from a park at night. Probably by the man Jen had seen with a gun. Nothing about this was all right.

Knox headed for her, arms opening at the last moment, before wrapping her and D.J. in a hug. "I'm sorry you're going through this."

She leaned into him, resting her head on his chest and cradling her son between them. "I don't know how to feel or how to process," she said, emotion welling in her chest and throat. "I'm glad for the evidence, because I know it's what we need, but I'm horrified by what this means." She struggled to even her breaths and calm her racing heart. "Do drag marks mean she's…" She paused, the constricting lump in her throat making it impossible to finish the gruesome thought.

"No. Madison was most likely unconscious, but alive at the time," he said, answering her unfinished question. "Otherwise, there wouldn't have been a reason to take her."

Jen nodded, finding logic and hope in the awful explanation.

As long as Madison was alive, there was still time to save her.

"This is all good news," Knox said, his breath blowing against her hair. "The lab will send folks down here to make casts of the shoe prints for analysis. They'll come back with height and weight estimates of her abductor. Tech will work on getting her phone unlocked. And with a little luck, the security camera recorded the whole thing."

Jen pulled herself together and stepped away. Everyone had a job to do. Including her. She just needed her marching orders. "What now?"

"Now, we wait another few minutes for the crime

scene team to arrive. I have a few more questions for the folks I was just talking to, then you and I will take D.J. home and wait for more news. Sound good?"

"Okay."

Knox wrapped his arm across her shoulders, pulling her close as they moved toward the group he'd been speaking with before she called him away.

The warmth of him soothed her, and she allowed herself to breathe easier. Whatever happened next, at least she wasn't alone.

Another memory found its way to the surface of her mind, and she slowed her pace. "There was a dark sedan here that night," she said, turning to point to where the car had been. "At the end of the gravel road, nestled up against the trees."

Knox looked in the direction she pointed, then sent another text. "Can you tell me anything else about the car?"

"No." She frowned. "I figured it was abandoned. The lights were off, and I was focused on finding Madison."

He nodded and pocketed his phone, then pulled her to him once more.

She melted into him with each slow step, trying not to think of how much she'd like to keep Knox in her life after Madison was safely home again. She wanted him as her friend, as a companion and confidant. Maybe even as her lover. She wanted Knox however she could have him, because he made her feel whole. And he'd made her feel better in the short time they'd been together than she had in a very long time, and he'd done that during two of the worst days of her life.

"Things are going to be okay," he said softly, reading her mind once more, and knowing precisely what she needed to hear.

A dark sedan appeared on the park road, several yards away, and Knox stiffened at her side. "Is that the car you saw last night?" he asked, voice tense and laced with caution.

"I—"

Before she could think or answer, the passenger window of the car rolled down and the driver's extended arm came into view, with a handgun pointed at them.

Knox was in motion before her brain could make sense of what was happening. He gripped her shoulders and pulled her sideways, nearly yanking her off her feet in the process. "Get down!" he bellowed.

She struggled to keep her feet beneath her, and the gunshots sounded as she stumbled.

Each round was fast and loud. Screams rose into the air, and for the first time since D.J. had been born, Jen hated having him on her chest. She needed to hide him, to tuck him behind her and get him out of the line of fire, but there was nothing she could do.

She wrapped her arms around her baby in the sling and pumped her legs with purpose, working to keep pace as Knox dragged them behind his nearby truck for safety. The window above them exploded, raining the broken glass over them and into their hair.

Tires squealed and an engine roared in her ringing ears as the car raced away.

In the distance, cries of emergency responders wound to life.

In her arms, a stiff and red-faced D.J. screamed and arched his back in panic.

In that moment, Jen's tears began to fall.

KNOX SETTLED JEN and D.J. into his office at the sheriff's department an hour later. His brother, Cruz, had picked them up from the carousel, after Knox and Jen had given their verbal statements. His pickup was on its way to the shop for a new window.

Meanwhile, Jen had provided a written account of the park shooting while Knox had followed up on the lead about the car. There had been a dark sedan outside Katie's house when they left too.

He watched as she played with her son, finally calmed after the awful experience. Her smile was present but false. D.J. didn't seem to notice, but Knox had learned to differentiate between the looks. The one she wore now was meant to put others at ease, usually her son. The expression was a good facsimile, but he could see the strain in her eyes and tight set of her jaw.

Jen glanced in Knox's direction, and he longed to reach for her. To comfort her and hold her. The urge was becoming impossibly difficult to deny, and he'd found himself indulging it far too often. How many times had he put his arm around her? Hugged her? Taken her hand or set a palm against her back? He had no right to do any of those things, yet she never denied him. Never stiffened or sidestepped. In fact, the opposite always happened. She relaxed into his touch, and his heart expanded further every time.

A knock on the open door drew his gaze from Jen to his brother, Cruz, leaning against the jamb.

Cruz smiled his ten-thousand-watt smile and crossed his ankles. "How's everyone holding up?" he asked, sliding his eyes from Knox to Jen and D.J.

His older brother had caught him staring at the woman in his care, and was amused. "We're good,"

Knox said. "Thanks for the ride earlier. I didn't realize you were still here."

Cruz shrugged. "I had a few things to follow up on." His private investigations firm kept him in regular contact with local law enforcement, so that wasn't a surprise. Still, Knox couldn't help thinking his brother appeared to have an agenda.

Jen smiled, the expression still not reaching her eyes. "We were lucky today. Thanks for getting us out of there," she said. "The carousel is officially ruined for me. I don't care if its renovation is legendary."

Cruz grinned. "How's the little one?"

"Perfect," she said, turning her son on her lap to face him.

Cruz made a few goofy faces and sounds at D.J., before winking at Jen and heading to Knox's desk.

Knox wondered if punching his older brother in the eye might keep it from winking at Jen again, then he laughed at the ridiculous thought and sighed. Clearly, he needed more sufficient rest, and possibly some good old-fashioned Kentucky bourbon. Because he was not himself.

Cruz sat on the corner of Knox's desk, one smug foot dangling, the other planted on the ground. "Any word on the camera footage?"

"Not yet," Knox answered. He double-checked his text messages and inbox, just in case he'd missed the update. He hadn't.

"Want me to look into it?" Cruz asked. "I'm guessing you'd like to get home."

Knox nodded. "Thanks." The Jefferson County Sheriff's Department was small by any standard, but especially when compared to the sheer amount of geographical area the deputies covered. And MX-10 had been running them ragged for the past couple months. As a result, they'd been calling Cruz and his partner, their cousin Derek, in more often.

"No problem," Cruz said. "Anything else?"

Knox rubbed his throat, mind racing over the day. "Maybe," he said. "I can't be sure, but I think the sedan in the park was the same one I saw parked on the receptionist's block earlier. The one outside Katie's place had a temporary tag in the window, but I don't know if this one did," he admitted, hating that he'd missed such an important detail.

His mind had been on Jen and D.J. instead of in lawman mode. Normally, he could remain calm through anything, because he wasn't worried about getting hurt. He never had been. Maybe that was a personality defect. Maybe it was a sign of damage done to a kid who'd lost his mother too soon, or a man who'd lost too much overseas. But he'd never feared for himself, and that fact made him a better lawman. He wasn't hindered by self-concern. When push came to shove, Knox could shove hard, and take in the most minute of details while he did.

But not today. Not with Jen and D.J. in danger.

Today, his body had responded on instinct, and the only thing his mind could manage was *Not them. Please, not them.*

Cruz tented his brows. "You followed the receptionist from her place. You think the shooter followed you?"

"Maybe," he said again. Truthfully, he wasn't sure of anything anymore, and he hated the tangling of his thoughts almost as much as the fact they'd been shot at.

He'd never been tailed without knowing before. And a screwup like that could've cost Jen and D.J. their lives.

Jen shifted, drawing the brothers' attention, and her gaze settled on Knox. "Did you learn anything from the folks you gave the burgers to?"

Cruz twisted on the desktop for a better look at Knox. "I almost forgot you head down there on weekends with food. What did they say? Anyone see anything?"

"Yeah," Knox said. "Actually they did, but nothing helpful. They tried though. I'll give them that. They saw a man dressed in black and carrying a gun. He wore a ski mask, so they couldn't describe his features. He was alone when they saw him, and came within a few feet of the group, gun brandished, before moving on."

Cruz made a disgusted sound. "He was probably looking for Jen's roommate, and she was hiding by the carousel. He must've found her after that."

"That's my guess," Knox said.

His brother's clear green eyes flashed. "All right then," he said, stretching onto his feet. "I brought you a loaner car and saw to it that your window will be fixed and the pickup returned to your place when it's ready. If you need anything else, give me a call." He produced a key fob from his pocket and set it on Knox's desk, then tipped his invisible hat and sauntered out the door.

Jen watched him leave, curiosity on her brow. She turned her attention back to Knox a moment later and grinned. "Your brother is nice."

He narrowed his eyes. "Yeah." Knox loved and respected his older brother more than just about anyone on the planet, so the odd sense of jealousy that hit with her words caught him off guard. He didn't like it.

She wouldn't be the first person to prefer Cruz to Knox. Most folks did. Cruz had that effect on people, especially women. They liked his confidence, his attitude and his swagger. Knox considered himself a likable guy, but compared to Cruz, he was a surly curmudgeon.

"You look a lot alike," Jen continued. "Are you ever mistaken for twins?"

"Not since we were kids," Knox said, a smirk creeping over his face. "Once I gained two inches on him, he was mistaken for the younger brother though. I thought it was funny at the time, but the closer I get to thirty, the more appealing being the younger brother has become."

She smiled. "Were your personalities always so different?"

That observation gave him pause. Jen had only spoken to Cruz a few minutes on the ride from the park, then a few more just now. "What do you mean?" he asked, before he could think better of it. Of course she'd noticed the differences between brothers. He and Cruz were like night and day. And Jen missed very little.

"I'm not sure," she said. "He might've been putting on a show for my sake, maybe to cheer me up," she clarified. "But he seems to be a charmer in the most charismatic sense of the word."

"That's Cruz," Knox said, smiling at her careful but accurate word choices. "People love him, and he loves that people love him."

She laughed. "And what do people think about you?" she asked.

Knox felt his resting grouch face return. "I'm too serious, and I need to relax. I'm steadfast and capable, but not the brother to have around if you're looking for a lot of jokes and small talk."

Jen nodded, accepting Knox's self-description, while he tried to figure out why he'd said so much.

"I think we're done here," he said, breaking the strange, suddenly palpable tension. "If you're ready, we can grab an early dinner and head back to your place. We've completely missed lunch."

She stood and nodded. "Okay."

He took the diaper bag before she could slip it over her shoulder, then he reached for her hand.

"Knox?" she asked, turning her palm against his and lacing their fingers.

"Yeah?"

"Is it okay if you're my favorite Winchester brother?" she asked.

A careful smile lifted Knox's cheeks, and a bubble of hope expanded in his chest. "Yeah."

"Good," she said, nodding as she raised her eyes to his. "Because I prefer steadfast to small talk."

Chapter Eleven

After dinner, Jen gave D.J. a bath, then strapped him into his bouncy seat so she could take a shower. She spent a prolonged amount of time attempting to wash away the awful day. The water and baby giggles went a long way to removing her tension.

Knowing Knox Winchester was in her living room, fully capable of protecting them all, and possibly attracted to her too, sent a flutter of comfort and joy through her core. She'd seen the interest in his eyes several times, though he hadn't said a word to confirm or deny it. But their connection was so much deeper than the danger they'd been in or the case they were working. Life was easy with him at her side. The time passed too quickly and always with warmth and laughter.

She stepped into the hall several minutes later, dressed in fresh yoga pants and a T-shirt. Her towel-dried hair was twisted into a high loose bun.

Not surprisingly, Knox had cleaned up the take-out containers from their meal while she and D.J. were busy. He'd also turned on the living room television and selected the local news station.

Jen pressed her eyes shut, sending up silent prayers for a new development on Madison's case. This was the end of the second day she'd been missing, and every hour she remained gone was an hour closer to the point where most missing persons didn't make it home.

D.J. cooed, opening Jen's eyes, and she carried on, shoulders back and chin up. She stopped at the front door to check the new locks once more. The deadbolt and knob had both been changed. She added the chain for good measure, and hoped Knox would consider staying another night or two. She doubted she'd be able to sleep otherwise.

"We're back," she announced when Knox looked up from his phone. "Sorry it took so long. You didn't have to clean up."

"I wanted to, and you should take as long as you need," he said. "Feeling any better?"

"A little." She set the bouncy seat on the floor near the couch and gave D.J. a snuggle before buckling him in once more. "Now, I just have to call off work so no one worries, and there's enough time to replace me. My next class isn't until the day after tomorrow, but I'm going to let them know what's going on, then bow out for the rest of the week." She bit her lip as a horrible thought arose. "At least I hope this will be over in a week." She grabbed her phone and dropped onto the cushion beside Knox.

His arm went easily around her. "We're going to do everything we can," he said.

She made the call with as much confidence and positivity as she could muster, despite her boss's well-intentioned questions and concern. Then disconnected with a sigh.

Knox wrapped his arm a little tighter, urging her to lean on him. "How'd you get a job teaching swim classes at the community center?" he asked. "I feel like there's a story there."

She pressed her lips together a moment, before reluctantly admitting the unconventional truth. "My dad was a swim coach until his heart attack, so I grew up in the water. Swimming is just about the only thing I'm qualified to do, and I do it pretty well."

Knox smiled. "Have you always wanted to coach like your dad?"

"No." She nearly snorted at the idea. Not that she didn't love her job. There was just so much more behind the decision to work at a pool. "I started swimming competitively before I could write my name, legibly anyway. I was five. I got a full athletic scholarship for college after high school, then I blew out my shoulder in training one day, and that was that. It didn't heal right. My times climbed. My scholarship disappeared, and I had to figure out who I was and what I wanted to do with my life if I couldn't swim."

Knox was still and quiet. Probably trying to decide what to say, so she pressed on.

"People hear about male athletes going through things like this more often than women. It happens, but it's not quite so newsworthy. I had a hard time finding women to talk to about it, and I grew bitter. I rebelled. Pushed everyone away who I suspected might try to comfort me. I felt like a failure and wanted to wallow." She smiled. "That was all wrong, of course. I see that now, but I didn't then. Thankfully, I met Dylan before I did anything too crazy, and I gave in to the wonders of a first love. Life with him was a whirlwind. It was exciting and ever-changing. We traveled when he was on leave. Always a new town. New adventure. Then sometimes he was gone for months. It was hard not knowing where he was or if he was okay. Then one day he was just gone."

She felt her breath shudder as she exhaled. "My parents warned me against the engagement. In fairness, they were right. I barely knew him. But Dylan made me feel alive. I hadn't felt so free and peaceful outside the water in a long time. Still, they didn't approve, and they made sure I knew."

"How are you and your folks doing now?" Knox asked.

"Okay. They call about once a week and check in. They adore D.J., and wish I lived closer." She gave a short humorless laugh. "They think it isn't safe for two women and a baby to live alone."

"Is that why you haven't called to tell them what you're going through?"

Jen sighed. She dreaded their next call. Having to tell them what was happening would be awful. They'd say they told her so. They'd be terrified and her dad would probably be on a plane to collect her before she finished her story. She'd almost called them last night, when she couldn't sleep, but she knew she'd never get the words off her tongue. "They invited me to come home to Florida while they were in town for Dylan's funeral, but I wasn't ready to think about starting over again. The concept seemed too big. And I didn't want to leave Dylan. I thought I'd visit his grave every day." She gave a soft smile. "I do not."

"He wouldn't want you to," Knox said. "No one wants that for their loved ones. Would you?"

Jen rested her head against his chest, knowing he was right. "No."

She reached for Knox's hand and let herself imagine a life with him. Silly as it was. And with too many scary things happening all around them. She indulged the fantasy, and it felt like home.

KNOX PULLED JEN in close. She melted against him as always, and he appreciated the complexity of her. So strong and still so loving. He hated knowing her family was so far away when she needed them. The idea of seeing her get on a plane to Florida made him feel hollow, but at least she and D.J. would be safe there. "You really should find a way to visit."

"Yeah." She tipped her head back and cast a shy look in his direction. "Maybe the next time you have some vacation days, you can visit them with me."

Knox felt his insides twist at the thought of taking a trip with Jen, especially one so important. So he set his mind to make it happen.

"Anyway," she said with a sigh, "I've always worked at pools since then. Sometimes I coach youth leagues or teach adult lessons, but right now I specialize in Water Babies and mommy-and-me classes, because I can take D.J. with me."

Knox tipped his head to hers, resting his cheek against her crown.

"Should we call the clinic and make an appointment to speak with the doctors?" she asked, changing the subject back to the crisis at hand.

"Definitely not," he said, determined to keep her out of harm's way moving forward. "Deputies will take care of that. Abel's name was on the list at the park, and they'll figure out why. Right now, my job is to keep you and D.J. safe, and your job is to let me."

He didn't have a single guess about what the names meant or how they were related, and it was sure to make him insane. There was nothing more grating than an unanswered question.

Jen reached for his free hand and pulled it across her middle, snuggling in for comfort. She angled her body and tipped her head to look at him. "What do you think Madison was trying to tell us with that list?" she asked.

"I don't know, but the sheriff's department will figure it out," he assured.

"Then we'll hop on a plane to Florida?" she asked, her tone teasing.

"Absolutely," he agreed, trying not to think about her sweet breath blowing across his face.

She was so impossibly close. He'd barely have to move to press his mouth to hers. Her gaze dropped to his lips, and his reckless heart gave a heavy thud.

This isn't the time, he reminded himself, especially considering what he still needed to ask her.

He'd planned to talk to her as soon as she and D.J. came back from the shower, but he'd let himself get distracted, and the time was only getting later. "Before we go to Florida," he said softly, his self-control waning, "how do you feel about spending tonight at my place?"

Chapter Twelve

Jen easily agreed to spending the night at Knox's place. She hadn't cared where they stayed, as long as he was with her, and she knew D.J. would be safe. She also couldn't complain about getting more time with Knox, whom she couldn't seem to get enough of.

D.J. had fallen asleep before she'd managed to finish packing, so they'd agreed to leave after he woke. Until then, she gathered the things they might need.

"Don't worry about all the baby equipment," Knox called from the living room, where he'd volunteered to break down the portable crib for transport. "My auntie and uncle keep one of everything baby gear–related at their place for when they babysit. And their stuff gets toted around, house to house, as needed when new kids come on board."

Jen stopped folding onesies for D.J. and backed into the hallway between the bedroom and living room. "Did you say when new kids come on board?"

He flashed a crooked smile from her living room. "My family was big by anyone's standards two years ago. Today, we could qualify as our own country."

"Winchester Country, huh?" she asked, returning to her packing. "Sounds wild."

"You have no idea."

She finished in the bedroom, then turned out the light on her way back to the living room. "I think this is everything," she said, setting the final duffel bag with the other things already stacked near her front door. She tried to imagine temporarily moving into Knox's home and failed. Squinting, she realized she hadn't asked a very important question. "Where do you live?"

Knox was a deputy sheriff. His jurisdiction covered the entire county. He might not even live in her town for all she knew, and she suddenly couldn't believe she didn't know.

"I'm about twenty minutes from here," he said. "On the outskirts between Great Falls and West Liberty. Not too far to run back for anything you forget."

That seemed acceptable, and incredibly comforting, because she wasn't sure what she'd need for an indefinite amount of time away from home. She and D.J. had never left the apartment for more than a few hours.

"Are you sure this is okay?" she asked, suddenly second-guessing his offer to move a new mom and her baby into his home. The bag in the kitchen, filled with infinite baby food jars, bottles and formula cans, was bigger than D.J.'s diaper bag, and that had his favorite blanket in it. "We're going to overrun your bachelor pad."

Knox laughed, then gave her a warm, sincere look. "I'm glad to have you both for as long as you need. I wish it wasn't under these circumstances, but I wouldn't trust many other people to keep you safe, so this works out just fine. Besides," he added, watching her over the half-collapsed crib between them, "I'm looking forward to getting to know you better."

Her cheeks warmed, and so did her heart. "Me too," she said. "You're my hero, Knox Winchester."

He chuckled. "Glad to hear it. I don't plan to have my title revoked anytime soon, so I'd better get back to work." He rooted in her little pink-and-black tool kit for something to use on the portable crib.

She'd purchased the item at a garage sale when she was pregnant, and it was a great crib, but it was old and testy. Not always easy to set up or tear down. She'd decided months ago it was easiest to leave it set up at all times, and just drag it from room to room as needed. Madison sometimes helped her carry it with D.J. playing inside. If it hadn't been for Madison, Jen probably would've moved home to Florida with her parents. Her life would be completely different. And Madison would still be in Missouri. And she would be safe.

Knox left the crib and moved across the space in her direction. "You okay?"

She nodded, but struggled to meet his eye, hoping he wouldn't see the wash of emotion on her face.

"Hey," he said, stopping a few feet in front of her. "I've been thinking. You've had a lot happen to you since we originally met. You lost Dylan. Had a baby. Your family's halfway across the country." He waited for her to meet his gaze before going on. "Aside from this mess with Madison, how are you really doing?"

Jen bit her lip and forced herself to hold his eye contact. No one had asked her how she was doing, not really, in a very long time. "I'm okay," she said, and unlike a long period of time during and immediately after her pregnancy, she meant it.

"Things must be hard without Dylan," Knox said.

She shrugged. "Sure. I was lucky to have him in my

life, even if it was only for a little while. He was easy to love and exactly what I'd needed while I figured out who I was or wanted to be without swim."

Knox nodded, crossing his arms and resting his backside against her counter, intently focused, as if her words were the most important ones in the world. And he needed to concentrate. "And who are you now?"

She smiled. "I'm strong," she said. "In different ways than I was before. New ways. More ways. I'm capable. I'm happy, and I'm content. D.J. is hands down the best thing that has ever happened to me, and being with him fulfills me in ways I never could've imagined before. I wasn't ready for a pregnancy, or for motherhood, but I wouldn't trade a moment of it for anything. I don't feel like I'm searching anymore. I feel like I am who I was meant to be, and I like this person."

Knox scanned her face with his gaze, examining her, evaluating her. And she couldn't help wondering what he saw there.

"What?" she asked finally.

He shook his head. "I think you're incredible."

"I try," she said, offering a shy smile. "There wasn't any choice once I learned I was pregnant. D.J. needed a mother."

Knox nodded. "What do you need?" he asked, still watching her with careful, evaluating eyes.

She gave a soft laugh. "I just need him to be safe," she said. "Anything other than that is icing."

"So, tell me about the icing."

Jen smiled. "I'd like to find a partner in this life someday. Someone to grow old with, to fight with, to make up with." She paused, thinking carefully about what she'd say next. "I want someone I know will always have my back, whatever comes. And I want a role model for D.J. A father figure who can do the things with him that Dylan can't. I think Dylan would want that too."

Knox nodded. "He would."

"But not another military man," she said, the words popping free without much thought. "No more men who live for exciting, special-ops, dangerous missions in far-off places. That was for a younger, child-free me."

Knox frowned deeply, his enviable light and good humor gone. "Explain, please."

She frowned back at him, ruffled by his reaction to her truth. "Because I've changed." She motioned to D.J., snoozing in his bouncy seat. "Everything has changed."

"And you wouldn't want a partner whose life was regularly in danger," he said, evidently forlorn at the thought.

"No." She shook her head. "Not that. It's more about the deployment. Because I'd really like to find someone who will always be around." She smiled, a small self-deprecating smile. "I've gotten selfish in the last year. I want a man who'd be here for me and D.J., every day. A man who wants to be here. Day in and day out, for the good and the bad. I want a full-time partner in my life."

"So, you wouldn't mind a partner who had a danger-ous job?" Knox asked. "Even if he worked long hours and his shifts varied?"

She smiled, and heat flooded her once more. "Not as long as he showed up for D.J. and me when it counted."

His frown eased. "So, a standard lawman, for ex-ample," he said, eyes twinkling, "would be acceptable, but not a marshal or agent who might have to go under-cover for long stints of time."

"Correct. I want the whole boring, wonderful, run-of-the-mill family experience."

"Like a man who coaches D.J.'s Little League and attends Scout meetings."

"I'll lead the Scout meetings," she said. "Obviously."

"And the swim classes?" Knox asked, his smile growing as he spoke.

"We can split those."

"Got it," Knox said, nodding. "And how will you know when you've found this guy?"

A wicked smile twisted her lips, and she shot a teasing look at her friend. "Because he'll be all-in from the start, and he'll want more than just my body."

He pressed a hand to his chest and groaned. "Let's keep it clean, Jordan. I'm still trying not to picture you in a swimsuit."

She laughed, and he went back to the crib. "Do you need some help?" she asked, following in his wake.

"Absolutely." He waved to the mostly flattened piece of baby equipment. "Unless I'm missing something, this seems to be completely stuck."

As she suspected. "Screwdriver," she said, offering him her open palm.

"Flathead or Phillips?" he asked, not bothering to lecture her on the obvious fact there wasn't anything on the crib in need of that particular tool.

"Either."

Knox handed her a flathead. "All right. Show me what I'm missing."

She felt along the padded blue cover for the rusty joint hidden just out of sight, then whacked it with the handle of her screwdriver, and the side swung down.

Knox clapped slowly in appreciation. "Nice."

She returned the screwdriver, and their fingers touched. Heat raced up her arm to her chest, and she stepped closer on instinct, eagerly seeking more.

Knox's gaze darkened, and his hands settled on the curves of her waist. "Thank you for your help," he said, tugging her closer still. "I was ready to chuck the whole thing out the window, but you knew just what to do."

"It's what I do," she said. "I'm a problem-solver."

He grinned.

She looked up at him, and the heat pooling in her core seemed to be reflected in his eyes. She'd nearly kissed him on the couch, when their mouths had been so close she could feel his breath on her face. Something had stopped her then, making her think it wasn't the right time. But she was more positive with every exchange that Knox was a man worth kissing. He was a man worth holding on to.

His broad palms skimmed her back. One set of strong fingers gripped her at the waist, pulling her against him, while the other hand glided up her spine to cradle her neck.

Her back arched in response, and her breath caught as his gaze lowered to her parted lips.

D.J.'s sudden cry sent a bout of nervous laughter from her lips, and Jen spun on her heels to collect her whimpering son. He never woke upset, and her heart clenched at the probability the day had left a dark spot on his psyche somehow. She cooed and rocked him, holding him close as she dared a look at Knox.

He leaned against the armchair a few feet away, unmoving. His eyes danced as he rubbed a forefinger across his lightly stubbled chin. A playful smile curved his lips.

She considered a number of silly comments about the way she'd jumped, as if she was a child who'd been caught doing something wrong.

But Knox's smile fell before she could find the right words, and he grabbed the television remote from the coffee table. "Jen," he said, raising the volume on a newscast as he moved in close to her side.

A breaking-news report had begun, complete with a red ribbon stretched across the bottom of her screen. The words *Death in Downtown* curled icy fingers into her gut.

The pretty blonde reporter tossed her hair and feigned sadness at the camera. "...sad to report a fatal accident at a busy downtown intersection earlier today. Eyewitnesses say that the driver ran a stoplight at the intersection of Jefferson and First Avenue. The car was then struck by a city utilities truck and forced into on-coming traffic, where it rolled several times before colliding with a tree. The car's driver, and only passenger, was ejected and pronounced dead at the scene. She is the only known fatality at this time."

Jen stared breathlessly at the remains of a small red hatchback on her television screen. Undeniably, the receptionist's car.

Chapter Thirteen

Jen wobbled and reached for the island to steady herself. The red hatchback they'd followed from Katie's home through downtown looked nearly annihilated on screen. A mass of emergency responders filled the area, and roadblocks were set up to control traffic and onlookers.

"She's dead," Jen whispered, her stomach knotting and her breaths coming in short shallow pants. "I feel sick."

Knox moved to her side and lowered before her, enough to catch her eyes. "May I hold D.J.?" he asked, gently taking the baby from her arms. "Thank you. Now, why don't you have a seat on the couch? I'll get you some water."

Jen let him lead her to the sofa, then she pulled her legs to her chest while she watched the onscreen horrors unfold. "The accident happened earlier today," she said. "How long do you think it was after we lost track of her? Did the cruiser ever catch up?"

Knox returned with a cold bottle of water and passed it to her. "I'll send a text and see what happened."

She dragged her gaze from the television to Knox, who was confidently comforting her son in one arm and texting with his free hand. His expression was impossibly calm despite the unthinkable turn of events.

Her thoughts were muddled as memories of the clinic's receptionist flickered in and out through the shock. The photographs on Katie's mantel came to mind. "Her poor son," she whispered, nausea rising at the memory.

"Drink," Knox said, motioning to the bottle in her hand. "I think it's time we get moving as soon as you're feeling steady." His gaze drifted to the television. "I want to get you both back to my place."

Jen's intuition spiked. The look on Knox's face said everything he hadn't. "You don't think the crash was an accident," she said.

"I don't know." Knox locked his eyes on hers. "The timing is questionable, and I can't help wondering if you're in more danger than I imagined. I'll feel safer once we're at my place." He cuddled D.J. close and tipped his cheek against her son's hair.

She nodded, taking another long drag on the bottle before pushing onto her feet. She wouldn't keep D.J. anywhere potentially unsafe. "So there isn't any chance that this was a horrible coincidence?"

"Few things ever are."

Jen stuffed her feet into waiting sneakers, then went to grab her purse, phone and keys.

Knox's phone dinged, and he swiped a thumb across the screen to read the message. "I've got confirmation that Katie's accident is being considered as connected to Madison's disappearance." He looked up with a nod. "That's good news. It means Madison's picture will be posted on local and state news and social-media channels. A whole lot more people will know she's missing, and our chances of finding her improve."

Her heart hammered, and hope rose in her chest.

The news reporter's voice drew Jen's attention back to the screen. "...this afternoon's fatal downtown traffic accident may not have been an accident, after all. Reports of a severed brake line have begun to roll in, but the Jefferson County Sheriff's Department is refusing to comment."

Jen's breath caught as the screen went dark.

Beside her, Knox lowered the remote to the counter and fixed her with a stare. "Ready?"

She nodded, and they gathered the things she'd stacked near the front door.

Of course Knox had predicted Katie's crash wasn't an accident. It was his job to get ahead of things, to be astute and cautious. Jen wondered what else he'd been right about. The pills hidden in her bathroom came to mind. "This is about the baggie of MX-10. Isn't it? You were right about that too."

Knox held the door while she passed. He locked up behind them, then ushered her quickly to his truck. "I was wrong when I thought Madison was using those pills," he said when they were safely in his truck. "I can see I misjudged her now, but I'm willing to bet she learned something about MX-10 that she shouldn't know, and Katie knew it too."

THEY RODE IN silence until eventually arriving at a small brick ranch with black roof and shutters. The lot was sizable with mature trees and a tire swing in the massive oak out front.

The home was cute and quaint, situated at the end of a long gravel lane off the county road. Jen took in the property details, gently illuminated by landscape and security lighting. Black mulch beds were polka-dotted with neatly trimmed shrubs and brightly colored flowers.

A large garden stone, situated near the porch steps, had two neatly scripted words across its center.

Welcome Home.

Knox climbed out and opened the extended cab's door to collect D.J.

Jen fixed her eyes on the inviting front porch, large welcome mat and quaint red rocking chair. A matching red barn sat several yards away in the lush green grass. She smiled at the little structure. He probably kept a lawn tractor and gardening tools inside.

Clearly, when Knox Winchester wasn't being a deputy sheriff, or her personal hero, he was a regular guy with an adorable home and a plot of land he tended.

He strode onto the porch with her baby in one arm and several bags looped over his shoulders. "You okay?" he asked, casting a look her way.

"Yeah." She followed, warmed by the unexpectedly domestic scene. She hadn't given much thought to where Knox lived, but she also hadn't expected this. She would've assumed he had an apartment like hers, if she'd expected anything at all. A single-man lair of some sort. Either utterly messy or cold and efficient due to his demanding job. The home and land before her were something else entirely.

He ushered her inside from his place on the porch, an inviting smile on his lips, and her baby snuggled contentedly against his chest. She imagined the scene unfolding a dozen times, each with Knox and D.J. growing older. Then flashes of Knox teaching D.J. to ride a bike on the gravel lane, pushing him in the tire swing under the oak tree and playing catch on the large front lawn. Her eyes and nose stung with unexpected emotion, and she covered it with a yawn.

The ideas were silly and impossible. A result of her strung-out state. And they were also more than she'd dared to dream of since losing Dylan.

"Come on. I'll give you the ten-cent tour," Knox said, as she passed him in the doorframe. "Think you're ready?"

"Yes." The answer was honest, and she knew it covered much more than a tour.

KNOX ROSE WITH the sun the next morning. He'd barely slept and was eager to get started on a new day. Hopefully, the next twenty-four hours would bring authorities closer to finding Jen's missing roommate than yesterday had. His heart had gone out to Katie, her family and especially her poor son. If only she'd clued Knox in to whatever was going on with Madison and what she knew about the MX-10, maybe Knox could've saved her. He'd run through the possibilities a thousand times. She might still have run, might not have let him take her into custody. Heck, depending on what she'd said, he might not have offered to take her anywhere, and she still would've gotten into an unsafe car the next time she left home.

He stretched a T-shirt over his head and pressed the heels of his hands against his eyes, hating the utter helplessness he felt. And despising the creators and distributors of a street drug that was taking far too many lives.

Knox shuffled into the hallway, ready for a pot of coffee and some food, when the sound of running water slowed his pace. The bathroom door was closed, but the soft scents of steam and soap curled into the hall. Apparently, Jen was already awake too. Hopefully, she'd managed more sleep than he had.

A squeaky baby sound drew Knox's attention to the portable crib he and Jen had set up inside her room. D.J.'s legs were in the air. One sock on and one bare foot grasped in his chubby hands.

Knox snorted and changed directions. He crept into the guest room for a look at the little brown-haired butterball.

D.J. squeaked again at the sight of him, and Knox chuckled. D.J. released his foot and stretched his arms into the air.

"Well, good morning to you too," Knox said, enchanted by the wide toothless smile. He lifted the pint-sized bundle from the crib and nestled him against his side. His diaper made the dry papery sound of a newly installed model, and his pajamas had been swapped for some kind of kiddie-sized baseball uniform. The look made Knox laugh. "I guess you were awake before your mama got into the shower, and she prepared you for the day first." That seemed in keeping with what Knox knew about her. Always putting others first. Making her son priority one. Knox had nothing but respect for that.

He turned for the door and carried D.J. into the kitchen. "I hope your mama won't mind if you help me with breakfast," he said, propping the baby on one hip while he set the coffee to brew. Next, he buckled D.J. into the portable high chair Jen had packed and scanned the counter full of baby bottles and foods. "I guess you get a bottle every morning?" he asked D.J. "It's made with water and some of that powdered formula, right? What about food?" He went back to the counter and lifted the hoard of foodstuffs. "Cereal?" He shook the box, then a few flakes onto his palm. "You eat this mixed with water?" Knox frowned and stuck out his tongue.

D.J. laughed.

Knox prepared a bottle, following the instructions on the formula can, then he started on a meal for the grown folks while the kid enjoyed his drink.

Once the oven had preheated, Knox placed a frozen casserole inside to bake. Next, he selected a knife and chopping board, along with several pieces of fresh fruit.

The pipes of his old home shuddered as he sipped his steaming coffee, signaling the end of Jen's shower. Knox did what he could to push images of her bare skin from his mind with excruciating effort. Knowing she was naked on the other side of the shared kitchen and bathroom wall was more temptation than his suddenly active imagination could handle.

D.J. patted his high chair tray, drawing Knox back to the moment.

He smiled at the thought of endless mornings like this one. Mornings when Jen and D.J. were here by choice and not as a matter of safety. He recalled her words about wanting a life partner, and someone who'd be a father to D.J. in Dylan's absence.

Knox's chest tightened as he let himself imagine filling both those roles. What would it be like if Jen and D.J. were his, and he belonged to them as well? Fishing trips with his family, and D.J. in the camp chair beside his. Laughs over shared meals, and late nights of showing Jen exactly how much she meant to him.

Soft footfalls drew his attention to the hallway beside the kitchen.

Jen appeared in black stretchy pants and a crimson top that exposed a sliver of skin when she raised a hand in greeting. Her hair was up again, and miraculously dry, somehow having eluded the shower. "Sorry," she said, looking unexplainably guilty. "I didn't mean to take so long. Normally, D.J. doesn't mind. I hope he wasn't crying. I can usually hear his whimpers from a mile away."

Knox poured a second mug of coffee, then lifted it to her in offering. "He's in a great mood. When I saw he was awake, I brought him out here with me for some man time."

She rolled her eyes and smiled. "How's that going?"

"Pretty well," he said. "I taught him to change the oil in your car before that bottle."

Her smile widened.

"Hungry?" he asked. His eyes skimmed her flushed pink skin, unbidden, and he jerked them back to her happy face.

"Starving." She smiled as she made her way to D.J. "Thank you for making him a bottle."

"It's no problem. I've got a casserole in the oven for us, and I'm making a fruit salad. I wasn't home for the last day or two, so I need to use this up."

Jen returned to Knox's side and selected a plastic bowl and spoon from D.J.'s meal supplies. "You don't have to do all this. Babysitting. Cooking." She waved the airplane-shaped spoon between them. "Letting us stay here is already too much."

He shot her a bland expression. "Please. My auntie keeps my freezer filled with more casseroles than one man could ever eat. She loves us with food, and clearly thinks I'm helpless."

"And the fruit?" she asked, resting her backside against the counter to his right.

"I like fruit."

She laughed, and the tightness in his heart unfurled.

He watched as she whipped up some mush with the baby cereal flakes, then opened a tiny jar of bananas and carried the meal to D.J.

Jen kissed her baby's head before taking the seat beside his chair. "I think it's sweet your auntie makes you casseroles. It shows how much she loves you. How many Winchester bachelors are there?"

He thought about all the weddings and engagement parties he'd been invited to in the last year and grimaced. He'd never even taken a date. Truthfully, no one had held his attention in a very long time. And no one had ever captivated him like Jen. "Only one," he said over his shoulder, lifting one hand as he pulled the casserole from the oven with the other. "Technically, I suppose there are two. We have another unmarried cousin, Nash, in Louisville, but he's too far away for Auntie to deliver meals or worry about. Plus, Nash's folks are in town with him, so she doesn't have to worry about the poor, helpless veteran and US marshal."

Jen spooned D.J.'s breakfast into his open birdy mouth. "How old is he?"

"Cruz's age," Knox said. "Maybe a year older."

Her brows furrowed, and her lips parted as she delivered each bite to her son.

Knox grinned as he plated their breakfasts and ferried everything to the little table.

D.J. bounced in his seat, legs kicking and arms flung wide, gobbling up the meal as quickly as his mama could provide it. His wide brown eyes tracked Knox's arrival.

Jen glanced up as Knox sat. "I fell asleep thinking about Florida last night," she said. "You were right. It's time I take D.J. to see my family. As soon as I know Madison is okay."

He smiled, glad for her sake and her family's, but feeling the loss at the mention of her leaving. "I think that's good," he said. "After all this, you'll need some time to recuperate. I'll keep a close eye on Madison so you won't have to worry."

Her brows rose. "You'll have to get someone else to do that," she said, scraping D.J.'s cereal bowl with a little plastic spoon. "You're coming with us."

A wide grin spread across Knox's lips and his heart gave a heavy kick.

The moment was cut short by his doorbell.

Whoever was out there had the world's worst timing, and he was nearly positive it was his brother.

Knox swiped the screen on his phone to life and checked the front porch camera.

Cruz waved cheerfully back.

Jen laughed, apparently spotting the image. "Is that Cruz?"

Knox stood with a sigh. "Welcome to Winchester Country, where you're always fed and rarely alone for long."

Chapter Fourteen

Cruz waltzed in, as carefree and attention commanding as usual.

Knox checked the driveway for signs of additional Winchesters before locking the door behind him, because his family typically traveled in packs. Satisfied his brother was alone, he followed him to the kitchen.

"Mornin', Jordans," Cruz said, waving to Jen on his way to make silly faces at D.J.

"Good morning," Jen replied, glancing at Knox with a grin.

"Breakfast sure smells good," Cruz noted, taking a seat beside the high chair. "I've been up since before dawn. Barely had more than coffee." He patted the flat stomach he was eternally proud of, then shook a monkey-shaped teether for D.J.

Knox rolled his eyes, already arranging a fresh plate for the interloper. He watched Jen for her reaction. She wasn't part of the family now, but if there was hope of her sticking around long-term, she'd have to deal with his family's nosy, pushy, loving but ever-present ways.

"Were you just in the neighborhood?" Jen asked, smiling as he entertained her baby.

"Just checking in," Cruz said.

Knox ferried the full plate to his brother.

Cruz straightened, abandoning the teether at the sight of fresh fruit salad and their auntie's casserole. "You always know exactly what I need."

"You literally told me you hadn't eaten," Knox countered, taking his seat at the table.

Jen laughed softly as Cruz dug in. Her soft, warm expression at the men's exchange spread across the space to his heart.

"Anything new on the case?" Knox asked, redirecting his attention to Cruz. "My phone's been oddly quiet since last night."

Cruz shook his head. "Not much. I stopped by the sheriff's department to deliver some findings on another case this morning, then asked around about the car accident and Madison while I was there. Mechanics confirmed the car was sabotaged. There was a clear slice to the brake line, nothing that would likely happen in the course of natural use or wear and tear. Also some damage to the steering column. Together, the issues would've made it tough to steer and impossible to slow down by the time she reached the fatal intersection."

Jen set her fork aside with a clatter. "Her driving was exponentially erratic as we followed. I thought she was just getting more upset."

Cruz bobbed his head. "That was probably true too."

Jen cringed, and Knox stifled the urge to cover her hand with his.

"I'm headed over to the clinic from here," Cruz said. "A couple deputies are planning to conduct interviews today. I figured I'd hang around, see who comes and goes. Stake the place out. Pose as a patient. Maybe overhear something of use."

Knox nodded. "I like that idea. Any chance Derek has time to get in on this?"

"He's busy." Cruz smiled. "Taking a look around Katie's house as we speak." Cruz stuffed another forkful of food into his mouth.

"Who's Derek?" Jen asked.

"My partner," Cruz said, as Knox answered, "Our cousin."

"He's a bit of a snoop and a fantastic lock-picker," Cruz added, sounding proud as usual.

Knox offered his usual, wholly ignored, warning look.

Cruz and Derek had been known to, on occasion, overlook what was legal in favor of what was helpful, especially when lives were in danger.

"A lock-picker?" Jen asked, her face scrunched in distaste, or confusion, Knox wasn't sure. "You mean he's breaking into Katie's house?" She flicked her gaze to Knox for an explanation.

Cruz waved his fork dismissively. "No. He's looking for clues about who would've hurt her and taken Madison. Nothing messy or invasive. Derek's quick and thorough. He'll be in and out without a trace. Anything he finds useful, he'll share with the sheriff's department immediately."

Knox pinned him with an unamused stare. "And how will he claim to have gotten wind of this potentially useful information this time? Considering the home owner is dead."

Cruz grinned. "Why don't we jump off that bridge when we come to it?" he suggested, mixing metaphors and tossing in a wink for good measure. "I'm sure he'll tell them the honest truth. The door was unlocked when he went inside."

"After he picked the lock," Knox said.

Cruz turned a pained expression on Jen, whose smile had returned at the increase of brotherly banter. "Knox is a fantastic lawman."

"He is," she agreed, flashing him a bright, warm smile.

"He can't always condone our actions," Cruz said, "but never complains about our respectfully gained results."

"Helpful and lawful aren't the same things," Knox said.

"Are you going to turn him in?" Cruz challenged, ending the conversation his usual way.

Knox rubbed a heavy hand over his face. "I'm on vacation."

"You would've made a great private eye." Cruz turned his face toward D.J. before Knox could work up an effective frown.

"I make a great deputy," he countered. "I hope someone is interviewing Katie's ex." And that the ex wasn't involved in her murder, or with MX-10. If her son's father went to jail, it would leave the child parentless, something no kid deserved.

"I'm sure they've got that covered," Cruz said. "You badge-types are always on the ball. Speaking of, I hear the autopsy will be today. That's fast. So this case was clearly made a priority."

Jen tensed, and Knox didn't have to ask to know what she was thinking. The words were practically written on her face. Her roommate was missing and likely in the hands of the same person or people who'd arranged Katie's death. This case was absolutely a priority.

"What are they looking for in the autopsy?" she asked.

Cruz flicked his gaze to Knox, then back. "MX-10, I'd imagine."

Knox rested his elbows on the table and clasped his hands. "Katie mentioned being in trouble before. If she has old ties to the drug community, it's possible she fell victim to the new and expanding web these pills are creating."

Jen stood with her plate and carried a half-eaten breakfast to the sink. "I'd still like to know the purpose of the list on the wall at the park," she said softly. "Madison's name was on there, and I think she left us that message for a reason. She could've been running, or hiding, or doing anything other than scratching a random stack of names on a weathered piece of plywood, but that was how she spent her time before being dragged away. I want to know why."

The quiver in her voice pulled Knox from his chair. The look in her eyes towed him across the room to her side. "I'm sure the sheriff's department is working on that too," he said. "If the doctors are being interviewed today, then there should at least be some speculation about those names soon, especially considering Abel was one of them."

"Do you think that could be a coincidence?" Jen asked. "There are lots of people named Abel in the world."

Knox could see the true questions behind her words. *What if this is another dead end? What if the one tangible clue we have is useless?* He fixed her with his most reassuring gaze. "Anything is possible, but I don't believe in coincidences. How many people does Madison know by that name?" Knox asked, stepping carefully closer. "How many do you? Other than this doctor, I don't know any, and his name was right beneath hers on that list, separated by a single line. The deputies know that's significant, and they will figure it out." He waited for Jen to lift her gaze to his. "We will find her," he promised.

Jen nodded, and the small rapid movements sent a cascade of tears over her cheeks. Then she stepped forward and hugged him.

Knox's arms went easily around her, and the collision of emotions that followed was nearly enough to wipe him off his feet. His heart had been broken at the sight of her tears, but the rush of joy that came with her embrace, and the fierce urge to protect her, and D.J., whatever the cost, was almost more than he could bear. Definitely, unlike anything he'd ever experienced. This wasn't their first hug, but it felt like an important one, and he held her a little more tightly because of it, like the treasure she truly was.

When the time was right, he would tell her how he felt and hope like crazy she felt the same way.

Cruz sauntered past them with an empty plate and a smile. His cool green gaze caught on Knox's and his brows raised. A small teasing smile played on his lips, but he kept whatever he was thinking to himself. Wisely.

Cruz had recently fallen for a woman he was protecting, and it had altered his world irrevocably. Knox wouldn't have believed it was possible to see his big brother so wholly taken by one woman, but there wasn't any denying the truth when they were together. And he practically worshipped the baby growing inside her. Couple those facts with his nosy nature and there was little doubt he already knew what Knox was thinking.

Jen slowly eased her grip, probably feeling their guest's entertained stare.

"Well," Cruz said, clasping his hands before him and rearranging his features to hide the knowing look he'd given his brother. "Thank you both for a delicious meal. I'm going to see what I can overhear at the clinic and report back when I have something worth bothering y'all."

Jen stepped away, wrapping her arms around her middle.

Knox felt her absence instantly and deeply.

"I appreciate what you're doing more than you can know," she said.

Cruz nodded, a rare expression of sincerity replacing his ever-present smile. "Don't mention it," he said. "This is what we do. I know it's not easy in your position, but try to rest and relax. You're in good hands." He cast a teasing look at Knox. "Figuratively and literally."

"Get out," Knox said, pointing to the door.

Cruz went with a laugh, then stopped in the threshold. "I mean it about the rest," he called back. The familiar glint had returned to his eye. "Sleep while you can. Auntie Rosa and Uncle Hank got wind there's a baby here last night, and I'm honestly in shock they didn't beat me to your door this morning."

Knox wrapped an arm around Jen's shoulders and pulled her back to his side.

She looked up at him, a bit of confusion on her brow,

clearly not understanding the gravity of Cruz's statement. "What?"

"I'm pretty good with bad guys," Knox said, "but I'm not sure I can protect you properly from my family."

Cruz's laughter trailed him to his Jeep.

Chapter Fifteen

Jen laughed when Knox's auntie and uncle arrived only minutes after Cruz departed, proving the brothers right. They only stayed long enough to say the family cabin was clean and the fridge was full in case they needed it. Then they hugged Jen and fawned gratuitously over D.J., before hurrying off to look after a grandchild so their son and his wife could spend the day alone.

His auntie promised repeatedly to be back soon, while her husband towed her toward their truck.

Jen requested a quick trip to her apartment after mention of a cabin. Thankfully, Knox had agreed. Packing for a few days at Knox's house had been one thing. Packing for a potential stay at a mountaintop cabin was something else completely. If things came to that, she wouldn't be able to pop over to her place and pick up anything she forgot, or even make a quick trip to the store if something ran out. In fact, Rosa had declared the cabin remote, and advised that internet access would require a cell phone hot spot. Worse, cell service was spotty.

For now, Jen rubbed her forehead and struggled to think of everything she and D.J. could possibly need, while reminding herself not to worry. She was an excellent planner, and they were in good hands with Knox.

The memory of his aunt's and uncle's warm smiles and tight hugs slipped sweetly back to mind. The way they'd cooed at D.J. had swelled her heart and strengthened her resolve to see her parents as soon as possible. D.J. deserved to have as much love in his life as possible, and she didn't want him to miss out on his grandparents for a minute longer than necessary.

Knox's auntie Rosa had cupped Jen's cheeks with gentle care and promised they'd get to know one another soon. It'd seemed a simple, friendly thing to say on the surface, but Jen had wondered about the way the woman had looked at Knox before she'd made the declaration. As if she might've seen something in him to suggest he'd want Jen and D.J. around when this was over. She'd no doubt seen that in Jen. And the possibility he felt the same way warmed her from the inside out. In fact, staying in Knox's life permanently, or as long as fate would allow, was a fantasy she'd indulged many times over the last couple of days.

The knob on her front door turned, and she smiled as Knox stepped inside and pocketed the key to her new locks. "Anything else?" he asked.

"Just these toys, and a couple of my favorite books," she said. "And I want to bring along a few things from the medicine cabinet. Just in case."

On that note, she headed to the bathroom in search of D.J.'s thermometer and infant Tylenol. If her baby got sick while they were hiding out, she needed to be prepared. And if her over-the-counter pain and fever reducers didn't help, she was hauling him off that mountain and straight to his pediatrician. Period.

Knox followed her as far as the bathroom doorway. "Good thinking," he said. "The cabin has a fully stocked first aid supply for adults, but I don't think anyone's gotten around to adding the basics for kids. I shouldn't be surprised you're the one to think of it."

She smirked at his reference to her preparedness. Planning ahead was a basic personality trait of hers that had been exacerbated by fear and uncertainty following Dylan's death. She had no idea what was coming on any given day, but she'd learned that preparing for everything she could think of helped her feel more in control, and when she had the things she or D.J. needed at the exact moment one of them needed it, she felt like she could handle anything else that came their way.

She paused to run mentally through their days, thinking of all the things she and D.J. used and needed. "My mail." She always brought the mail up on her way in from work, and it filled the small box quickly, thanks to an abundance of advertisements and junk correspondence no one wanted. "There isn't any time to ask the post office to hold it. Maybe Mrs. Hancock will?" Her building manager had been so kind and helpful already. Maybe she wouldn't mind checking Jen's mailbox and holding the contents until Jen returned, or shoving it under her apartment door.

"Do you want me to check with her while you finish up here?" Knox asked. "I'd planned to touch base with her before we left anyway. I want her to contact the sheriff's department if she notices anyone hanging around the building or otherwise behaving suspiciously."

"Okay," Jen said. She handed him the small pouch

of infant medicines and a thermometer. "Will you put this with the last bag on the island?"

"I'll take it all to the truck and be back in a minute," he said, curling long capable fingers around the bag.

She walked him to the door and turned the deadbolt behind him, the way she had two other times already.

D.J.'s soft snores rose from the living room, where he'd fallen asleep in his swing. Enjoying his last ride, for a while anyway, to its fullest.

Jen's contented smile fell as she recalled the reason she and D.J. weren't staying at the apartment. It wasn't just that they could be in danger; it was that Madison already was in danger. The resurfaced memory of her roommate's absence hit like a fist to her gut, as it did every time the thought came to mind. The possibility that whoever had taken Madison from the park had hurt her, or worse, was a near-constant terror, and each time she forgot about it, if for only a few minutes, a shameful guilt followed. Jen and D.J. had the Winchesters to comfort and protect them. Madison, wherever she was, had no one.

Thoughts of Jen's time with D.J. and Knox at the coffee shop returned to mind next. They'd been retracing Madison's steps, and Coffee Cat had told them about a notebook Madison kept. Jen hadn't had time to look for them earlier, but there was plenty of time now.

Jen hurried into Madison's room and scanned the space for anything she might've carried around and written on. News of Katie's car accident had redirected and scrambled Jen's thoughts the last time she was home, but suddenly the notebook was all she could think about. Figuring out what Madison had been writing down could be the piece of information the local sheriff's office needed to locate her and stop the criminal who'd taken her from hurting anyone else.

A single hardcover journal lay on Madison's desk beside her bed. A delicate imprint of blue waves stretched across the bottom and a yellow sun graced the top. Jen flipped the book open, then thumbed through it quickly, in search of notes or doodles.

The pages were thin and tinted the colors of a sunset. Each was neatly lined in black without a single other marking.

Jen fanned through the pages twice for good measure, then set the book aside and opened Madison's desk drawer.

A pile of spiral notebooks was stacked inside.

She removed them one by one to discover that, unlike the desktop journal, every page of every notebook was filled with writing. There were personal notes to Bob, before and after his death. Diary entries. Lists of things to do before she died. Poetry about how easily loved ones can disappear.

Jen groaned at the unpleasant notion of reading her best friend's private thoughts and letters to her fallen husband, but there wasn't any other way. And it could take hours to figure out which notebook was the one she carried regularly to the café, or if it was even in this pile. So she lifted the stack onto the desktop. "Looks like you're all coming with me," she whispered. Luckily, she had a partner to help evaluate every word, note and tittle.

She raised her eyes to the mirror hung above the desk and sighed. An image of Madison with her arms around Jen and D.J., only hours after he was born, had been taped to the gilded frame. She plucked the photo away and tucked it into her back pocket. If she also brought a magnet, she could stick the image to Knox's refrigerator door and see it anytime she needed a boost.

She turned for the hallway when a sound, like the breaking of glass, froze her temporarily in place. Her heart jerked into a sprint as her mind worked to make sense of the noise.

Her apartment door was locked, and she was alone in the space, with a sleeping infant who certainly didn't break anything. Could Knox have returned and she hadn't heard him? Could the sound have come from outside?

She stepped into the hallway, instincts on high alert, and cell phone at the ready, listening for the sound to repeat.

"Knox?" she called, moving slowly along the corridor, eyes locked on D.J., snoozing soundly in his swing.

Silence gonged in the apartment, and she wondered briefly if she'd imagined the whole thing.

The creak of a floorboard assured her she hadn't.

Her steps faltered as her view of D.J. became suddenly interrupted by a broad figure dressed in black.

Jen opened her mouth to scream, but the intruder raised his handgun and stopped her.

Across the room, a breeze blew in through the open window, and she recalled the sound of breaking glass. She'd doubted herself, and she shouldn't have. She should've called Knox immediately, but it was too late now.

The man pointed to the window, unspeaking. His cold dark eyes raged behind the black ski mask. His tall frame was tense. Edgy.

Because he knew, Jen realized, that his time was

limited, and Knox would be back soon. He'd probably been watching her apartment, waiting for the opportunity to move on her.

She wasn't sure if that awareness made her safer, or put her more at risk. *A man with a gun was dangerous.* But a nervous man with a gun seemed significantly worse.

Her mind raced to assess the situation.

She couldn't go out the window and leave D.J. alone in the apartment.

And she absolutely couldn't take him with her.

The intruder grabbed her shoulder and shoved her toward the window. He still hadn't spoken, and she wondered why. Did he think she'd recognize his voice? Or that speaking would wake the baby? And if he was worried about making too much noise, would he really use the gun?

Her gaze caught on D.J. as she bumped against the edge of the couch. "My baby," she whispered, a risky idea forming in her mind. "Please," she begged, spinning to face the gunman, hands raised in surrender. "Don't do this. My baby will be alone. His father died in Afghanistan before he was born. I'm all he's got." She didn't have to fake the tears that rolled freely from her eyes. And she didn't try to stop them. Her neck and cheeks heated. Her stomach coiled.

The man released a low guttural sound, then lunged at her, likely planning to throw her out the window if necessary.

She dodged the incoming blow, but pretended to fall. "Please!" She roared the word this time, letting her emotions take over, and not attempting to get up or run.

If she was lucky, the man would leave rather than be caught by Knox.

"Don't hurt my baby!" She sobbed, bowing her head and pressing her hands to her scalding cheeks.

"Get up," he seethed. "Now." The words were a gravelly whisper and barely tamped threat.

Her limbs itched to obey, but she braced herself instead, calling on every last ounce of bravery she could summon. She just prayed her body would remember what it had to do, even if her mind was too scattered and panicked to focus.

The man bent to grab her, and she snaked her legs out to tangle with his. Then, in the way Dylan had taught her, she jerked the man off his feet.

And screamed, "Help!"

The thud of his collapse at her side nearly rattled her teeth. His weapon bounced free from his grip and skittered across the floor.

D.J.'s cries rose into the air, and she projected her voice to match his.

"Help!" she screamed, flipping onto her stomach and grabbing the fallen handgun. She flicked the safety off and pointed the gun at her intruder when he reached for her once more.

He turned his palms out, showing his surrender.

Behind her, the front door burst open and smacked against the wall. "Jen!" Knox bellowed.

She dared a glance in his direction, and witnessed his expression flow from fear to rage in the space of a heartbeat.

The sound of breaking glass drew her eyes back to the man in black once more. Now on his feet, he flung himself through the open window and onto her fire escape with a bewildering crash.

"Are you okay?" Knox asked, gripping her shoulders and searching her eyes.

"Yes."

He scanned her trembling body, before removing the gun from her frozen hands. "You're okay. I'm here," he assured, setting the weapon on her counter.

"Go," she said, her tears flowing anew. She thrust a hand toward the window. "Catch him."

Knox moved to the window in two steps. "He's almost to the bottom of the fire escape," he said, pulling his cell phone from one pocket and pressing it to his ear. "Lock the door behind me," he told her, blowing past her and into the building's hallway.

She slammed the door and flipped the locks, not needing to be told twice.

The sound of his fervent footfalls in the hallway outside brought her back to the moment at hand. She freed D.J. from his swing and hoisted him into her arms, then moved the gun to the end of the countertop, near the broken window.

Jen rocked and shushed her baby, kissing his soft curls and keeping watch, the broken window in view, and the gun in reach.

The next person through her window would be leaving with an injury.

Chapter Sixteen

Two hours later, Knox, Jen and D.J. were back at his place. He'd fielded a dozen calls from concerned family members while their statements had been taken by his fellow deputies at Jen's apartment. He could thank his brother's and uncle's police scanners for that. Cruz and Derek had decided they'd meet him at his house to go over the details in person. Which roughly translated to his big brother worrying unnecessarily and wanting to see for himself that Knox and the Jordans were unharmed.

Knox had reluctantly accepted, knowing the alternative was futile, and he'd warned them to keep it brief. The aftermath of Jen's shock had paled her skin and set her teeth to chatter. She needed rest, and that would be impossible while surrounded by people rehashing what she'd been through.

Thankfully, she seemed to slowly unwind at his place, apparently feeling safe and comfortable. Knox would've appreciated those facts more if his tension hadn't continually ratcheted since he'd first heard her scream. He'd allowed a gunman to break into her apartment while he was just down the hall, speaking to the building manager. He'd never imagined someone would climb the fire escape three floors and break a window, but he should have.

He should've thought of everything. Jen's and D.J.'s lives had counted on it.

He dragged a hand over his hair and forced himself to take long deep breaths, willfully slowing his temper and pulse. Jen's attacker was long gone. She and D.J. were safe. That was all that mattered.

He selected a pair of water bottles from his refrigerator and carried them to his living room, where Jen rested on the couch. Her teeth had stopped chattering from the excess and misplaced adrenaline and her cheeks had regained their color. Those details eased a measure of his tension, and he exhaled fully for the first time in hours.

"Thanks," she said, accepting the offered drink.

D.J. lay on his back before her, feet in the air and tugging off one sock with his busy little hands.

Knox watched as she sipped the water, slowly at first, then in deep thirsty pulls. "How are you feeling?" he asked. She'd barely allowed the medics to glance at her when they'd arrived at the apartment. She'd insisted on giving her statement immediately, and afterward she'd simply brushed the EMT off. Thankfully, the intruder had only shoved her and had never really gotten a chance to harm her. Knox wasn't sure he could've handled it if things had turned out differently.

According to her statement, Jen pegged the man at six feet tall, trim and with brown eyes. She also said he'd smelled of spearmint. It wasn't much of a description, but it was more than Knox could offer. He'd only seen the man for a moment before he dove onto the fire escape and ran away. If Knox was supposed to be Jen's personal protection, she needed to put a help-wanted ad in the paper, because he stunk.

"I'm going to be okay," she said, answering the question he'd nearly forgotten he'd asked. "All things considered, I'm still here with you and D.J., and I can't complain about that."

Knox tried and failed to return her small smile. His brows furrowed in frustration instead.

"How about you?" she asked. "You're awfully quiet."

He rolled his head to stretch the tense and aching muscles along his neck and shoulders. When that didn't work, he gripped and kneaded the knots with aggressive hands. "You shouldn't have had to defend yourself or face him on your own. I should've been there and I wasn't. And I hate it."

Jen sighed. "I figured that's what was bothering you."

"Can you blame me?" he asked, unable to hide the frustration in his tone. "I had one job."

She rolled her eyes. "Protecting me isn't your job. Getting to the bottom of this situation is, and that was what you were doing. We both believed I was safe inside my apartment, and you were letting Mrs. Hancock know to be on the lookout. You were spreading awareness and setting down a framework for finding this guy. That is your job. I'm smaller than you, but that doesn't make me helpless."

"That's not what I meant," Knox said. "This isn't a male/female thing. This is me feeling ashamed that I didn't do the one thing I promised to do. It might not be my exact job description, but I promised to protect you. And I never break promises. At least, not before now."

She cocked a brow and studied him.

"Hearing you scream," he said slowly, the sounds returning to him in a haunting echo. "Hearing D.J. cry. Knowing you were in trouble." He paused to wet his lips and check his composure. "That twisted something inside me so tightly I could barely breathe." He pressed a fist to his chest in illustration.

Knox had experienced all kinds of fear in his life, but none of it had compared to the possibility he'd be too late to save Jen and her son. He'd struggled to unlock and open her door, his thick frantic fingers devoid of agility. And he'd been sure all was lost on the other side.

The scene he'd walked in on had thrown Knox, almost as much as it had probably confused her assailant. Jen had a gun, and a man dressed in black was splayed on her floor.

It had taken longer than it should have for Knox's feeble mind to catch up.

She'd taken the man's gun.

And knocked him on his backside.

An unexpected chuckle broke through his pressed lips.

"What?" she asked, eyes narrowing.

"You attacked your attacker," he said, still awed. "And you won."

"I did," she said. "I can thank Dylan for that. He insisted I learn a few basic self-defense moves. He never wanted me to be a victim."

"You certainly aren't that," Knox said, crossing his arms and nodding. "I miss him, you know?" Knox hadn't seen Dylan in nearly two years before his death, but they'd stayed in touch online, and the distance hadn't seemed so big, nor had it diminished their friendship. He'd understood Dylan's need to keep fighting, and Dylan had understood Knox's desire to come home and protect folks in new ways.

"I miss him too," Jen said.

Knox watched as Jen stroked her baby's arms and cheeks. He admired the protective expression in her kind and loving eyes. "It took a lot of bravery to do what you did today," he said. "Knowing what to do is different than being able to do it when you're in danger. The guy had a gun. You still took him down." A torrent of pride swelled in his chest, and his smile widened to match hers.

"Well, I have a baby now," she said. "I had to do something, and I couldn't afford to be afraid. Not if it meant D.J. might pay the price for my hesitation."

He nodded, admiration growing impossibly further in him.

"Now what are you thinking?" she asked, scooping D.J. into her arms. "Here. Sit. You're making me anxious."

Knox obeyed, taking the seat at her side. "I was thinking I like that you can handle yourself," he admitted. "I hate that I wasn't there for you, but I'm darn glad you didn't need me."

"Is that right?" she asked, a hint of disbelief in her voice. "I thought you hero-types tended to feel less manly when women saved themselves."

He laughed. The sound broke from his lips unexpectedly, and she laughed in return. "I'm just glad you're both okay. I don't care who did the saving."

Her expression softened, and her lips parted. "Yeah?"

"Yeah," he agreed. "And you won't catch me sneaking up on you anytime soon," he admitted, earning another broad smile.

"Smart man."

Their eyes met, and their smiles fell as the air around them seemed to charge.

D.J. set his cheek against his mother's collarbone and closed his eyes.

Jen snuggled her baby closer, and Knox felt the last of his resolve slip away. The little family before him had gained an unprecedented hold on his heart, and he wanted more than anything to let Jen know. He'd put off telling her for a dozen reasons, but being honest about his feelings, regardless of her response, seemed like the right thing to do. And if she didn't reciprocate, he was man enough, friend enough, to accept that without question or argument.

"What's wrong?" she asked.

"Nothing." He forced a smile and reminded himself he was a grown man, a former soldier, a lawman. Someone known for his bravery, and someone who shouldn't be afraid to tell the truth, even when the potential result posed a risk to his heart. "There's something I need to tell you," he said, willing the words from his lips.

"Okay." She shifted to face him, her expression somewhat…hopeful?

The doorbell sounded, changing his intended words to a growl.

Jen smiled. "Welcome to Winchester Country."

He groaned. "That makes it sound too fancy," he said, shoving onto his feet. "I changed my mind. I think we're more like a traveling circus."

The bell rang again as he strode into the foyer and opened the door to greet his guests.

Auntie Rosa patted his cheek as she and Uncle Hank bypassed him in search of his houseguests. They paused briefly to scan the area, then headed for Jen and D.J. By the time Knox made it back to the living room, his uncle had the baby in his arms and his auntie had pulled Jen into a hug. "We heard what happened and wanted to see you were okay with our own eyes," Auntie Rosa said, squeezing Jen tight.

"We're okay," Jen answered, stepping out of the embrace with a gentle smile. "We were lucky, and I'm glad we have somewhere safe to stay."

His auntie turned a bright smile on her husband. "All of my men are fully capable protectors and defenders, but Knox takes it to another level." She swung her attention to her nephew. "Always so serious. Always prepared to fight." Obvious pride flashed in her eyes. "It's nice to see him with something of his own to fight for."

Knox coughed, and tried not to give his auntie the pointed look she deserved. Jen might've been a champion swimmer, but Rosa was a world-class meddler. "Cruz and Derek are on their way," he said. "If you stick around a bit, you can get your hands on them too."

Auntie Rosa beamed. "I love when my family gathers. I can dole out hugs in bulk."

Jen laughed, then moved to Knox's side and slid her arm across his back. She rested her head against him, and his heart gave a heavy kick. "It's nice to have family near," she said softly, watching as his auntie turned to fuss over D.J. in Uncle Hank's arms. "I didn't realize how much I missed this."

"The fussing and intrusion?" he teased.

His auntie clucked her tongue, clearly eavesdropping. Jen laughed. "Yes. All of it."

Across the room, his aunt and uncle fluttered and

buzzed around her baby, attempting to comfort him or make him smile.

"He loves all this attention," she said. "Look at that big gummy smile."

Knox slid his arm across Jen's shoulders. It was true. D.J. was clearly in heaven.

The doorbell rang again, and Knox went to greet the newcomer.

Cruz waltzed passed. "Derek's a few minutes behind me. Hey, Jen."

She lifted one hand in a hip-high wave. "Hey."

Cruz kissed Auntie Rosa and shook their uncle's hand, then performed a lot of goofy baby talk for poor D.J.

Jen looked on in obvious delight. "It's really always like this here?"

"Every day," Knox said, rubbing a palm against his cheek. "Not usually at my house, but in general, yes."

Cruz spun to face his brother and clapped his hands together sharply. "I didn't overhear anything useful at the clinic, but I noticed that only one of the doctors was there. Martz, I think. He showed up a couple hours after the staff. Shots and blood draws went on without him until he arrived. I called Derek when I heard you were attacked," he said, shifting his gaze to Jen. "He'll be here any minute to fill us in on his day."

As if on cue, the doorbell rang.

Cruz let Derek in and followed him back to the living room, where all eyes turned to his cousin.

"Well?" Cruz asked, falling onto the armchair and wedging one foot over the opposite knee. "I hope you learned more than me. My reconnaissance mission was an indisputable bust."

Derek greeted his mom and dad and the Jordans before turning a look of discouragement on his partner. "I didn't find anything useful at the receptionist's house, so I spent most of the day outside Dr. Abel's home on Willow Bend Lane. His car was in the garage when I got there and I took a peek around the perimeter. I sat in my truck and waited, but I never got eyes on him. No one came. No one left. I headed this way when I heard what happened at the apartment. I don't see how it could've been him if he was home the whole time, but I suppose he could have another car."

"Did you run a registration check with the DMV?" Cruz asked.

Derek shot him a bland look.

Knox took that as a yes, but Derek didn't elaborate.

Jen deflated onto the couch. The lightness in her eyes a moment earlier extinguished. "Do you think he stayed home today because he knew the deputies were interviewing at the clinic?"

"Maybe," Derek said. "I don't know what those doctors are up to, but it feels like something, and my instincts are never wrong." He shot Cruz another pointed look. "My contact at the DMV is pulling up Abel's vehicle registration."

Cruz nodded.

Jen looked to Knox, and he moved to her side. "I get the same feeling about the doctors," he said. "I don't like that Abel's name made that list. At least we can mark him off as the gunman. He couldn't have been at my place and at his. Any word yet on the other names?"

Cruz ran a hand through his hair. "Officially? I haven't heard anything, but they were all common first names."

"Clinic patients?" Jen guessed.

"Maybe," Cruz answered.

Knox gripped the back of the couch near Jen's shoulders, sorting through the new information. "Well, staying home won't keep the deputies from interviewing Abel, so that tactic will only work for a short while. They'll likely head over there when they finish downtown."

Jen swiveled on her seat, catching Knox in her suddenly wide gaze. "Can we go to his house?" she asked.

"Dr. Abel's?" he asked.

"Maybe he'll talk to me," she said. "Maybe he knows something that can help us. We assume he's a guilty party, but he could be afraid of someone else like Katie and Madison were. Maybe that's why his name made the list."

"That's a lot of maybes and unknowns," Knox said. Which equated to a lot of risk. And he didn't want Jen anywhere near another source of danger. She'd been lucky to survive a gunman already today. "I think we should consider the offer to get out of town and move to the cabin. These guys can go knock on Abel's door and see if he's hiding from someone other than the sheriff's department."

Her jaw set, and his brother chuckled.

Derek rose and clapped a hand on Knox's shoulder. "I know I just met your girl, but that looks like a hard no to me."

Knox shook his cousin's hand away and glared at him, before catching his auntie's eye.

She'd apparently wrestled D.J. from Uncle Hank's grip and was busily smothering the baby with tickles and kisses. She raised an eyebrow. "Hank and I don't mind waiting here with this little sweetie if you all need to go somewhere for a bit," she offered, unhelpfully.

Knox groaned. He'd hoped that the risk involved in taking D.J. to a potential criminal's home would put an end to discussion on the outing.

Instead, all eyes turned to Jen.

Knox gritted his teeth while she deliberated. Maybe she wouldn't be comfortable leaving her son with someone she barely knew.

She pressed her lips together for a long moment. "Are you sure you don't mind?"

His auntie beamed. "Not at all. We'd stay here with this little man until he was eighteen if you wanted. I have my grandma supplies in the truck, stroller included, so we'll start with a long walk. I'll pack a picnic! Bananas and bottle for baby. Fresh fruit for Hank and me."

Delight crossed his uncle's features a moment before he blurred past Knox on his way out the door, presumably to fetch the stroller.

Cruz headed in the same direction. "Sounds like a road trip," he told Jen. "And you've got a three Winchester escort. Couldn't be any safer."

She rose and hurried after him.

Something told Knox this wouldn't be the last battle he lost against Jen and her accomplices, aka his too-accommodating family. And a smile spread across his face at the thought.

Chapter Seventeen

Knox followed his brother and cousin to Dr. Abel's home in West Liberty, one town beyond his jurisdiction as a deputy sheriff. He parked along the curb behind Cruz's big white Jeep and waited for the private detectives to climb out. He wasn't any happier about ringing the doorbell with Jen in tow now than he had been when they'd left his place, but she was adamant, and he was stuck.

She climbed out and rounded the hood to his side, nervously rubbing her palms against her thighs.

Knox offered her his hand and the most confident look he could manage. "Ready?"

She nodded.

The home was impressive and situated in the elite West Liberty Hills. The unique Frank Lloyd Wright–design style spoke volumes about the likely price tag, and the owner's desire to make a statement. Tall windows. Flat roofs. And an overall aesthetic that blended the home with the landscape. Private practice physicians made good money, but Knox wasn't wholly convinced the pay was enough to afford the sprawling property before them. He couldn't help wondering if MX-10 had somehow helped make the purchase possible. He made a mental note to find out how long the doctor had lived there.

Jen squeezed his fingers as they crossed the street.

Derek and Cruz had already disappeared, presumably checking the perimeter.

"Do you want to knock, or should I?" she asked.

Knox pressed the doorbell in response, eager to get this over with and hoping the guy didn't answer. His gut told him at least one of the doctors was trouble, and he needed to keep Jen as far away from trouble as possible. He couldn't bear to fail her again.

The bell chimed deep inside the home, but no sound or movement followed. He tried again, then turned to Jen, preparing to make his case for ending the mission.

A flicker of movement in his periphery swung Knox's attention to the attached garage. Derek stood in the driveway, his ear pressed to the closed door.

Jen frowned. "What's he doing?"

"I'm not sure," Knox said, tugging her away from the front door for a closer look at Derek. Knox lifted his chin in question when his cousin met his gaze.

"I smell exhaust," Derek said. "And I think I hear a car running."

Cruz appeared from around the corner, his expression dark as he lowered his face to the junction of garage door and driveway. "I smell it too. Call an ambulance," he said, shooting a look at Knox, before turning away.

Derek jogged to the nearby utility door and tried the knob. When that didn't work, he kicked the door in.

Jen squeaked as wood splintered, and the barrier banged open.

Cruz followed Derek inside.

"They shouldn't go in there," she said, staring wide-eyed as exhaust billowed through the busted door.

Jen might not have put the details together yet, but Knox had. Whoever was in Abel's garage wouldn't be any danger to them now.

Knox held her hand as he reported the facts to local dispatch.

The large door rolled slowly upward, and Cruz reappeared, T-shirt and arm pulled across his nose and mouth.

The sound of breaking glass was followed by the settling of a car engine, and Derek appeared seconds later. He doubled over at the waist, coughing and struggling for clean air.

"Abel?" Knox asked.

Cruz shook his head once. "He's gone. Probably been that way for a while now."

And Abel made death number two in as many days.

Not a good sign for Madison.

Jen thanked her lucky stars for the thousandth time that she hadn't brought D.J. along with her. If it hadn't been for Knox's aunt and uncle, she probably would've, and she couldn't imagine having him there now. Not with another tragedy nearby.

She'd been sure Dr. Abel would shed some light on what was happening. And that he wasn't the one trying to hurt her, so things were supposed to turn out okay. Having the Winchesters present had bolstered her confidence. All they'd needed, she'd thought, was to get Abel talking. That would never happen now.

Instead, another life had ended, and she was gutted by the senselessness of it all.

Her life had been beautifully ordinary only a few days before, but everything had changed. Madison's life had become entangled somehow with MX-10, and the drug might kill her without her ever taking a single pill.

Knox's shadow fell over Jen as he returned to her side. "My cousin Blaze is on his way," he said. "He's a West Liberty homicide detective. He was handling something at the prison, but he's leaving now. We've confirmed the man in the car is Dr. Abel. Cruz and Derek are going to wait out here. Why don't we take a look inside?"

She glanced over her shoulder at the picturesque home.

"We won't disturb anything," he said. "I'd just like you to see if you recognize anything as Madison's. Some sort of indication she's been here."

Her muscles tensed at the request. "You think she might've been here?"

"I think it's worth a shot," he said.

Jen followed Knox through the garage to the interior doorway, careful not to look in the direction of a small black Mercedes.

Knox held the door for Jen with his forearm. "Try not to touch anything."

She nodded, having no intention of leaving her mark upon the poor man's possessions. Her mind raced to the family and friends he'd left behind. Of all the people who'd get the awful call she had when Dylan died unexpectedly. Like Katie's family had yesterday.

The home's interior was as beautiful and well maintained as the exterior. Inviting, wide-open spaces were lined in tall narrow windows, most without blinds or curtains, allowing unobstructed views of the neatly manicured landscaping outside. The decor was minimal, but obviously high-end. Large furniture pieces had been neatly arranged in groupings and clusters throughout the rooms, creating the overall look of a magazine shoot instead of someplace a man had actually lived. Probably the work of an interior designer.

"Was Abel married?" Jen asked, realizing the home was far too large for one person, but far too tidy for a young family. Maybe the kids were grown? Or he was divorced? Maybe that was why so many spaces seemed more for show than function. A single person could likely only use a portion of the square footage with any regularity.

"I'm not seeing any signs of a roommate, spousal or otherwise," Knox said, leading the way through the main areas. "Shoes on the mat are all men's in the same size." He pointed to the entryway they'd passed through, then to a grand foyer on the left, where a pair of picture frames bookended a sculpture on an entryway table. One of the photos was of him and an elderly couple, possibly his parents. Another, of the doctor and a boat.

Knox ducked into an open bathroom in the hallway, then returned with a pair of tissues and offered one to Jen. "If you have to pick anything up."

She accepted with a nod.

The distant sound of sirens trickled into the sprawling home, a striking contrast to the bellowing silence around them.

Knox had shifted seamlessly from casual companion and protector to lawman. The change was visible in his stance and stride, the set of his jaw and the look in his eye. All evidence of the playful man she'd been with moments before was now wrapped tightly in a uniform and badge. Even if neither were physically with him.

He moved methodically through the home, a trained and sweeping gaze likely seeing more in a moment than she could if given an hour. Their first official stop was a home office with a library. Floor-to-ceiling windows graced the far wall, spilling natural light over hard-wood floors, a massive mahogany desk and two walls of soaring bookcases. Under other circumstances, Jen would've been in love.

She inched toward the desk, feeling awkward and intrusive. Nothing of Madison's had been visible so far, and Jen wasn't sure what to look for otherwise.

She lifted a pen using her tissue as a barrier against her prints, then used the pen to open drawers and poke through the contents.

Knox concentrated on the bookshelves.

Nothing in the giant desk looked useful or seemed amiss, and she closed the final drawer with a sigh.

"Here," Knox said, urging her across the room with a tip of his head. "I've got something." He dialed his cell phone, then pressed it to one ear. "Hey," he said into the receiver. "There's MX-10 in the home office. About fifty pills." His eyes shut briefly. "No surprise there."

Jen followed his gaze when he opened his eyes.

He'd pulled a set of books away from the shelf and revealed a series of plastic baggies behind them, each with a small number of tablets like the ones found hidden under the sink in her apartment. "Looks like these were counted and ready for distribution," Knox said, sliding the phone back into his pocket. "Now, was this guy just a dealer? Or did he have a hand in the production too?"

Jen stepped away from the evidence, needing to put some distance between herself and the drug that seemed to be getting people killed. "How did you know they were there? There are thousands of books in here. A hundred shelves."

"These books weren't flush with the rest, but they're clearly part of this series," he said, pointing to the other tomes still standing on the shelf. "Plus, this shelf and set of books were clean, but the other shelves and books had a thin layer of dust on top. They'd obviously been recently moved, used or otherwise disturbed."

She considered taking a closer look, but decided to accept his word on the subject. Her mind had already jumped to a more important issue. "Abel's name was on the list at the carousel, and now he's dead," she said.

A look of understanding and compassion crossed Knox's face. He abandoned the stash of MX-10 in favor of meeting her near the door. "Why don't we check the rest of the house for signs of Madison?" he suggested. "Deputies will be here soon to handle the evidence. Meanwhile, we can check the property for places Madison could be held."

Jen's heart rate jerked into a sprint as she took his hand. Together, they backtracked to the garage, then started their exploration again. This time, opening every door, closet and cupboard.

"Madison!" she called, no longer able to contain the need to run, and Knox let her go.

He kept pace at her side, and together they cleared every floor, from attic to basement, before darting outside to check the grounds.

The street was full of first responders and emergency vehicles when they jogged into the yard. The late-afternoon sky was awash with carousels of red and blue. Uniformed men and women streamed in and out of the garage, across the tidy lawn and along the barricaded road at the end of the drive.

Jen's heart sank as Knox forced the door on the pool house open, revealing yet another unoccupied space. The last one on the grounds to check.

The feeling of loss hit like a brick, stealing her breath and stinging her eyes.

Once again, Madison was nowhere to be found.

KNOX CLOSED HIS front door for the last time at nearly midnight, hours after their return from Dr. Abel's home. The day had been long in every sense of the word, and his capacity to keep moving had dwindled almost completely. Thankfully, there was a fresh pot of coffee and plenty of questions to keep his tired mind engaged.

And there was Jen, who needed him to be strong.

She sat on the couch in her pajamas, looking cuddly and warm. She'd had a long shower after finally getting D.J. to sleep, and she'd emerged looking somewhat more relaxed. She should've been exhausted too, but her expression signaled fear more than fatigue.

Knox couldn't blame her for that. He was starting to seriously worry about her friend too. The bodies were adding up, and Madison had been missing for several days. More than he was comfortable with after seeing his share of missing women cases. The facts so far didn't set the stage for a happy ending.

Knox headed to the kitchen for coffee and hot tea, running mentally over all the details that had arrived in the last few hours.

Abel's death hadn't been labeled a homicide yet, but

Knox's cousin Blaze suggested it was only a matter of time. The fact MX-10 was found in the car with the victim, and the initial coroner's report cited conditions pointing to drug use, Knox had to agree. The working theory was that Abel had taken some pills before getting into the car, likely with a little help. He'd passed out, then inhaled the exhaust fumes to the point of asphyxiation.

Deputy Wence was processing the gun used in the break-in at Jen's place and hoping for prints or ballistics to guide the investigation. The serial number had been scratched off, but if the gun had been used in any previous crimes, they would soon know.

The related conversations with Derek, Cruz and Blaze had been heavy and long, but Jen had listened carefully and asked excellent questions. Having her with them while they'd hashed things out had felt good. Natural. And his family members hadn't missed his pleasure in that fact. He'd seen it in their expressions as clearly as he'd felt it in his bones.

Knox carried a cup of hot tea and a mug of coffee to the living room, then set the tea on the coffee table for Jen. She'd switched from coffee after finishing her shower.

Knox drank deeply from his mug, then took the seat at her side. "How are you holding up?"

She gave a soft, humorless laugh. "Terribly. I'm shaken, terrified and getting angrier all the time. I hate that all this is happening."

"That's understandable," Knox said. "Stuff like this doesn't typically happen to law-abiding citizens. I'm sure it's confusing and infuriating." Knox set his mug aside. "You can talk to me about that if you want. Whatever you're feeling is valid. This is a lot to take in, and nearly impossible to process. I've investigated plenty of cases similar to this one on the surface, but something's not adding up this time."

"Agreed," she said, straightening with interest. "Aside from the fact Madison shouldn't be part of any of this, I keep wondering why Dr. Abel would get behind the wheel doped up. That doesn't make any sense. If he thought the sheriff's department was closing in on him for something, why not get rid of all those pills in his office? If a bad guy was threatening him, why not run? He had enough money to leave the country if he wanted."

"All good questions," Knox agreed.

"Do you think someone put the pills in his car and office to frame him?" she asked. "Why would he take a bunch of pills, then go sit in the car and inhale fumes? Seems like overkill to me. Don't both acts produce the same result?"

Knox nodded. "I suppose if he was an addict, he might've wanted one last high, or maybe he was just in a terrible headspace. He might've felt out of control, depressed or panicked, and he acted on it."

Jen reached for her tea, considering his words, but not arguing with them. "I guess. Speaking of bad headspace. Do you think Derek will be okay?"

"I think so," Knox said.

Derek had left shortly after Auntie Rosa and Uncle Hank. He'd blamed himself for not knowing Abel was in the car in the garage, when Derek had been right outside all day. A man had died only a few yards away, and Derek hadn't had any idea. He could've saved him, and that would haunt Derek for a long while to come.

Knox knew because, logical or not, he'd feel the same way in Derek's place.

"Winchesters are made of some pretty tough stock," he added, appreciating Jen's concern for his cousin more than she could know. "He'll get through this. But I can see where he's coming from. We all do our best to be omniscient. We try to predict other people's motivations and reactions in order to maintain control, especially in difficult situations. It can be tough when we miss something. Especially something this big."

Jen sipped her tea, then set it aside. Her pensive expression faded slowly, and she turned to lean against his side.

His arm went around her on instinct, and it felt like the first true breath he'd taken in hours. He loved the way she felt in his arms, the way she fit so perfectly in his life and with his family. It was possible, he realized, that he was falling in love with Jen.

"Madison can't be dead," she whispered. "Because I can't lose someone else I love, and she's already been through too much. It just can't happen. She has to come home."

Knox pulled her closer. "No one is giving up on her," he promised. "Every new clue, each incident and uncovered fact, is leading us closer. It's just hard to see the progress when you're standing in the middle of the action. It might seem as if we're spinning in circles, but we are moving forward. I promise."

Jen twisted free of his arm, and tucked her legs beneath her, studying his features closely. "Madison's photo is all over the news, but no one knows where she is. No one has seen her since the night she was dragged away by a gunman in the park. Hope is getting a lot harder to find."

Knox reached for her hand, twining their fingers and giving an encouraging squeeze. "She's out there somewhere, and someone knows how to find her. All we have to do is keep looking. I'm here for that," he promised. "I will single-handedly turn over every stone in this county if I have to. Blaze and his brother, Lucas, will do the same in West Liberty. Plus, we've got Derek and Cruz. It's an all-star team," he said with a confident grin.

She smiled, and his heart ached to pull her against him once more. How was she so darn perfect for him and how had he not told her yet?

"I'm glad you're with me," she said, expression softening. "I'd be completely lost if you hadn't decided to stay with me that first night and kept me with you every day since." She averted her eyes and bit into her lip, drawing his attention to her mouth. "I know you're just here as some kind of obligation to Dylan," she said, "but it means a lot to me. Probably more than it should."

"No," he interrupted. "That's not why."

She stilled and her brows rose. "Then you're here because it's your sworn duty to protect and serve."

"I'm on vacation," he whispered, bracing himself once more and willing the right words to come.

She smiled.

"It's true," he continued. "I heard you ask for me at the department, and I could never walk away from anyone asking for my help, but it became a lot more than that pretty quickly."

Her lips parted, and something akin to hope crossed her beautiful features.

"I knew I liked you that first night at your apartment," he said. "I also knew I shouldn't, because you were in trouble and needed a protector, not a boyfriend. But you're smart and kind, with a big admirable heart. I wasn't ready to leave when I easily could've gone. I used your potential need for protection as a reason to stay. And the longer we're together, the more I don't want to go."

Her blue eyes widened in pleasure, and a chill rippled over his skin. "What if I want you to stay?" she asked, sounding a little breathless. "Even when this is over?"

"Then I'll stay," he answered simply. "I've grown unreasonably attached to you, and your son."

Her lips twitched, fighting a small smile.

Knox's heart began to pound.

"Is that what you wanted to tell me earlier, before you were interrupted?"

"Yes. And I know the timing is terrible. You're in the middle of something awful. Emotions are high. The future is uncertain. The last thing I want to do is make you uncomfortable with my proclamations."

Jen's gaze dropped to his mouth, silencing him instantly. "Knox," she said, "the only thing making me uncomfortable right now is the fact you still haven't kissed me."

Chapter Eighteen

Knox felt his brow furrow, even as a wide smile spread over his face, and he lowered his mouth to hers. The confusion about how he could be fortunate enough to gain her desire vanished when their lips met, and all he could think about was the taste of her. Heat flooded over him until what he'd planned to be a respectable and chaste exchange quickly deepened.

Jen's arms wound around his neck, and she rose onto her knees, bringing them closer.

He inhaled her sweet scent and devoured her delicious moans.

The warmth and weight of her body against his sent his heart and mind into the atmosphere. And he knew it was a turning point from which he would never fully recover.

His hands spanned the width of her back, and he glided his palms along her spine, memorizing and cataloguing every dip and curve. His fingers trailed a path over her ribs until his thumbs found the underside of her breasts, warm and enticing beneath the thin cotton shirt.

She sucked an audible breath in response.

Knox stilled. He pulled back an inch and looked into

her wide blue eyes. "Are you okay?" he asked. "Is it too much? Too fast?"

Jen shook her head, a dazed but pleased expression on her beautiful face. "I'm in absolute heaven."

He smiled at her description of the moment.

"There had only been room for one man in my life since the moment I realized I was pregnant," she said. "Until now."

A familiar swell of pride bloomed in his chest. The knowledge she wanted him in her life was mind-boggling. A complete aphrodisiac and one heck of an ego boost.

He dropped a line of grateful kisses along the column of her throat, alternating gentle nips with comforting swipes of his tongue. He cradled her head in his hand when she arched, exposing more of her flushed skin.

Her narrow fingers found the hem of his shirt and dragged it upward, forcing him to release her long enough to strip the material away.

His muscles flexed and contracted beneath her teasing fingers, and he longed to return the favor.

She broke the kiss again too soon. Then, apparently reading his thoughts, she removed her shirt with one sharp lift of her arms.

To his immense shock and extreme pleasure, she'd forgone a bra.

A guttural moan ripped through him as his hands returned to her sides. He gripped her tightly and lifted her over him until her thighs bracketed his. Then he lowered his mouth to her bare skin and lavished her with kisses.

Jen's fingers knotted in his hair, and a series of sexy encouragements fell from her lips. "I'm not going to break," she said, arching into his touch. "I want you. And I don't want you to hold back."

Knox raised his eyes to meet hers once more. Eager to please them both, but hesitant to ruin the moment by pressing his luck. "I don't want to rush you, and I'm in no hurry."

Jen pulled his mouth back to hers and lowered fully onto his lap.

His obvious, undeniable arousal was a testament to how much he wanted her too.

Then she rocked her hips, and Knox's inner gentleman left the building.

JEN DRAGGED HER eyes open later, temporarily confused by the scene around her. Silver rays of moonlight streamed through Knox's bedroom curtains and over her thoroughly sated body. The scent of him on her pillow, and on her skin, drew a pile of vivid, beautiful memories into her mind.

She'd asked him not to hold back, and he'd responded by raising the bar on intimacy for eternity. Definitely the smartest request she'd ever made.

A small laugh broke on her tongue, and she rolled to see if she'd woken him.

The sheets beside her were mussed, but cool and empty.

The home was quiet, save for the sounds of soft male singing in the kitchen.

She stretched onto her feet and tugged one of Knox's T-shirts over her head, then padded quietly toward the tune, shamelessly proud. She'd made Knox Winchester sing.

The refrigerator door was open as she entered the

kitchen, lending a cone of soft white light to the space. Knox straightened and peered at her over the divide. A low cuss ripped from his mouth. "Are you wearing my shirt?"

Jen grinned. "I guess I should've asked. I can take it off, if you'd like."

"Get over here." Knox shut the fridge and pulled her to him. He kissed her lips, then set her on his countertop and offered her the bottle of cold water in his hand.

"Couldn't rest?" she asked, sipping gently, and hoping he hadn't gotten out of bed because he didn't want to sleep with her.

Uncertainty doused her warm thoughts like ice water, and she crossed her arms over her chest in embarrassment. In some ways, waking up together was as intimate as anything they'd done before falling asleep. Maybe she'd gotten carried away. Maybe she was the one who'd moved too fast.

Maybe Knox was one of those men who didn't do relationships.

"Why are you single?" she asked, ripping the proverbial bandage off her heart before she became more injured than necessary.

Knox's easy smile halted her emotional spiral. "It's been a long time since I found someone who interested me more than my work."

She contemplated the deeper meaning, hoping but unsure. "I see." He was on vacation now, and it was probably stupid of her, but she was determined to soak up every available ounce of him until he went back to work. Better to have a few days of bliss in his arms than to go their separate ways later, and wonder what it would've felt like to be the one he kissed good-night.

She set a palm against his bare chest and worked up a small smile. "Does that mean I have your attention now?"

Knox's eyes went dark as he stalked closer, removing the bottle from her hand and nudging her knees apart with his hips. He gripped her thighs and brushed his lips against hers. "Jen," he said with reverence. His palms slid beneath the hem of her shirt, and he pulled it over her head, leaving them skin to skin once more. "You have all of my attention, for as long as you want it."

She released a long happy breath, hoping there was a scenario where that would be true long-term. His sharp green eyes appraised her when she hesitated, then she pushed the doubts aside and kissed him deeply.

His responding growl rumbled beneath her roaming hands.

"I really like your attention," she said between kisses, feeling a smile spread his lips.

"It's all yours," he confirmed, leaning her back on the counter with an appreciative, hooded stare.

She arched sharply in response to his talented, confident touch.

"Keep that up," he said, "and I'll call in tomorrow and resign."

She clutched his wrist as desperation rose in her once more. "Keep that up," she countered, "and I will gladly let you resign."

Then she fell apart before he could argue.

Chapter Nineteen

The bed shifted beneath Jen, rousing her once more. A phone buzzed softly nearby.

It only took a moment for her to realize Knox was still with her. He'd brought her back to bed, and he'd stayed through the night. Her heart leaped as she turned in search of his handsome face.

But he'd already rolled away, sitting on the bed's edge, the phone pressed to his cheek.

"Yeah?" he answered roughly, the husky growl of sleep in his voice.

Jen held her breath, fighting the pang of uncertainty. She'd never been in a real relationship until Dylan, and being with him had been nothing like being with Knox. Life with Dylan had been a series of flirtations and teases, dates and romps. Their time had been easy, carefree and youthful. She'd only truly begun to let her whole guard down a short while before his death, and he'd never seen her at her worst. Knox had met her at her worst and lived with her in a state of emotional and physical dishevelment all week. The stakes were impossibly high, and everything around them felt intense and heavy.

"No," he said quietly to whoever had called. "I'm up.

Just trying not to wake Jen or the baby." He twisted at the waist for a look in her direction. An expression of surprise was replaced by a smile when their eyes met.

She breathed again, attempting to look at ease, and likely failing miserably.

Knox rose, then leaned across the bed to press a kiss against her forehead. "All right," he said into the phone's receiver. "We'll be here." He disconnected the call and tossed the phone onto the bed. "It's breakfast time with the Winchesters," he said. "Cruz, Derek and Blaze are on their way over. Sounds like they're bringing food. All we need to prepare is coffee."

He pulled a shirt over his head, then froze when their eyes met once more. "What's wrong?" He scanned her face and tense form beneath his sheets. "Is it us?" he asked, motioning vaguely between them, a frown marring his brow.

"Maybe," she admitted, wanting to be truthful, but hating the catch in her voice. "I don't regret last night, but this is awkward, right?"

Knox returned to the bed. "How?"

She pressed her lips, then blew out a sigh. "You were Dylan's best friend. I was his fiancée, and your family knows that. What will they think?" She averted her gaze. "Not that there's any reason for them to know."

Knox stretched out on the bed beside her, propping his head on one hand. "We both loved Dylan. That connection will always be between us, and it's unusual, but it's not wrong."

She huffed a small breath, eyes stinging suddenly with unexpected tears.

"You told me yourself that you aren't the same woman he knew," Knox said, earning the return of her gaze. "You've changed. And even if you hadn't, I know he'd want you to be happy. I want you to be happy. And, Jen, I would never do anything to intentionally make you cry." He reached for her cheek and swiped away a falling tear.

She covered his hand with hers and held it to her cheek. "Thanks."

Knox nodded, searching her face for something more. "After my mama died, there were times when going on without her was even harder than losing her, if that makes any sense."

"Yeah," Jen said, swallowing past the lump in her tightening throat. "It does."

"I think we owe it to the ones we've lost to keep on living," Knox said. "To do good in this world, to find joy and make them proud." He swept sleep-wrecked hair from her cheek and smiled. "I'm not here to push or rush you, and I understand if you're seeing things differently by light of day. It won't weaken my dedication to protecting you and Dylan Jr."

Jen pressed a kiss to his palm, infusing the act with her gratitude. "What about your family?" she asked. They would surely need to explain themselves to a family as involved in one another's lives as his. Wouldn't they?

"We'll tell them as much as you want to tell them, when you're ready to tell them, but I've got to be honest with you. They're all detectives of their own accord, and a bunch of shameless gossips where family is concerned. I'm sure they already know."

A bolt of alarm burst through her at the thought. They knew? "About this?" she squeaked, and clutched the sheets more tightly to her chest.

Knox laughed. "About my intentions."

"Your intentions?" she repeated, loosening her white-knuckled grip on the material. A self-deprecating smile twisted her lips. "With a woman managing a missing friend and a baby?" She shook her head. "There's no pressure here. I know I come with baggage."

Knox's expression turned cold. His brows furrowed and his lips pulled down at the corners. He lifted her chin with his fingertips and trapped her in his piercing green gaze. "You aren't pressure, Jen. You're a prize. You got that?" He dropped a kiss on her forehead, cheeks and nose, repeating the pattern until her smile returned.

"Okay," she agreed.

"Good." He rolled away and rose fluidly from the bed, then cast her a wicked grin. "Now hurry up and get dressed before my family finds you in here naked."

KNOX REFILLED COFFEE mugs while keeping tabs on the conversation with his brother and cousins, as well as one eye on Jen and D.J. The Winchesters were spitballing, brainstorming and attempting to piece together what they knew about the MX-10 epidemic and its apparent connection to Madison, Katie and Abel. As well as the names on the list at the carousel. Jen was playing on the living room floor with her son, while thumbing through the stack of notebooks she'd taken from her roommate's desk.

Blaze tapped a finger against the open folder before them. Autopsy results, complete with photos, lay on the table beside the emptying plates of fruits, cheeses and muffins his wife, Maisy, had sent along. "The coroner found no evidence of emissions in Abel's lungs," Blaze said. "He was definitely dead when he got into the car."

"No surprise there," Derek said, exchanging a look with Cruz. "The question now is how'd a dead man get into a car and start the engine?"

Knox set the pot back on the coffee maker and resumed his seat at the table. "So, we've got two murders. Katie's and Abel's."

"Yeah." Blaze scrubbed a hand over his unshaven face and stretched back in his seat. "The list at the park had both Madison's and Abel's names on it. She was taken. He was killed. Katie's name wasn't on the list, but she's also dead. So where does that get us?"

Cruz frowned. "Incomplete list?"

"All three victims worked at the clinic," Derek said. "So there's an undeniable connection to that location."

Knox nodded. "Agreed. Could the other names be additional staff?"

"Nope," Cruz answered. "I got a list of employees from the sheriff's department after they finished with their questioning. Derek and I are assisting officially now, on reconnaissance and research. I'll be running background checks on the other employees, but my money's on that other doctor, Martz."

"Any chance we know if the names are patient names?" Knox asked, knowing it was a long shot, considering the regulations surrounding privacy and health care.

Blaze shook his head. "It'll take a warrant and a miracle to get access to patient names."

Derek tipped his chin at Cruz. "Maybe you can use your pretty face and some sweet talk to grease a few lips at the office. The clinic employees know their coworkers are dying. Find a staffer who'll tell you if there are patients with the same names as those on the list. You don't have to ask for last names. No sensitive information. Just do they or don't they have at least one patient by each name."

Cruz sucked his teeth, contemplating. He'd made sport of using his charm and personality to get whatever he wanted until a short while ago, when he'd met Gina. He'd grown a bit of a conscience since then that Knox normally appreciated. At the moment, his opinion was on the fence.

"I can ask," Cruz said. "No promises. And whatever I learn won't hold much weight."

"Agreed," Knox said. "The names were fairly common. It's reasonable to assume we'd find matches in any group larger than a couple dozen. The clinic probably sees hundreds of folks every year."

Blaze nodded. "We can run on the assumption they were clients, or at least affiliated with the clinic, for now. That gets us to the likelihood that the drugs are linked to the facility as well. It'll be easier to get a warrant to search the premises than the patient files. So, I'll work on that." He swiped his phone to life and tapped the screen, presumably setting the ball in motion for a warrant.

Knox cast another look into the living room and caught Jen looking back. She smiled, and it reached his lips as well. When he returned his attention to the table, the other men stared in open curiosity. Cruz smirked, but nodded slightly with smug approval.

As predicted, his family saw everything.

Blaze set his phone aside and rolled his shoulders. "In a twisted way, Abel's death might be good news for

Madison. A second associated murder is pushing her missing person case to the top of the local law enforcement priority list."

Jen's attention snapped to Blaze. "Have you learned anything new?"

Blaze nodded. "I had a feeling this case was headed my way, so I contacted the guys over at the sheriff's department, and they brought me up to speed. So far, I learned the boot prints near the carousel were a size larger than any of the boots found in Abel's house, and the treads didn't match. So he wasn't the one who took her, and wasn't likely the gunman you saw in the park."

"Or the one in my apartment," she said, putting the facts together.

"Not according to time of death," he agreed.

Jen rose onto her knees, and the memory of seeing her do the same thing last night flashed into Knox's mind. In the next moment, she'd kissed him like she'd longed for it. And things had only gotten better from there.

Cruz leaned in close and positioned his mouth near Knox's ear. "You need a little privacy for those thoughts?" he whispered. "Maybe a napkin to wipe up the drool?"

Knox snapped back to reality, then locked his jaw when both Cruz and Derek laughed.

Thankfully, neither Blaze nor Jen seemed to have noticed. They hadn't missed a beat in their exchange.

"You think Abel got the pills through the clinic somehow?" she asked. "Maybe his dealer is the one who took Madison. She might've found out what was going on and told Katie." Her eyes flashed with fear. "Tell me there's a chance whoever killed Abel and Katie hasn't already..." She trailed off, unable to finish the awful thought.

That the killer behind two known murders might have already committed a third.

Blaze offered a patient but confident look. "We'll find her."

Jen lowered back to the floor with a nod. She scooped her baby into her arms and buried her face in his soft curls. Then returned to the pages of Madison's notebooks once more.

Knox longed to go to her, but sensed she needed a little space and time. Especially in the presence of his family. So he forced his attention back to the discussion at hand.

Where was the MX-10 coming from? Who had killed the doctor and receptionist? And where was Madison?

The conversation was slow and heavy, like wading through quicksand, examining known evidence for an aspect or detail they'd somehow overlooked. The need for new information was increasingly painful. And an hour later, nothing in the case file had moved them forward in their search for answers.

"Knox?" Jen said, drawing his eyes to her once more.

Her attention was fixed on a page thick with writing, and her lips were parted, as if she'd paused midthought.

"What do you have?" he asked.

She raised a bewildered expression to the men at the table. "I think I found the original list from the carousel." She turned the notebook around in evidence. "Madison wasn't finished writing at the park. The last name on this list is Dr. Martz."

Chapter Twenty

Jen paced the living room with D.J. fighting sleep against her chest. She rocked and bounced to soothe his whimpers and complaints as much as to burn her restless energy. Knox's home had been a tense flurry of activity after she'd shown the Winchesters Madison's notebooks. The detective and PIs were gone now, but her pulse still raced from the crash of voices and activity that had ensued.

The men had swarmed her, examining the notebook in her hand as well as all the others Jen had brought from Madison's room. They'd photographed multiple pages, then torn them from their flimsy spiral binding.

Knox had scanned and printed copies of every page of interest, then secured the sheets inside clear plastic sheaths for their protection. His brother and cousins had made phone calls, spoken in acronyms and stormed around, setting plans based on the new information, before blowing out the door one by one. Each on his own mission.

The general commotion and deep rumbling of authoritative male voices had worked D.J. into a fit, and Jen had spent her time distracting and calming him. She'd missed most of what had been said, and eventually had to leave the room to help her baby find his calm. Now, the home was quiet. Knox had walked his brother out and D.J. was nearly asleep, though determinedly resisting.

She only wished she could sleep as well. Her insides were tight with worry and her mind spinning with unanswered questions, old and new. Wouldn't it be nice to be rocked to sleep and wake up at a different place on her timeline. Even a few hours from now, when her nerves had calmed and her son was rested. It would be even better to wake when Madison was home safely and the worrying was done. Jen was tired in her bones and in her soul. She'd been that way for more than a year, if she were being honest, and the only time she'd felt any true respite had been in Knox's arms.

She wasn't sure if that made her weak or something worse, but it had been true nonetheless. She'd underestimated the value in feeling safe, seen and cared for when her life had been filled with feelings like those. She wouldn't be so quick to take anything for granted in the future.

The front door opened, and Jen started, frozen temporarily in place.

Knox lifted a hand in apology. "Sorry." He secured the locks and rested his hands on his hips, thoughts racing behind troubled green eyes. "Blaze is on his way to talk with Dr. Martz at the clinic," he said. "Derek's going to try the doctor at his home. Hopefully, one of them catches him. They'll be in touch to coordinate the interview."

"And Cruz?" Jen asked, pressing a kiss to D.J.'s forehead when his soft snore reached her ears.

"Cruz is also on his way to the clinic, but he plans

to schmooze an admin out of as many details and insights as possible." Knox grinned and shook his head, as if there was more to that story, but he didn't go on.

Instead, he headed for the kitchen table, still covered in printed photos of the notebook pages. The originals had gone with Blaze.

"If we're right, and Martz is involved with MX-10 in any capacity, it'll ruin him professionally," Knox said. "If he's the one making and distributing the pills, he's looking at more than the loss of respectability and his medical license. He'll be put in jail and held accountable for the lives he's ruined, not to mention the ones he's taken."

Jen returned to her seat across from his. "You think Dr. Martz is the killer."

The tension in his limbs and jaw confirmed as much, but Jen needed to hear him say it. There wasn't any room left in her cluttered, terrified mind for guesswork or assumptions.

Knox nodded. "Abel's and Katie's deaths, Madison's abduction and your recent attack."

"Okay," she said, steeling her nerve and pushing past the dream of sleeping until the worst had passed. Fighters didn't hide, and she'd never been anything else. "What can we do? Don't say sit tight and be patient," she said. "There has to be some way we can help, even from here."

Knox flexed his jaw several times before he met her eye again. "How are you at online research?"

She smiled. "I can find people on social media as needed, and if I know the city where they live, I can usually find a little more."

Interest lit his gaze. "Such as?"

"Their home address, using the local auditor's site, assuming they bought their home. With that information, I can find images of their home with Google Maps, and sometimes the interior as well, if the sales pages haven't been removed from the realtor sites."

Knox leaned forward on the table. "Marital status?"

"Sure. If it's not noted on their Facebook profile, I can check public records. Marriage license applications and divorce filings are all public record," she said.

"Do I want to know why you know how to find all that?" he asked.

"Women are frequently endangered, injured or killed at the hands of a date or spouse," she said. "We're taught that practically before we're out of diapers, so I've long made it a practice to know who my friends and I are trusting with our lives before heading out on dates or getting serious with anyone. Some guys are just married liars too, so there's that."

Knox performed a slow blink. "I forgot who I was dealing with for a minute," he said. "My apologies." He tried and failed to suppress a smile, and Jen sat taller in response. "Why don't you take another look at the list of names from the carousel wall and notebook?" he asked, selecting the photo of the page in question from the table. He set the paper in front of Jen. "See if you can find their social-media profiles and if there's a common thread Blaze or the deputies can pull. Now that we have last names to work with, maybe something useful will turn up. I'll review the staff's background checks," he said. "Looking for commonalities."

He rose and made a trip to his desk, then returned with a pair of laptops. He placed one covered in travel and sports stickers in front of her, then set a more seri-ous-looking black computer before himself.

Jen excused herself to settle D.J. in his crib, then returned quickly to the table, eager to get started. She eased the lid open and powered the device on, prepared to do her best to oblige and impress. A moment later, an image of Knox and Cruz with a woman who, based on the matching thousand-watt smile and pale green eyes, could only be their mother appeared. The men were younger, somewhere in their teens with floppy unkempt hair, sun-kissed cheeks and imperfect com-plexions. Knox had braces. Cruz was in a baseball jer-sey. The woman glowed with all the unapologetic joy of a mom thoroughly in love with her two perfect sons.

"She was healthy there," he said, drawing Jen's at-tention to him. "That was the last one of Cruz's ball games we attended together before her diagnosis. She was planning a family vacation, because he was leav-ing soon. Either to a career in professional baseball or to college on a full athletic scholarship, anywhere he wanted to play."

Jen glanced at the photo again, applying ages to the men. Cruz was a high school senior there, which made Knox barely old enough to drive. Why this was their last game together was still unclear. "Was it the last game of the season, or did you lose her before he grad-uated?" Jen asked.

"Neither." He smiled, a distant, unfocused look in his eyes, seeing something in his past she couldn't begin to guess. "He quit."

"Quit baseball?" Jen guessed, assuming he hadn't meant high school, but quitting a sport he was appar-ently so good at seemed equally unbelievable.

Knox nodded. "Yeah. She wasn't given much time, right from the start, so he and I made it our jobs to spend every minute we could with her. We attended every treatment. Missed a lot of school, but the teachers were understanding. They gave us extra time on assignments and made lots of provisions. Small-town benefits, I guess. Everyone knew and loved Mama." He returned his gaze to Jen, steadying himself, before going on.

Jen waited patiently, eager for the details but unwilling to rush him about anything so important.

"We held her hair back when the chemo made her sick. Shaved her head for her when she was ready. Cared for her when she was weak. And we were both there when she left us," he said. "Cruz sensed it before I could. Maybe because I was younger. Maybe he's just always been more in tune with people. He told her we'd be okay. That we had Auntie Rosa and Uncle Hank to keep us in line, and that she was the perfect mother. So, the work for Rosa and Hank wouldn't be hard. Then he said we'd see her again one day." Knox cleared his throat. "He handled everything like a man, comforted me like a dad, when he was just a kid himself. He joined the military instead of playing ball and sent money home frequently to help with her medical bills. I stayed with our aunt and uncle until I graduated. Then I did the same. Cruz seems like he's carefree, but he's the most conscientious, grounded and caring person I know. That's saying a lot because I know some pretty great people."

Jen's eyes misted, and she reached for Knox's hand. How had the women in his life before her ever let him get away? How could anyone know him and not love him?

She squeezed his palm, not even a little startled by the path her thoughts had taken. Her heart was already his. "Thank you for sharing that with me," she said. "I'm glad to get to know you better. And the fact you made time to let me, even in the midst of this—" she motioned to the laptops and case evidence peppering the table "—means more to me than you know."

His cheek lifted with a lazy half smile. "I want you to know me. And I want to know you." He lifted their joined hands and pressed a kiss to her knuckles before letting go and setting his fingers on his laptop keyboard.

She flashed him a bright smile, then turned back to the machine before her.

They worked in companionable silence for a long while before taking a much-needed break.

Knox pushed away from the table and stretched to his feet. "I would never survive a desk job," he said, rolling his shoulders and twisting gently at the waist. "Have we eaten since breakfast?"

"You had an apple," Jen said, suddenly famished at the thought of food and wishing she'd had an apple too. "Should we make something?" she asked. "We can discuss our findings over whatever mealtime this is?" She turned on her seat in search of a clock.

"I've got this," he said, heading for the fridge. "Did you have any luck connecting the people on the list outside the clinic?"

"None," she said. "Other than the fact they all live in the same county, which I could've guessed, given the fact they all chose a doctor here. That's where the commonalities seemed to end. There's a high school athlete, a local college honor student, a couple of professional dancers, a judge, an ophthalmologist and a few women who have home-based businesses." She arched in her seat, stretching her aching neck and shoulders.

Knox crossed his arms and rested his backside against the countertop. "All those professions sound high-stress," he said. "That might be the link between them. A dope-peddling doctor might've suggested he could help them relax." He pursed his lips a beat, as if considering his own suggestion. "I'll mention it to Blaze and the deputies."

She nodded. "What did you learn about the clinic employees?"

"They had a few things in common," he said. "None have criminal records, but they're all in precarious financial situations. Recently divorced, working two jobs, living alone in the area with loose or no known family ties. And aside from a phlebotomist with a certification, no one on staff has any specific qualifications. No college degrees. No extensive experience or training."

"Is that legal?" Jen asked, recalling all the people she'd seen in scrubs at the clinic. "No nurses?"

"No nurses, and it's legal," he said. "Anyone can check a patient in, weigh them, take vitals and complete charts. The phlebotomist draws blood and gives shots. Other than that, the doctors seem to handle things. It's possible Martz sought employees he felt would be loyal to him for the opportunity. I'm guessing a more than fair wage helps seal lips as well."

Jen frowned. "I'd say it's awful and shameless to manipulate people in need, but I suppose he's done much worse. And I can see how Madison fit the bill. She's new to the area, has no family nearby and struggles with the loss of her husband."

"By design, it should've been easy for any of the

employees to look the other way if they saw something questionable going on," Knox said.

"Easy for anyone except Madison."

He nodded. "I'm guessing that's exactly how all this began. She might've had a suspicion that needed to be confirmed before going to the police. I can see why she didn't clue you in on what she was up to."

Jen's lips curled into a slight smile. "She always does the right thing. I should've known her painstaking goodness had something to do with the trouble she's in. I hate that I ever doubted her," Jen said. She hadn't gone all-in thinking Madison had slipped up, but she had wondered, initially, if Madison had made a wrong decision somewhere along the line. Trusted a wrong person, or otherwise inadvertently started the ball rolling downhill.

Of course her friend had seen something dangerous happening and wanted to stop it.

Knox's phone rang as he removed a loaf of bread from the pantry. "Yeah?" he answered, gaze drifting to Jen as he listened to the caller. "Sounds good. We'll meet you there. We were just about to eat anyway."

Jen's stomach tightened and her muscles tensed. His expression was unreadable. Was he attempting to cover bad news?

He pocketed the phone, then put the bread away. "Wence says she's headed to Coffee Cat to interview employees in about an hour. She thought we might want to sit in on some of the discussions. How do you feel about getting a bite to eat there while we wait for her to arrive and get started?"

Jen rose with a smile. "Give me ten minutes to change D.J. and pack his bag."

"I've got the bag," Knox said. "You do you. I'll handle this. Bottles. Diapers. Monkey rattle and those weird puffed cereal bits. Yeah?"

Jen paused, grateful and warmed once more by Knox's easy willingness to help, even when the task was small and she hadn't asked. "Thanks."

He winked, and her heart gave a heavy kick.

She would be lost and miserable if he left when Madison returned, so she hoped like crazy that he might want to stay.

Chapter Twenty-One

Traffic was thick and slow around Coffee Cat. The sidewalks teemed with people, and Jen felt the familiar pangs of fear return.

"What's going on?" she asked. "Is it always so congested at this hour?" She checked the time on Knox's dashboard clock and groaned. No wonder she was hungry. It was twelve thirty.

Lunchtime.

"Yeah," Knox answered belatedly. "There are a lot of popular restaurants on this block."

"Great." She swung her gaze in search of a parking spot but came up empty.

Knox circled the block, then doubled back in the opposite direction on a second pass.

The clinic parking lot was on her right.

"You see that?" he asked, pointing through the windshield. "All those men and women in black ball caps and windbreakers are deputies."

Jen followed his gaze, not seeing the hats or jackets at first, then becoming hyperaware. There were three men in black windbreakers just outside the truck, and another two near the corner. They blended with the moving crowd, when she wasn't looking for them, but now that she was, it was easy to see they weren't going anywhere. They were meandering. Maybe searching for something.

Or someone.

Knox drummed his thumbs against the steering wheel. "Something's going on."

Jen trailed one of the deputies with her gaze as he threaded his way through the pedestrians, head turning slowly side to side.

Knox cursed. "Hold on."

The truck darted forward a few feet when the light turned green, then rocked to a stop on a wide patch of concrete at the corner of a large full parking lot. He released his safety belt, then stretched an arm behind the seat and came up with a small domed emergency light. "There." He set it on the dashboard and turned it until the Jefferson County Sheriff's Department sticker was visible through the windshield. "I might still get a ticket, but I can't keep circling the block. I'll go insane. Plus, I want to know what's going on."

Jen frowned. "I'd be more worried about being towed than getting a ticket. Will that little thing really help?"

He turned a mock-offended look her way, one hand still resting on the light. "This is an official mini-beacon," he said. "Not a little thing."

"Oh." She fought a smile. "I see. I'm very sorry."

He nodded, then opened his door.

"It's just that my cousin had one of those in her room for karaoke dance parties when we were eleven," Jen said as genuinely as she could manage.

Knox pointed a warning finger at her, then unfastened D.J.'s harness and lifted him from the car seat.

"Your mama thinks she's funny," he told her baby. "Good thing she's so cute."

Jen snickered as she met him at the grill of the truck, then accepted her perfect baby boy from Knox's careful hands. "I was only joking," she said. "I think your little flasher is adorable."

Knox snorted. "Don't let my family hear you say that."

She produced a wicked smile, then slid D.J. into the sling and headed for the coffee shop.

Knox easily kept pace. He slid his hand around hers and pulled her to his side. "Once we get in line, I'll text Wence and see what she can tell me about all the deputies down here. We'll wait to see if the interviews are still on schedule, or if they're being postponed, and if so, why?"

"Any guesses about what's happening?" Jen asked, fear scraping at her bravado once more. What if someone else was hurt, or worse? And what if that person was Madison?

Knox opened the coffee shop door for her, then took the place in line at her side. "Other than they seem to be looking for something or someone, no," he said. "The absence of uniforms makes me think they're trying to be discreet."

Jen turned to the menu board, trying not to think of what the new information could mean for Madison. Her stomach growled at the sight of all the delicious options.

Knox set a palm against her back as they inched forward. "Chicken bacon ranch panini. I think those might be my new four favorite words."

"I'll try that too," Jen said, thankful the long line was moving quickly.

Knox pulled his phone from his pocket and began to dance his thumbs across the small screen.

Jen scanned the busy café and hummed to D.J. while she waited for news from Deputy Wence.

"Next," the woman at the counter called, motioning Jen ahead.

"Two chicken bacon ranch paninis and two bottles of water," she said, unwilling to interrupt Knox for a drink order.

She paid the bill, then moved to the end of the counter.

Knox ghosted along at her side, eyes fixed on his screen.

"Okay," he said a moment later, pocketing the phone and stepping into her personal space. "Wence says someone called in a tip about Madison. They claim they saw her on the news, and think she's being held in the building near the clinic."

"Which building?" Jen said, her attention jerking to the window overlooking the street. "Is she okay?"

He shook his head. "We don't know. A team is clearing each building floor by floor. The deputies outside are watching for suspicious activity. In case whoever took her tries to move her."

"Chicken bacon ranch paninis," a man behind the counter called. "Two waters."

"Here." Jen raised her hand and Knox accepted the tray.

Together, they moved to the only open table, a two-seater near the far wall.

Knox angled his chair for a view of the window, and Jen followed suit.

"Where's the team now?" Jen asked, pushing her

sandwich into the center of the table, her appetite suddenly gone.

"I'm not sure. They cleared the clinic and every floor above and below it first, then moved next door," he said. Knox lifted his sandwich absently, gaze trained on the window, as if he might see something his fellow deputies could not.

They stared in silence at the crowd outside, peppered with undercover deputies. Knox demolished his sandwich, while Jen held tight to her son. This could be the day she finally saw Madison again. She prayed with each passing moment her friend was still all right.

A sudden flash and resounding boom rattled the glass and caused the people outside to scream. Some ducked, bracing their hands over their heads. Others ran. Smoke billowed from the alley near the clinic.

D.J. jolted, then thrashed and cried.

Jen's ears rang. The air ripped from her lungs. Had she just witnessed an explosion?

Did she just lose Madison to a bomb?

Knox rose to his feet.

The windows of a building across the street were gone, broken and shattered. A dozen car alarms blared to life.

Knox cursed, cutting his attention between the frightening view outside and Jen as she moved to join him.

The chaos outside the café seemed to double as the moment of initial shock passed, and people began to panic.

"Go!" she said, rocking and clutching her frightened son. "Help them. We'll be right here." Terror slid like ice through her veins, chilling her from the inside out.

Madison could have been near the blast. She could be one of the injured people. "Go!" Jen repeated when Knox didn't immediately move. "Be a hero." She forced a smile, worry for him sinking in as she realized what she'd asked.

A prolonged moment later, he dipped his chin and snapped into lawman mode. "Don't leave this building. Stay with the crowd. Call me if you see anything I need to know."

He waited for her nod of agreement, then broke into a sprint, weaving seamlessly through the cluster of patrons who'd moved to the window for a better look at the destruction.

Jen inched slowly away, back to the table where she'd sat with Knox before the blast.

Would there be another explosion?

Would the next one take Knox too?

The fire of panic burned up her neck and across her chest. It boiled in her gut and seized her breaths. The panic attacks she'd experienced regularly following the news of Dylan's death returned in full force, with one massive grip.

Until the blunt press of a gun barrel against her spine rocketed her straight back to clarity.

"This way," a low male voice instructed, wrapping an arm around her shoulders and leading her toward the back door. "Atta girl," he crooned. "You wouldn't want a bullet to make its way through you and into that sweet baby."

Chapter Twenty-Two

Knox raced across the street, stopping to check on drivers and passengers involved in fender benders as a result of the nearby explosion. "You okay?" he'd asked, knocking on windows and waiting for the stunned commuters to nod or respond verbally. "Hang tight," he told each victim. "Help is on the way."

He raised his phone and called dispatch, then gave a running tally of folks in need of assistance, issuing orders to bystanders and seeking signs of the black hats and windbreakers.

Where were all the deputies?

Sirens registered through the commotion. First responders were on their way.

"Winchester!" a familiar voice called through the dark acrid smoke.

Deputy Van appeared, moving in Knox's direction. "Looks like a Tannerite-induced explosion," he said. "Lots of noise. Broken windows. Some unfortunate projectile injuries." He squinted through the hazy air at the fender benders and pedestrians unlucky enough to have been near the windows when they shattered. "But the bulk of the damage was contained. The explosives were set up in an unoccupied portion of the building. No distinct signs anyone had been there, but the area is still contaminated with debris." He gripped the back of his neck, still visually searching the streets. "I'm not sure what the point was supposed to be. Some kind of distraction, maybe. While he moved the missing woman?"

A pair of ambulances screamed their way into view and parked as close to the destruction as possible, with complete disregard to signs for the tow-away zone.

Knox stiffened as Van's words sank in, and he swung his eyes to Coffee Cat, where he'd left two very important people and a good chunk of his heart. The reality of the situation hit him like a second bomb.

The explosion wasn't a distraction meant to cover Martz's movement of Madison. It was meant to cover the abduction of another woman altogether.

"Jen and her baby were in that coffee shop," Knox said, breaking into a sprint without further explanation.

He flew back across the street, holding out one arm to stop slow-moving vehicles as he cut around their hoods and onto the packed sidewalk beyond. Too many minutes had passed since he'd left her. How long had it been? Six? Eight? More? He squeezed through the cluster of onlookers gathered in the café's open doorway, knocking shoulders and calling out apologies before landing soundly in the center of the small nearly vacated dining area.

Jen's panini and water sat on the table untouched.

She and D.J. were gone.

JEN HELD TIGHT to her son as Dr. Martz yanked her from the seat of his black sedan and shoved her forward, into the forest. A massive old house sat in the distance. Too far to reach without being shot by her abductor. Its dark windows and sunken porch suggested no one had likely lived there in a long while anyway. It wouldn't be a safe haven or refuge. Just a different place for her abductor to finish what he'd brought them there to do.

He'd parked the car on a deserted gravel lane, thickly lined in overgrown trees that obscured the county road. Pillars of crumbling brick stood near the mailbox, topped with an ugly urn-like sculpture and engraved with a word, maybe the owner's name, that age and neglect had nearly chiseled away.

"Move it," he demanded, nudging her shoulder once more.

Jen took baby steps, trying not to upset him while she scrambled to come up with an escape plan. She'd thought being driven away from town by a killer had been the most terrifying experience of her life. But walking into the forest with him was impossibly worse.

They'd driven for nearly an hour on unfamiliar country roads, passing very few homes and no notable landmarks.

If there was a blessing in the midst of her horror, it was that they'd arrived without incident, and D.J. had fallen asleep in her arms. The doctor's car had lacked a proper infant seat, and the combination of smooth roads and a car's engine had put her baby out like a light.

The irony of a safe arrival to the destination of their intended demise wasn't lost on Jen, but she appreciated it anyway.

Martz had been silent, but fidgety, as he drove, checking his rearview mirror often and watching her intermittently. He let the handgun resting on his lap speak for him.

Jen shuffled forward, nudged regularly by Martz's

gun, and D.J. blew spit bubbles and babbled against her chest as she panicked internally. She eyeballed fallen limbs and sizable rocks, wondering if she could reach and swing one at her captor before he could manage an accurate shot.

Ultimately, she didn't dare try.

Tears stung her eyes as she imagined what might happen next with each crunch of fallen leaves underfoot. Only the darkest, most horrid things came to mind. "You don't have to do this," she whispered, willing herself to speak for the first time since Martz had found her in the café. She hadn't wanted to provoke him before, but the time for plotting an escape was up. She had to try anything she could, and talking to him was her only option.

"Shut up and keep walking," he said quietly, a note of regret in his tone. "I should've just shot you the night you drove through the park looking for Madison. This could've been over days ago."

"I won't tell anyone what happened," she pressed, ignoring his demands. "I swear it. You might hurt my baby if I tell, so I would never. You can leave us here in the woods. Get a head start on leaving town and evading the sheriff's department. Start over somewhere else. I don't have a phone." Martz had made sure of that. He'd chucked her cell phone through his car window before they'd ever left town. "I can't call for help," she continued. "It will take me forever to make my way back to civilization."

"Shut. Up," he repeated, breaking the words into two sharp sentences.

The car shrank behind them, and her fear grew. "What are you going to do to us?" she asked, knowing and hating the obvious answer. "You don't have to add two more murders to your charges. Killing your partner and receptionist was bad enough. Killing a baby isn't going to help things when they catch you, which they will if you don't leave us here and get out of town."

"I haven't killed anyone," Martz said, scanning the forest with a solemn gaze. "I didn't tamper with Katie's car. Robert did. And I didn't kill him. He was a junkie, hooked on his own drug. I just put him in his car to buy myself time to think. A lot of good that did me," he grouched. "Autopsies are supposed to take weeks. I don't know why all of this is going wrong."

Jen fought the urge to scream as her mind raced to process his claims. "Dr. Abel was the one selling MX-10?"

"He's the mastermind," Martz said, begrudgingly. "The creator, distributor and user. It was supposed to supplement his income after he was taken to the cleaners in his divorce. He'd been making the pills for himself for years, which was probably why his wife left him in the first place." Martz shook his head. "I was an idiot for agreeing to let him handle business through our practice. Now he's dead and I'm left holding the bag."

A measure of hope rose in her. If Martz wasn't the cold-blooded killer she thought he was, would he still shoot her and her child if they tried to run?

The hope collapsed as she imagined making an attempted escape.

Even if Martz hadn't killed Katie or Abel, he was undoubtedly the one who'd attacked Jen at her apartment. The familiar spearmint scent on his clothing had turned her stomach as they'd driven, and it hung heavy in the air between them now.

"What did you do to Madison?" she asked, pressing the words around a painful lump in her throat. "She's my best friend, and I don't understand what happened."

He ignored her, and she pressed on.

"Please. I need to know."

Martz moved to stand in front of her, blocking her path and pointing the gun at her face.

Her hands flew up on instinct, and she turned her back to him, putting herself between the gun and her baby.

Rustling leaves and brush drew her attention over one shoulder.

Behind her, Martz dropped a mass of vines and branches onto the ground, revealing a rusted metal door set in a small embankment. Probably an old storm shelter belonging to the decrepit farmhouse she'd seen. He stuffed the gun into his waistband and gave her a firm look. "Don't try anything, or I'll hurt him." His gaze dropped to her middle, where her arms wound over D.J., still angled out of Martz's sight.

He removed a padlock, then heaved the creaking door wide with effort and pointed into the blackened tomb. "Get in."

Jen gaped and considered her escape options once more. She wouldn't make it back to the car or road before he shot her. But if she went inside, would she ever get out? "What is it?" she asked, the question blurting from her lips.

Where was he putting her? What was in there? And how long could she and her baby survive without food or water?

"Watch your step," he said, ignoring her question.

"Don't make me force you, the way I forced your friend. She wasn't carrying a baby."

Jen stilled. Her gaze drifted to the dark hollow. "You brought Madison here? Is she still in there?" How many days had it been? Could she still be alive?

His grimace turned to exhaustion as he motioned with his gun. "I won't ask nicely again."

Jen didn't doubt him, so she steeled her nerves and took a step inside.

The door slammed behind her, and D.J. cried.

She shushed her baby in the darkness, listening as the metal lock clanged against the door, being returned to its place. Then she turned in the impossible blackness, afraid of what awaited her and recalling Martz's mention of Madison. "Hello?" she whispered, listening intently for sounds of another person, and hopefully nothing else.

A low moan and strange scratching sound answered back. A moment later, a cough.

"Madison?" Jen pressed her palms to the cool cement walls and used one pointed foot to feel for steps. She counted four wooden treads, committing each to memory in case she needed to backtrack in a hurry.

On solid ground again, she concentrated on the scratchy sound, both familiar and not. And let the small glow of light draw her forward.

The air was cool and earthen, raising gooseflesh on her arms and assaulting her senses.

"Madison?" Jen asked again, trailing her fingertips along the wall. She sang quietly to calm D.J. and distract her own panicked mind.

The scratching sound began again, and the light slowly brightened.

Madison's dark form came into view, curled on the ground, head resting on one arm like a pillow.

"Maddie!" Jen rushed to her friend's side and lowered herself to her knees, elated and terrified at the sight of her. "What happened? Are you hurt?"

Madison's filthy face and closed eyes made the second question unnecessary.

Something was very wrong.

"Hey," she tried again, stroking hair from her friend's overheated cheeks.

Madison twitched her hand, and the sound began again. A small crankshaft light glowed in Madison's fist, storing energy and creating light with every grip and release of her hand.

Had she been doing that all these days? Just to stop the darkness?

"You shouldn't be here," Madison said. "Take D.J. away."

Jen nearly sobbed in relief and horror as she snuggled her still-whimpering son. "I can't. Martz locked us in. Now we have to find a way out."

Madison grimaced. "I think I broke my leg. He pushed me down the steps. I hit my head and landed on something sharp. I might have a concussion. My leg's hot, infected, I think."

Jen bit her lip as she recalled the heat in Madison's cheek. She settled a hand on her forehead for confirmation. Her friend was burning. "May I?" Jen asked, taking the light from Madison's weak grip.

Jen squeezed the crank fast and hard, captivating D.J.'s attention and bringing the small glow into maximum brilliance behind the aged plastic shield. She swept the light over her roommate's curled body, lingering on her red and swollen leg. Jogging shorts revealed a deep gash on the thigh above the knee. Whatever she'd been cut with had left a serious wound, and there was no doubt about the infection. "Okay," Jen said. "Time to get out of here."

Madison coughed, then groaned. "The door is locked. I tried."

Jen powered up the hand crank, keeping her rhythm steady and moving the cone of light around the room. "What do we have to work with?"

"Not much," Madison whispered, her eyes drifting shut once more. "I drank the little water I could find. I'm sorry."

"You did the right thing," Jen said, mentally adding dehydration to the tally of injuries and issues with her friend.

A set of rickety wooden shelves clung to one wall, angled, as if they might give up their load of ancient canned goods at any moment. A decrepit table, covered in mildewed papers and books, stood a few feet away, an open first aid kit on top. Madison had likely rifled through the kit once she was able to find it, before infection had set in.

Jen turned in a circle, illuminating an empty jug on its side near Madison's head, presumably the water she'd consumed. She cringed at the thought of her friend's fear, pain and despair. To be alone in the dark, injured and hurting. Hungry and fevered. She couldn't imagine what Madison had been through, and she needed to get them out of there.

Madison coughed, and Jen returned to her, revving the hand crank for light. "I'm so sorry you and D.J. were pulled into this," Madison rasped. "I tried so hard to keep you out of it."

"I'm not caught," Jen said, mustering as much bravery as she could manage. "I'm rescuing you."

Madison gave a small brittle laugh. "I didn't know what to do when I realized the doctors were making and selling MX-10. I took some pills home as evidence to help prove my story, but I got scared. I waited too long to call the police." Her voice went thin, and she stopped to cough some more, before pressing on. "Once Martz came for me, I couldn't shake him. I ran to the park and hid, but he had a gun. I knew he'd kill me. I tried to leave a list of the people involved. People they'd hurt or sold to, but I didn't get to finish my note." Fresh tears ran silently over her cheeks. "I botched everything. Now look at us."

Jen squared her shoulders. "You haven't botched anything," she said. "This isn't over." She could save them. She just had to think.

"Madison?" she asked, gaze falling on the badly infected cut on her friend's thigh. "What did you cut yourself on?"

"I'm not sure," she rasped. "It was dark. I found my way in here, then felt around for another door. I found the flashlight, first aid kit and water. Then I lay down to rest my head and things got fuzzy."

Jen moved back toward the shelter's entrance.

"Don't leave," Madison called, her voice suddenly panicked.

"I'm not leaving," Jen promised. "I want to see what you fell on. I need something to break us out of here. The shelves might work, if I can take them apart. A shovel or something metal would be better."

"Take me," Madison pleaded. "I don't want to be in the dark."

Jen doubled back and knelt beside Madison, who looped a fevered arm across her shoulders. "Ready?" she asked.

Madison screamed as Jen tried to hoist her upright.

"Okay," she whispered, consoling Madison and D.J. at once. "Wait." She lowered Madison to the ground and let her take deep breaths. Jen collected the newspapers and spread them on the ground at Madison's side. "Can you roll onto your side?" she asked.

Madison complied with effort, and the opened papers became a pathetic makeshift backboard.

"I'm going to try to drag you," she said. "I'll go slow, and I'll stop if it hurts." She handed the light to Madison, then dipped into a squat.

D.J. huffed and complained, cheeks red and bottom lip jutted.

Jen gripped the ancient papers and tugged gently, until Madison began to move.

One small step at a time, they made their way toward the stairs, adjusting and replacing sheets of paper as needed, until they reached their destination.

She fell onto the ground at Madison's side, kissing D.J. and panting from effort. "Well, that was easy," she said.

Madison moaned. "My leg is definitely broken."

"But you're alive," Jen said. "The sheriff's department has been looking for you, and there's a manhunt underway for Martz. We're going to be okay. We just have to get out of here, so we can be found." She pulled the crank light from Madison's grip and swept the area.

An overturned metal box came into view against the far wall.

"Bingo." She hurried to see what was inside. The container was empty, but her eyes misted with hope and relief at the sight of a single long screwdriver lying nearby.

Jen pulled D.J. from the sling and returned to Madison's side. She spread the sling on the cold dirty floor like a blanket, and lay D.J. on top. "I need you to stay awake and protect him," she said to her friend. "Can you do that for me one more time?"

Madison chuckled, then moaned. "You just got here. You already want a babysitter?"

"It's not as if you're doing anything else," Jen said, smiling as she faced the rusty door. The metal was in bad shape along the edges and ground, deteriorating from age and weather. She could definitely work with that.

Jen jammed the business end of the tool into the worst-looking section of metal and levered a chunk of rust away. A pinhole of light shined through, and she turned to share the joy with her friend.

But Madison had tipped over beside D.J., her eyes closed and face slack.

Jen had to work faster.

Madison's survival depended on it.

Chapter Twenty-Three

Knox kicked the dumpster outside Coffee Cat and fought the urge to scream.

The commotion out front had drawn attention for blocks, but the real devastation had occurred silently and without notice. Martz had walked into the coffee shop and ushered Jen and D.J. away. No one had even noticed. All eyes and phone cameras were focused on the fender benders and smoke. If not for security cameras at a bank on the opposite end of the block, there would've been no indication about what had happened to Jen and her baby.

Even now, knowing who'd taken them, there was little to suggest where they'd gone.

Every deputy in Jefferson County was on the lookout for the black sedan. The car's temporary license plate number, a fake, on a car registered to someone in another town, was thankfully picked up by bank cameras. A description of the vehicle and passengers had been broadcast to highway patrol across the region. And like her roommate before her, no one had a clue where Jen had gone.

"All right," Derek said, stepping into Knox's strike zone and pushing his phone into view. "I've got something. There's a property about an hour from here that was owned by Martz's granny before it passed to his mom, who uses a different last name. The mom lives in Phoenix, so the house is family owned and, as far as I can tell, empty. Local patrols have been dispatched. It's a long shot, but right now it's all we've got to go on, and you look like you're about to combust. I'm going to check it out. You want to come along?"

Knox nodded. "Yeah." He reached for the phone, to get a closer look at the map, while he followed Derek to his truck. "I can't keep standing around here when they could be getting farther away every second."

The cousins were on the road within minutes and cruising away from town.

Knox changed the view on the map of the property in question, trading an overview of general directions for a satellite view. He zoomed and scrolled the immediate area. "An abandoned home seems like a good place to store a couple of missing women."

Derek grunted. "I thought the same thing. Wouldn't be a bad place to set up a drug enterprise either."

Knox stilled as a broken-down and faded sign became visible on the small screen. The paint was chipped and the wooden frame barely standing, but the remnants of words and familiar green leaves tightened the knots in his stomach. "Was this place previously a mint farm?"

Derek shot him a questioning look, gaze dropping briefly to the cell phone. "His mother's family raised mint before the whole industry moved to the Pacific Northwest, but that was more than sixty years ago. How'd you guess that from the satellite view? I only found the information by happenchance while confirming it was his mother's property."

Knox traded Derek's device for his own, dialing dispatch with purpose. "The gunman in Jen's apartment smelled like mint."

JEN GRIPPED THE baby sling with both hands and hefted it from the floor. She'd filled the material with the heaviest cans of ancient food she could find, and broken away as much of the rusted door as possible. Now, it was time to get out of there.

"One," she said, swinging the sling for momentum. "Two. Three." She swung the makeshift battering ram against the door with a body-jolting thud. The metal groaned and strained under the hit.

"Again," Madison said, before beginning to cough once more.

Madison had moved in and out of consciousness throughout the day, oscillating between speech and incoherency, her fever seeming to rise.

D.J. cried continually. He was wet, hungry and scared, but Jen couldn't help him. She couldn't help any of them without her bag of well-planned emergency staples. What good had all the hours of forethought done her when something like this had happened? Just like the bomb that had taken Dylan and Bob, there hadn't been any way to prepare for this.

So, she swung.

The sound and impact reverberated down her arms and spine. Her joints ached and her muscles protested. Her head hummed with the dull pain of physical and mental exertion.

Again, she told herself. *Again.* And she swung.

And she swung.

And she swung.

A great shifting screech broke through the cascade of desperate sobs and tears, sending her back down the steps at a run.

A large section of metal gave way, collapsing inward and falling toward her.

"Whoa! Whoa! Whoa!" She leaped down the steps and dove at her son and Madison, shielding them with her body and taking the brunt of the collision with her back. Her hands planted on the wall where Madison's back rested, her knees dug into the floor.

D.J. remained, miraculously, untouched in the space beneath Jen's arched torso.

Pain screamed up Jen's back and shoulders, the sharp rusty edges of the panel surely taking skin and flesh in the attack.

Her son's cries filled her ears as she shifted the heavy metal away and rested her head on the filthy floor beside D.J.

The dimming crank light lay under the steps, fallen and nearly forgotten.

Moonlight and fresh minty air rolled in through the hole above them.

KNOX EXITED DEREK'S truck at a run, grabbing the first uniformed person he saw and demanding details.

According to the local detective, a search party had just arrived and was dividing to explore the eighty-acre property, on foot and with all-terrain vehicles, but the encroaching night would be a problem. The house had been confirmed empty by the initial set of dispatched officers, but a set of recent tire marks were visible upon their arrival. The detective confirmed the tracks were likely made by a sedan or other midsized car.

Knox scrubbed anxious hands over his head and locked them there, elbows pointed skyward and a desperate prayer in his heart. Jen was determined and resourceful. If there was a way to signal searchers for rescue, she would find one. *Where are you?* he asked silently, willing the night to give her up.

Eighty acres was a formidable amount of land to search in the best of conditions. Twilight had made things more complicated.

A sea of spotlights bobbed and swam in the fields near the old farmhouse. The first sets of volunteers and lawmen were beginning their hunt.

A chill in the air raised the hairs on Knox's arms and climbed up the back of his neck. The scent of spearmint rose on the breeze like an apparition.

And in the distance, a small fragile cry reached Knox's ears.

"D.J."

JEN HUGGED HER baby to her chest as she dragged herself up the wooden stairs and into the night.

Madison lay on the floor behind her, unconscious, as she had been since Jen reopened her eyes after the hit with falling metal. Madison hadn't responded to Jen's pleas, and the impossibility of dragging her up the steps on newspaper had forced Jen's hand. She didn't want to leave her friend behind, but she also couldn't sit and wait for rescue. As it was, she didn't know if Madison would survive. Every hour and every minute counted.

Jen willed her feet to move, the piercing pain from her injured back cutting deeper with every step. She couldn't find the voice to comfort D.J., so she held him more tightly as he screamed, hoping he could feel her love, even if she was in too much pain to speak.

Every inch of progress took her farther from Madison and farther from the horrid tomb where they'd been left to die. But the oppressing darkness of the nighttime forest felt almost worse. She was alone now, and this new tomb was vast. What if she wandered in the wrong direction? What if she became hopelessly lost? What if she failed them all?

Her tears fell on D.J.'s hair, and she stifled a sob.

It was time for her to be strong.

The thunder of footfalls froze her in place, and for a minute she imagined Martz returning. Could he have come to check on them? And if so, would he let them live if he found they'd escaped?

Pinpricks of lights appeared on her right, dancing like fireflies over distant fields, barely visible through the dense forest trees. Was she hallucinating?

She stared at the lights, wondering if she should go toward them or maintain her path. Uncertainty rooted her, confused her, terrified her. A wrong choice could cost lives.

And then, above the screech of her wailing son, she heard her name.

KNOX JOGGED TOWARD the sound of D.J.'s cries, his heart in his throat, and his cousin at his side. A dozen volunteers and local law enforcement followed.

"Jen!" he called.

Derek echoed her name, and the others behind them did the same.

The forest was dark and treacherous, impossible to

see clearly or navigate properly, even with the mass of flashlights in his rescue party. He couldn't imagine doing it alone, with a baby and no light source. Heavy brush slapped his legs and briars caught on his jeans as he ran, calling her name with every breath.

They took wrong turns, following the sounds of D.J.'s muffled cries, distorted by trees and distance. Until suddenly the wails grew louder.

They were on the right track and Knox ran harder, faster, determined to reach her before she spent another moment scared and alone.

Then suddenly, Jen called back.

JEN OPENED HER eyes to the offensive fluorescent lighting of her hospital room. She'd been treated to nonstop check-ins from medical staff and nosy but well-meaning Winchesters since her admission the night before.

D.J. had been examined and released into the custody of Knox's auntie and uncle when Knox had refused to leave Jen's side. His aunt and uncle had nearly needed resuscitation from overwhelming joy. Jen had been a little drugged at the time, but she thought she'd seen Auntie Rosa skipping away.

"Good morning," a husky voice said, yawning deeply after the greeting. Knox shifted in the utilitarian hospital chair beside her, attempting to get comfortable. His hair was tousled and his cheeks were dark with two days of stubble. His clothes still smelled of the outdoors, but thankfully not of spearmint.

"Hey," she whispered, falling deep into his kind green eyes. "You didn't have to stay."

He leaned forward, pushing hair from her forehead

and planting a kiss in its place. "You're here," he said. "Where else would I be?"

She smiled, and Knox exhaled.

"How do you feel?" he asked.

"Better than her," Jen said, shifting her gaze over his shoulder, to the bed where Madison slept. A dozen machines beeped and blinked around her. IV bags hung from multiple hooks, each running necessities direct to her veins. "She almost died," Jen whispered. "Dehydration. Sepsis. A broken ankle and tibia."

Madison's surgery had taken hours. Her leg had needed to be re-broken and reset. The infection in her thigh had spread severely and nearly killed her. The concussion had been the least of her many problems, and the emotional trauma from her experience would likely be around long after she'd physically healed.

Knox tipped his head, bringing his face back into Jen's view. "She's alive because of you."

"We're all safe because of you," she challenged.

He wrinkled his nose. "Technically, Derek deserves the credit for finding Martz's family property," he said, "but we never would've found you or that storm cellar at night if you hadn't done what you did. And Madison wouldn't have made it until morning."

A single hot tear formed at the corner of Jen's eye.

Knox swept it away with the pad of his thumb. "Martz was caught near the state line. He's in custody, and given the extent of his crimes, he won't be free again for a very long time."

"Good." She nodded.

Knox smiled, but the expression grew tentative. "I think you and D.J. should stay with me while you heal. At least until Madison is released. You can rest and let me take care of you awhile before you go home and try to meet all of your friend's needs too."

Jen glanced at her friend once more. "Her folks are coming for her," she said. "They'll be here this afternoon."

"Then I guess you can stay with me as long as you want," Knox said.

He raised her hand in his and kissed her fingers. "I hate that you're hurt, but I'm so grateful the metal that damaged your back didn't break it. You should've seen yourself when we found you. I thought you'd been shot."

There'd been a lot more blood than Jen had realized before being hoisted into the ambulance. Under proper lighting, the gore was real, and she couldn't even see the wounds on her back.

The three-by-four-foot piece of door that chased her down the shelter steps had ripped large sections of skin away from her back and left deep cuts that had required extensive stitches. She'd received skin grafts too, but the injuries weren't nearly as bad as they could've been. And she was eternally thankful D.J. hadn't been harmed at all. Not a single bruise or scratch on his perfect little self. That was all that really mattered.

Knox stroked her hand with warm fingers. "I thought I'd lost you," he said. "I know it's probably too soon to say this, but I wasn't sure what I'd do without you," he said. "You feel like the missing piece to a puzzle I thought I'd finished."

Jen's throat constricted, and her chest ached at his welcomed words. "And D.J.?" she asked, unable to return his confession with the truth of her heart until she heard the whole story. Because she wasn't just one person anymore, and the smaller, handsomer part of her was far more important than the rest.

Knox frowned, and her stomach dropped. "Didn't he tell you?" Knox asked.

Jen pressed her lips and shook her head, smashing the bubble of hope and waiting for his explanation.

"D.J. and I already talked about this," he said. "While you were sleeping, we negotiated arrangements for the bigger bedroom. I won, since I plan to share it with you, and that just makes sense. He agreed, but is demanding to meet the other kids in this family before making a final decision, and he's asked me to get him out of that nasty mush you feed him for breakfast. Beyond that, he says he trusts your judgment."

Jen covered her mouth as emotions began to rise once more. "It's not too soon," she whispered. "I feel it too, and I want to be with you. Long after I've healed," she said. "Way, way after."

Knox's brows rose. "You sure about that?"

She nodded, the motion feeling erratic and wild.

"You sure it's not just the IV talking?" he asked. "Because I'm thinking the three of us can get a really long-term situation going."

She bobbed her head again, speechless and reaching for him.

Knox rose to lean over her. He stroked her cheek and tipped their foreheads together. "I love you," he said, then kissed her lips with adoration.

She relaxed into the perfect moment, enveloped in his precious words.

A commotion in the hall spread her lips into a smile. "Visitors?" she asked.

Knox checked over his shoulder, then turned back with a pleased expression. "Yeah."

"Your family?" she guessed.

"Maybe soon," he said. "If you're interested in my offer, I've got something I need to ask your dad."

"Baby!" Jen's mother called, rushing past Knox to her daughter's side.

Her father trailed behind, a look of distress and relief mixing on his brow. He stopped to shake Knox's hand. "Thank you for calling," he said. "It was awful nice of your family to arrange our airfare. We couldn't think straight after receiving this news."

"Of course," Knox answered. "She's quite a hero. I know she's been missing you both, and while I wish the circumstances were different, I'm glad you're here."

"Mama?" Jen asked, receiving an onslaught of hugs and kisses, as if she were a child.

Then Jen remembered what it felt like to be a mother, and she hugged hers back a little more tightly.

Epilogue

D.J. toddled over the warm dry sand in dress shorts, a white button-down shirt, bare feet and suspenders. The pageboy hat his grandpa had placed on his head only a few minutes before sat painfully askew.

"That hat is coming off," Jen whispered.

Her father chuckled. "Look at him go. He's a natural beach boy. I'll bet he's one heck of a swimmer."

D.J. face-planted, as if on cue, and the hat rolled into the sand.

"He's a total tadpole," she agreed. "He's still getting his land legs."

Her dad laughed and set his hand on her fingers resting in the crook of his arm. "I'm glad you're here," he said, eyes misty and full of emotion, the way they'd been when he'd arrived in her hospital room, nearly a year before.

"My folks live here," she said sweetly, setting a palm against his smooth cheek. "Where else would I be?"

Those words had meant everything to her when Knox had first said them, and she'd made it her mission to live by them. From now on, she would always be where her family needed her. And today, they needed her on this beach. Her father's health severely limited his ability to travel, so she'd volunteered to come to him.

Thankfully, Knox's family shared his motto, and they had no problems traveling. They didn't even mind baking in the hot Florida sun.

Before her, three rows of ten chairs each had been arranged in the sand outside her favorite resort. An aisle divided the guests but not the people. Her mom held Auntie Rosa's hand in the front row. Uncle Hank swept a crawling D.J. into his arms and shook the fallen hat before placing it back onto his head. Then he flew Jen's son like an airplane to the grapevine altar laced with white silk and roses.

"Are you ready?" her father asked, voice cracking on the words.

"I am," she said, tightening her hold on his arm. "I love you, Daddy. And I love him too."

His expression crumbled at her gentle use of the childhood endearment. "I know you do, baby girl. If I didn't, I wouldn't let you go."

With that, the music changed, and they began their walk past family and friends.

Madison accepted Jen's bouquet when she arrived. Her deep blue dress sparkled against the matching sea behind her. She'd made a full recovery, and moved back to Missouri, where her parents had overseen her care. And she'd met a professional football player, also in recovery, treating his blown-out knee. Maybe she was just a sucker for uniforms, because they would be married at Christmas.

Knox's green eyes flashed as he drank her in before taking her hands. "You're beautiful," he whispered, and her cheeks heated with pleasure.

Their exchange of vows stole her breath, almost as completely as the man before her had stolen her heart.

"I now pronounce you," the pastor declared, "husband and wife."

A chorus of cheers went up before them.

The line of groomsmen at Knox's back, Cruz, Blaze, Lucas, Derek and the last remaining Winchester bachelor, Nash, gave a collective "whoop!"

Madison and the groomsmen's wives clapped and cheered.

The guests rose and began to scatter.

Across the sand behind the altar, a gaggle of children ran wild, and precariously close to the surf, monitored by four delighted grandparents and an army of loved ones, hurrying to catch their offspring.

"Welcome to the circus," Knox whispered, planting a much deeper and more intimate kiss on Jen's lips as they stood alone at the altar.

The pastor took his cue and slipped away.

Jen pulled back, arms draped over her husband's shoulders. "I believe this is Winchester Country," she corrected, marveling at her incredibly good fortune. "What do you think about a few minutes alone before the reception?"

"Alone?" Knox bent immediately and swept her off her feet, into his arms. "It's the only thing I've thought about since you showed up in that dress."

She laughed.

"If we make a run for it, we might have six or seven minutes before anyone notices we're gone," he said, breaking into a jog.

She giggled and buried her face into his neck. "Actually, I assigned each of my bridesmaids a task that will waylay and detain the family for a minimum of thirty minutes."

Knox growled with pleasure as he pressed the elevator button with gusto. "Another reason I love you, Mrs. Winchester," he said, backing her into the empty car when it arrived. "My smart, sexy little Scout."

She arched against him as the elevator rocketed them upward. "Wait until you see what I've got in my honeymoon bag," she teased, certain no amount of time alone with him would ever be long enough.

* * * * *

COLTON'S
DANGEROUS
REUNION

JUSTINE DAVIS

He thought they'd give him a... that he'd get something out of his will they didn't always get out of theirs. The firsthand certainty that he'd helped children even twice scared and lost than he'd been was as somehow more... somehow... most of... about his work.

Chapter One

Gideon Colton was delivering a roundhouse shot to the well-used punching bag in his workout room when the call came in. It was on the third ring by the time he got his gloves off and picked up his cell phone. When he saw it was the office, given that it was well after hours on a Friday night, it made his adrenaline kick up more than punching gym equipment ever did.

Somewhere, a kid was in trouble.

"Gideon?" came the query when he answered.

It was Marcy, his rule-bound boss at the children's services office. He bit back the question "Is that who you called?" and merely asked, "What's up?"

"Need you to go to the county MC," she said, using the common office terminology for Lark's County Medical Center.

In his job, this was never a good way for a conversation to start. But he'd known what he was taking on when he'd decided to forgo the legal and law enforcement careers that so many of his siblings had chosen and go for more hands-on helping. He'd had to endure a lot of groaning about their brother the social worker, but he knew they understood. They might tease him, but he was a Colton, and when it came down to it, his family had his back.

He thought they also knew he often got something out of his work they didn't always get out of theirs. The firsthand certainty that he'd helped children even more scared and lost than he'd been was something more important to him than anything else about his work.

"What's the case?"

"His name's Charles Webber. Charlie. Five-year-old male, probable abuse victim in the hospital. Mother Ellen has been admitted, father Rick is in custody."

Gideon suppressed an old, familiar shiver. How well he knew what it was like to have your life turned inside out. It had been hard enough for him, and he had been older than Charlie. And he'd still had his siblings and his mom, a home free of abuse.

"How badly is he hurt?"

The unspoken subtext was clear, and they all knew it: How fast did he have to move? Was the child likely to die, so he needed to race to get there before it happened, to try and speak with him? This part made his gut churn, but it was part of the territory. Part of that emotional territory his siblings teased him about.

All except Rachel.

Yes, his sister got it. As the district attorney, she got it, not just because she saw what it did to him to deal with those cases, but because she steeped herself in the grim details of the cases she prosecuted. Maybe that was why they were so close. That and only being two years apart, plus being two of the only three singles, as they called themselves, among their multiple-birth siblings.

Whatever it was that had bonded them, it had made Rachel ask and Gideon immediately say yes to her wish for him to be her baby Iris's godfather. In this case, he knew it would be more than just ceremonial because of the absence of Iris's father in the picture. It wasn't even an issue for him; helping his sister with sweet little Iris wasn't a chore, it was a bright spot in his life, and one that he'd needed after—

"It's not critical," Marcy said, thankfully pulling him out of the memory before he strayed down a well-worn path. "But they'll be keeping him overnight at least. I'll send you what details we have."

"Copy," Gideon said before ending the call.

He flipped out the light in his home gym as he left, headed for his bathroom and took a rapid shower. Mentally he moved installing that lap pool he wanted a little higher on the to-do list; he would have loved to be able to put in fifty or so this morning. He'd never quite left behind that competitive swimmer he'd once been.

But no time to dwell on that now. There was a hurting little boy waiting, alone and no doubt scared.

He didn't bother with his hair other than to comb it back, dried off and dressed quickly. He chose casual clothes that would be less intimidating to a five-year-old than a formal suit: jeans, a heavy knit sweater and, after a glance outside to confirm it was still snowing, the waterproof sheepskin boots Rach had bought him for his birthday a couple of years ago.

All the while his mind was racing, calculating. The kid would definitely be scared, if not terrified, afraid to do anything, afraid to say anything. Doing or saying something, whether it had been him or his mother, had probably brought this on. If the boy knew his mother was also in the hospital, he'd be scared for her, too. Gideon would no doubt have to climb a wall to get through to him. But he'd give it his best shot.

You're so good with those kids, honey. You need to have a dozen or so of your own.

You just want a herd of grandkids, Mom.

Your point?

He smiled as he headed for his car, remembering how Isa Colton had given him a raised eyebrow as she'd responded. It was the only thing to smile about in that exchange. Because when it came down to it, he wanted those kids. Well, not a dozen, but definitely one of each, and maybe a couple more. Children who would never know the kind of trauma the children he worked with knew all too well.

He truly liked kids. The way their minds worked and how each one was different, even among siblings, endlessly fascinated him. Hadn't his own family proved that last bit?

But for himself, he wanted kids who would grow up happy. With no major trauma, no betrayals by the people they should be able to trust the most. No beatings at the hands of those people. No emotional grinding down until they believed they were worthless.

Or, in his own case, no finding out the father you'd loved was a liar and, worse, a crooked judge who had destroyed so many lives in so many ways. Innocent lives.

As he opened the garage door, he steered himself off that old, worn route he'd been dealing with since his own father's little enterprise had crumbled around them all. No, he thought as he got into his SUV, his kids, if they ever arrived, would know their father, know he was what he appeared to be and that he loved them enough to make sure they had a good example in life. His kids would never have to face some dark, hidden, ugly secret about him. Ever.

No, they'll just have a father who has to keep avoiding thinking about things like his own father and the one who got away.

And that brought him back to the other problem. Because having those kids required a partner who felt the same way. And that was something he seemed doomed to never find. Or if he did find someone, he always managed to blow it. As usual, when the subject sneaked into his mind, Rachel's words from a couple of years ago played back in his head.

Gid, you know I love you, but you have to stop falling for a woman—or at least telling her you've fallen for her—at the drop of a hat.

I don't wear a hat.

Good, because as fast as you're dodging the point, it would fly off.

The irony was that, while she was right in general, the instance that had brought on that observation had been...different. That time, he really had been in love. He knew because of how different it felt than all the previous times. He finally understood the difference between infatuation and genuine love, the kind that lasted a lifetime.

But it hadn't mattered. By the time he'd realized it, he'd already scared her off. Sophia hadn't just walked away; she'd practically run. The one woman who had taught him a lesson he'd needed to learn—the hard way. The woman he'd fallen for on every level. The woman who'd guaranteed he'd never mistake a temporary passion for real love again. The woman who had left a scar on his heart that had hardened at least some part of it.

The woman he would never, ever forget.

He was almost glad of the snow as he pulled out of his driveway. It meant he'd have to be a bit more careful, and he needed the distraction from his thoughts. Like thoughts about how his dating life had been virtually nonexistent since the night Sophia had blasted him with her disbelief and left. He felt like the boy who cried wolf must have, saying he was in love so many times that nobody believed it when he truly was. Except, in his case, it had never really been a lie; he just hadn't known the real thing. Until Sophia.

He focused on the distinctive sound of his snow tires on the pavement, hoping it would divert his mind. When that didn't work, he was back to going through his list of things that needed doing at home. He'd known when he'd taken on the big, forty-year-old house that the renovation wasn't going to be fast, if only because he wanted to either do or oversee it all himself.

And he'd made a lot of progress in the house, located about a half hour from the house where he'd grown up. The rabbit warren of small rooms downstairs was now a spacious great room with a big fireplace, adjacent to a modern kitchen—not that he cooked much—and there was a media room that even his brothers envied, along with his dedicated home gym. Upstairs he'd expanded the master bedroom, taking up one of the adjacent bedrooms to use as a retreat with a fireplace and a flat-screen, with some hazy idea of future harried parenting and needing a place to escape to. The master bath was next, but he hadn't decided what path to take on that yet.

Then there was the outside. One of the reasons he'd chosen the place was the size of the property around it. Almost five acres, and bordering open land with a view of the tall, reddish-orange plateau that overlooked the town of Blue Larkspur. If he wanted to go up another story, he'd probably have a view of the river the state was named for.

It seemed like the perfect place for a family. He'd even envisioned one of those climbing, sliding, swinging combinations he'd seen in parks, maybe built like an Old West cavalry fort just for fun.

Yeah, for that family you don't, and may never, have.

And somehow he'd ended up back on that topic he'd been trying to avoid.

His phone chimed an arrival, the file from Marcy, most likely. He was halfway to the medical center, so he decided to wait until he got there and parked rather than pull off the road now. When he arrived he found a spot around the corner from the small ER, where he was guessing the boy still was. If not, he'd track him down inside.

He pulled out his phone and called up the email and the attachment. The list of domestic violence calls to the Webber house told a sad story. He was surprised he or one of his colleagues hadn't been brought in before now, although as was sadly so typical in these situations, the wife had apparently defended the abusive husband and denied what had happened. But this time there had been a witness, a neighbor who had finally had enough. She had made the call and was, according to the file Marcy had sent, more than willing to testify if necessary.

He put the phone back into his jacket pocket, stepped out into the chilly night air and headed for the door to the ER. He was, unfortunately, well-known to the staff here. Some were even friends. And he was glad to see one of them, Eric Kearney, manning the desk at the moment. The tall, lanky young man glanced up when he heard the door open, spotted him, then nodded and waved him over.

"Charlie Webber?" he asked. Gideon nodded. "Glad it's you. That's one scared kid."

"I was told the mother's been admitted. Serious?"

"More than bruises. She'll be here for a while," Eric said, and Gideon left it at that, knowing regulations made it impossible for him to elaborate unless and until Gideon got legal access to her records.

But child abuse was different. And there was already a police report, which made it official and triggered the protected information section that lifted the restrictions in such cases.

"The boy?" he asked.

"You have a case number?"

"I do."

What he learned then turned his stomach. Any child abuse case was rough, and when he read the list of Charlie Webber's injuries—new and old—it was all too familiar. But when he saw the vital statistics, he felt the familiar anger start to stir. "Damn, he's little."

Eric nodded. "Under the normal range in both height and weight for his age."

Gideon pulled up the arrest report Marcy had sent. "And his father's six foot and over two hundred pounds," he said, his jaw tight.

"Sometimes I'm sorry they bring them in alive." Gideon's gaze shot to Eric's face, and he saw his own anger reflected there. "I know, I know," Eric said. "I shouldn't feel that way, but…"

"If there's any class of subhumans that deserves it, it's this one," Gideon agreed. Then, to take the edge off them both, he looked at his friend. "But we both know if he showed up here hurt and needing help, you'd help him."

"More fool me, eh?" Eric said, with a wry smile.

"More dedicated you," Gideon corrected.

Eric shrugged and said, "Just take care of the kid, okay? He's in room B."

Gideon nodded, pondering his approach as he headed toward the exam room. He hoped they hadn't left the kid in there alone. He had to be terrified by everything happening to him. Apparently his father— no, check that, he was no more than a sperm contributor—had still been threatening both the boy and his mother, even as the police carted him away.

He was still going through his repertoire when he got there, so he paused outside the door. He'd probably have to adjust on the fly, but right now he needed to decide on an opening, something he could start with that wouldn't scare Charlie any more than he already was. Something that could maybe even be a distraction.

The asking-for-help bit might work. It had before,

in similar situations. Coming in and asking if the boy knew where the bathroom was; that was basic and distracting. And saying he was lost, that might help. The idea of an adult being lost was sometimes a way to reach a kid who was feeling far beyond lost.

Decided now, he stepped up to the doorway. There was a narrow vertical window above the door handle, through which he could see the shape in the hospital bed. Charlie was even smaller than he'd expected, and with one eye swollen almost shut and one arm bandaged, he looked helpless. Gideon had to bite back that anger that wanted to overwhelm him.

He knew his family and friends mostly assumed he didn't want to get involved in law enforcement because he was too softhearted. But Gideon knew that way down deep, it was *this*. This deep, consuming anger at the brutality of some of humankind. If he'd been the one to encounter this piece of debris masquerading as a human and a father, he'd probably have beaten him to a pulp. It had taken him years after his own dad's disgrace and death to regain his inner peace and what his mother called his sweet soul, but at times like this he felt like that furious child again.

But, honey, don't you see? It's that big heart of yours that makes you feel that way and want to help.

As her words echoed in his head, Gideon didn't know if she was right. He only knew he didn't just want to help; he had to. It was the only thing that made what he'd gone through worth anything.

He pushed open the door. The little boy in the bed looked over. He didn't seem quite as frightened as Gideon had feared he'd be. Probably because, thank goodness, they hadn't actually left him alone in here. There was a woman sitting on the edge of the bed, her back to him, her slender brown hand holding the boy's pale one. As the boy looked up, she twisted to look over her shoulder at him.

Gideon stopped dead in his tracks. Stared, forgetting to breathe. Or forgetting how.

It was *her*.

The woman he to this day spent too much time thinking about.

The woman he had never forgotten and would never forget. *Sophia.*

Chapter Two

It had occurred to her that it might be him. From the moment the police officer had told her they'd called in a social worker who specialized in working with traumatized kids, Dr. Sophia Gray-Jones had wondered.

Hoped? She wasn't sure. She only knew she had no right to hope.

She had even been the tiniest bit afraid it would be him. After all, she was the one who had ended their brief but intense relationship two years ago. Abruptly and harshly. That she regretted it, that she considered it just might be one of, if not the biggest, mistakes of her life, didn't matter. She knew that the moment she saw his face, his expression, go utterly cold when he saw her. She hadn't just burned that bridge; she'd blown it up down to the foundations.

Now, thinking of some of the things she'd said to him, it was no surprise to her that he was looking at her as if she'd crawled out from under a wet, slimy rock. Contrasted against the way he used to look at her, as if she were the answer to a prayer, it was beyond chilling.

On some level she noticed he looked different in other ways. Bigger. Stronger. He'd always had an impressive chest and pair of shoulders, but tonight they looked even more powerful, and she didn't think it was just the heavy sweater he was wearing.

Upping the workout yet again? You're in great shape already. Believe me, I know.

Maybe I want more...endurance.

You've got plenty of that, too.

The memory of the teasing exchange—and what had followed—sent heat rippling through her. But coupled with that was a strange sort of longing that got tangled up with what else she knew. What he'd told her on their third date, when a friend from his gym had stopped by their table and she'd first realized how serious he was about his regimen.

You don't seem like a typical gym rat. Why the focus?

I don't want to fight anyone.

She remembered frowning at that answer, not seeing the connection. And then he'd explained.

If I look strong enough, intimidating enough, people— especially the abusers I encounter who might be thinking about it—might hesitate to tackle me. That can buy me time, maybe enough to talk them out of it.

Most abusers are cowards at heart, she'd said.

True. Which is why it often works.

And if it doesn't?

She knew she would never forget the look in his eyes, those lovely blue eyes, then. Or the simple answer that had warmed her, heart and soul.

I'll do anything a kid needs me to.

"Dr. Sophia?"

The tremulous little voice, using the name only allowed to her patients, pulled her out of the pit of regret she'd slid into. The boy had been utterly silent since she'd arrived after the ER staff had called her as Charlie's physician. He'd shut down, and she hadn't been able to coax more than a nod or a shake of his head out of him since she'd arrived.

She looked back at the little boy, seeing the fear in his soft brown eyes. Right now helping this frightened little boy was all that mattered. And there was no better person to do just that than Gideon Colton. She'd never met a gentler man or anyone who was more understanding with kids than Gideon. And they took to him easily, because he always seemed to find the way to reach them as individuals. She wasn't quite sure how he knew what approach to take with each one, only that he did, and he got to them in ways even she as a pediatrician couldn't match.

"It's all right, Charlie," she said soothingly. "This is Gideon. He's here to help, and he's very, very good at it."

"He is?" The boy's voice was faint, but at least he was speaking.

"He is. The best I've ever known."

She knew she was pouring it on thick but told herself it was for this child's sake. And it had the added advantage of all being true. Thankfully, she hadn't had to deal with this firsthand; she'd not had a patient who was an abuse victim in her private practice. But she knew Gideon, and how much he cared. Not to mention that…she owed him this much. At least.

When she turned back again, he wasn't even looking at her. He was focused on Charlie, who was looking back at him warily. "You're big," the boy said, sounding as guarded as his gaze as Gideon walked to the other side of the hospital bed.

"Sometimes that's a good thing," Gideon said, very quietly, bending down. "I can keep people away if they're mean, or mad."

"You mean...at me? Even if it's my..."

Sophia knew when the boy's voice trailed off that he'd being going to say "my father." She shifted her gaze to Gideon, to tell him, but he was already there. She should have known.

"Especially if it's your father, Charlie. He has no right to hurt you. Or your mother." He straightened then, drew himself up to his considerable height. Six foot one and built, he was impressive. And she somehow knew he was making himself look as large as possible to the injured boy. And when he spoke, it was with a grim determination that even a five-year-old couldn't miss. "And I will make sure he knows that."

Sophia saw something change in the child's eyes then. A flicker of something. Awareness? Appreciation? Hope? Yes, that was it. That quickly, Gideon had given the child hope. She doubted Charlie had ever had someone in his life willing to stand up to his brutal dad, let alone look as if he could actually do it.

But the hope faded quickly. "Are you a policeman?" Charlie asked, almost sourly. "They never do anything."

"Sometimes they can't, buddy. Not until a line is crossed."

And until a woman takes a stand for her child. Sophia was a little surprised at the vehemence of her own thought and amended it to add, *If she can.*

But she suspected this had happened before. Charlie had come to her as a new patient three weeks ago with a case of strep throat, and she'd noticed a fading bruise on his arm. She'd asked about it, and his mother had said the boy was just playing ball and got himself banged up. It hadn't looked like the typical grab-and-twist mark, so there hadn't been enough to justify reporting it, although she'd made a note on the chart. Along with the notes that he was small in both height and weight for his age, something she was concerned about but figured she could address once he was over the infection.

Now Sophia knew better. She never should have let it go, not even for that short period. Never should have assumed she would see the boy again and could address it then.

She had a hard time comprehending the idea that a mother could have allowed her child to be injured like this. It was one thing between adults, but your own child? Didn't that change…everything?

"A line?" the boy asked, eying Gideon, still wary.

"Hitting you is crossing that line."

The boy studied him for a moment. Sophia held her breath, waiting, knowing it was the child's decision. Then, with a touch of that sourness that no five-year-old should have, he said, "He's hit me before."

"And nothing happened then, right?" Gideon said.

"No." The boy's face twisted, and he raised his uninjured arm to wipe at his eyes, then looked away as if embarrassed they'd seen the tears. "The police came, but my mom sent them away. She told them it was a accident."

"Was it?" Gideon asked softly.

"No." And then, in the most wrenching voice she'd ever heard, the child whispered, "She lied. She said it was my fault." His head came up then. "But it wasn't! I didn't do anything bad. I just asked…"

When the tiny voice trailed away, Sophia said, just as softly as Gideon had, "Asked what, Charlie?"

He looked up at her, his eyes still wet with unshed tears. "If I could have a dog."

She felt her own eyes begin to tear up. This really hit home for her. She'd never been allowed the dog she'd wanted, either, but her father had certainly never hit her for asking. She searched for something to say but couldn't find any words to deal with the answer to such a simple, childlike question being a blow from his father. Then Gideon spoke again.

"Why do you want a dog, Charlie?" His question surprised her.

"I just… I thought… I could pet it. And talk to it. It would listen to me. It wouldn't yell at me. It would be like a…friend."

Sophia could almost hear her heart breaking. Gideon pulled over a chair and sat beside the boy's bed, having made his point about his size and power, she supposed. He leaned forward and casually rested his elbows on the bed. "What about a human friend?"

Charlie shook his head. "I had some, but they're afraid of my dad, so they don't come around anymore."

"I'm not afraid of your father."

The boy's eyes widened, and Sophia saw hope flare there again. In that simple statement, Gideon had again reached the child.

"But you're a grown-up. You wouldn't want to be my friend."

"You know," Gideon said with a smile, "that's one thing about being a grown-up. You get to pick your own friends."

Sophia had a sudden flash of memory, of a day they'd been down at the riverfront, just walking and talking. Their second…meeting, she guessed, since it had been a chance encounter, not a date per se. He'd gotten a phone call and excused himself to take it, then regretfully told her he had to leave.

"Former case," he'd said.

"Former?"

He'd nodded, then shrugged as if it were nothing when he explained, "They all have my number and know they can call if they need to."

"The kids? Even after the case is closed?"

He'd given her a steady look then. "When I tell them I'm their friend, I mean it. It doesn't end just because the case is handled."

And that, she admitted now, had been the moment when she'd first looked at Gideon Colton as something more—much more—than just a guy she'd run into at the coffee shop.

Chapter Three

Charlie didn't quite believe him. Not yet. But he would. Gideon would see to that.

His mind was racing ahead, planning. And trying not to let the presence of the woman he'd never forgotten distract him. Although it was nearly impossible when she looked...like she looked, and that lovely, throaty voice of hers still sent shivers and heat up and down his spine.

He clenched his jaw and made himself focus. He would need to talk to the mother, then the cops, then Marcy again with his assessment. With the mother here in the hospital and the father...well, where he belonged, they were looking at foster care, at least temporarily. And he knew just the place, if they had room. He'd make a call himself; the Knights liked him and would help if they could. It wouldn't be official, not until it came from the office, but he could lay the groundwork, at least.

"What should I call you?" Charlie asked, and Gideon felt a pop of relief. The boy might not realize what a step that was and what it implied—that he would need to know what to call him—but he did.

"Gideon is fine. Or Gid, if it's easier."

The boy frowned. "I'm s'posed to call grown-ups by their last names." He shot a sideways look at Sophia. "But she lets me call her Dr. Sophia."

She would.

He'd been trying not to even think about her presence, but it was impossible. By necessity he'd encountered a few pediatricians in his work, but never had he seen one who exuded care the way she did. In fact, he'd heard that about her long before he'd ever met her. Looking back now, with as much detachment as time had given him, he supposed that was part of the reason he'd fallen so hard, so fast. He'd already known going in that she had a reputation for being dedicated to her patients. His sister Aubrey had told him that before he'd ever run into Sophia the first time. Apparently Sophia had joined in enthusiastically when the Gemini Ranch, which Aubrey ran with their brother Jasper, hosted a special event for seriously ill kids. Several of her patients attended, and she had come with them, seemingly delighted to be able to see them outside a medical setting.

She's wonderful with them, Gideon. And they clearly adore her, which tells you a lot. Just like it does with you.

He'd wondered then if Aubrey had been just talking or matchmaking. If it had happened now, he'd have no doubt; she was so deliriously happy with her Luke that she wanted to see every one of her unattached siblings in the same sweetly rocking boat.

And as he looked at the woman he'd known was exactly what he'd wanted in a wife and mother to his children, the old pain built in his chest. He clamped down on it hard. The effort put a chill in his voice when he answered the boy's comment.

"Then you're very lucky she lets you call her Dr. Sophia."

To his surprise, Sophia winced. Then he winced inwardly himself as he realized he'd just told a child in the hospital after a beating from a person he should be able to trust most that he was lucky. He'd let his personal feelings intrude and rushed into it headlong. As he seemed to want to do with everything.

Hell, no wonder she'd dumped him.

With an effort he wrenched his mind back to the matter at hand. Gideon settled in to talk to Charlie more, about outside things—what he liked to do, what he wanted to do in the future, if only to assure the boy there would be a future for him, and it would be better. And gradually Charlie opened up a little, although slowly and cautiously, evidence of how shell-shocked the child was.

He vowed anew he wouldn't let his own frustrations interfere with the job he had to do. He summoned up the indelible memory of how, as a child, he'd not only had to deal with his father's death, but the revelation that the man he'd loved and looked up to had been a horrible fraud.

And one of the worst things had been that he'd never been able to confront the man who'd sired him. No, he'd only had to live amid the debris left behind, watching his mother struggle, seeing the Colton name, once respected and almost revered in town, practically destroyed. It had taken a mountain of hard work and twenty years for his elder siblings to regain the respect of Blue Larkspur. The family had established the Truth Foundation with the intention of righting every wrong their father had done by investigating and, if possible, helping exonerate those he'd sent to prison. That included his final case, that of convicted drug smuggler Ronald Spence. But they'd only been able to find a few leads in that case. So although they hadn't given up and wouldn't, they had expanded into helping anyone whose case they believed in and had gone a long way toward that goal. That he wasn't as actively involved as Caleb and Morgan sometimes made him feel guilty, but he helped when and where he could—had even come across some cases they'd ended up taking.

The irony of that thought wasn't lost on him. Hadn't he just recently spent an emotional hour or so convincing Aubrey, who felt guilty herself over not being more involved with the foundation, that it was all right? To not feel that way, that she had a huge job seeing to Gemini and she had to take care of herself, too?

Great advice, bro. Maybe you should take it yourself. The taking care of yourself part, I mean.

He knew that, despite their teasing, his family saw the toll this work sometimes took. And they were good about it, not pushing him when he was exhausted from it. But they all seemed to have settled on the perfect solution, which was, according to them, a woman who truly deserved him.

He'd never asked if that meant as reward or punishment.

HE WAS AMAZING. Utterly amazing.

Sophia watched, rapt. Gideon had taken a child too

terrified to speak and now had him talking about how he one day wanted to fly in an airplane—to escape, perhaps?—how he was learning to read and liked it, and, heartbreakingly, how he had wanted to be an astronaut someday, but his father had told him he was too stupid.

The only stupid one here, Charlie, is me, Sophia told herself. *This man wanted me, and I refused to believe it and threw him away.*

She'd regretted it ever since. No one she'd dated before or since had made her feel the way he had. Which was probably why the others had never gone beyond more than one date, a polite good-night, end of story.

She'd spent some long, sleepless nights thinking about if something was wrong with her. Oddly, it had been a patient who had opened the door for her. It had been a young girl who had never known her father, who'd asked her somewhat wistfully what hers was like.

"He's a professor. Smart, and very respected."

"I meant, what was he like to you, when you were my age? Did he hug you and want to hang out with you?"

She'd been taken a little aback, but something in the girl's expression had made her answer with the truth instead of some platitude. "No. No, he didn't. He's not overly affectionate." *Or at all.* "But he provides for us, sees that we have all we need."

"But didn't you need hugs?"

Yes. Yes, I did. "That," she'd said, leaning down to give the girl a hug herself, "is why I collect them from my patients."

So she'd successfully changed the course of the uncomfortable conversation, but it had opened a floodgate in her mind. She thought she'd long ago accepted that her father was not one of those parents who exuded warmth and love. He doled out accolades when he felt they were earned and affection by the calendar. Her graduations from high school and even college had earned only a nod because they'd been expected. Her acceptance to medical school had earned a nod and a brusque "Good." Her graduation from there had, at least, gotten her a hug and a smile, and she'd even heard him telling someone on the phone with a note that had almost sounded like pride in his voice.

He'd never told her, of course.

The affection was just as rare, a hug on birthdays and Christmas, and once when she'd been in the hospital for appendicitis, the event that had inspired her wish to go into medicine. Or rather, brought the person who'd inspired her into her life. Dr. Beharry had done the near-emergency appendectomy neatly and efficiently. And she knew, somewhat ruefully, that the way he had spoken sternly to her father when he had complained the surgery had interrupted an important seminar had impressed her ten-year-old self enormously. Anybody who had the courage to stand up to her father like that was someone she wanted to be like.

But she wasn't. She simply tried, again and again, endlessly, to live up to expectations. Her mother's were rigid enough, but her father's—and seemingly every other man she'd dated—expectations were perfection, and she'd never managed to achieve that.

You don't have to be perfect, Soph. Just be you.

Gideon's long-ago words echoed in her head now. She felt moisture sting her eyes as she sat there, watching him and that scared little boy, and realized just how much she had thrown away because she hadn't been able to believe that this man loved her just the way she was. Hadn't been able to believe he was so open with his feelings when, with every other man in her life, she'd had to practically beg them to show even a little emotion, a little feeling.

But the expression on his face when he'd first stepped into the room and seen her was seared into her mind. He hated her now, would never forgive her for tossing away what he'd offered as if it were worthless. And she couldn't blame him.

But their respective careers meant that it was likely that they would occasionally…collide. Like now. And when they did, it would be because a child like Charlie needed their help. They had no right to let their—be honest, *your*—personal issues interfere with that, she told herself. Kids like Charlie needed and deserved their full attention. As he was getting now, from Gideon. So he would get it from her, as well. She'd be completely professional, regardless of Gideon's presence. She'd learned to keep her emotions on a leash, and she would do so now.

Even if the only man who had ever made her want to slip that leash completely was sitting within reach.

Chapter Four

"You're looking regal, as usual." Gideon leaned back in his chair, rather pleased with the nonchalant tone he'd managed.

Sophia stared down at the cup of coffee on the small table before her. He remembered how she'd laughed the first time he'd said it. But it's what she had made him think, the day he'd encountered her with her mass of curly black hair pulled up atop her head. He couldn't help thinking it looked like a towering crown, which had brought on the remark, which had made her laugh, then. And it had been a rich, luscious laugh that lit up her gorgeous hazel eyes.

And now those eyes were staring down into that coffee cup as if it held the answer to world strife.

He saw her take in a deep breath, and then she raised her head. What, she had to steel herself just to look at him?

Like you had to, to ask her how she'd feel about going for a simple cup of coffee, just to discuss the case?

He'd suggested a place away from the hospital, thinking it would be more comfortable. Charlie was his case now, and that meant they were going to have to work together, at least for now, until he was healed. It would be easier if they weren't constantly on edge around each other.

It would be easier if she didn't tie you up in knots simply by existing.

She'd agreed easily enough, and the short walk down the street had been fine, with chat about the snow, which had stopped before it made the sidewalks impassable, and the chance of more in the offing. But once they'd arrived, had their drinks and sat down, she'd gone rather quiet. And he suddenly saw the flaw in his thinking: she might have been happier on the familiar turf of the medical center.

You never did think straight around her.

She ignored what he'd just said about her appearance—he supposed he couldn't blame her for that. "You'll be handling Charlie's case?"

Okay. Business it is.

He should have known. She was the one who had ended it, after all. And rather brutally, leaving him reeling. He'd probably been out of sight, out of mind for her soon thereafter, but for him it had been a rough haul for a while.

But none of it was little Charlie's fault, and that had to be his focus now. His own hurt feelings over a broken heart were nothing compared to what that child was going through.

"Yes," he said. "I've got a foster family in mind for him. I'll be calling them first thing in the morning." Still sensing her tension, he tried a smile. "They have a sweetheart of a pup, too. Milo is practically a therapist himself. And is a therapy dog."

She did smile then, although he had the feeling it was still a nervous one. "Do you think they'll take him?"

"If they possibly can, yes. They're good people."

She sighed. "I should have made a report the first time he came to me."

He heard the guilt in her voice. So that was it. She had always been so hard on herself, such a perfectionist, that he should have guessed missing this would eat at her. He wasn't sure what compelled him to try and ease it; it wasn't like he cared how she felt. Not anymore.

"From what I saw in the file, there was no basis at the time. He was there for an illness, wasn't he?"

"But he had that bruise."

"Of undeterminable origin. And almost faded. You couldn't have known."

"I should have known from the way he acted. So withdrawn."

"First appointment with a new doctor." He raised an eyebrow at her. "And a beautiful one, at that."

She let out an audible breath. And gave him the barest of smiles. But it was something. And it seemed to breach the dam, as it were, because she relaxed a little. But what had happened still lay between them, and this process with Charlie was going to be a personal nightmare if they didn't put it behind them. So after a moment, when he was sure he could manage a chipper voice, he spoke again.

"So, your practice is going well?"

She looked up sharply, as if startled. But she'd always been willing to talk about her work, which was her passion. Hadn't he spent hours wondering if she was capable of dedicating as much of herself to anything else? Or, particularly, anyone?

"Yes," she said after a moment. "Very well, thanks."

"I knew it would. You're too caring for it not to."

He hadn't meant it as a criticism, but he saw something flash in her eyes that made him think she'd taken it that way.

Don't you ever think about anything but work?

I have young lives in my hands.

The old exchange ran through his mind, not for the first time. He remembered he'd felt a bit of a jab when she'd answered, thinking that in a way, he also had those young lives in his hands. He hadn't thought she'd meant it as an attack on him or his work; that defensiveness just seemed to be automatic with her. No matter how hard she worked or how much she accomplished, it was never enough.

And you think the best way to care for them is to run yourself into the ground? Be so tired you can't think straight?

He'd only wanted her to go away with him for a weekend. She'd lost a young patient nearly a month before and was so troubled he'd thought a complete change of scene might help. So troubled that he'd done what he rarely did: pushed. And later, looking back, he thought that was probably the beginning of the end. Because he'd pressured her to do something she was apparently incapable of doing. *Relaxing*, it seemed, was not a word in her lexicon. He'd always thought he held himself to a pretty high standard when it came to dedication to his work, but he couldn't hold a candle to her.

He wondered if she even remembered the exchange. Probably not. She'd been too wrapped up in "I should haves" to think about a little thing like saying no to a weekend away.

Or maybe it had just been a weekend away with him she hadn't wanted. Maybe she'd never really felt it, what he'd felt. He'd never had the chance to ask. And as he sat there looking across the table at her, he thought about asking now but couldn't think of any way that didn't sound inane, ridiculous or downright pitiful.

What is it you wanted that I didn't give you?

Did you ever feel how I felt?

Did you ever love me?

Besides, it was ancient history now, and none of it mattered. She'd obviously put it—them—far behind her. And if he'd never quite been able to do that, that was his problem. His mother, who loved every one of her dozen children beyond measure, had firmly told him if Sophia couldn't see what a prize he was, she didn't deserve him. But that's what a mother was supposed to say, wasn't it?

"—quite the reputation."

He snapped out of his fruitless thoughts, but too late to hear her entire sentence. Which was unlike him; he was usually very attentive. With her, he'd been glued to her every word.

"Reputation?" he repeated, hoping it would net him an explanation that wouldn't betray he hadn't heard a word, so mired had he been in might-have-beens.

"Yes, you have. Among many of my colleagues. You're their first thought if they have a situation like Charlie's."

"But not yours."

Damn, he hadn't meant to say that. Where had all this come from? At this moment he felt as if he hadn't moved an iota beyond that day when she'd kicked the supports out from under him and left him floundering.

"Mine more than anyone," she said quietly. Then, after a deep breath, she said, "No matter what happened between us, I have never, ever doubted your dedication, Gideon. It's one of the things I admired most about you."

Admired. Past tense. So whatever she felt, she didn't feel anymore. Or it was all she'd ever felt. It didn't really matter which—the end result was the same. Which was…the end of any personal connection.

With an effort he shoved his unruly emotions back into the hole he'd thought them safely buried in, until the moment he'd walked into that hospital room and realized it was her. It had been the shock, that was all. He really wasn't still a whimpering mess after all this time; he'd just been caught off guard.

Business. Stick to business until you get it together.

"What do you know about Charlie's family situation? Anything seem more significant now, looking back?"

Sophia blinked, as if startled by his suddenly brisk tone, but she didn't say anything about it. She looked thoughtful for a moment, then slowly nodded. "I remember having to really insist she bring him back for a recheck so I could be certain the antibiotics cleared up his strep. And when they did come back in, she was very antsy and insisted they had to leave quickly, which in itself isn't so strange, but Charlie… He said they *had* to be home before his father."

"And he said it like that? That kind of emphasis?"

She nodded. And then she let out a breath and closed her eyes for a moment. "I really should have guessed—"

"Stop. That gets us nowhere. You only saw him twice, then?"

She nodded. He wondered how she was supposed to have guessed on so little evidence, but then he knew she'd always held herself to a ridiculously high standard.

He'd just never known why.

Chapter Five

They were actually talking, Sophia thought. A little carefully at first, maybe even strained, but it had gotten easier. They'd gone through everything they both knew about Charlie's case and then had strayed onto more personal things. Not their relationship, of course. But they talked of what they'd been doing since that day when she'd brutally put an end to them.

She'd talked about her practice and how it had grown. A couple of honors she'd received, although that sounded too much like trying to impress him, so she didn't dwell on the subject. She did enough of that with her father. Something she had never fully realized until Gideon pointed it out, that day after another disappointing phone call with the man.

When are you going to quit living to impress your father?

Stung, she'd fired back at him. *About the same time you quit trying to make up for what yours did.*

He'd looked startled, then thoughtful before nodding. *Point taken.*

He'd said it quietly, no male bluster or denial that she was right, that his situation was different, or any other kind of belittling of her argument. And that had been the first time she had wondered what it would be like to live with a man like that, a man who didn't judge or work from the assumption he, of course, was always right and you had to live up to his impossible expectations.

She quickly diverted her thoughts before she said something foolish, and diverted the conversation to him. He updated her on the family project, the Truth Foundation, something she'd always admired; the Colton family was determined to make right what they could of their disgraced father's horrible actions. The case they'd just taken on, that of one Ronald Spence, had been the last conviction their father had handed down before his death. She couldn't imagine what it must feel like, to find out your father had feet not of clay, but of viscous mud. Her own father was difficult, but she had absolutely no doubt he was who he was.

Then, unexpectedly, he asked, "Did you ever go back and do that specialty course you wanted to?"

Sophia was surprised he remembered that. She'd wanted to broaden her knowledge of pediatric infectious diseases after a patient of hers had nearly died from a complication related to simple measles.

"I… Yes, I did. And it's helped prevent similar issues a couple of times."

He nodded as if he'd expected nothing else. She wasn't sure what that meant. But it enabled her to ask something of him, something she'd thought about every time she read about the event in the news.

"Did you ever do your bike climb of Pikes Peak?"

He blinked, as if he was as surprised as she had been that she remembered. "I did. I even finished."

"That's quite an accomplishment. Fourteen thousand–plus feet."

He gave her a crooked smile. *That* crooked smile, which had always made her pulse give a little kick. "The last quarter mile, from Devil's Playground to the summit, about killed me."

"Only getting about half the oxygen you get at sea level? I can't imagine why."

The smile became a grin. "The rest was a breeze, though."

"All nine miles straight up?"

"Piece of cake," he said, with an expression that told her he knew perfectly well it was a big lie, and knew that she knew it, too. "But I stick to easier mountain biking now. I think I'm going to try Kokopelli's Trail this summer."

She stared at him. "Easier? Isn't that the one that goes all the way to Utah?"

He nodded. "Loma to Moab. Hundred and forty miles or so."

She managed not to gape at him, but it was a near thing. "Maybe you should think again."

"It won't be that bad, if I can keep my speed up. Cut a couple of days at least off the average five or six."

"Oh, why don't you just do it in a day, straight through?" she asked sweetly.

He lifted a brow at her. "It's been done. I think the record is a little over eleven hours."

"That's…twelve miles an hour? On a mountain

trail? That has, if I recall correctly, no water available along the way?"

He grinned again. "True. So you need someone to meet up with you along the way with water. But there are some nice downhill bits where you can make good time."

"Ah," she said dryly. "Now I get it, you want those grueling downhill runs."

"Might be part of the appeal," he admitted.

She studied him for a long moment. "Why, Gideon? Why the need to push yourself so hard?"

He didn't look away. "It's more a matter of hanging on to my sanity."

"I think I understand that," she said slowly. In its way, his work was as stressful as hers. Kids came to her when something wasn't right with their bodies, and to Gideon when something was wrong with their lives.

"If I didn't have a physical outlet for the emotional strain and stress, I would have quit long ago." Then he eyed her rather pointedly. "Did you ever find one? Or is your answer still to just work harder?"

And there it was, one of the biggest reasons she'd pulled back from him. Because for all his dedication and expertise, Gideon had never let his work utterly control him. Other things mattered to him. His family mattered to him. And he mattered to his family, a lot, while she'd spent most of her life having to excel, striving for her father's grudging approval. Which, once over the flood of tangled emotions, she'd realized was probably the reason she hadn't been able to believe in Gideon's swift declaration of feelings for her.

"I work out," she said, hoping it didn't really sound as much like a slightly whiny protest as it seemed to her.

"Oh," he said.

What did that mean? Was he doubting her? Thinking she should do more? Maybe take on something extreme, like his mountain biking? Just because Blue Larkspur was in the midst of prime mountain biking country, that didn't mean she had to take it up, did it?

And why was she second-guessing every exchange like this?

You know why. It's because of who it is with.

She ordered herself to stop. They were sitting here over a casual cup of coffee; they'd had legitimate business to discuss—Charlie—so this wasn't a date or anything close to a date, nor would there ever be another date, so there was no reason for her to be all wound up like this.

Even if he was the one who got away.

The only one in her life she truly regretted.

GIDEON FINISHED HIS COFFEE, whose temperature had dwindled to lukewarm. Only then did he glance at the time and realize how long they'd been sitting here. Time always had seemed to slip away so quickly when he was with her. That, at least, hadn't changed a bit. Nor, it seemed, had she. She was still brilliant. Still driven. Still a perfectionist.

Still beautiful.

He'd forgotten how many colors were tangled up in her hazel eyes. How the luscious brown of her skin made those colors seem even more vivid. How the simple, small gold hoop earrings she always wore emphasized the delicate shape of her ears.

She stood up suddenly, as if his checking the time had been a cue.

"I need to go back and check on Charlie before I leave."

He felt a burst of both regret and relief, an odd combination he didn't want to try and figure out just now. So he got to his feet as well. "Good idea. Let's go."

THE BOY WAS huddled on his side in the hospital bed, not quite in a fetal position but close. Gideon hoped he was asleep, but the boy's big brown eyes, looking a bit like a puppy he'd once found abandoned in a pile of trash, opened as they stopped beside him. That dog had been almost immediately adopted into a loving home. But Charlie was still, legally at least, bound to the parent who had done this to him.

Sometimes it seemed to him the system dealt with animals better than children.

He managed a smile at the boy. It was up to him to see to it that there never a repeat of this episode. And he'd do whatever it took to make sure Charlie never ended up like this again, in a hospital, hurting, because his father was an out-of-control brute.

"You came back," Charlie whispered, sounding surprised.

"I promised I would," he said, knowing what the boy's surprise told him about the child's faith in promises. "And I keep my promises. I'll be here in the morning, Charlie. That's another promise."

The boy looked hopeful but not convinced.

"He does keep his promises," Sophia said softly, keeping her gaze on the boy. Which was probably a good thing, since if she was looking at Gideon, he'd be trying to read into it, to find exactly what she'd meant. Or how many ways she'd meant it. Sophia Gray-Jones was nothing if not…nuanced.

"My dad won't come back tonight, will he?"

The fear in the child's voice sent that now familiar jolt of chill and hot anger through him. *If he does, he'll regret it.*

"You're safe here," Sophia assured him.

"When can I see my mom?"

"I hope tomorrow," she told him. Then she added, clearly to avoid breaking a promise to the child after what Gideon had told him, "But that's not a promise. I'll check in on her before I leave tonight. How's that for now?"

"So will I," Gideon said. "And tell her you're okay. Can we tell her you'll be sleeping, so she won't worry?"

After a moment, the boy nodded, somewhat reluctantly.

"Good. Go to sleep now, honey," Sophia said quietly, reaching out to stroke the boy's hair.

"Will you be back tomorrow, too?"

"I will. First thing."

"'Kay."

There seemed to be a hint of sleepiness in that last word, so they said nothing more but, by mutual, silent agreement, waited until the boy's eyes drifted closed.

Ellen Webber actually was asleep when they got to her room, although Gideon guessed she'd been sedated. She was in worse shape than Charlie. If there was any resemblance between mother and son it was obscured now, by bruises and swelling and bandages.

"Oh," Sophia whispered, sounding rather odd. And when he looked at her, her eyes were closed and she was shaking her head.

"What?" he asked.

Her eyes snapped open. "I was just admonishing myself not to rush to judgment. I'd been thinking unkind thoughts about Charlie's mother for allowing him to be hurt like that."

"You thought she hadn't defended him?"

She let out a breath. "I think all I saw was that little boy hurt."

"The way you focus on your patients is one of the reasons you're as good as you are at your job," he said, feeling both that she deserved the honest truth and that she needed it just now.

She looked up at him, and he was suddenly aware of how close they were, almost touching. Suddenly remembering other times, in other days, when he'd lost himself in the sheer pleasure of just looking at her.

"Your kindness knows no bounds, does it, Gideon?" Her voice was so quiet and held a decidedly tremulous note.

And just as suddenly as those memories had come a moment ago, he couldn't take this anymore. Couldn't take her compliments, after she'd thrown him—them—away. "But my tolerance has developed limits," he muttered.

And with a last glance at the woman in the bed, but no look at all at Sophia, he turned on his heel and left the room.

Chapter Six

Sophia was glad her first appointment the next morning wasn't until nine, which gave her time to stop by the hospital on her way to her office in the building next door.

What she wasn't glad about was the horribly restless night she'd had. And no matter how she tried to tell herself it was only natural that she was upset that one of her patients had been hurt in such an awful way, she knew it was more than that. Knew that the final capper on her mood had come in the form of Gideon Colton.

They'd slipped into talking so easily, after the first expectedly awkward moments. One of Gideon's stellar attributes—and skills—had always been the simple fact that he listened. No, not just listened, but *heard*. And he understood the difference between asking for solutions and just needing to vent. Although he still had to ask sometimes.

You want me to try and fix this, or do you just need to let it out?

She remembered so well when he'd said that, toward the beginning of their relationship. She'd so appreciated that he'd asked that she ended up requesting—and actually taking—his advice about what to do about the landlord who wanted to double her office rent. As he'd promised, merely dropping the name of the Colton and Colton law firm did the trick, and the increase was suddenly at a manageable level.

"It shouldn't be necessary to do that, though," she'd fumed.

"Agreed," he'd said. Then, casually, "You might want to look around for a different location, in your own time and on your own terms. Your landlord talks a lot about equality and how she's for helping the disadvantaged, but when it comes to her own wallet, she's suddenly a grasping tightwad."

She'd been a little blown away by the fact that not only had he talked to his lawyer brother and sister, but he had apparently researched her landlord enough to confirm what she'd always suspected about the woman—that she was a big-mouthed hypocrite. She'd barely known Gideon a month, and she'd already known he was one of the most understanding and generous men she'd ever met.

And shortly after that, she'd decided he deserved a perfect woman, something she always strived to be but never succeeded. So when he'd told her he wanted a future with her, she'd run. She simply couldn't believe it could be that easy, that she could have a happiness she hadn't had to earn every step of the way.

Thanks a lot, Father.

Sophia shook off the memory and the intrusion into her mind of the man who had shaped her, and not always in the best way. His demands for perfection had driven her to the success she'd had, but they had also, in a way, constrained her. She didn't know if she would ever get past that. And it had taken losing Gideon to get her to realize it.

After checking her weather app and seeing winter was winning the annual battle with spring again today, she dressed in warm wool slacks, her favorite green blouse—which she picked because it was her favorite, not because Gideon had once remarked on how the color picked up the green in her eyes—and a pair of warm, shearling-lined boots. Then she gathered up her purse and heavy coat and headed for the small garage attached to her townhome.

It wouldn't be long before it would be warm enough to walk to work, one reason she'd chosen this place, along with the spacious great room area and the near-luxurious master bath. Sometimes, when the people next door had a loud, late party, or when the traffic out front awakened her, she longed for someplace quieter, but for now the proximity was a decent trade-off. And now, on this day that threatened more precipitation, she went for her car, glad she had left the snow tires on for another unpredictable month.

She'd started college in Denver, with the Front Range of the Rockies a sight she was used to. She was still struck by the difference between there and here, where the towering plateaus were the norm, rather than the skyscraping peaks. It struck an entirely different kind of awe in her, but it was awe, nevertheless. She loved her home state, in all its varied beauty.

She'd called the medical center when she'd first awakened from her too-restless sleep, and the just-then-oncoming day shift had retrieved his chart, then come back on the line and told her Charlie had had a restful night. That surprised her a little, but the nurse assured her that his record indicated no medication had been administered other than a mild pain reliever. She sounded just harried enough with the shift change that Sophia let her go; she'd see in person how Charlie was in just a few minutes.

She focused on her driving, knowing her night of little sleep—and with what she did get punctuated by sad, regretful dreams—was not the best start to her day, either for her work or for being on the road. But she made it to the hospital without incident and found a place to park near the entrance closest to the wing Charlie was in. The instant she stepped out of the warm car, she reached back for her puffy jacket; if it was more than a degree above freezing, she would be surprised. But it served to wake her up fully, and she sucked in a deep breath of the clear, biting air.

Once inside she encountered the same nurse who had been there when Charlie had come in yesterday, just a few yards away from the boy's room.

"Hi, Doc," Eric said cheerfully, his usual form of address.

She'd heard some people sternly correct him, telling him he should address them more respectfully— *You should address me as "Doctor," young man*—but she found the nurse's unfailingly cheerful mood more than worth it. And had told him so, after witnessing that particular encounter.

"Frankly," she'd said, "I tend to call those folks the old grouches."

They'd both laughed, and she knew she'd made an

ally. And it had come in handy more than once; she knew her patients got Eric's maximum attention when he was on the floor. And that was what she cared about most.

"How's Charlie, Eric?" she asked when he stopped beside her.

"Good, actually. Unless you disagree, he can be released."

"I'll check him out, but start the paperwork. How did he do last night?"

"He had a nightmare early on, but after that I think he felt pretty darn safe the rest of the night."

"Safe?"

"Yeah. He—" Eric broke off as his name came over the paging system, with the urgent code attached. Then he just nodded his head toward Charlie's room. "You'll see. Gotta go."

"Go," she said, understanding. She'd wanted to ask about Charlie's mother, but that would have to wait until after she had seen the boy. She continued walking down the hall to his room. She opened the door, stepped inside and stopped dead. Looked at the scene before her in surprise, then realized with a tug deep inside that she should have known.

Charlie was still asleep. Soundly, it appeared, lying on his side facing the chair beside the bed. The chair in which a tall, broad-shouldered man was stretched out, his long legs crossed at the ankles. On the rolling table beside him was the debris of some fast food, including a large bag that made her suspect he hadn't been eating alone. The conclusion was obvious. After a nightmare—only to be expected—and a meal that had probably been a treat for the boy, Charlie had slept well because he indeed had felt safe.

Because Gideon Colton had spent the night at his bedside.

The scene before her blurred a little in the instant before she felt the sting in her eyes. This, this was what she'd thrown away because she'd been afraid. This kind of quiet strength, this kind of do-the-right-thing rectitude, this kind of loving heart. It had been hers for the taking and she'd rejected it, out of her own fears and doubts.

Gideon would never forgive her for that, and she didn't blame him one bit.

It was a moment before she was able to move. As she neared the chair, she saw his hair was a bit tousled on top, as if he'd repeatedly run his fingers through it. Her own fingers curled, and she had to remind herself she didn't have the right to do the same, not anymore.

She stopped beside the chair and the bed. A glance at Charlie told her he was still quietly asleep. When she turned back to Gideon, he opened those gentle blue eyes and looked up at her. She could have had this, too, this sleepy-eyed look to go with the night-mussed hair. The ache that thought caused deep inside her made her chest hurt. As a doctor she knew what physiological reaction was happening, but right now the only word she could think was *heartache*.

"Hi," he said quietly as he got to his feet, his voice just-waking-up rough. Yet another thing she could have had, that lovely, low, almost gravelly sound tickling her ears every morning.

Her throat was so tight she couldn't get a word out.

Which might be just as well, considering the only words that were clamoring to get out were words of apology, words of regret and words begging for another chance. A chance he would never give her.

She nodded at him, because that was all she dared do. Then shifted her gaze to Charlie, who hadn't moved.

"He had a rough start, but he's slept well since about eleven," Gideon said.

She looked back at him. Tried not to think about how tall and strong yet gentle he was. Swallowed past the tightness. Drew in a breath and managed to speak, almost levelly. "Because you stayed. All night."

He shrugged as if it were nothing. "He was pretty rattled after a bad dream about what happened. And about his father showing up here to hurt him again."

She suppressed a shiver. But then something occurred to her. "But you left...before I did." The last thing she wanted was to remind him of how angry he—Gideon, who was so rarely angry—had been when he'd gone.

He let it pass, as if he didn't want to remember it, either. "I saw the drive-through open on my way out and thought he might like something."

"So you loaded up and came back?"

He nodded. "And he gobbled up that burger and fries and drank a milkshake like he hadn't eaten in a week." He grimaced. "Maybe he hadn't. He's so damned small."

"I know." She sighed. "His mother insisted he was just a picky eater. And he's not blatantly malnourished, although I planned to run some tests."

"Withholding food as punishment isn't unusual with abusers."

Guilt shot through her. "I know that, too."

"I wasn't accusing. He was brand-new to you. You couldn't have known."

And there, she thought, was Gideon Colton in a nutshell. Even hurt, even angry, he was still fair. Ever and always fair.

"Thank you. I'm not sure I deserve it, but thank you."

"You're never sure you deserve it," he said.

She amended her earlier thought. Understanding and fair. He'd always had that knack for seeing things from both sides. She remembered it had been Gideon who had gotten a supposed victim in a domestic abuse situation to trip up and admit she had purposely tried to provoke her husband into striking her, so she could rake in a small fortune in a divorce. While he was naturally inclined to believe the woman or child in such situations, something about this case hadn't smelled right to him, and he'd persevered until the truth had come out.

"You're here."

The tiny, wondering voice turned them both around.

"We promised," Gideon said. And Sophia wished more than anything in that moment that the "we" had meant what it once had. Because Charlie wasn't the only one Gideon could make feel safe.

Charlie gave them a shy little smile that tugged at her already aching heart. She carried the memory of that smile with her all day, as she went through her appointments. And the knowledge that Gideon had spent the night in that uncomfortable chair, just so that little boy he'd just met wouldn't be scared when he woke up. Perhaps it was that that made her leave as soon as possible that evening to go back to the hospital. And she was not at all surprised to see Gideon there again, nor was she surprised when he merely shrugged and said he'd been able to make some arrangements from here so he could stay close. Charlie's wider, better smile told her how much that had meant to the child.

Sophia had just opened her mouth to say she'd go in a few minutes to check on his mother when a bang as the door was shoved all the way open made her jump. She smothered an instinctive startled cry.

But Charlie didn't. He screamed. Which told her who this was, this man in the doorway.

His father.

Her heart was hammering. Her vision had narrowed down to the obviously furious man coming through the doorway. An image of Ellen Webber, battered almost beyond recognition, shot through her mind. Her instinctive distaste for violence was one thing, but facing it personally, in the here and now, shifted everything.

For an instant she was frozen with fear, but then one thought rose uppermost in her mind. She had to keep him from getting to Charlie. No matter what it cost her. Because she would sacrifice anything to keep that terrified, too-little boy from any further harm. But in the next instant, before she could even remember how to move through her fear, she realized she didn't have to. Because she, and Charlie, suddenly had a bulwark. A solid, unyielding barricade between them and the threat.

Gideon.

Chapter Seven

Gideon knew who the man was instantly, by Charlie's terrified reaction as much as the fact that the boy had his eyes and the same facial shape, and the same sandy-brown hair.

He could also sense Rick Webber's anger, not that it took much, given it radiated from him in waves that were almost palpable. He was an intimidating sight and must have seemed overwhelming to a child. Because he was not just tall but broad, burly. A big guy.

But not too big to handle.

Gideon moved swiftly, putting himself where he would block the man's line of sight to Charlie and at the same time keeping Sophia behind him.

"Who the hell are you?" Rick demanded.

"The man responsible for your son right now, Mr. Webber," he said, purposely keeping his voice low, quiet, his tone even polite.

"No one's responsible for him but me."

"In a way, that's absolutely true," Gideon said, in the same even tone. *Because you're responsible for him being here, you SOB.*

"What BS story did the kid tell you?" Webber demanded. Without waiting for an answer, he shifted his derisive gaze to Sophia. "Or maybe she told you some tale that I abused him. She and his damned mother probably got together and made it up. Women always stick together."

"When they're not clawing each other's eyes out," Gideon said amiably, trying to get the man to think he was on his side. He felt Sophia stiffen behind him and reached back with one hand to hold her back, stop her from jumping into this and setting the man off.

The words seemed to throw the man, and his brow furrowed as he tried to figure Gideon out. "Like the cats they are," Rick finally agreed, warily.

"Too bad we need them. You know, to have our sons. But then it's up to us to train and discipline them properly."

Something flickered in the man's eyes then, and Gideon's gut was telling him he was on the right track. It figured—the sorry excuses for fathers he encountered too often thought they had it right, that severe punishment for any violation was the only way, that showing kindness or love was weakness, no matter the circumstances.

That it was likely the way they themselves had been brought up didn't excuse it, in his view. Because he'd encountered just as many men who had broken the chain, who had understood what was wrong and re-made themselves to fix it, vowing never to be the kind of person their own parent, be it mother or father, had been. In a way, that's what he and all his siblings had done, wasn't it? Even though Ben Colton hadn't physically abused them, he'd broken their hearts and harmed innumerable other people's lives.

Gideon sensed Sophia moving, probably to comfort the boy.

"You stay away from him, or you'll be sorry," Webber said, pointing at her. Then he turned back to Gideon. "I want my son back," he demanded. Charlie whimpered.

"Understandable," Gideon said. *Not going to happen.* "In fact, Dr. Gray-Jones here was just going to make a call to secure…the release paperwork."

He put the slightest emphasis on the word *secure*, and with the pause after the word, he hoped she was as quick on the uptake as she'd always been.

She was. And judging by the deference in her voice when she spoke, she also understood what he was doing. "Yes, I was about to make that necessary call. Let me get it started so you can get out of here."

She turned to the phone beside the bed. Out of the corner of his eye, Gideon saw that she didn't let go of Charlie's hand to do it. And that the boy's cheeks were wet with fearful tears.

And he knew he'd do whatever it took to keep this child out of this bastard's hands.

He focused again on Webber, who was watching Sophia suspiciously. He needed the man to believe they were going to turn Charlie over to him, just long enough for security to get here. And he needed to distract him from what Sophia was saying, albeit very quietly, on the phone just a few feet away.

"Too bad some people don't appreciate how hard it is to be a good father, huh?" he said conversationally.

"My father, now he was a tough one. He had standards we had to live up to." *Standards he gave up on long before he died. He might not have beaten us physically, but he did enough damage that we're still dealing with it twenty years later.*

"Exactly. You have to be tough," Webber said, and Gideon saw his body language change just slightly, become less tense, as if he were slightly less on the offense. Gideon kept talking, saying anything he could think of that he thought might appeal to the man, all the while thinking of the parents he knew who were just that: tough, but never, ever straying into abuse.

He almost had the man talked down when the door swung open behind Webber. The instant he saw the uniformed security guard, he spit out a string of curses and lunged toward his son. Gideon heard Charlie's heart-rending cry and Sophia's exclamation in the instant before he took that one step that would put him directly in Webber's path. The man seemed startled, as cowards often were, when Gideon moved toward him instead of backing away in fear. But Webber didn't stop; he kept coming toward the bed where his son cowered.

In a swift move, Gideon grabbed the man's outstretched right arm at the wrist. Stepped aside just enough to let him barrel past him, letting Rick's own momentum carry him forward. In a split second that arm was well behind him. Then Gideon moved one step toward him, swiveling the captured arm as he went. In another second it was jammed tightly behind Webber's back. He yanked upward until the man yelled and tried to pull away. His grab for his son was momentarily forgotten.

A security guard had entered during the scuffle and was staring at him with raised brows. "I heard about you. Didn't believe it until now."

Webber swore again, viciously. "That's my son, and I'll get him back no matter what you do. You can't stop me."

"Pardon me," Sophia said, her voice so icily polite Gideon thought it must have brought down the room temperature a few degrees, "but I believe he just did."

Gideon felt an unexpected jolt of pleasure at her words. And when the security guard took Webber's arm, the one he was holding, he let go, happy to be free of the task he'd never wanted.

"You beat my father."

The tiny voice came from the bed behind him. Gideon couldn't be sure about the undertone in it. It wasn't unusual for an abuse victim to abruptly switch sides when it came down to their abuser being taken into custody. The immediate threat over, all other fears, carefully inculcated over the years, seemed to take over.

All the usual explanations and placations crowded into his mind as he turned around, but then he saw Charlie was looking up at him almost in awe, even as the guard led the boy's still struggling father out of the room.

"To protect you, Charlie," Sophia said softly.

The boy nodded, wide-eyed except for the one that was purple now and almost swollen shut. "My mom tried, but he's too big, too strong." His gaze fastened back on Gideon. "But you're stronger."

Going with his gut again, Gideon said, "And I'm on your side. Nobody else's, Charlie. Yours."

He saw the boy's eyes suddenly take on a sheen and knew it was tears. This was a new, novel idea for the child. Which made him angry inside, but he buried it. He wanted nothing more right now than to hug the kid. Gently of course, given the bruises. He wondered if the kid had ever—

A loud crash followed by shouts came from in the hallway.

Gideon spun around and dashed for the doorway, his gut clamoring. Several yards away, he saw what he'd feared. The young—and clearly inexperienced—security guard was sprawled on the floor, looking dazed. Another nurse was down, leaning up against the wall, as if she'd been shoved into it and slid down. A cart of supplies, he guessed the source of the crash, lay on its side, the contents strewn across the floor.

Webber was nowhere in sight. But he didn't need to be for Gideon to understand; the line of turned heads and gaping stares all aimed one direction, toward the door down at the end of the hallway labeled Fire Escape. He knew it emptied out into the main parking lot, with a hundred ways to run from there.

He was on the verge of taking off, had even taken a step that way, when a small voice stopped him.

"Is he coming back?"

Gideon turned around and looked back at Charlie, whose eyes were still wide with fear. And in that moment he knew he had to stay and leave rounding up Rick Webber to the pros.

"He's gone, Charlie," he said as he walked back to the bed. "Out the back door."

Charlie looked relieved. Gideon left it at that, knowing that eventually the child would realize that if he was on the loose, his father could come back looking for him again. But time enough for that; for now he left it there. He wouldn't lie to the kid; he never did that, but that didn't mean he had to blast him with reality at a time like this, when he was so vulnerable.

Charlie would have to face it soon enough.

Chapter Eight

Sophia hated the way she was shaking now that the immediate threat was over and did her best to mask it. But the violence of that encounter had rattled her. If it hadn't been for Gideon…

And Charlie lived with this. She wondered if his father had always been like this, or if something recent had set him off. Decided it didn't matter, as nothing excused what he'd done.

And he would likely have done worse if Gideon hadn't stopped him. She'd done a turn in the ER, and she knew all too well how bad things like this could get. But Gideon had stopped him so smoothly and easily she'd practically gaped at him like the security guard had.

She turned her head to look at him, over where he'd walked to the other side of the room to make a phone call. Actually, this was about his third phone call. But he had stayed in the room, with Charlie, as if he somehow knew the boy needed him there. Needed to know his protector was still here.

That old conversation ran through her mind again, in bits and pieces this time, since she was so rattled.

I don't want to fight.
And what decides you?
If a kid needs me to.

Well, this kid had needed him to. To be honest, so had she. And he'd done it. He'd done it and kept them both safe. The way he'd somehow made himself seem even bigger, even if it was only the stance he took, drawing himself up to his full, imposing height, was amazing enough. But all those workouts, all that gym time clearly hadn't been just to accomplish that, but also for working on moves like the one he'd just done here. Him ending the confrontation neatly and smoothly suddenly made infinitely more sense to her.

And she had the feeling her blanket distaste and disapproval of violence might need a bit of adjusting if she was going to avoid total hypocrisy. You couldn't expect to be protected if your protector didn't have the tools and skills necessary to do the job.

And Gideon definitely had the skills.

He put away his phone and looked over at her. He made the slightest motion with his head, as if to call her over there. She patted Charlie's hand, gave him a reassuring smile, then stood and walked over to Gideon.

"There's an APB out now on Rick Webber," he said quietly. "It was a condition of his bail that he not go anywhere near his wife or Charlie."

"Why was Webber even out on bail in the first place?" she muttered, half to herself.

"That," Gideon said sourly, "you'll have to take up with the justice system. Or, as my DA sister calls it, the lack-of-justice system."

"I wish that was funnier."

"Me, too. But that tells us how off the rails he is, if within hours of getting out he's here hunting for Charlie, knowing what will happen if he gets caught."

"And he was caught," she pointed out. "Thanks to you."

"Too bad it didn't stick."

"That," she said flatly, "is the fault of security here."

He tilted his head slightly as he looked at her. "You're really mad."

"I am. Webber should never—"

She stopped as two men stepped into the room, one the ER doctor from last night, the other older, with silver hair and a ramrod-straight bearing. "Well, there's the guy to talk to," Gideon said.

"Head of security?" she guessed as the man paused while the doctor went over to check on Charlie.

He nodded. "All yours, if you want."

"I do." She gave him a sideways look. "You'd be too nice to him."

"Don't be so sure. I may have spent all my nice on Webber."

She blinked. "That was nice?"

"Compared to what I would have liked to do to him? Absolutely."

Sophia bit back her next words, which would have been "You are the most amazing person I've ever met." She didn't have the right to say such things to him, not anymore. So instead she crossed the room to the silver-haired man who had come in with the doctor. The man—Sorensen—who took one look at her expression and held up his hands.

"Outside," she whispered fiercely, and the man didn't quibble but backed out into the hallway.

"I understand," he said quickly. "I'm not quite as furious as you, but close."

"That man never should have gotten this far in the first place," she snapped.

"I know. You're absolutely right."

She was so angry she was having trouble tamping it down, even when the head of security agreed with her. "If Gid—Mr. Colton—hadn't been here, he could have gotten to Charlie. Could have grabbed him and made it out that back door with that innocent, abused child."

"I'm aware."

"And then for your employee to let him get away like that is unforgivable."

"It's his third day on the job. He says that all he knew was it was a disturbance. He was trying to show initiative by responding quickly. Before he heard the part about it being somebody who'd been arrested for putting two people in here last night."

"Excuses?"

The man shook his head. "Explanations. There is no excuse. And it will be dealt with."

She felt a sudden qualm. The guard had been so young. And his boss's words were now sinking in, about the guard trying to respond quickly, to help. "Are you going to fire him?"

The man studied her for a moment. "Are you going to demand it?"

She couldn't. "No. But some very stern words and more training seem in order."

"Agreed on both. I'll handle it personally."

"Thank you."

Again he studied her before saying, "I've heard about you, Dr. Gray-Jones."

"Have you?"

"Heard you'll go to the wall for your patients. Which is really all I need to know."

With the feeling she'd been handed one of the larger compliments of her life, she watched Sorensen walk away.

Gideon was at Charlie's bedside when she went back into the room. For a moment she couldn't see the boy and the bed itself looked empty. Her heart skipped a beat then. Until she took another step and saw that the reason she couldn't see Charlie was because the child was sitting up, his arms, including the bandaged one, thrown around Gideon. And Gideon, who towered over the child, was holding him carefully with one arm, gently stroking the boy's hair with his other hand.

"It'll be all right, Charlie," he was saying, very softly. "It might not be right away, and there'll be some hard parts ahead, but in the end, I swear to you, it will be all right."

Sophia hastily backed up, out the door she had just come through. She leaned back against the wall outside, fighting the rush of tears that threatened. That man, she thought. That wonderful, strong, gentle, kind, loving man. She could have had him, had him in her life, for life. She knew that now, knew that when Gideon Colton made a vow, he would keep it. And that would include a vow to love, honor and cherish.

"You all right, Doc?" She opened her eyes to see

Eric, the nurse she'd spoken to earlier, looking at her with concern. "Is the kid?"

In the moment before she could trust her voice, she reached out and patted the concerned young man's arm. Then she said, "I'm fine. And Charlie couldn't be in better hands right now."

Eric smiled. "Gideon? You've got that right. The guy's amazing with the really scared ones." He gave her a crooked smile. "He happened to be here once when they brought in a traffic accident victim, a girl whose parents weren't here yet. We couldn't get her calmed down—she was hurting and screaming for her mom. It wasn't a case of his, or anything Gideon would normally deal with, but he heard her crying. And being Gideon…"

"He stepped in," she said softly.

Eric nodded. "He had that girl smiling inside of five minutes. And even as we put stitches in, he had her laughing."

"I believe it."

After Eric had gone, she took another minute to compose herself before stepping back into the room. Charlie was lying back down in the bed now, although it was raised at the head so he could eat his apple pie. She suspected Gideon had picked that up when he'd brought the rest of the food. It would be like him to think of a treat for the boy. Although apparently a real meal itself was a novelty for the poor little guy.

Gideon turned and took a couple of steps toward her. "Did you leave the man standing?"

She'd been so distracted by her emotions and seeing him with Charlie that she'd almost forgotten about the security chief, Sorensen. "Yes. Of course. I think he'll see that something like that never happens again."

Gideon nodded. "I've dealt with him. He's a good man. He—"

He broke off when his cell phone rang. He excused himself, answered, listened for a moment, then said, "Give me a couple of minutes, then send them back."

Sophia wondered whom he meant, but she stayed quiet as he turned back to Charlie, who was licking his fingers now. "Hey, buddy, remember my friends I told you about?"

Charlie's big brown eyes widened. "With the dog?"

He nodded. "They're here now. They'd like to see you."

"To see me?" The boy sounded astonished.

Gideon nodded. "Is that okay?"

Charlie looked even more startled—to even be asked if something was okay with him, Sophia guessed. "Yeah, I guess," he said after a moment, still sounding uncertain.

"I think you'll like them. Especially the furry one." He handed the boy a napkin from the bag as he looked back at Sophia. "And you'll probably want to talk to at least one of them. We won't do this without your sign-off."

Belatedly it hit her what and whom he was talking about—the foster family. She glanced at Charlie, who was now industriously wiping his fingers. Then she looked back at Gideon. "These are the potential fosters?" He nodded. "The father," she said. "I'll need to be sure he can be as gentle as he needs to be right now." *As gentle as you are.*

"Tim Knight is great with kids, and the best with scared ones," Gideon said softly. "He—"

He stopped at the sound of footsteps outside. Footsteps…and something else. A gentle tap came on the door, and Gideon went over to pull it open. She saw him bend down a little, grinning. "Excellent."

When the newly arrived visitors stepped into the room, Sophia saw Charlie's eyes go huge. But then he was smiling, so widely she knew it had to be hurting his face where his brutal father had struck him. But he clearly didn't care; his gaze was fastened in obvious delight on the big golden retriever, wearing a vest that identified him as a certified therapy animal, who came into the room.

The animal obviously knew why he was here and headed straight for Charlie. He raised up and put his front paws on the bed, inched forward, and plopped his head down on those paws, and looked beseechingly up at Charlie as if a pat from him would mean the world.

"Charlie, meet Milo," Gideon said. "And if you don't pet him right now, I think he's going to cry."

As if on cue, the dog let out a begging whine. Charlie instantly reached out and stroked Milo's head. "Don't cry," he said, soothingly. Milo sighed happily and wiggled closer.

Sophia stared at the pair, thinking what a small miracle had been wrought here, when a battered child who had needed comforting was suddenly the one doing the comforting. She knew what a huge thing that would be for the boy, how much it would lessen that helpless feeling.

Gideon introduced her to the couple, Tim and Stephanie Knight, and before she even had to ask, the man said, "Given the circumstances, I presume you'll want to talk to me?"

She knew within a few minutes of stepping outside to talk to the man that these people were everything Gideon had said they were. "I can't thank you enough for coming so quickly."

"Gideon Colton calls, we jump," Mr. Knight said easily. "After what he did for us, it's the least we can do."

She gave him a curious look. "What he did for you?"

"He didn't tell you?" He smiled and answered his own question. "Of course he didn't. Man never toots his own horn. He saved our family."

She blinked. "He what?"

"While he was on a case a few years ago, he came across our daughter. She'd run away after getting into some trouble in school and falling in with the wrong crowd. It wasn't even his case, but he brought her home and worked with us until we got through some things. He put in a lot of his own time, and Amy, our daughter, really connected with him. He saw that in her and kept working with her."

The man smiled. "Gideon saved us, out of the goodness of his heart. And he gave us, especially Amy, a calling. That's how we got into fostering. Turns out she really has a knack for it. When she tells her foster siblings she knows they feel lost, she means it. And they know it."

"I...see." She wasn't surprised. At all. It was just so... Gideon.

The man who'd loved her. The man she'd pushed away.

Chapter Nine

"I'll see you soon, Charlie," Gideon said.

"Promise?" the boy asked, his tone the one of some-one who would believe it if he said yes.

"Promise."

Gideon was glad that he'd made this point at least to the child, that he kept his promises. The boy seemed much less fearful now. He knew it was in large part the golden retriever that seemed to have glued himself to Charlie's side. That animal was truly a miracle worker.

"But in the meantime," he said, "you've got Milo to look out for you, and you can help look out for Milo."

The boy looked intrigued at the idea that he could look out for anyone, which was what Gideon had wanted. Charlie went along with the Knights easily enough, although he stayed close to the gentle dog.

Gideon turned around to see Sophia watching the quartet leave, her brow furrowed. She was still unset-tled, he could see that in her expression and the fact that she couldn't seem to stop pacing the floor.

"He'll be all right," he assured her. "They've got a really good security system, and although it may not look it, Milo is a great alert dog, and he guards kids fiercely. Plus, the police are aware, so they'll keep an eye out, too, especially since Webber violated his bail terms."

She gave a shake of her head. "I'm sorry. I'm just so angry that he got in here at all."

"Understandable."

"If you hadn't been here, he could have grabbed that poor boy."

For a moment Gideon just looked at her. Then he said softly, "And if I hadn't been and he'd tried, he'd have had a fight on his hands, wouldn't he? With you."

She let out an audible breath. "Nothing like the fight you gave him. That was pretty smooth, Mr. Colton. Not even any bloodshed."

He smiled at that. "The reason for all those hours in the gym." Then, on an impulse he almost immediately knew he should have resisted, he said, "Come on. I'll give you a ride home."

She straightened. "I can drive."

"Didn't say you couldn't, just that maybe you shouldn't right now, if you don't have to." *Not to mention Webber's out there somewhere.* "And it's on my way, unless you've moved."

"I haven't," she said, her voice a little tight.

He could sense she was resisting the idea, and just when he thought he was going to escape his own foolishness in suggesting it, she unexpectedly gave in. They walked out of the now-empty room together.

Kind of like walking away from our now-empty relationship.

He nearly rolled his eyes at himself but instead inwardly called himself seven kinds of an idiot. It was over, in the past. And now he was going to have to have regular contact with her again for a while. It would be much better to treat her as someone with whom he had only a professional relationship. Then once Charlie was safe and in a stable place again, he could go back to pretending she didn't exist.

Except he'd never quite managed that.

"You were wonderful with him."

The quiet words snapped him out of his thoughts. He glanced at Sophia. She was looking down at the floor, not at him. Which gave him a chance to really look at her. She was wearing *that* blouse. The one he'd really liked on her because it set off the green flecks in her hazel eyes.

The one he'd really liked taking off her.

He jerked his gaze away.

"But then," she went on, still looking down as if they were already outside, where there might be slippery ice under her feet, "you always did have a way with kids."

A way you didn't want. Kids you didn't want. Mine, at least.

He gave himself an inward shake. "Part of the job," he said coolly.

She did look at him then. "Part of you."

She sounded almost…regretful. The inner barriers that had become a little shaky in her presence sprang back up to their full height. And he snapped out an order to himself. *Oh, no, you don't. You are not going down that pointless road.*

He didn't say anything as they pulled on jackets, and he stayed silent all the way out to his car. But then it was like a flashback, sitting behind the wheel

with Sophia in the passenger seat. It had been a different car then, but she was just as close. And a lot more
quiet than she had been. Back then, when they'd been
together, she had talked easily, in the way a person did
when they were getting to know someone. And everything she'd told him then had made him like her more,
until he was convinced he'd finally found the real deal.

Convinced too easily. Don't forget that part.

The sour remonstration rang in his head, and so he
stayed as quiet as she was as he drove. It was an odd
feeling, to drive this road he'd driven so often, always
with the determination to ignore her street, but this
time be actually looking for it.

They hit the red light at the main intersection near
the hospital. *Figures. Longest stoplight in town.*

"I liked Mr. Knight," she said, sounding as if it were
simply to break the silence.

Well, that was safe enough. "He's a good guy. Salt
of the earth, as my mother says."

"She knows them?"

He nodded, not looking at her, although there wasn't
much cross traffic to pretend to be watching. She didn't
say anything more, and after a moment the probable
reason why hit him.

"Thinking she's no judge of character?" Once more
the words were out before he thought. She had always
had that effect on him, and it seemed she still did.

"I didn't say that, or even think it," she said quietly.
"I've never blamed your mother for...what your father
did. Everyone has their blind spots."

Especially me. "Oh? What's yours?" He hadn't

meant it to sound as sarcastic as it came out, but damn, she put him on edge.

"Mine," she answered in a low, quiet voice, as if she hadn't heard his undertone at all, "is sometimes being unable to recognize what's right in front of me."

It was so pointed, so achingly said, that he couldn't help wondering if she'd meant it as *personally* as it sounded. If she'd been talking about him. Them.

This time, with the help of the traffic light changing, he bit back words that would have been dangerous to say. He wasn't about to make any assumptions, not with this woman. He'd done that once and it had blown up on him spectacularly. He might have been slow on the uptake, but you didn't have to teach him the same lesson twice.

He made the turn onto the street that ran along the park. Her townhome, less than a mile away from her office, looked out over the park, and he knew during the spring and fall she often walked to work. There was still too much snow on the ground for that, though, and more than once they'd had some pretty fierce snowstorms in early spring.

Not much had changed since he'd last driven this route, in the opposite direction. Not that he remembered much about that trip. He'd been too busy processing the fact that the woman he'd fallen for like a ton of bricks had just cut him off at the knees with her pronouncement that it was over. That it just wasn't working.

That she wasn't for him.

You can do better, Gideon.

Of all the corny, insincere platitudes, that had to

be the worst. He would have preferred to hear that she just didn't love him, or even like him, to that crap. Or even that she couldn't deal with his family history. And he knew how far gone he'd been when even that was preferable.

The streetlight she'd always complained was too bright, since it was right outside her upstairs bedroom window, was still there and still lit. He'd never minded, in fact had liked the way the overflow of light enabled him to see her in ways she had been surprisingly shy about. Had loved the way it slid over her skin, gilding the rich brown with golden light.

Oh, that's smart, Colton, start thinking about that.

There was a parking spot free almost under that light, and he took it, even though it was a few yards from her house. He shut off the engine and opened his door. Heard her start to say, "You don't have to—" but kept going as if he hadn't. He'd see her to her door, with the manners that were one of the few lessons worth learning his father had taught him.

She was already getting out when he got around to the passenger side of the car. He stayed carefully back—he didn't dare risk any actual contact—and shut the door when she was clear. Their path lit by that blessed streetlight, they strolled toward her walkway. She was once again studying the ground, although the sidewalk itself was free of snow. He didn't see any sign of ice, and it felt to him as if the temperature was a few degrees above freezing.

They reached the bank of mailboxes that served the row of townhomes, and he was hit with a flashback that nearly stopped him in his tracks. One evening, he'd brought her home after a dinner out. She'd stopped to pick up mail and found an envelope from the mother of a former patient, one she had sadly had to refer to a cancer treatment center. The envelope contained a card and a photograph, a thank-you message and the picture of a smiling young boy who was, the card said, now in full remission.

She'd been deliriously happy. So happy she'd practically danced her way to the door. And once inside she'd turned to him and poured some of that happy all over him, in the form of sweet, hot kisses.

It had been the first night he'd spent with her, under the golden glow of that streetlamp coming through her bedroom window. A night that was seared into his memory, vividly and hauntingly. No matter how hard he tried to forget it.

She didn't even pause this time, just kept going, still looking down. He had to snap himself out of the memories and keep walking to stay even with her. Clearly she wasn't bothered by the past, at least not the way he was. But then, dumping him had been her idea, so why would she be? Whatever she'd expected, whatever she'd wanted in a man, he hadn't been it. And he wasn't it now, and the less time he spent thinking about it, the better. It was old, worn ground, and thinking about it never changed anything. He should have learned that lesson by now, and—

He stopped dead. Broke every vow he'd made in the last ten minutes. Grabbed her just as she was about to step onto the walkway. Her head came up as he pulled her back. She gasped, tensed, and he knew she'd seen what he'd seen. The man, peering through the window beside her front door.

Webber.

Chapter Ten

"Stay back, out of sight," Gideon whispered as he led Sophia to a small alley between her town house and the next one. Sophia nodded without speaking, although she was a little surprised she could hear his whisper over the sudden hammering of her heart. And then Gideon turned as if he were going to head back to the walkway leading to her door.

And Webber.

"What are you doing?" Her whisper was much fiercer than his had been. His had been a quiet order, hers a startled protest. Because she already knew the answer to her question—he was going after Webber. "Gideon, don't. Don't confront him."

He turned back, stared at her. "He came here, looking for you. Who knows what he would have done if you'd already been here? Or if you'd walked up on him alone?"

"Call the police. There's always somebody not too far from the hospital." In the glow of the streetlamp, she could see his rigid jaw.

"You call them," he said. "I'm just going to watch what he does."

"Just watch? Not go after him? You *promise* that?" She chose that word purposely, after how he'd made a point of it to Charlie.

He hesitated, she heard him let out a compressed breath, then he said, "Yes."

She could breathe again. A Gideon Colton promise was golden. She made the call, giving the most concise report she could manage as she watched him walk over to the corner of the building and cautiously look around. The dispatcher was thankfully aware of what had happened at the hospital earlier and very quick on the uptake.

And then her words froze in her throat as Gideon took another step, then another. In plain view. Was he going to break that promise he'd just given? Break a promise to her, for the first time ever? Not that she had any right to expect him to consider a vow to her any different than one to anyone else, but even if it wasn't, he still kept them. Always.

And then he stopped. But he hadn't wanted to, she could read that in his body language. He sagged a little, turned and came back to her. "He's gone. He headed back toward the alley. I didn't hear or see a car."

She relayed the information to the dispatcher, who gave her an ETA of a couple of minutes.

"You know what they say," Gideon said grimly after she ended the call and told him. "When you need help in seconds, the police are only minutes away."

"Thank you," she said.

He blinked. "What? For an old joke?"

"For keeping your promise. I know you wanted to keep going."

"He came after you. At your home."

He was, she realized with a little jolt, furious. Cool, calm Gideon was furious. Because he felt for sweet little Charlie and wanted his abuser in custody? Just on general principle, because Webber was on the loose and hunting someone? Or…because it was her? She didn't know. But she did know which one she should not believe, for her own sake. Thinking Gideon still cared enough to be so angry on her behalf was beyond foolish. She'd destroyed whatever he'd once felt for her. This was just Gideon being Gideon, always for the underdog, in this case an innocent child who had already had to endure more betrayal than any child should.

After giving the arriving officer what little information they had, Gideon asked the very question she'd been wondering about herself. How had Webber known where she lived? The cop said she would look into that and call her if she found anything. Once they found Webber, it would be up to the judge to order him back into custody for violating the terms of his bail, and the officer thought that, with this new evidence of stalking, that wouldn't take long. In the meantime, she suggested Sophia find someplace else to spend the night until they were able to round up Webber.

"She'll be with me," Gideon announced. Startled, Sophia stared at him. He wasn't looking at her; he was looking at the officer, but his jaw was set.

"You," she said rather pointedly, "are in the phone book."

At least, she assumed he still was. It wasn't like she often went looking for him. Well, maybe when that old-school paper phone book came and there wouldn't be a search record of it to haunt her. That was how she'd known he moved after they'd split, to someplace north of town that seemed very far out to her.

But he always had been listed because, he'd said, he wanted "his kids" to be able to find him if they needed to. And she'd always been torn between thinking that idea noble, or then again foolish, given some of the cases he dealt with.

Cases like Charlie Webber.

The way Gideon grimaced at her words told her she was right. "All right," he muttered. His brow furrowed for a moment, then cleared. "We'll go to my mom's place. She's off at the ranch, so we won't bother her."

"The Colton house?" the officer asked. "That's a good choice. Good security there."

"Yes. We've all seen to that."

Sophia was certain they had. She knew all the Colton siblings worried about their mother living alone, especially with the debris left behind after their father's fall from grace.

But that didn't mean she was happy about the idea of going there with him. Alone, without even his mother to be a buffer. Although maybe she should be glad about that. She'd managed to blow up their relationship before she'd ever met Isadora Colton, but she imagined the woman knew about her. And what she'd done to Gideon.

"—and grab whatever you need, while Officer Fulton is still here."

She tuned back in abruptly. How like Gideon to already know the officer's name. She hadn't looked beyond the uniform and badge to the name tag perfectly lined up above the left chest pocket. Or maybe he already knew her, from previous cases. The man made friends wherever he went, it seemed. People could sense he was honest and could probably tell he was bighearted and kind, too. He just gave off that vibe.

Until someone helpless, like Charlie, needed him to be something else.

The best of both worlds.

As she went inside—smothering the spark of outrage she felt that Webber had been here at all with the thought of how much worse it would have been had he gotten inside her home—she tried to chivvy herself out of the self-critical mood. But it seemed to be well upon her at the moment. The facet of her father's character she'd least wanted to emulate, and yet here she was, turning it on herself.

Her only saving grace on that front was that unlike the father who had learned the cool distancing from his own father—her grandfather—she refused to pass it on. She'd vowed from the beginning that her patients would never feel the way her father had, as if no matter what they did, they couldn't measure up. And she did what she could to make sure their parents didn't do it, either.

You also vowed you'd never pass it on to your children. The children no one has ever wanted with you. Except Gideon. Who wanted a whole brood of them.

She yanked her mind out of that useless ditch and gathered up what she thought she'd need. Then she stopped. What if they didn't catch Webber right away? What if this went on for days? Weeks, even? What then?

She couldn't think about it. Because if she did, she'd

end up thinking about spending all that time with Gideon, and she'd be a mess.

Why did he have to be as gorgeous as ever? No, even more gorgeous. He'd been fit then; he was a powerhouse now. A perfect, very masculine powerhouse, from those beautiful blue eyes to those broad, strong shoulders and chest, to the trim waist—and the no doubt even more pronounced six-pack of abs—narrow hips and tightly muscled backside, to the—

She derailed that train of thought before it swerved around to another part of him she most definitely did not want to be thinking about, especially if she was going to be alone with him tonight.

Alone with him tonight.

She stared down at the bag she'd already packed half-full. She hadn't even consciously decided to go with him, and yet here she was packing.

You could go to a hotel. You should *go to a hotel.*

She stood there, considering. There were a couple of places in town, and a half dozen B and Bs scattered around. And if they were full, there were the ski resorts not that far away, although there was still enough snow there they might be full, judging by one of her teenage patients who had broken an ankle there just a couple of weeks ago. She'd insisted on coming directly to Sophia, despite the forty-five-minute drive back to Blue Larkspur. That was the last time she'd been in the emergency room, having met the family there.

Until tonight.

"Sophia?"

Gideon's voice came from the doorway. As if he would come no farther, would not step into her bedroom. And Sophia. Not Soph, as he used to call her. Only Gideon had ever called her that. Only Gideon had ever been *allowed* to call her that.

This was too much. The thought of spending even one night alone with him was dangerous and…tempting. Oh so tempting.

"Are you ready?"

Too ready.

She bit off the thought. He was doing her a favor. Watching out for her in a potentially dangerous situation, simply because that's who and what he was. A guardian, for whoever needed one. And right now, that appeared to be her. And noble soul that he was, he wouldn't let their breakup interfere with that.

Because Gideon Colton lived by his own rules, even if it cost him.

Chapter Eleven

Sometimes, bro, you're too good for your own good.

His sister Rachel's oft-repeated observation seemed to be playing in an endless loop in Gideon's head as he drove west toward the house he'd grown up in. The ten miles from the city center had never seemed so far. But on some level he knew that when they got there and he was facing a night alone in a house with Sophia, it would feel like the shortest drive in history.

He didn't often regret these impulsive decisions he made. Usually they were to help a kid he couldn't see any other way to help at that moment in time. But this, this was an impulse he just knew he was going to regret.

Regret? Spending tonight—and maybe more—with the one woman you've never been able to get out of your system? The one who still sends your pulse into overdrive the moment you see her? The one who dumped you like a hot rock when you dared to tell her the truth about how you felt?

Great. Now in addition to Rach's lectures, he was chewing himself out over his own stupidity.

He tried to derail his train of thought. Instead of

thinking about her, he should be wondering why the hell the guy whose goal was usually to avoid a physical confrontation—all that working out did have a purpose, after all—had felt so compelled to go after the obviously out-of-control and violent Rick Webber when he'd turned up at the town house door. But that brought him full circle, because the only reason he could think of, the only reason that made sense, was that the threat was to Sophia. Which meant that, when it came to her, all bets were off.

When they'd been together, he would have just accepted that as part of the deal; when you loved someone, you saw to their welfare. But now there was no reason he should feel that way, and no explanation for why he had. No explanation he could or would accept, anyway.

So much for mental diversion.

Plan, he told himself. He needed a plan, and he needed to stick to it. After all, the house was big. He could put plenty of space between them. It had five bedrooms and two other rooms that could be used as such. And he'd slept in most of them at one time or another; when there were more than a dozen people in the house, you made do. And whenever one of the older siblings moved out, the big bedroom shuffle had begun. He never really had had a spot of his own for long, something he'd vowed would never happen to his own kids.

Yeah, those kids you wanted to have with her and now wonder if you'll ever have at all.

He tried not to think about that, either. Except to occasionally wonder if the multiple-birth tendency had been passed on to him and his siblings. Which usually sent him back to pondering the tangled mess that his family had been. After starting with twins and then triplets, a lot of people would have quit right there. Most people, probably. And they surely would have stopped before they got to an even dozen. But if they'd stopped at those first five, he wouldn't exist. Nor would Rach, Jasper, Aubrey, Gavin or the "kids," as they all teasingly referred to the youngest set of twins, Alexa and Naomi. And that would be a great loss.

And again he wound up pondering his mother, and how she must have felt to have the man she'd built this huge family with, the man she'd trusted enough to marry, turn out to be not just a liar but actively corrupt. He couldn't even imagine that level of betrayal. It was part of what had shaped them all, and made he himself determined to never stray to the dark side, as Rach called it.

He knew his mother was proud of the way her children had pulled the Colton name out of the morass their father had left it in. Every one of them had worked hard at that, whether or not they were directly involved in the Truth Foundation. There had never been a whisper of their father's kind of corruption around any of them, and that was an accomplishment they should all be proud of.

It didn't really register until he saw the sign marking the start of the Green Valley subdivision that he'd driven this entire way without saying a word. Nor had Sophia said anything. Maybe she was feeling as edgy about this whole idea as he was. She certainly wasn't happy about it. But then, who would be, under the circumstances?

When he made a turn, he noticed she started to look around. He was fairly certain he'd told her this was where the family home was, but he didn't know if she'd ever been out here. She'd told him her townhome was only the third place she'd looked at to buy, and it was the location close to her work that had decided her. She'd probably hate his place, half an hour from here and out in what his more city-bound siblings called the boonies. But that was exactly why he'd chosen the place; he needed the peace away from it all. And after Sophia had broken up with him, renovating the older house had been the one thing that kept him motivated.

The farther they went into Green Valley, the farther apart the houses became. The family place was on an acre and a quarter or so, which added to the sense of wealth of the neighborhood.

"Nice," she murmured as she looked around.

So she wasn't opposed to space, at least. Maybe she would like his five acres, after all. Not that it mattered if she did or didn't, of course. A bit rattled that he was even wondering if she'd appreciate his place, he answered what he wasn't sure if he'd been meant to hear. "Looks that way."

"Only looks?" She gave him a sideways glance. "Bad memories, I suppose."

"More good than bad, after." He didn't explain after what. Anyone who knew the tiniest bit about the Coltons—hell, anyone who lived in Blue Larkspur—would know what he meant.

"Did your mother ever consider leaving?"

He shook his head. "Not really. The place was custom built to her preferences, and she loves it. And after things fell apart, she didn't want to change anything for a long time."

"What happened was a horrendous amount to have to process," she said.

"Not to mention she couldn't afford the upkeep," he said sourly. "Not with ten kids from six to sixteen still at home and suddenly no income, except a small inheritance from my grandparents."

She looked startled. "Your father didn't have life insurance?"

"He did. A lot. It was given to his victims. She never fought it. We all felt they were owed it."

"So it runs in the family."

His head snapped around. The car slowed as he took his foot off the gas. "What, exactly?" he asked, a little stiffly. If she meant his father's corruption, and the mentality that allowed it, that opened up a whole new vista on why she'd figuratively chucked him out on his ear.

"The nobility," she said, looking puzzled enough that he knew he'd veered off on a course that had never occurred to her. He should have known. She wasn't one to blame the son for the sins of the father.

"I'm not noble," he muttered and picked up the pace again.

"I don't think you get to decide that," she said in that thoughtful way he had always loved about her.

And thinking about the ways he'd loved her was the second stupidest thing he'd done tonight. After bringing her here.

SHE HAD NEVER been to Green Valley, though she'd heard about it, knew it was one of the most desirable locations in Blue Larkspur. Several of her patients lived out here. In fact, when she and Gideon had been together, she'd learned one of them lived close by and knew his mother. Mrs. Hernandez, Gabriella's mother, had been aghast all those years ago, as most of the town had been, at the revelations about Judge Colton, but she'd admired his widow for how she'd stepped up and kept the big family going, despite the devastation her husband had left behind.

That had gotten her to thinking, as such things often did, about her own mother. How would she have done in the same circumstances? Sophia didn't know, but she suspected it would be one extreme or the other: she would either fall apart or blossom. However, the very thought of her stern, upright father committing the kind of acts Ben Colton had was ludicrous. Impossible.

Exactly as Gideon and his siblings no doubt thought. As his mother herself no doubt thought.

As she looked at the houses here that had such large lots, it occurred to her to ask, "Does your mother go to the ranch a lot?"

"Not all that often," he answered, not looking at her as he negotiated the curving, tree-lined road. "But she's there this week for her birthday. A spa week, Aubrey calls it."

Aubrey, she knew, was his younger sister. She ran the Gemini Ranch with her twin brother, Jasper. She'd met them both when she'd been out there for the event they hosted annually for seriously ill children. It had been a joy to see those kids act like ordinary kids for a day, swimming, meeting cows and goats, and riding horses, a first for many of them.

"Sounds lovely."

"Mom says they pamper nicely."

She smiled. "From what you've told me, she's earned it."

As soon as she said it, she wished she could pull it back; discussing what he'd said to her, back when they'd been together, when he had been so open with her and told her whatever she wanted to know, didn't seem like the thing to do now. Not when she could see so clearly how badly she'd hurt him.

But he answered easily enough. "She has. If she'd fallen apart after Dad, who knows where we all would have ended up? Caleb was her right hand, but she was a rock."

"That took a lot of courage," Sophia said. As an only child herself, she couldn't begin to imagine what his mother had faced—such a betrayal, then death, and to be left with all those children to care for.

She thought the smile that curved his mouth then one of the sweetest she'd ever seen. She'd almost managed to put out of her mind how wonderful that smile was. "I think she found out she's more fearless than she ever realized."

"Now that's a very silver lining in a very dark cloud."

He glanced at her. "Interesting" was all he said.

"What?"

"That's exactly what she said. That if there was a silver lining to any of it, it was finding out how strong she could be when she had to."

Sophia opened her mouth to say she'd like to meet her, but then the implications of that hit and she bit back the words. She'd not be meeting Gideon's mother, for this or any other reason.

Chapter Twelve

Gideon entered the code on the keypad by the gate, part of the security system the family had had installed just recently, for the peace of mind of all of them. When the gate had opened far enough he pulled through, then waited for it to close behind them before he started up the long, curving driveway and into the underground garage.

"When is your mother due home?" she asked suddenly, in the tone of someone a bit uneasy about being here.

"Not until tomorrow." He gave her a sideways look. "You're safe. She doesn't mind houseguests."

There, that got things in the right place in his mind. She was simply a houseguest. And not only that, she was only here under duress, essentially. Between those two things, he should be able to keep his thoughts—and his suddenly unruly body that remembered the bliss he'd found with her all too well—in line.

He hoped.

"Coming in through the front door is more impressive," he said, aware he was chattering but unable to stop, "but this is easier."

"Fine" was all she said.

It didn't hit him until they were inside that his family home would likely strike her as old-fashioned and probably a bit shabby. Her own place was sleek, contemporary and a lot newer. He saw her looking around but couldn't discern her thoughts from her neutral expression. And found himself needing to explain.

"We all pitched in and had the kitchen and family room updated a few years ago, since that's where she and all of us spend the most time. But the rest is a bit tired."

"I think it looks lived-in and loved," she said quietly.

He blinked. Stopped walking. She stopped beside him. "I thought you wouldn't like it. Your place is so…"

"Modern? Stiff?" She grimaced. "Heartless, compared to this."

He stared at her. "If that's how you feel, then why did you choose it?"

"Convenience." She sighed. "My place is just where I go when I'm not at work. It's not…a home." She gestured at the wall where Mom had hung photos of them all, which in their case was a huge display. "This is a home."

He felt a strange tightness in his throat. "It is. Despite everything, it is. My mother saw to that. She didn't really want to change anything and couldn't afford to, anyway, so she kept everything as it was."

"Change isn't always good."

"Sometimes it would be." He grimaced. "Sometimes we all wish that now that she could afford changes, she'd do it. Some things, like touches my father insisted on, make it feel like a shrine to something that never was." He ran a hand through his hair wearily. "She really loved him." *Too bad the man she loved never really existed.*

"And she clearly loves all of you. Maybe that's what the shrine is meant for."

He'd never thought about it quite like that, that as much as their father's, it was her family and her children's history she was clinging to by not changing a thing in this place.

"Maybe," he said, looking around as if with new eyes. Sophia had always been good at that—giving things that just slightly different outlook that made you consider other possibilities.

"I never had a home that feels like this," she said, with a touch of wistfulness that made the lump in his throat expand. "My father wouldn't allow anything to be kept if it was worn or less than perfect, even if it was loved."

Including you?

He'd never met Professor Harold Jones, and she hadn't talked about him much when they'd been together. He'd thought after they broke up that she'd known they would and so hadn't shared anything like that with him. But now he found himself wondering if she didn't talk about him because it was too painful. He'd known she was driven, not just to help her patients but to be the best at it. He'd never thought much beyond that, never wondered if there was something beyond her instinct to care and heal that pushed her. Now he wondered if that compelling impetus had a name.

"He'd have a tough time here, then," he said. "Every piece has a history. And the wear and tear is part of it. That's Mom's favorite chair, where she sits to read or make notes. Over near the door, that's the key rack all us kids got together and bought for her when I was about thirteen, because she's brilliant but cannot keep track of her keys. Didn't help. The bookcases there, around the fireplace? A shelf for each of us, and we got to put whatever we wanted on it."

"What was on yours?"

"Books," he said succinctly, with a raised brow. That got a slight smile out of her, which he counted as a win.

"Specifically?" she asked.

The eyebrow came down as he wondered why it mattered. Now, anyway. Maybe it would have back then, but they'd never quite gotten to the sharing childhood memories stage beyond the surface questions: where did you grow up, go to school, what did you want to be kind of thing.

"Most of them I had then are still there. That wizard kid." She smiled again. "And after, I saw the *Lord of the Rings* movies. I was too young to appreciate the writing and decided I liked those better. I had a figure of the Balrog next to the books. My mom hated it, but I thought he was cool, with all the fire."

"She hated it, but you were allowed to put it out there?"

He shrugged. "It was my shelf, she said." She looked almost amazed, and he knew he'd gotten a glimpse of her own childhood, whether she'd meant to betray it or not. So lest she think he'd gotten away with everything, he added, "My video game controller was there, too, although I wasn't allowed to play as much as I wanted."

"Good for your mom on that," she said. "Some things need limits."

"She never put one on the reading, though."

"What about what you could read?"

"She watched but rarely stopped me, or any of us," he said. "Usually it was 'You can read this, but later.'"

"I think I would like your mother."

The moment the words were out, her eyes widened, as if she hadn't meant to say them. He wasn't sure why that would be. Unless she was thinking in the context of meeting the parent of someone you were dating. Which made no sense at all. And was something he was so not going to think about. At all.

He had a sudden image of how this might have gone, back then. Back when they'd been together. What would he have said to that then?

Yes, you would.

She's the best.

No, he knew he would have gone straight to *She'd like you, too.*

Because his mom had known how he'd felt about Sophia. As if she'd somehow sensed this was different. As if she'd known this situation was real.

Problem was, Sophia hadn't known it. Or hadn't believed it. Or hadn't wanted it.

Or him.

With an effort he focused on shoving all those thoughts aside, compartmentalizing as he often had to with his work, to keep it from eating away at him 24/7. If he hadn't learned how to do that, after a long, serious counseling session from his boss years ago—

Gideon, this job will eat you alive if you don't learn

how to turn it off when you can—he doubted he would still be functioning.

So he flipped that switch now. She was just someone needing temporary shelter, that's all. He turned his mind to the minutia, to getting her things into the guest room just down the hall from the family room and kitchen—the only rooms that looked like perhaps they at least belonged in this century, and that had the added benefit of never having been his at any point. There was a three-quarter bath attached, which when he asked, in a nicely businesslike voice, he thought, she said was fine. He thought about explaining the old-fashioned furniture but decided they'd pretty much covered that and let it be.

"I'll leave you to settle in," he said, in that same not-quite-impersonal tone, "and I'll go see what's available to eat. You must be hungry."

"Not yet," she said, "but I will be."

Again her eyes went wide. And made him wonder if she was hearing some sort of suggestive alternative meaning. Wonder if her mind had gone where his had before he'd slammed that door on it.

He walked over to open the bathroom to make sure it was tolerably clean and tidy; sometimes, since it was the closest, anybody who'd been working outside came in here to clean up. It looked fine to him, although he wasn't the stickler some were. Sophia? Maybe. The only times he'd been in her bathroom he'd either been in a hurry to get back to her or…she'd been with him and there had been absolutely nothing else on his mind except the beautiful woman in his arms with a stream of water flowing over her luscious curves, water that was cold compared to the heat she kindled inside him.

Needing to be out of here—*now*—he spun around on his heel. And careened right into Sophia, who had followed him over here. For an instant she was pressed against him, and that heat he'd just been thinking about burst to life in reality. She stared up at him. Her lips parted.

There had been a time when that would have been an invitation. An invitation to kiss those delicious lips, to probe that sweet mouth, until they were both mad with it and ended up back where they'd begun, on the nearest bed. Or the floor if they couldn't make it that far. For that matter, up against the wall had its appeal as well.

That mental compartment door rattled loudly, and he had to kick it shut this time. He backed away from her. She looked as if she was about to say something, and no matter what it was, he didn't want to hear it.

He didn't dare risk saying anything himself, so he simply left the room and headed out to the kitchen. He didn't know how long he stood there with the refrigerator door open, staring blankly, unseeingly, at the contents.

Should have opened the freezer; it might have cooled you off more.

He gave a sharp shake of his head, made himself focus. He doubted there would be much here, since Mom was off at the ranch, and he was right. So he ended up at the freezer anyway. And there found what he'd hoped for, the family favorite pizza, which she always kept on hand for impromptu movie nights when a few of them ended up here.

He heard Sophia come back into the family room. She didn't head toward the kitchen. He wondered if it was because he was in here, then shoved that thought into the compartment, wishing he had some kind of thought sealer to put around the damned door that seemed to be leaking.

He pulled out the big, square box, making a mental note about replacing it. *And that'll stick about as well as all the mental notes you've been making tonight.*

He checked the suggested temperature and then set the oven. Maybe he'd build a fire; Mom usually turned the heat down when she was going to be gone for long, an economizing measure she'd had to learn and then had just kept up.

He opened the box and slid the round tray out. And realized belatedly he hadn't even asked her if she still loved pizza.

"Pizza okay?" he called out without looking. "It's about all that's here, since Mom's been gone."

"Fine," she said.

It registered that she'd answered from some distance, and when he did look up, he saw she was over looking at what the family laughingly called the rogues' gallery. All of them were there at least twice—one childhood shot and one as an adult—plus some group shots of them all, so it made for a full wall. He was almost dead center in the columns, with six ahead of him and five after. And that's where she was, and he could tell by where her gaze was fastened that she was looking at the shot of him hugging the shaggy, floppy-eared dog who had been the adored family pet when he'd been a kid. It was his mother's favorite picture of him. Probably because it had been taken before everything had fallen apart, and he looked like the happy, carefree child he'd been.

He couldn't seem to stop himself from walking over to her.

"That's Denver," he said. "Named after the singer, not the city."

"He looks so sweet," she said softly.

"He was a great dog," Gideon said, forcefully assuming it was the animal she was talking about. "My best friend, for a long time. And the only thing that got me through, a couple of years after that picture was taken."

"I never had a pet," she said, sounding more than a little wistful. "Except a goldfish for a while."

"My mother said once—I think when one of my brothers wanted a snake—that a pet is something you can pet. So I don't think a goldfish counts."

"I was never allowed anything else."

"Let me guess," he said sourly, "your father?"

She nodded. Didn't look at him. He opened his mouth to make a comment on what he thought of the man, then shut it again. He'd never met her father and never would. Nor did his opinion of him matter one iota to her.

Because he didn't matter one iota to her.

And it irritated him that he had to remind himself of that; he'd thought that lesson pounded permanently home years ago. *What the hell does it take to*

get through to you? She didn't want what you were of-
fering, then or now.

And when he went to start that fire on the hearth,
he did it with more energy than it needed, prodded by
that irritation.

Because, damn it, she still got to him.

Chapter Thirteen

"Who's this?" Sophia asked, nodding toward the photograph of a baby in the column to the left of Gideon's. It was beneath the shot of his sister Rachel, whom she recognized because she'd seen photographs of the woman who served as the county district attorney.

He straightened from the hearth, where a warming fire was starting to crackle. As he stood she was reminded anew of just how tall he was, towering over her own five-seven by at least a half a foot. He walked over to her, with that smooth, long stride, to see what she was looking at. When he did, a soft, loving smile spread across his face.

"Rachel's daughter, Iris. My goddaughter."

That didn't surprise her. She'd known he was close to his sister, just two years older, and she remembered speculating that it wasn't just that they were close in age, but at least in part because they were two of only three of the twelve Colton siblings who were single births.

"Lucky girl," she murmured.

And meant it; she knew Gideon would take that position seriously, and if that child ever needed him, he would be there one hundred percent. And there were countless kids who had passed through the system at some point who could attest that she could have no better defender.

He shrugged. "Right now it consists mostly of trying to get her to laugh when she's cranky."

Like you used to do with me? Oh, Lord, that man could make her laugh. Even if she came home totally stressed or depressed, Gideon could somehow eventually have her laughing. And then he'd kiss her, and the incredible fire between them would leap to life, and—

"I didn't know she'd gotten married," she said hastily, before she could say something stupid.

"She didn't," he said tersely.

Okay, apparently she had said something stupid. "Oh."

He let out a compressed breath as he stared at the baby's picture. "We don't even know who Iris's father is. Rachel won't tell anyone."

Sophia looked at him then, saw the touch of irritation in his expression. Thought of what she'd learned—and envied—about this family. Silly, perhaps, because of the hell they'd endured, but despite what Ben Colton had put them through, they'd had something she'd never had. And still had it. Each other. She supposed they had their squabbles, but if a threat came from outside, the Coltons stood together.

"Maybe," she said very neutrally, "she's afraid her brothers will go beat him up."

His head snapped around. He stared at her for a moment. Then gave a rather rueful grimace. "Can't say the thought hasn't occurred," he admitted. "But I have to accept that Rach has her reasons."

Respect.

That was the first word that popped into Sophia's mind. Respect for each person's autonomy. Their right to make their own decisions. Even if it wasn't what he or his siblings or even their mother might want for them.

As opposed to her father, whose primary rule was pretty much his way or the highway.

No wonder Gideon was the wonderful guy he was.

And no wonder you were too stubborn and stupid to believe in him when you had the chance.

"She's adorable." She nodded toward the column of photos to the right, her gaze this time fastened on one that she guessed was all the boys in the family. They all looked grumpy at being forced to stand and pose, except Gideon, who was smiling at the person behind the camera. "And so were you."

He shrugged again. "I outgrew it. She won't."

She turned to face him then. And it took all of what nerve she had left after a rough evening to say levelly, "No. You didn't."

A reaction to her heartfelt words flashed across his face. That expressive face that she'd once been able to read so well. But now it vanished so quickly she couldn't tell if it had been surprise or…anger.

She wouldn't blame him if it had been the latter. But she couldn't bring herself to regret that she'd said it. Because it was nothing less than the truth. Gideon had always been a good-looking man—those eyes of his were breath-stealing—but now he was even more so. As he'd exhibited tonight, he was strong enough to fight, yet cool enough to only do it to protect. And that only added to his already considerable appeal, at least in her mind.

Too bad she'd had to lose him to realize just how rare a thing she'd had within her grasp.

She was more aware of that than ever here, in this house where he'd grown up. She'd meant what she'd said. Some people might think the house was a bit dated, but she thought the scuffs on the floor and the worn edges on the tables and chairs just showed that a family had lived and loved here, that it had been a home, more of one than she herself had ever known. And she felt a little stab of awe that Isadora Colton had managed this, had held that big family together, after a blow that would have destroyed a weaker woman, would have shattered weaker bonds than those she'd built with her children.

"Did your parents love each other?" She asked it before she thought, but Gideon didn't seem offended.

"They did. We never doubted that, even…after. Sometimes I think my mother still loves him, despite it all." He ran a hand through his hair. Sophia's fingers curled as she remembered how much she had loved to do that. "Or maybe," he went on, "she just misses the idea of her marriage."

"I can understand that. My parents merely tolerate each other."

He gave her a sideways look. "Was it always that way?"

"As long as I can remember," she said. "Ironic, isn't

it? I remember as a teenager thinking you can have the love or the stability, but not both."

"You don't really believe that, do you?"

"No," she admitted. "I've seen too many loving parents to believe it always has to be one or the other." She looked around the family room that had clearly been just that, for a family. "Are there rooms here you weren't allowed into?" she asked. "As a kid, I mean."

He gave her a curious look. "Not allowed? No. A couple of rooms we had to knock first, but it was our house, our home. That's why Mom fought so hard and worked so hard to keep it. After."

"You'd had enough upheaval in your life. That's a fierce kind of love," she said softly, admiring the woman she'd never met.

"Yes." His mouth curved up slightly. "She kind of dotes on all of us. She'd do anything for her kids."

It was after the pizza—which she had missed, she realized, since they'd had it often and, as with many things, she avoided the things that reminded her of him—that she'd looked back toward the picture wall. And asked the first thing that popped into her mind, something she'd rarely done in her life, except with him. Because he made her feel safe? She didn't know; she only knew it happened, as it did now.

"Who took that group shot?"

She realized the moment he went very still that she shouldn't have asked. She also realized that many men would just clam up and refuse to answer if they didn't want to. But that wasn't Gideon's way. And so she tried to salvage the situation by answering it herself.

"Your father."

"Yes."

His voice was stiff. She stifled a sigh. The relative ease they'd achieved had vanished. Or rather, she'd blown it up with her ill-advised question.

But then Gideon changed, in a very Gideon-like way. He leaned back in his chair across the table from her, fiddling a bit with the one remaining crust of the last pizza slice he'd eaten. And then he looked at her, meeting her gaze steadily with those bright blue eyes, and said quietly, "Neither one of us has had much in the way of fatherly support, have we?"

She blinked, drew back slightly. "My father's always been there."

His eyebrows rose. "Yes. Usually to tell you what you're doing wrong, or how you've disappointed him."

"He's just a perfectionist."

"Sophia, from all you've said, he's as cold as that lingering snow outside. A normal father would be so damned proud of what you've accomplished in your life he'd be buying billboards to shout how great his daughter is."

She nearly gaped at the incredible compliment. But again, that was Gideon; she had hurt him, badly, but he still never denied the truth or his respect for her work. And she had the sudden feeling that as much as she admired that about him, she'd never fully understood how deep it went. How on earth, with the father he'd had, had he managed to turn out with such a deep sense of what was right? Or was it perhaps because of his father? Maybe that had made him determined to never bend his principles.

"I'm still better off than you," she said softly. "At least my father is still alive and could change."

"Where there's life, there's hope? Really? After all these years, you think he's going to change?"

"What else should I do?" she asked, a little stung. This was a Gideon she hadn't seen before, a little sharper, edging on sarcastic. And she couldn't help wondering if she'd done that to him.

Because it's always all about you, right?

"I don't know," he said, dropping the uneaten crust. "Maybe fire him from the position of deciding what you should do in your life? Revoke his permission to criticize?"

"I think that's a lifetime position," she said with a grimace.

"Only if you keep paying him."

She blinked. "Paying him?"

"By showing him what he says matters."

"But he's my father."

"And the infamous Judge Benjamin Colton was mine." He got up abruptly. As if he'd simply had to move. He moved away from the table, into the family room toward the fireplace. She rose herself, watching him, seeing that his jaw muscles were tight. "If we had let that rule us, none of us would have survived. So we acknowledged what he'd done, made amends where we could—and still do, with the foundation—and moved on."

"You have." She walked over to him but stopped a safe couple of feet away. "When this town thinks of the Coltons now, it's of all of you, not your father. But my situation is different. My father may be…strict, and demanding, but…"

"But what? He's never humiliated you?"

"No." She tried to stop there, but as so often with Gideon, the words she tried to hold back came pouring out. "If anything, I've—"

"Stop right there. If you so much as hint that he has reason—any reason—to be ashamed of you, I'll—"

He abruptly bit off whatever he'd been going to say.

"You'll what? Go beat him up?"

One corner of his mouth lifted wryly, but it was nowhere near a smile. "Can't say the thought never occurred."

She knew the repetition of his earlier phrase, when he'd been talking about his much loved sister, was intentional. But what that meant now, she had no idea. She was still too blown away by her own reaction to the very thought of Gideon confronting Harold Jones on her behalf. It almost took her breath away. The only thing that could hit her harder would be if he'd meant that repetition because of how he felt about her. But she knew better than to believe that. Didn't she?

She felt suddenly weak in the knees, felt herself wobble slightly and sank down to the couch, grateful for the warmth the fire was putting out.

"Sophia?" He was sitting close beside her instantly, concern in his voice. Ordinary concern, she told herself. The kind he had for anyone, because that's who he was.

Reaction, she added. That's all this was.

And even as she thought it, Gideon said gently, "You've had a rough time. Little Charlie hurt and so scared, his father bursting in like that, and then daring to show up at your home. It's no wonder you're rattled."

His soothing tone accomplished what he'd intended. He always seemed to know, not just what to say, but how to say it. How he'd handled Charlie was proof of that.

She studied him for a long, quiet moment. Tried, almost successfully, to quash the longing that was building inside her, the wish to take back that day when she'd ruined it all with her fears and doubts. Where would they be now if she had not, as he'd said, given her father the right to decide what she did in her life? If she hadn't gone along with his insistence her work was more important than anything else, including family? Even now, as an adult, she was still trying to win his approval. A task she was beginning to believe truly impossible.

While Gideon had never, ever left her in doubt of how he felt. How much he'd admired her—her herself along with her work.

How much he'd loved her.

And she hadn't been able to believe him.

"I am rattled," she admitted. "While you are rock-solid calm." At this point she wasn't even trying to hide the admiration in her voice. "You were, through it all."

He shrugged. His go-to when he was uncomfortable or embarrassed, she knew. And that it was usually at praise or a compliment had never been lost on her. "I've had a bit more practice dealing with those kinds of situations," he said, as if what he'd done was nothing special.

"And those kinds of people. Like Charlie's father."

"Yes."

"Don't belittle how well you do it, Gideon. There's a reason you're the one they call in those situations."

"It's my job."

"It's also your calling. As much as becoming a doctor was mine." She gave him the best smile she could manage, although she suspected it was a little crooked. "We both have that taking-care-of-people gene, I guess."

It had made him chuckle when she'd said it before, back when they were together, the idea of a doctor talking about a made-up gene. But this time there was no laugh, no smile. Instead he was looking at her so intently she almost forgot to breathe.

Then he moved, and she did forget to breathe. Or couldn't, more likely. Because he moved toward her. Leaned in. The only sound in that moment was the occasional snap and pop from the fire, which warmed the air. Or maybe it was Gideon, warming her, as he always had with his mere presence. Giving her a kind of warmth she'd never felt before. Or since.

He kissed her.

Chapter Fourteen

Gideon knew it was a mistake the moment he did it. The instant his lips touched hers, it was as if the intervening couple of years had never happened. The fire within him roared to life as if it had only been banked, not extinguished, and he knew he'd been kidding himself all this time.

Yet he hadn't wanted to stop. The moment she'd made that old joke, he'd been plunged back to the time when it had been his right to do this, when kissing her had been the most luscious dessert he'd ever tasted. And suddenly he'd had to know if it still was.

It was.

Even as he savored it, he cursed himself for being an idiot. Hadn't he learned his lesson before, when she'd ended them as if what they'd found together meant nothing?

All the times he'd thought himself in love, all the times that had come before he'd realized it was the idea of love he'd fallen for, of love and a life and a family, were mere wisps of memory, fragments of a time when he'd been young and foolish. Sophia was the first and only time in his life that it had been real, down to the core, hot and fiercely real. The irony of that bit deep, that the one time he'd really, truly meant it, it had driven her away.

That was what he'd been driven to find out, what had pushed him to this foolhardy move. He would have been better off to still be wondering. At least he could have written it off with a casual "Guess I'll never know." But now he did know. Knew that it had been everything he'd remembered it to be.

And now he had to live with that knowledge.

He broke the kiss, pulled back. Realized the rapid breathing he was hearing was his own. Tried to stop it. Failed. In the end he could only stare at her, into those eyes flecked with green and gold. She was gazing back at him, wide-eyed, looking almost stunned.

Yeah, me, too.

"Sorry," he muttered. "I didn't—"

He cut himself off. He'd been going to say he hadn't meant it, but it would be a lie. He had. Because on some level he'd simply had to know. Had half hoped the kiss would be cool, unemotional, with nothing of what he remembered in it.

Instead it had been instant combustion.

"Are you? Sorry?" she whispered.

"No," he said with the honesty that had gotten him into as much trouble as it got him out of. "But I won't do it again."

It came out like a grim, certain vow. And he meant it. Didn't he?

"So… I'll have to."

She'd shocked him into silence now. He stared at her, summoning up every memory of the pain and loss he'd felt when she'd broken it off to keep from wishing she would. He wasn't going to go through that again.

"I'd recommend you don't," he said coolly.

And although the hearth didn't need it, he got up and stoked a different kind of flame.

"Was it…that bad?" she asked, sounding almost wistful.

He looked back at her as he tossed another log on the fire that was already crackling merrily as the resin in the wood heated and snapped.

"Which time?" he asked, not quite mockingly. Then regretted it when she winced.

If you'd asked him before he'd walked into that hospital room, he would have said he was over her. Or at least had relegated her to the past. But that past, the time when she'd thrown them away, obviously still rankled. It surprised him just how much. He wasn't snarky by nature and didn't like himself much when he was. But he still needed some distance between them, because he was not going to make the same mistake twice. No matter how much he wanted to kiss her again. And more.

So this time when he went back to the couch, he sat farther away. At least a foot. She was steadier now that she was sitting down, so she didn't need the moral support.

The support you stupidly turned into something else altogether.

She was looking at him warily, as if she expected him to snap again, when that was the last thing he wanted to do. But if he'd learned anything from the crash and burn with her the first time, it was that what he wanted or didn't want didn't matter much when it came to Sophia.

She'd made the decision, had decided he wasn't what she wanted, and that alone should have hardened his heart against her. But now it seemed that in all this time since, when he'd thought he'd been building walls that would hold against even her appeal, he'd apparently accomplished nothing.

"You said your practice was nearly full. What made you decide to see Charlie the first time, when he was sick?"

He practically blurted it out, and it was an obviously blatant change of subject, but at this point he didn't care. He just needed a distraction from the taste of her that lingered on his lips.

"My PA, Christopher, asked me to. He said Charlie's mother sounded so—" She broke off, her eyes widening. "I'd forgotten."

"What?"

"Christopher said Charlie's mother sounded desperate. That their previous doctor had moved away, and he was so sick she was scared."

Gideon went still. That was an excuse he'd heard too often, in cases where injuries from abuse had required changing doctors frequently.

"The alarm bells should have gone off right then, shouldn't they?" she said, sounding disgusted.

"A red flag, maybe," he said, keeping his tone neutral.

"Ellen Webber insisted she had Charlie's medical records at home, but she'd been so worried she'd forgotten to bring them. We contacted her at least twice, but she never brought them in or sent them." She gave a shake of her head and looked as disgusted as she'd sounded before. "I should have realized she wasn't just disorganized, as she claimed, but hiding something."

"Probably that there are no medical records. Because they never dared to go to the same doctor twice."

"They only called me because Mrs. Webber still had the empty prescription bottle in the bottom of her purse, with my name on it." She rubbed her hands, with those long, slender fingers, over her face, shaking her head yet again. "I should have known."

"You're not omniscient," he said. "You only saw him once, for an illness, not an injury. And only three weeks ago."

Her hands lowered. For a long, silent moment, she simply looked at him. Then, in a tone almost of awe, she said, "You are the most forgiving man I've ever met. I wish…"

Her voice trailed away. She lowered her eyes. He stared at her, focused on the twin dark sweeps of her eyelashes. She wished for what? Forgiveness? But that would imply she had—or at least thought she had—made a mistake. Wouldn't it?

He nearly groaned aloud. No one else on the planet—other than his father after the revelations and his death—had ever made Gideon spend so much time ricocheting around off his own thoughts. She tangled up emotions he hadn't even felt in ages. Hadn't felt since…her.

Yet as he sat there looking at her, he couldn't help but visually trace the delicate line of her jaw, the arch of her brows, her slender neck and that spot beneath her ear that used to make her go all quivery when he kissed it. Would it still? And if it did, would that response do what it had always done—send him surging to readiness with his next heartbeat?

She looked up then, and he didn't have time to hide his thoughts. If he even could have, they were so intense. Her eyes widened once more as she met his gaze. And the connection they had always had snapped to new life between them, so he knew in the instant before it happened what she was going to do. Follow her own words, spoken after he'd told her he wouldn't do it again.

I'll have to.

And she kissed him.

SOPHIA KNEW SHE would never have done it if she'd had enough control left. But tonight, what had happened with Charlie, then his father, and now being here, in this house, had pretty much blown up what control she had. And what little had been left had been seared to ash when he'd kissed her.

She'd told herself he hadn't meant to do it, was sorry he had, that he didn't really want her, he'd only been… curious.

She'd told herself that just because she erupted into full-blown fire at the feel of his mouth on hers didn't mean he felt the same.

She'd told herself that just because afterward he'd looked at her that way, his breath coming with an audible quickness, didn't mean his entire body was yearning for her the way hers was for him.

She'd told herself all this, and none of it, nor all of

it together, was enough to stop her, not when he was within her reach.

The way he went still almost did stop her. He didn't quite stiffen, or pull away, but it was close. That should have pounded home to her that this was not the man who'd loved her, not anymore. But less than a second after their lips met, he was her Gideon again—for the moment, at least. And she tasted him long and slow and deep, because the part of her mind that was still functioning was warning her this would be all she would get, all she would have to add to the storehouse of precious memories.

She reached up, putting her hands on his shoulders, savoring the breadth and strength of them. Memories flooded her, of what his skin felt like under her hands, how she used to love to watch the contrast between them as she traced the muscled lines of his chest and abs, the weight and heft of him when she reached lower to stroke and caress until they both couldn't handle it.

She had never been able to resist him. Which, in the quieter times after she'd put an end to them, she realized had been part of what had made her go through with the action she now regretted more than any in her life. The ferocity of what she felt for him, both emotionally and physically, had scared her. And scarred her.

And, above all, cost her.

He moved, slipping his arms around her, pulling her closer. She felt his heat, and it sent the blaze inside her rocketing along every nerve, waking up places she'd smothered the day she'd walked away from him. Even this slight sign of the wanting returned fired her even higher, and she felt every restraint slipping.

And then he was cupping her face, as he used to do to tilt her head so he could probe deeper, thrill her with his eagerness, as if she were a taste he could never get enough of. And he did it now, his tongue sliding over her teeth and then past them. As if she had no choice in it, her own tongue danced with his, stroked, teased, each touch turning that blaze into an inferno.

Whatever else had changed between them thanks to her fears, this had not. This fierce wanting, this half-crazed need, had been there from the beginning and was still there now. And the leash snapped, so definitely she almost thought she could hear it.

She didn't even realize how she'd been clawing at his clothes until he broke the kiss and stopped her, his jeans already half-unzipped by her eager fingers, fingers that wanted to stroke the amazing length and breadth of the starkly male flesh within her reach. And she couldn't deny the joy that leaped in her at this blatant evidence that he wanted her, too.

"You know how this ends." It was almost a growl, in that deep, rough tone she loved that only sent more fire leaping along every nerve.

"I hope so," she answered fervently and kissed him again, almost desperately.

He broke the kiss. "I'm not…prepared for this."

"It's all right, I am," she said, silently thankful that her dedication to her work had made her ensure no unplanned pregnancies would disrupt it. Not that it had really been an issue. Until now.

She kissed him again. And yet again he broke the kiss, but he still held her. "You've had a rough evening. Don't do this if you're going to regret it later."

This time his voice was that combination of gentle yet firm that she also loved. *Face it, girl, you love everything about the guy.*

And wasn't it just so Gideon that even now he would give her the chance to change her mind? Even as aroused as he clearly was, he wouldn't take anything not freely given. This was the man he was, had always been. And as the heat built to a peak, her heart melted.

"No regrets," she promised. And meant it. Because suddenly more than anything she wanted another memory to cling to. And she told herself that was all it was, because he'd made it pretty clear he hadn't and would likely never forgive her. And she couldn't blame him for that. So with a last warning to herself not to make any assumptions, that there was no way he could still care for her, she threw what caution he'd left her to the wind.

Chapter Fifteen

No regrets.

Gideon wished he could be as sure as she had sounded. But he was fairly certain he was going to regret this.

He knew he should stop, not just because of the regret that would ensue, but because he was on edge. It had been a rough day for him, too, and it always took him a while to come down after those rare occasions when he was forced to resort to physical intervention.

Physical. Right, that's all this was. The slaking of a need he'd apparently been ignoring for too long. Only sex. And it was just a bonus that he happened to be with the one woman who brought him to the boil faster than anyone ever had.

Plus, he had that promise. *No regrets.* And he knew her well enough to know that if he called her on that promise, she would keep it. She was honorable that way, this woman who had torn his life and hopes to pieces.

The irony didn't escape him.

You can sure pick them, bro.

That was what Jasper, Aubrey's twin, who ran the

Gemini Ranch with her and had seen Sophia that day with the kids, had said when he'd found out Gideon was dating her. He'd remembered her vividly. What man wouldn't? Gideon had come back with something along the lines of not taking dating advice from a guy who rarely got involved in relationships. He'd assumed at the time his brother meant she was beautiful, but maybe he'd somehow sensed what would happen.

But no one could have guessed they'd end up like this, here and now. But it was a dream scenario, right? Long dry spell, hot woman, one you already know the sex will be over the moon with, and a promise of no recriminations afterward. What more could anyone ask for?

What you asked for back then, which got thrown back in your face, maybe?

Nope, he wasn't going there again. He wasn't going to let his stupid heart lead him into disaster again. This was not love. It was physical, a slaking of need, that's all. That it happened to be with the woman who had drawn him like no other was just happenstance. Luck, even. He could admit that, couldn't he?

And then her hands, those dexterous, wonderful hands, slid down his body, slipped beneath the waistband of his jeans and stroked perilously close to taut, erect flesh that he would swear quivered in response. All caution, all internal warnings were blasted into the ether when her fingers curled around him, clasped him with the perfect amount of pressure.

It was the last straw. He gave up any attempts at restraint, at waiting, at patience. His own hands began to move. He needed to touch that silken skin of hers more than he needed his next breath. And to do that, the clothes had to be gone. Out of practice, he fumbled a bit.

He noted the delicate, lacy bra, in a slightly lighter shade of green than her blouse. That blouse he'd liked. At least he thought it was the same—he was no expert on how long women kept their clothing.

And you're no expert anymore at getting it off. It really has been too long, Colton, when you can't even unhook a bra.

But then she moved, slipping the straps off her slender shoulders herself, making it easier. And this sign of her willingness, eagerness even, fired him up all over again. He did the same, tugging his heavy sweater clear and tossing it aside. As his eager hands slid down to cup her breasts, those full, luscious breasts, hers slid over his chest, tracing every line of him as if she were making sure nothing had changed.

Only on the inside, Sophia.

And he had changed. He was tougher now, more careful. She had taught him that. The hard way.

But right now the only hardness he cared about was being painfully restrained by his half-open jeans. He shifted slightly and shucked them down with his hands. He didn't care if he was still half-dressed, and it seemed she didn't, either, because with their clothes tangled around them, she urged him on, touching him, guiding him, whispering only, "Hurry."

The single word fired him into a rush, like a starving man facing his final meal, wanting to savor yet driven to an urgency he couldn't deny. He pushed forward, sinking into her deeply, a shudder wracking him as her slick heat surrounded him. He groaned, unable to help himself. And then he simply had to move. She urged him on again, rocking beneath him so temptingly it drove him to a fever pitch.

It happened fast after that, and he was afraid he'd embarrass himself by losing the battle to hold back the moment he was fully inside her. But she was clutching at him, as if she wanted him deeper, all the way, and he thought he heard her say huskily, "Please."

He thrust once, twice, thought he could manage three, but then she gasped and he felt it begin for her, the rolling, rippling tightening of the muscles clasping him, milking him, and he let go simply because he had to. It rolled through him and he froze, unable to move as surely as he'd had to move before, aware of nothing but the pulsing sensation of pouring himself into her. It left him drained, and he no longer had the strength to hold himself up.

And in the moment when he buckled and sagged against her, he didn't care about anything else except that he felt more whole than he had since the night this woman had destroyed his world.

SOPHIA STIRRED SLEEPILY. If she'd been able to form a comprehensible sound, it likely would have been "Mmm." She was so comfortable and relaxed it didn't matter how cold it was outside; here she was warm and safe and she didn't want to wake up from those sexy dreams—

Her eyes snapped open.

They hadn't been dreams.

She felt the muscled length of Gideon beside her,

the soft leather of the couch behind her. The light in the room was from the windows, not the hearth, which told her it was morning and the fire had likely died down. But she didn't miss it, not with her own, personal heat producer pressed against her from shoulder to toes. Naked, muscled and even more beautiful than she'd remembered.

Dear God, they hadn't been dreams.

Every glorious, soaring moment had been real. His hands on her, driving her to heights only he ever had. His body driving into hers, hers clenching around him as she hit the peak only he had ever taken her to.

It had all been real.

And suddenly she was terrified. Not of what had happened; she would treasure the memory forever. But she was afraid that now it would end. That this one night would be all there was.

Ironic, she supposed, that the fabled morning-after regrets that hit her, the ones she'd promised not to have, were not because of what she'd done, but because she would likely never do it again.

You know how this ends.

Gideon's harsh, rough words rang in her mind. And it suddenly occurred to her that perhaps he hadn't meant them the way she'd thought. She'd assumed he'd meant if she kept kissing him like that they were going to end up exactly as they had, hot and fierce.

But what if it had a different meaning? What if he'd been telling her that what had happened between them last night would end, that this came with no declaration, no commitment, no promises, that it was just sex between two people who were great together physically but done emotionally, and she needed to know that?

What if it had been a warning? A warning not to read anything into something that was simple chemistry? Anything...lasting?

I know in your work you have to, but with us, before you go careening off into space with all the possibilities, maybe you could just ask?

More words from Gideon echoed in her head. It had been the first time he'd ever canceled a date with her, and via a terse text that said only, Can't make it. More later.

She'd spent the time when they'd planned on a nice dinner out eating junk food, while her mind indeed careened around between all the possibilities, from him lying hurt in a hospital bed—or worse, the morgue—to him not caring as he'd said he did, to the first step of him ghosting her. All her uncertainties, her doubts, instilled by not measuring up her entire life, came rushing back, and she'd worked herself up into quite a state.

When he'd shown up at her door later that night, she'd been angry, and all her thoughts had come tumbling out before he had a chance to say a word. And Gideon had just stood there and let her get it out before he quietly explained where he'd been.

When she'd found out he'd been with one of his former kids, who'd tried to take their own life that afternoon, she'd felt smaller than an ant. A grease ant at that. And couldn't apologize enough. Which was when he'd made that rather poignant request.

Was she doing it again? Assuming the worst, or at least thinking it? Or was she only being realistic? What was the likelihood he would ever forgive the way she'd ended it between them? Or that she'd ended it at all? He certainly wasn't acting as he had before she'd done it to them. He had been the same Gideon to Charlie, and he'd seen her as the caring professional he was, but to her personally he'd been edgy, reticent and cool at times. He—

And there she went again. She grimaced inwardly. It was amazing he'd lasted as long as he had.

He stirred beside her, and a sudden jab of fear hit her. When he woke up, would he be the one sorry? Would he wish he'd never given in? Would he recoil, wondering why he'd ever—

With an effort she stopped the flow. And did the only thing she could think of. She put her arms around him and held on.

GIDEON HAD FELT her wake up. As if there was some connection between them beyond the physical, he'd sensed her tension. After an amazing, delicious night, he hadn't wanted to face this morning, with all the things that seemed inevitable. The doubts, the embarrassment and, despite her promise, the regret. Because he knew there would be some. Because he was feeling it himself. Regret because he knew down deep he'd blown apart all the hard-won equilibrium he'd gained. Because all the mental gyrations he'd gone through, assuring himself he could take what she was offering and walk away unscathed, that it would somehow not be as incredible as he remembered or, silliest of all, that he could be the one with no regrets in the morning, had been just that. Mental dancing around because the bottom line was that he still, even after what she'd done, couldn't resist her.

And what does that say about you, Colton?

He didn't want to think about it.

And then she had put her arms around him and pulled him close, and now he couldn't think at all, at least not about anything except taking the chance for one last time with this woman who could fry all his circuits with a look. Because it would be the last time. The cool, calculating part of his brain knew that, even if his heart didn't.

The problem was, that was one of the circuits she usually fried first. And all it took was this, her holding him close, the feel of her body pressed against his, and he was on fire again, as fiercely as ever. It would have been pitiful if it wasn't so damned glorious.

As he kissed her, stroked her, and his body surged back to life, as eagerly as if the night before had never happened, he wanted to think his knowledge of everything she liked, everything that made her sigh or moan, had come back to him once they were together like this. But he knew it hadn't come back, because it had never gone. And the few times he'd tried a relationship with someone else since Sophia had left him in the dust had all been sabotaged by her memory before they'd even begun.

Some primal need rose in him as he slid into her welcoming body one last time, a need to imprint himself on her as fiercely and permanently as she had done to him. He went harder, driving, pounding, with every little sound of pleasure and assent that broke from her pushing him further. He wanted to hear her cry out with it, to know she was as helpless in the grip of this as he was, Ms. always-controlled, driven-to-perfection Sophia Gray-Jones.

It took every bit of control he had to last when she was practically writhing beneath him, when she was clawing at his back and gasping at every thrust. But he got what he wanted. When her body clenched around his in spasm after spasm, his name broke from her in an explosion of helpless, uncontrollable sound. It was the trigger he'd been waiting for, and he let himself follow her, exploding with a ferocity he'd never known before, even with her.

He was panting, with little shivers of sensation still rippling through him. Not bothering to even try to hide it, he collapsed atop her. When he could think even a little, it was only to realize he would never look at this couch in the same way again. He wasn't sure he would ever be able to look at it at all, once the inevitable happened and they went their separate ways again.

Something tickled at the edge of his awareness. He ignored it.

He pondered, no doubt uselessly, if it really was inevitable. Then caught himself, wondering what the hell was wrong with him, even starting to think like that. Hadn't he learned his lesson? Didn't he know better than to—

He froze. That something that had nudged his sated brain registered fully this time. It had been the sound of tires on the driveway. He knew that, because now he heard the sound of the garage door rising.

"Crap." It came out vehemently, unsuppressed.

Sophia scrambled out from under him. "Was that—"

"Yes. Mom's home."

Sophia gasped, started grabbing at her clothes. A split second later, he was doing the same.

A split second spent thinking that if she had been two minutes earlier, his mother would have heard Sophia scream his name.

Chapter Sixteen

Sophia recognized Isadora Colton instantly.

It wasn't just because the disastrous end of her marriage to the most corrupt judge Colorado had ever seen had resulted in photographs popping up all over when someone in the media revisited the past. Those pictures were decades old, after all. Although to be honest, she'd have to say the woman didn't look all that much older, which was amazing given everything she'd been through.

And okay, maybe she'd gone looking for the Colton name on occasion, during her many storms of regret over breaking up with him. And she might have lingered on any mention of Gideon's name—which was rare; he stayed under the radar and was usually only mentioned when it was a high-profile case he'd been involved with and had had to testify on—just to know that he was alive and well and doing his work with the dedication she'd always known he had.

And maybe she'd in the process seen the articles about how the graphic design company his mother had begun had risen from the ashes Judge Colton had left behind, articles that often included more recent photos.

But that wasn't why she knew her immediately. She knew her because she could see Gideon in her face, in the blue eyes that were so similar, even in her smile. She thought that even if she had simply passed her unknowingly on the street she might have guessed.

She knew from Gideon that his mother was utterly dedicated to her family. She had supposed early on this was why he was so good with kids; he'd had a stellar example. She'd envied him that; Deborah Gray-Jones had been cut from the same cloth as her father when it came to showing her emotions.

But she also admired what Isadora had accomplished, not only because she'd had to fight through the usual barriers to build a business, but because she'd had the additional baggage of her late husband's corruption to overcome. Sophia admired strength and perseverance and determination, and clearly Mrs. Colton had all three, not to mention enough smarts to take something she had a knack for and build it into a paying concern.

Ordinarily she would have expressed all that to her. But there was nothing ordinary about this meeting. Because she wasn't just a woman who had weathered a horrible storm and come out on top. She was Gideon's mother. Somehow that intimidated her, in a way no one other than her father usually did. Even all her own accomplishments in life didn't feel like enough to balance it.

And now Sophia was face-to-face with her.

Despite the fact that she'd managed to get dressed, mostly—her boots and bra were shoved out of sight under her coat that lay across a chair—before Gideon's mother got into the room, she had reason to be glad her skin was as dark as it was so the blush she could feel didn't show very much. A glance had told her Gideon had his sweater on and tugged down far enough to cover that his jeans weren't fully zipped before his mother stepped into the kitchen.

And that was the moment when the pretty blonde woman looked up from setting her keys on the counter—forgoing, Sophia noticed, the rack Gideon had pointed out near the door—and spotted them. And Sophia knew she wasn't wrong when she thought Mrs. Colton gave a quick glance at the clock on the big, stainless steel oven's control panel. Only then did Sophia herself look and see that it was not quite eight in the morning. So there would be no passing this off casually, although she guessed from the disaster her hair probably now was it wouldn't have been possible anyway.

"Well, hello," Mrs. Colton said, not trying to hide her surprise.

"Mom," Gideon said. "Didn't expect you back this early."

"Obviously," his mother answered, although there was none of the distaste that would have been in Sophia's father's voice, only a teasing sort of tone that seemed lighthearted—in fact, almost welcoming. She walked around the corner of the counter to stand before them, her gaze moving from her son to Sophia and back.

"How are things at Gemini?" Gideon asked, looking as if he knew he sounded a little lame, his attempt at distraction obvious.

"Maybe you should stop by and see for yourself. Aubrey says Misty is missing you. She's quite besotted, you know."

Gideon looked embarrassed. Misty? Sophia felt a sudden chill—had Gideon cheated on a previous girlfriend with her? Gideon cheating did not reconcile with what she knew of him, but…had she, what she'd done, changed him that much? Before she could go off on that tangent, her attention was drawn to his mother, because she had shifted her gaze, with those eyes so like her son's, to Sophia.

"Misty, by the way," Mrs. Colton said with pointed amusement and a raised brow that told Sophia her reaction had shown on her face, "is a horse. Since it appears you have reason to wonder."

She heard Gideon let out a compressed breath. Then, with a wry expression and looking more at the space between them than either of them individually, he said in the manner of introduction, "Isadora Colton, Sophia Gray-Jones."

The amusement vanished. Sophia saw the older woman go very still. Her eyes widened, and her gaze narrowed. And that answered the question that had popped into Sophia's mind when she'd realized who was here—she knew. At least, she knew who Sophia was and what she had done, and by her expression Mrs. Colton didn't like the idea that she was here, like this. Because Sophia could also see this woman was far too smart to be fooled into thinking anything else had been going on here other than…what had been going on.

Mrs. Colton looked from her to Gideon, who still

wasn't looking at either of them. "Gideon?" his mother asked quietly.

Sophia could almost feel him steady himself, and then he met his mother's gaze. It might be an awkward situation, but Gideon was no coward. "This was the safest place I could think of," he said. His mother's brows rose again, and he obviously realized how that could be interpreted, because he hastily explained what had happened yesterday. He finished with, "He found Sophia's home. So until Webber's rounded up, she needed a place to lay low, a place with some real security."

The moment he mentioned little Charlie and what had happened to him, his mother's expression had shifted completely. She went from wary to shocked to worried mother in the space of two seconds. And Sophia knew everything Gideon had told her about his mother was true. She was kind, caring, nurturing...and protective. Even about a little boy she'd never met.

"Of course. You must stay here until that evil monster is in custody." Then, suddenly businesslike, she added, "You haven't eaten yet, have you? I see you hit the pizza—"

"I'll replace it, Mom," Gideon promised.

"I know you will," she said sweetly, reaching up to cup his cheek lovingly. A gesture Sophia had seen but never gotten from her own mother. A gesture that had always seemed so loving to her, and one she'd incorporated into her work. And that had, in a strange way, taught her how much her own parents had missed, because that gesture sent the love behind it in both directions.

"So, what shall we have? I plan to go shopping later today, but—"

"We'll be fine," Gideon said. "There's leftover pizza."

His mother rolled her eyes at him. "That may be fine for you, but not me. I'll fix something."

"Mom—"

"Hush. I may not be the best cook in the world, but breakfast I can handle."

"You don't need to do that, Mrs. Colton," Sophia said.

The woman looked at her. And, after a moment, smiled. It was a kind, welcoming smile, and it startled Sophia how much it made her want to smile back. "Isa, please. Seems silly to be so formal at the moment."

Had it been her mother, Sophia would have assumed there was a dig hidden in the polite words. But looking at that smile, after seeing that loving touch between mother and son, she couldn't believe it of Gideon's parent. "All right. Thank you, Isa."

"And I'll call you Sophia, if that's all right? Or would you prefer 'Doctor'?"

Again, there was no sign of any kind of jab. Perhaps she was merely looking for it where it didn't exist because she expected it. "Sophia is fine."

Isa smiled at her again. "If I were as accomplished as you, I'd be throwing that doctor title all over the place."

Sophia couldn't stop her laugh. "This from one of the most successful graphic artists around?"

Isa's smile widened, as if she were flattered. "Thank you. Now I'll see what I can rustle up."

"May I help?"

"Thank you, but let me see what we've got first."

"Then... I'll go take a shower, if that's all right," Sophia said, feeling she needed a break from the intensity of her feelings about all this. And the shower. Although it would wash away the scent of Gideon that lingered on her, and she wouldn't welcome that.

She turned to go but stopped dead when she saw Gideon staring at her, brow furrowed. Not angrily, but as if he was curious about something. As she walked toward the guest room, she thought back over the exchange with his mother and tried to think if she'd said anything that would have puzzled him. Maybe it was that they'd had a civil conversation at all.

It wasn't until she was in the shower, trying not to think about how his hands had felt running over her skin, of how much she wished he was in here with her now, when she was grasping at anything to fight off images of Gideon taking her against this tile wall, that it occurred to her that they'd never talked about his mother's company. As far as she could remember, he would think she had no reason to know about it, unless she'd gone looking for it.

Which, in fact, she had.

And now he knew she had. No wonder he'd looked puzzled. A woman throws you out of her life, and years later you find out she's been keeping tabs on your family?

She winced, closed her eyes and tilted her head back, as if that would help. She found herself slowly shaking her head in denial. Of what, she wasn't sure.

Her own foolishness, not in letting this man slip away but in tossing him away.

And since she was in the shower and her face was wet anyway, she let a few of the tears that were welling up slide down to join with the water flowing down her cheeks.

Chapter Seventeen

"Are you sure you know what you're doing?"

Gideon stopped, having to make a conscious effort not to mash the half loaf of bread he'd picked up when his fingers wanted to knot into a fist. With another effort he relaxed them.

Did he know what he was doing? Hell, no.

What he did know was he didn't want to be here. He wanted to be in that shower with Sophia. He didn't dare look at his mother, because he was certain that wish would show in his face. To her, at least.

He shrugged, hoping the movement would ease some of the tension that was humming through him. "I figured you'd want toast. And there's peanut butter," he added brightly, hoping the reminder of one of his favorite childhood treats would deflect her.

"Do not toy with me, Gideon Colton. You know perfectly well what I mean. Just as I know perfectly well what went on here last night. Which gives me the right to know."

He put down the bread. "The right?"

"You used my home for your...your tryst."

The word almost made him smile despite everything. But realizing amusement would not be wise just now, he stifled it. Then he let out a long breath. "That wasn't the intention."

"And yet."

"Everything I told you was true, including that she didn't dare stay at her place with Webber on the loose, not after he'd already shown up there looking for her."

For a moment her expression shifted, as if a different kind of motherly concern had taken over. "And you were there, too, with that brutal man."

"His kind don't usually tackle people bigger than they are," Gideon said, his voice heavy with the weight of too much experience with people like Rick Webber. "They like to beat up on smaller, weaker people."

"I'm surprised you didn't tackle him."

Oops. The memory of what had happened before that encounter at Sophia's house, in Charlie's hospital room, flashed through his mind. Even though he didn't consider that a fight, more of a management situation, he doubted his mother would see it that way. So he went with the situation already on the table—the encounter at the town house.

"I promised Sophia I wouldn't."

She blinked. "I see."

"And I couldn't really go after him without leaving her there alone. He could have circled back. So like a good boy—" it came out rather sourly "—I waited for the police. Careful, like you always want."

"First time for everything." Her dry tone made him blink in turn. "Too bad that careful didn't last until morning."

And there they were, back at him and Sophia again.

He should have known better than to think she would be diverted for long. She didn't hold her big family together through chaos and then build a successful career by being easily sidetracked.

He sighed. "It just...happened."

"With the woman who broke your heart."

He didn't even try to deny that. His mother had that maternal perception that would tell her it was a lie. "We... It..."

He gave a sharp shake of his head. Somehow the fact that he and Sophia were combustible together, that she still made him hotter than anyone ever had, that all she had to do was look at him a certain way and his body rose to attention, did not seem the right thing to say. And in the face of that, Gideon did something he almost never did. He took the coward's way out.

"I'm going to go take a shower," he said, turning on his heel.

"By yourself?" she asked sweetly. Too sweetly.

"Yes," he answered through gritted teeth. Because his mother's arrival and reaction had brought home to him the conclusion he probably would have reached on his own eventually.

That he'd made a colossal mistake.

SOPHIA DID WHAT she could with what she had at hand to disguise eyes that looked—accurately—as if she hadn't slept most of the night. She took one last look, decided this was as good as it was going to get at the moment and dumped everything back into her makeup bag. Then, for a moment, she looked at herself in the mirror.

She looked fairly together. She'd had a lot of practice at rolling out in a hurry, knew lots of shortcuts and tricks to getting ready. She fortunately didn't have a great many emergency cases that required a middle-of-the-night rollout, but they did happen, and she couldn't waste time on the finer points of her appearance at moments like that.

Odd, how she was feeling the same way now. Not that it didn't matter what she looked like—it probably mattered more on this occasion—but that it was a sort of emergency. An entirely different kind but, for her at least, with the same sort of urgency one of those midnight calls had.

When she finally braced herself enough to leave the sanctuary of the guest room, she paused at the door to wonder how this all would have unfolded had they made it this far last night, then decided it probably wouldn't have happened at all, because even the short trip down this hallway would have been enough time for Gideon to come to his senses.

She moved on, only to be surprised and more than a little uneasy to find herself alone with Isa, who was bustling around in the kitchen. Gideon, it seemed, had also decided to take a shower. Not with her, sadly.

She gave herself a sharp shake. She needed to get that thought—indeed, any thought of Gideon in the shower at all—out of her head. *Find something to do. Anything.*

How many times had she chanted that refrain in the days after she'd walked away from him, from them? She had no idea, but if it was in the thousands, she wouldn't be surprised. Sometimes it had even worked, for a while. If what she found to do had taken some concentration.

Maybe something involving a sharp object. Her self-directed sarcasm made her mouth twist wryly.

Her tentative offer to help ended with her and that sharp object, cutting up an onion for some egg concoction Isa was putting together. "I don't do big meals very well, but breakfast I've got down," the woman said with a self-deprecating laugh.

Sophia tried to remember her mother ever admitting she wasn't perfect at anything and couldn't. She did remember several times when Deborah had researched some task furiously and then proceeded to do it herself as if she'd been born to it. Sophia had never had that knack. Except with medicine. It had spoken to her in a way no other work had. Thankfully it was an acceptable path to her mother, even to her father, although his approval for even that was gruffly given.

"The little boy, Charlie, he'll really be all right?" Isa asked, and there was no denying her concern for a child she'd never met was genuine.

"Physically, he will be." She grimaced. "Whether he stays that way depends on what happens to his father."

Isa gave a disdainful snort. "That man doesn't deserve the title."

Sophia agreed completely. No matter how harsh her own father was, he'd never struck her in anger. "No, he doesn't."

"Gideon will see to it that this doesn't happen again," his mother said confidently. "He'll keep him safe."

"He's...very dedicated."

"He is. I'm very, very proud of that boy."

"As well you should be."

Isa put down the whisk she'd been about to dip into the egg mixture in the bowl before her. And she lifted her gaze to meet Sophia's head-on.

"I'm very proud of him, and very protective. In some ways, Gideon needs it more than my other boys, because he's so honest and open and true and sometimes doesn't protect himself as much as he should."

Sophia's breath caught. There could be no doubt this was aimed at her. That piercing look made it obvious, even if the almost-stern tone didn't.

"I remember you," Isa went on. "I mean, I remember when he was seeing you. I'd never heard him talk about a woman the way he did about you. He was obviously attracted, but he also admired and respected you immensely. That was a combination I'd never seen from him before."

Sophia felt a rush of heat, an entirely different kind than last night. This was more the heat of shame, of regret, of downright remorse, leavened by the grim knowledge that it was all her own fault. Something that Isadora Colton obviously knew.

It took every bit of inner strength she had to hold the older woman's gaze, but she did it. "I felt the same about him."

"Did you? He loved you," Isa said bluntly. "And you hurt him, badly. I've never seen him so...wounded."

Sophia winced inwardly. "I know that, now. Then, I couldn't believe it. It was too fast, he was too wonderful, and I... I wasn't enough."

Isa drew back slightly. "Enough?"

"Good enough. Smart enough. Loving enough. He deserved a perfect, flawless woman, and that wasn't me."

Isa's expression changed then, something almost like sympathy coming into her eyes, those eyes so like her son's. "I don't recall perfection ever being one of Gideon's requirements."

"Not his. Mine." Sophia sighed. She'd known this would be awkward; she just hadn't known it would be so painful. "My father," she said ruefully, "taught me well."

"I'm sorry, but if your father taught you perfection is even possible, let alone required, he's a fool."

Sophia blinked. Her father had been called many things—mostly brilliant, accomplished, hard-driving, sometimes just hard or uncompromising—but he'd never, ever been called a fool.

Isa went back to whisking the eggs in the big bowl. "I have twelve children," she said, "so you'd think my odds of having a perfect, flawless one would be decent. But none of them are. I adore them all, but they're all this thing called human. Meaning *not* flawless. Each has their own weaknesses. As do I, as anyone can and would tell you," she added dryly.

Sophia was amazed the woman didn't sound bitter, after the way her life had been destroyed through no fault of her own. "But you've overcome them. Amazingly."

"Thank you," Isa said. "But I've merely learned to deal with them and hopefully sidestep when one rears its head. As have all my children. It's all a human being can do—know themselves and adapt the best they can."

Sophia thought she was probably staring at the older woman as if she were some never-before-encountered phenomenon. And to Sophia, in a way, she was. She wondered, rather longingly, what it must have been like to have such a kind, understanding woman as a parent.

"No wonder Gideon is who he is," she said quietly.

Isa looked up and smiled, taking it as the compliment she'd meant it to be. "He's an amazing person. But Gideon's biggest flaw is also his biggest strength."

Sophia knew exactly what she meant. "His big heart."

Isa stopped the whisking and again gave Sophia that straight-on, steady look. For all her gentle understanding, Isa was no pushover. If she hadn't been that way before, what had happened with her husband had certainly taught her how to take a stand and hold it.

"Sometimes too big for his own good. Please, Sophia," Isa said, and this time there was a pleading note in her voice that made the stern demeanor seem somehow more potent, "don't break that huge heart of his again. I don't want him hurt like that ever again."

Sophia felt moisture welling up in her eyes. She hated the thought that she had done that to the one man who had asked nothing more of her than to be herself and love him back.

"And," Isa added, "I don't want to see him lose what makes him able to give to those children the way he does now."

Sophia's breath caught in her throat. She'd never really thought about it quite like that, but it made sense that a heart battered by other things might not be quite soft enough to do his work the way he did, with the utmost care and concern for the children in his charge.

She had made a mistake more momentous than she had even realized, all that time ago. She thought about all the foolish hopes that had built since last night, hopes that perhaps all was not lost, that he might actually be able to forgive her, that they could rebuild what they'd once had.

But she realized now that, if he was even willing to try—a huge if—she had better be utterly and completely certain and committed. No doubts, no letting the scars of her own childhood interfere. No letting the memory of her father's critical assessments get in the way.

If your father taught you perfection is even possible, let alone required, he's a fool.

Could she let go of it? Could she silence once and for all that judgmental voice in her ear? She would have to. It had cost her the best thing that had ever happened to her once; would she let it happen again?

She could not. She would not. Because if she hurt Gideon's good, generous heart and soul again, she didn't think she could live with it. Or herself. Better she should wish that he was well and truly done with her, that for him last night had been an aberration, something to be left behind, forgotten.

For her, it would be a memory she would carry forever.

Chapter Eighteen

Gideon had to admit, his mother was good at this one. Her roasts might tend to be a bit overdone, her spaghetti a little underdone, but she had this egg thing down. A frittata, she called it; he just called it tasty and filling, with just enough kick to make it interesting. Yep, definitely good.

It was almost good enough to help him not look at who was sitting across the table from him.

It was nowhere near good enough to keep him from wondering what they'd been talking about while he was in the shower. When he was in the shower fantasizing like some overly hormonal teenager, obsessed with visions of a night that now seemed almost impossible to believe had really happened.

When he'd come out to see Sophia and his mother together in the kitchen, Gideon had frozen in his tracks, his breath equally frozen in his throat. But they'd seemed to be talking amiably enough, so he'd warily moved forward. When he got close enough to hear that the subject seemed to be the weather and the predictions of an approaching late-season storm, he relaxed a little. At least, as much as he could, given the circumstances.

In one way, he was actually glad his mother was here. It prevented—or at least postponed—one of those uncomfortable morning-after talks. Sophia had promised there would be no regrets, which meant at the least she wouldn't voice them if she had them. He doubted that had changed about her—if she made a promise, she kept it.

He, on the other hand, hadn't made any promises, about regrets or anything else last night. Which was a good thing, because he sure as hell was feeling them now. Regrets, confusion and tangled thoughts all warred with remembered sensations that made his body tighten all over again, hoping it would be asked to rise to the occasion again, and soon.

He'd thought he'd broken free, but he'd dived back in headfirst and was now dealing with the aftermath he should have known would come. And the height of last night's rapture made the morning-after crash even worse.

Remember that, will you? How many times do you have to be shown before it takes?

He wasn't sure the self-lecture was taking, so he got up to take his dishes to the kitchen. His mother appeared finished, so he grabbed hers, too, for which he got that motherly "well done" smile. *Oh, yeah, I'm housebroken, all right. Or maybe just broken.*

He tried to stop the monologue going on in his head. Focused on what he was doing. Sophia still had food on her plate, so he left it, wondering if her appetite was off after last night. He'd have thought they'd both worked up an appetite the size of Pikes Peak, but neither one of them had eaten like it.

After putting the plates in the dishwasher, he refilled his coffee mug. Stared down at the now half-full pot and contemplated his next move. Going back to the table and trying to find something else to look at now that he couldn't stare at his empty plate anymore didn't seem at all wise. So instead, mug in hand, he walked over to the glass French doors out to the back patio and spacious expanse behind the house.

He stood there for a moment, contemplating, then decided he might as well step out and see if he could sense how close that forecast snow was. He instantly buried, with the ease of long practice, the origin of the idea that some people could sense a storm coming. The origin for him, anyway. Which had been his father, who had claimed to have the knack.

He stepped outside onto the covered portion of the patio, and the brisk chill that hit him was the first step in the assessment. He only had on his sweater—the sweater Sophia had practically torn off him last night—so he should be able to judge. He went over to the thermometer that hung on the outer side of one of the support posts, carefully positioned away from the outdoor grill area. He'd been guessing forty and a fraction and nodded to himself when he saw the gauge read a hair under forty-one.

He looked out over the open, rolling land that comprised the rear portion of the acre and a third the house sat on. Memories swept over him, of happy days he'd thought would be endless, spent playing out here.

He remembered that last summer so well, the last

summer before reality had crashed in on them all. By then the firstborn, Morgan and Caleb, were nearly twenty and busy away at college, prepping for law school. The triplets had been solidly teenagers and already above doing much with their younger siblings. The twin babies of the family had been only six, too young to really understand what had happened.

But he, Rachel, Gavin, Jasper and Aubrey—they were all old enough to sense it. Old enough to understand the enormity of it, if only because they saw their mother's awful distress.

And later, when a lot of Blue Larkspur seemed to have no qualms about blaming the kids for the sins of the father, they'd drawn even closer together.

"This looks like a wonderful place to grow up."

He'd heard the door open behind him, and the light footsteps. He didn't have to look to know it was Sophia. The tingle at the back of his neck told him that. He was a little surprised, though. He'd half expected her to avoid him altogether. In fact, it had been one of the reasons he'd come out here, to give her the chance to do just that.

Strictly for her own sake, of course. Nothing to do with his need to avoid even thinking about the aftermath of what they'd done.

"It was," he said, glad that his voice sounded fairly level. "We had great times out here, playing in all that space. Lots of trees to climb, places to hide, just sheer room to run and roam."

"Our homes were too manicured for that. Once when I was eight, I accidentally broke a lawn ornament my father had placed near a fountain. That cost me a month confined to my room after school, and I had to write an essay for him about how careless and wrong I was."

Gideon stared at her. Then, with a slow shake of his head, he said, "A month? At eight? Was the thing worth a million dollars, or what?"

"That wasn't the point. The point was that it was my father's, and I broke it by being reckless."

"You, reckless? I don't believe it."

"It was my fault," she insisted. "I'd tried to lure a neighbor's dog into our yard so I could play with it." Her mouth twisted slightly. "I think that set him off as much as anything, the idea of a dog in his yard."

"*His* yard. What, as if you didn't live there at all?"

"If you'd seen that yard, you'd understand. It was like one of those formal gardens at big estates, with everything placed and trimmed just so."

"And God help anything that tried to grow in its natural way?"

She gave him a sideways look, as if she wasn't sure if he was talking about plants or her. He meant both, and he thought deep down she knew that. To him this mental torment was just a few steps short of Charlie's father's brutality—ironically once also over a dog— but she had never been able to look at her father rationally, like an outsider would.

Right, like you're an expert on that, Colton?

But for all his father's sins, he and his siblings had had something Sophia had never had, at least for a while. "Were you ever allowed to just be a kid?"

"Not if it interfered in any way."

He bit back the first words that jumped to his lips. He knew she had always had tremendous respect for her father, but he was starting to wonder just how much of it was founded in fear.

"You know," he said, very quietly, "there's more than one kind of abuse."

She looked startled, then shocked. "My father never struck me."

"Sophia, you're a physician. You know better than to say that that's the only abusive behavior."

"But—"

"Think about this for a moment. If an eight-year-old patient told you that story you just told me, what would you think? What would you think about her parents?"

"I'd think they were strict." Then she gave him another of those sideways looks. "And I'd take that over corrupt."

Gideon drew back sharply. He supposed he'd had that coming, given how hard he'd been pushing on a subject he knew she was sensitive about. But that didn't make the stab any less painful.

"Point taken," he said stiffly. "Excuse me. I need to make a call."

She looked as if she regretted what she'd said. "I was hoping you'd show me around out here." Her words weren't an apology but seemed at least like a peace offering.

He found he wasn't in the mood for a peace offering.

"I need to call the police to see if you can go home."

She looked like he had felt when she'd made her jab. So did that make them even? And how had the pair that had spent the night as they had been reduced to sniping at each other over their fathers, of all things?

He didn't know. But right now he felt like he didn't know much.

Chapter Nineteen

"Sorry, man, she can't go home yet. But he's been spotted once."

Gideon grimaced at his cell phone as if the bad news that Webber was still at large was the device's fault. "Where?"

"Gas station downtown, near the Corner Pocket," Detective Benitez said.

Gideon mentally placed the popular bar and billiard hall. He'd not been in there in a long time, but he was aware of it, being as it was run by an ex-con. Insider trading didn't usually even skirt the edges of his work, unless it was a parent being sent off, so he'd simply filed it away as part of knowing his turf.

And it was nowhere near either here or Sophia's place. And a good twenty miles in the opposite direction from his own home.

"Gassing up?" he asked.

"Yeah, and went inside for some food. Patrol got the call, but he was gone by the time they got there. We pulled the surveillance video and saw he'd talked to the clerk a bit more than if he'd been just paying, so I went to talk to him. He said the guy was mouthing off about who kept him away from his injured son because his bitch of a wife was lying about him, as usual."

Gideon went still. Did the guy mean the security guard he'd then overpowered? Or...him?

"Wait," Benitez said when Gideon asked, "do you mean you actually had physical contact with this guy? The report only said you were there and intervened."

Gideon explained exactly what had happened in Charlie's hospital room.

"Good for you," Benitez said. "But that means he could have meant either one of you. In fact, it sounds like he probably meant you, since the rent-a-cop didn't do such a great job of keeping him anywhere."

"Did he say anything else?"

"Not about that. We got his direction of travel when he left the station, but he could have gone anywhere after that. But I'll go talk to the clerk again. Now that I know you had an actual altercation with him, maybe something else will click."

"Any idea how he found the townhome?"

"Actually, yes. The officer who was there took it very seriously and went through some street cam footage. On her own time, I might add. She came up with what looks like Webber checking out the neighborhood, including the doctor's house, about three weeks ago. Then a week later, it showed him walking by within minutes of her arriving there, I'd guess coming home after work."

Three weeks. Right after Ellen had taken Charlie to Sophia. But long before Sophia would have been aware there was a potential problem, so that she might not even notice someone following her.

And her name was on the mailbox. Was Webber that out of control, that he'd walk every street near the hospital looking for her name, then follow her to confirm, just to know where the woman who had dared to help his son lived?

Of course he is.

"Thank Officer Fulton for me," Gideon said. "That was above and beyond, and I appreciate it."

"We try. Especially in cases like this. I know you said it was a domestic, but white guy stalking a Black woman adds another layer to this whole thing." When the call ended, he slipped his phone back into his pocket. Stood there for a moment, amid the cluster of big-toothed maple trees his mother had had planted for the fall colors. He and his siblings had liked them for the good places to hide. They were bare of leaves now, but next month the cycle would start.

He slowly realized he was getting cold. At first he welcomed it, for the distraction if nothing else.

He knew Sophia had reacted defensively to his push about her father. The push he didn't even know why he'd started. Why did it matter at all to him why she let Harold do that to her? Nothing about her should matter to him anymore. She wasn't part of his life any longer. Wouldn't be in the future, because despite last night, nothing had changed. Not really.

And she'd struck back with the one weapon he couldn't counter. The one weapon that did the most damage. Which she knew. And had to have intended. So obviously she wasn't worried about how hurt he'd be.

What did you expect? That a night of hot sex would

change everything? That she'd want you back? Hell, she never really wanted you in the first place, and all the steaming-hot sex in the world won't change that.

Even as he stood there, almost savoring the chill, he knew that wasn't completely accurate. She'd wanted him, all right. You didn't mutually combust like that if the desire wasn't on both sides.

She just hadn't wanted what came with him. Hadn't wanted what he'd wanted with her.

He'd spent a lot of time after she'd broken it off trying to figure her out. It had been after he'd mentioned the kids he wanted some day that she seemed to have started to withdraw. Which made no sense to him. It seemed only logical that a pediatrician had to love children and consequently want some of her own. Didn't it? So he'd spent a lot more time wondering about that, if it was simply him she didn't want to have a family with, an idea that made him not want to ask the question directly. Or if it was his last name and the scandal attached, which she'd never seemed to hold against him. Or if it was that those kids would face more challenges being mixed race. Or if it was that her father wouldn't approve, for any one of myriad reasons he felt sure a man of such disciplinarian nature could come up with. Maybe it was he who wouldn't tolerate his daughter and a son of the infamous Judge Colton. And he had such sway over Sophia that—

He broke off his thoughts as he realized he was shivering. He didn't want to go back inside, which reminded him of all the times when he'd pretended he didn't hear his mother calling him to come inside and clean up for dinner. But then his father had called, his big judge's voice booming out, and he knew he'd better obey, just like those criminals in his courtroom knew.

His mouth twisted into a bitter, one-sided smile. He really had believed that, then. That his dad was the arbiter of what was right in his world, and maybe the entire world.

Sometimes growing up sucked.

SHE WISHED SHE hadn't said it. She knew it was a low blow, but she'd had to stop that criticism of her father. She had to stop it so she could think. Because that last thing he'd said, about what if an eight-year-old patient had told her the same story she'd told him about breaking her father's statue, had struck hard. Because deep down she knew what she'd think, as a doctor responsible for her patients. She wouldn't just be thinking strict.

She'd be thinking cruel. Maybe even cruel and unusual.

Which would have had her looking that child over carefully for any signs of physical abuse.

The idea of her father ever striking her was absurd. He never had. He never would. But did that make what he did do any less harsh? Just because he hadn't taken that next step that too many parents did, did that make what he did do all right? Acceptable? How much was acceptable, given his views on raising children of color in this world, something Gideon might not understand?

She paced the floor in the guest room she'd retreated to when he'd walked away to make that phone call. She knew she needed to know the result of that call, but she wasn't quite ready to face him again. She found herself hoping that the police had rounded up Webber for personal reasons in addition to the obvious ones. Selfish, perhaps, but if they had, she could go home. Away from here, this home that had clearly been a haven for children who'd been through their own kind of hell. Away from the home Isa Colton had built through sheer determination and devotion to her huge brood.

The kind of home and haven that she had never had.

And what did that say, that she felt wistful about the lives of the Colton children, even in the aftermath of their father's downfall?

Face it, it's not just this place you want to get away from. It's Gideon.

She knew it was true. Because every time she looked at him, it was pounded home to her what she'd thrown away. Every time she saw the guardedness in those beautiful blue eyes, that wariness that hadn't been there when they'd met, she knew she'd put it there. She'd taken that open, caring, bighearted soul and she'd battered it, without even realizing what she was doing. What she was turning her back on.

The potential for exactly the kind of home and haven she was feeling wistful about.

She sank down onto the edge of the bed. The bed she'd never slept in. She wrapped her arms around herself, even knowing it would be no comfort. And certainly not the kind of comfort being wrapped in Gideon's arms was.

But then she wasn't sure anything on earth could match the warmth, comfort and safety being wrapped in Gideon's arms gave her.

A self-lecture began in her mind, and she forced herself to her feet. She walked into the attached bathroom; steeling herself to do something she wanted to avoid always seemed to work better when she had to face herself in the mirror. She wasn't sure what that said about her—she only knew it worked.

She would make sure she looked all right. She would leave the temporary shelter of this room. She would face Isa Colton and thank her again for her hospitality.

And she would face Gideon. Apologize for the snide remark. And hope he could, if not forgive her— again—at least put it behind them. Otherwise the time it took to get Charlie's situation safely resolved was going to be awkward and painful over and above what it already was.

Hopefully he'd gotten word that Rick Webber had been apprehended and she could go home, and so could Gideon. Home to wherever that place out in the hills was that she'd never set foot in or even seen. Because she had consistently resisted the urge to drive by, just to see. It was too far out of town to be able to go past and claim it accidental. Which in turn would have likely made her presence obvious. It would be hard to claim she was just passing by when only people who lived out there used the road, since it was not on the way to anywhere else.

She realized she'd been standing there, trying to imagine what his place was like, and had no idea for how long. That man rattled her like no one ever had. Only with him had she found herself lost in lingering imaginings, wonderings and, since Friday night, longing.

Who are you trying to kid? You've been longing for him from the day you sent him packing.

And there was no recovering from that kind of mistake.

Chapter Twenty

This shouldn't feel so odd. Gideon had spent many a Sunday at his childhood home. Everybody tried to get here and spend a day with Mom at least once a month. Well, except for the triplets, who could be anywhere at any given time: Ezra wherever the army sent him, Dominic probably undercover in some unsavory place and Oliver wherever the next business opportunity had taken him. But for Gideon, Blue Larkspur was home, where he wanted to stay. He wasn't about to let his father take that away from him, too.

But today it felt strange. As if he'd not been here in much longer than it had truly been. As if he were seeing the place for the first time in a very long time. And he didn't kid himself about why. It was the presence of Sophia, who truly was seeing it for the first time. The way she looked around, pausing before the photo wall for long moments and simply looking at all the pictures hanging there, scanning the shelves that flanked the fireplace, and frequently walking over to look out the windows in different directions, as if the vista that rolled out from the house was something unique instead of what he'd grown up looking at and playing in every day.

It clearly was unique to her. Which figured. What was natural beauty and a pleasure to him likely seemed wild to her, given her description of her father's preferences.

Demands, you mean.

He watched her now, standing by the French doors of the family room, looking out. The sun was at the perfect angle now, and she looked painted with the golden light. With that crown of hair and her perfect posture—she was still stunning, even after all she'd been through.

And he still wanted her. Right now, watching her with that sunlight pouring over her, he wanted more than anything to resume what they'd spent last night doing. Preferably in a bed this time, and without any interruptions.

And more, he wanted it for a long, unbroken string of nights.

So you're going to let that rule you? Haven't you learned anything?

He turned away from the vision at the doors. Needing to move, to do something—anything—he headed down the hall to his mother's office, where she'd gone to do a little catching up from her week away.

The wood-paneled room with the floor-to-ceiling shelves had once been his father's office—austere, masculine and feeling almost weighty with its air of importance. His mother had determinedly taken it over, and while the wood still gave it a substantial feel, the feminine touches she'd added—flowers here, colorful prints of her own graphics on the walls and several sentimental items collected over the years on the shelves now, in place of the row upon row of heavy law books they had once held—had made it her own. Most of the time he had to think to remember what it had looked like before.

She was at the computer on her desk, which made him smile. When he'd been a boy, she'd always claimed she was useless with technology. But now she ran a monster system with a graphics processor that would make a professional gamer envious, and she did it with ease. She looked up when he tapped gently on the half-open door.

"Just doing a final check on that presentation we're doing tomorrow," she explained with a smile. Then her expression changed from professional to motherly. "Are you all right?" He shrugged. She frowned. "That's no more of an answer now than it was when you were a child."

"I will be," he said, even now unable to lie to her. None of them really could, because they all knew how much she'd been lied to by their father. How much they all had been.

"Sophia is lovely."

"I noticed," he said dryly.

"And accomplished."

"That, too."

Isa looked back at her screen, hit a couple of keys, and it went dark. Then she swiveled around in her chair to face him. He could practically see it coming.

"I see why you fell so hard for her."

He stopped himself midshrug, since she clearly

wasn't in the mood for dodging. "Ancient history. I know better now."

"Do you?" she asked, so pointedly he knew she must be thinking about how they had spent last night.

"It was just circumstances, Mom. It won't…"

His voice trailed off. He'd been about to say it wouldn't happen again, but he remembered how hot he'd been moments ago, just looking at her standing in the sunlight, and was a little too afraid he'd be making the vow a lie.

"Just keep yourself safe, Gideon," his mother said softly. "Your heart is so big, so generous, that it leaves you open to terrible pain when someone lets you down badly."

And she would know. He wondered, as he often had, if his mother had any hopes of her own about finding love again. But this didn't seem the time to ask. He sucked in a deep breath and let it out slowly. "I hope I'm older and wiser now."

"And some of that wisdom you got the hard way, thanks to her."

He did shrug then, because he had no answer to that.

"But—" his mother stood up as she went on "—now that I've met her, talked to her a little, I don't think it was…intentional."

His brow furrowed. "She was pretty intentional the night she told me we were done."

"I just meant not in the way it is for some women, who just like to play with emotions and go from man to man to do it."

He had to admit she was probably right about that. Sophia wasn't like that; her decisions had an entirely different source. But all he could manage to say was "Maybe not."

Isa walked over and stood right in front of him. "The end result was the same, though, and that would be hard to forgive."

She said it so fiercely that it made him smile. "Hard for me, or you?"

"Yes. Anyone hurts my children, they'll hear from me."

This time he couldn't speak because his throat was tight. She had ever and always been their fiercest defender. He swallowed, and then said softly the only thing that really mattered. "I love you, Mom."

She threw her arms around him and hugged him. "And I love you, Gideon. Ever and always."

He hugged her back, and he felt no small amount of awe and reverence for this amazing woman who had withstood more than should be asked of anyone and had had the strength to stand for them all when it seemed the world was against them.

He felt her jump when the doorbell, a chime loud enough to be heard almost anywhere in the house, rang. She gave him a worried look. He shook his head. Webber surely didn't know where they were; he also wouldn't have the gate code or be able to get past the alarms the family had set up here without triggering one. She didn't seem convinced.

"Trust me, Webber wouldn't ring the bell," he told her wryly.

She visibly suppressed a shudder. "Sometimes I hate that you have to deal with those kinds of people."

"Not my fave thing, either." She turned as if to start

for the door. "Check the camera first?" he suggested, knowing his gregarious mother's first instinct was always to just go welcome any visitor.

"Oh, of course." She turned to look at the doorbell video camera display sitting on the eye-level bookshelf. "Oh!" she repeated, this time in an entirely different tone. She sounded almost...flustered. Curious, Gideon tilted his head so he could see the screen himself.

His own eyes widened when he recognized Blue Larkspur police chief, Theodore Lawson. The man's impressive height, broad shoulders and silver hair were unmistakable. If there really was such a thing as Ezra's often-referred-to command presence, Chief Theo Lawson had it in spades.

"Well, now," he said in amusement, "there's someone who has all the right...codes."

His mother took a swipe at him, playfully but with a blush coloring her cheeks. And a new, intriguing idea occurred to him. Rachel had called the man a silver fox, which he supposed was no worse than the men who called her a blonde bombshell. But now he was wondering if perhaps his mother, who had never seemed to look at another man after Ben Colton had died—something Gideon never quite understood, after everything his father had done—might have finally recovered enough to at least be attracted to someone else.

She could hardly make a better choice than the chief.

"Didn't realize you had a date," he said, raising a brow at her.

"Don't be silly, it's not a date. I don't even know why he's here. Unless—" her gaze narrowed on him "—it's about your situation."

That, Gideon realized, was entirely possible. "Could be," he admitted.

"Then you can go to the door. I have...something to do."

She left the office and vanished down the hall toward her bedroom, leaving Gideon staring after her, puzzled. He stepped through the doorway himself and almost collided with Sophia.

"I... There's someone at the door." She sounded a bit nervous, so he hastened to reassure her.

"It's Chief Lawson," he said, nodding toward the screen on the shelf.

"Oh."

"He's probably here about Charlie's case."

Sophia looked surprised. "Personally?"

"He's that kind of guy. Hands-on. He's why when there's a job opening, Blue Larkspur PD has more applicants than they can handle."

He headed for the door quickly; the chief had already waited longer than he should have. But Gideon knew the man knew how big the house was; after all, he'd helped them choose the security system for the place. And he'd been here more than once for various things. He knew all the Colton siblings, although obviously he knew Rachel, as the DA, best, given she had the most frequent dealings with Blue Larkspur PD. And as he pulled the door open, Gideon was trying to remember how his mother had acted on the occasions the chief had been here. He couldn't. He'd have to ask Rach. She'd have noticed. She was tuned in like that.

Oblivious. That's what you are, oblivious.

"Gideon," the chief said with a nod as the door opened.

"Sorry, sir," Gideon said. "I was back in the office."

"No problem," the man said as Gideon gestured him inside. "I was in the area and thought I'd stop by and make sure you were all right and give you an update. The boy's doctor is here as well?"

"She is," he said and led the way into the family room. "No progress on Webber?"

"Not yet," Lawson said, sounding clearly unhappy about it. Gideon grimaced, not sure how he felt that they needed to stay put for the moment.

"He's got to have a hiding place somewhere," Lawson went on. "We know he has no family in the area—from what we've learned, he's estranged from what family there is."

"No surprise there," Gideon said grimly.

"No. But we'll find him. And we'll confirm this is only a domestic situation, that there's no other motive involved. I won't have a respected member of my community like the doctor a victim of unreasoning hate."

No wonder he liked the guy, Gideon thought. "Have a seat. Coffee?" he asked. "Mom just made a fresh pot."

"She's back from the ranch?" Lawson asked.

"This morning," Gideon said, trying not to think about the circumstances and what she'd almost walked in on.

And then it struck him: how and why did the man know where his mother had been? Not to mention he'd sounded almost…eager when he'd said it. But before Gideon could dwell on that, Sophia was there. He introduced them hastily. The chief shook her hand with care and gave her a rather courtly nod.

"I'm sorry you had to deal with this," he said. "Obviously Rick Webber should never have been let out on bail."

"Not your decision," Sophia said kindly, returning the nod in that equally regal way of hers.

He and Sophia went to sit in the family room while Gideon got coffee for them all. He needed a minute so he could rein in the memories of what had occurred on that same couch last night. He wondered if Sophia was remembering, too, or if she'd put it completely out of her mind.

He gave himself an extra moment, then went out with the three steaming cups.

"You said you had an update?" Gideon asked as he recovered from the little shiver that had gone through him when he handed Sophia her cup and their fingers brushed.

"I spoke to Mrs. Webber this morning," he said.

"She's awake?" Sophia asked.

He nodded. "They backed off the sedation, and she was pretty clearheaded. She confirmed what happened, that her injuries and her little boy's were directly caused by Rick Webber."

"Is she protected?" Gideon asked. The memory of how the battered woman had looked, lying helpless in that hospital bed, had taken up permanent residence in his catalog of unpleasant images.

Lawson nodded. "We've got an officer stationed there, and we will until Webber is captured." He glanced at Sophia. "Apparently it was all brought on by the boy having the gall to get sick and require your services."

Gideon saw Sophia's eyes widen. "Men like him

hate having anyone new involved with the family," he said to her, "because it heightens the likelihood they'll be found out."

"And from what our investigator has learned so far, Webber had managed to keep his true nature pretty well hidden."

"Some men can," Gideon said flatly.

He sensed rather than saw Sophia look at him. He didn't look at her. He didn't want to see sympathy in her eyes. He was long past wanting that from anyone, but especially her.

The chief only nodded. "Mrs. Webber said he was furious when he found out she took Charlie in. But she'd read enough to know his strep throat could cause serious problems if not treated."

"It can," Sophia confirmed. "Ear infections, sinus infections or worse. Like rheumatic fever, which can cause heart problems. Or a kidney disease."

"Exactly. So she went against him. And this was the result."

"But will she testify to that in court?" Gideon asked; he'd seen far too many cases where the victim was too cowed and fearful to take a stand when it came to their abuser actually being criminally prosecuted.

"That I can't say. We'll do our best to support her." He took a sip. "Your mother makes good coffee."

"Yes, she does."

The man didn't say anything more, but Gideon thought a particularly pleased look flashed across his face for a moment. Then he was back on topic. "As for Mrs. Webber, I'd say if anyone can convince her to hold strong, your sister can."

Gideon smiled. "Yes, she can." Rachel was a genuinely caring person, and as the county district attorney, she was excellent at just that—keeping uncertain witnesses steady.

Lawson studied Gideon for a moment over the rim of his coffee cup. "I'm told we owe you for the Webber boy's safety."

Gideon shrugged. Then, to his surprise, Sophia said, "He kept Charlie's father from kidnapping him right out of the hospital. And he did it without ever really striking a blow."

Gideon stared at her. She'd sounded almost…proud.

"I heard," Lawson said. Then he looked back at Gideon. "Peace through strength, I think the saying goes. I've always admired how you put that into practice."

How the hell had this become a pat-Gideon-on-the-back party?

He didn't know. All he knew for sure was that while the chief's approval pleased him, Sophia's praise rattled him. And it took some fairly stern self-lecturing to keep himself from reading into it.

And even sterner self-lecturing to remind himself why what she thought of him didn't matter anymore.

Chapter Twenty-One

Sophia had seen but never met the police chief until now. She'd always thought he had the perfect appearance and bearing for the job, and he seemed to have the ideal approach and mentality as well. But having never met him in person, she had only the slant the news coverage had given her to go by, and she knew better than to take that as gospel.

"One other thing," Lawson was saying now. "Judging by something Webber said to the clerk in that store, he thinks you're a cop."

It made sense to her; Gideon had stopped the man, so he would likely think that. But she saw Gideon's brow furrow. "What did he say?"

"He told the clerk some muscle-head cop stopped him from getting to his son." Lawson smiled, and Sophia had to admit it was a great smile. "It has to be you, because I've seen the security guard."

Gideon looked embarrassed, but he was grinning. "Thanks. I think."

Lawson nodded. "Clearly he doesn't know who you really are or why you were there. And his wife says he's not particularly computer savvy, to search you out. So

I'd say you're pretty safe to go home. He's not likely to go looking for a guy he thinks is a cop—especially one that already took him down—not when he knows we're looking for him. I'm guessing he's focused completely on finding his son at this point."

Gideon nodded. "Good. Then we can focus on keeping So—Dr. Gray-Jones safe."

The chief didn't react to the abrupt change in what he called her, but she didn't think he'd missed it. She certainly hadn't, and it was an effort not to plunge into a whirlpool of speculation about what it meant. "Yes. Here would be best, probably."

"I can't just stay here," she protested. "I have to get back to work tomorrow. I have a full day of patient appointments."

"It will only be temporary," the chief said reassuringly. "We'll have him rounded up soon."

"I will not," she said firmly, "be frightened out of doing my work. I have children depending on me."

Chief Lawson studied her for a silent moment. Sophia saw his gaze flick to Gideon for a second, then it came back to her, considering. She didn't know what he was thinking, but she had the feeling the man was probably pretty accurate when it came to assessing people.

"I can assign someone to you for protection," he finally said. "But we're a small department, and that's one less person looking for Webber."

"We'll handle it," Gideon said abruptly. "Caleb has people he uses who do security for them when they need it on cases, to protect clients or witnesses. I'll call him."

Sophia knew Gideon's brother Caleb was one of

the founding attorneys at Colton and Colton, one of the premier law offices in town. And also one of the founders of the Truth Foundation, that family-wide effort to get justice for the wrongly convicted, in part to address some of the harm Judge Colton had done. She also knew that while Gideon did what he could, setting victims up with counseling options and helping them get new starts, he'd always said he wished he could do more.

But then, Gideon always wished he could do more when it came to helping people. It was one of the reasons she'd fallen in love with him.

One of the many.

She wasn't particularly fond of this idea of having some kind of Colton guardian. But apparently she had no say, because Gideon got up, pulling out his phone as he walked over toward the glass doors she'd been looking out of when the doorbell had first rung. Owing Gideon and his family on top of...everything was hard for her to swallow.

She stole a glance at him, over by those doors. It had given her such an odd sense of peace, looking out over the hills and trees. She'd grown up amid buildings and houses and had thought this would feel isolated to her. It did, but she was realizing that isolation didn't necessarily have to be bad.

It was certainly wonderful last night, wasn't it?

She quashed the thought, but not before a burst of heat shot through her at the memories. Memories she knew she would carry forever.

But she couldn't help dwelling on how very typical of Gideon what was going on now was. Despite everything, here he was arranging for her protection. Not because he still cared for her—she was determined not to let her mind wander into that minefield—but because that's who he was. A protector. Someone who wanted the best for her. And that took a very special kind of person. Some might think social work a soft, squishy kind of job for a man, but Gideon showed that was a lie.

When he had to be strong, he was. Rick Webber had found that out, to his dismay. She almost smiled at the thought of what a shock that must have been to the abusive bully, to be stopped without even a punch thrown.

"One thing I should tell you, Doctor," the chief said, and Sophia looked from Gideon back to the man at the other end of the couch, "is that when I told Mrs. Webber you were with Charlie when his father showed up at the hospital, she was quite moved. And surprised, since you'd only seen him the one time."

"He's still one of my patients." She gave a sad little shake of her head. "And I should have realized the situation he was in then."

"With no real visible signs of anything untoward? Have superpowers then, do you?"

She blinked. Looked at this powerful man, who was smiling back at her beneficently. In this moment he reminded her of Gideon, with his talent for turning things around, putting them in a different light. And a little of her tension eased.

"That's a wonderful knack you have, Chief," she said sincerely.

"Helps when it's the truth," he answered. Then, at a sound from the opposite side of the room from where Gideon was still on the phone, his gaze shifted.

And his expression changed completely. He'd been kind to Sophia, in a very professional manner. But now something warm, welcoming and almost…wistful came into his lovely green eyes. Longing, Sophia thought suddenly.

And then Gideon's mother stepped into the room, and Sophia thought she understood. She wondered if Isadora Colton had any idea this man was in love with her.

"Thanks, Caleb."

"It'll probably be better, actually. Our guy won't have any of the restrictions a cop might."

"Good point." Gideon liked the sound of that, having private protraction dedicated only to keeping Sophia safe. Thankfully, Caleb had someone he trusted and had used before.

"How soon do you want him?"

"Tomorrow's fine. We'll hunker down here at Mom's until morning, then I'll take her to her office and your guy can take over."

"No problem," his brother said.

But then, that's what Caleb always said when it came to his family. After their father's ignoble fall from grace, Caleb had stepped up in a way few would. He'd put everyone else's needs first, at no small cost to himself. And then, when they hadn't needed him quite so much, he'd thrown that ferocious energy into the Truth Foundation. That after a marriage and a couple of relationships that had fallen victim to his dedication to those things, Caleb had apparently found happiness with, of all people, the cousin of his ex-wife, was a relief to them all.

"How's Nadine?" Caleb had recently gotten engaged to the activist and jewelry maker after he'd helped prove an oil company was trying to take advantage of her ailing father. He endured his brother's enthusiastic words with a wry smile touched with a bit of longing. He didn't begrudge Caleb; how could he, after the way he'd stepped up when his younger siblings had needed him? But still, it made him feel even more lost, at least on the relationship front.

"You heard from any of the triplets lately?" he asked briskly when Caleb wound down.

"Our world wanderers? Yeah, I talked to Dom a couple of days ago. He's on an assignment, as usual. But he mentioned he'd talked to Ezra. Apparently he's getting leave soon and plans on heading home for a while."

"Well, that's good news. I'll tell Mom."

"Do that. With," Caleb added in his most lawyerly tone, "the proviso that something could always happen to mess it up."

"Of course," Gideon said. All the siblings had banded together to protect their mother from any more pain in her life whenever they could. They all felt it was the least they could do after all she'd done for them.

He thought of her reaction to Chief Lawson, and his to her, and wondered if he should bring up the subject. Maybe one of his siblings had noticed something as well.

Or maybe he should just keep his mouth shut; he was obviously not an expert about such things.

When the call ended and he walked back to the seating area around the fireplace, he saw his mother had taken the chair directly opposite Chief Lawson. And that she had changed clothes. Pretty duded up, as Jasper would say, for a casual Sunday afternoon at home. She was wearing her favorite, she said most flattering, sweater, one that Naomi had bought for her in Los Angeles because it perfectly matched her eyes. She had put on earrings, the ones he himself had bought for her on a trip to Denver last year.

But most noticeable was the color in her cheeks as she stole the occasional glance at the man sitting across from her.

Her reaction when she'd realized who was at the door came back to him, and once more the question rose in his mind. And he realized he was hoping it was true. Above all she deserved to be happy again.

After the chief took his leave a while later, and his mother took an inordinately long time walking him to the door, Gideon was trying to figure out how to broach the subject when Sophia did it for him.

"He's a very impressive man," she said to his mother.

"He is," Mom agreed, and that quickly, the color returned in her cheeks.

"I think we need to talk, Mom," Gideon said, eyebrows raised.

"No, we don't," she said, a little too hastily. "We're just friends, that's all. He's been very helpful to us all, Gideon, you know that."

"Yes, he has. He's a rock-solid, good guy."

"Yes. Excuse me, I need to…do something."

She disappeared back toward her office with the air of someone escaping an awkward situation.

"Interesting," Sophia said neutrally.

"Yes," Gideon said, still looking toward where his mother had vanished so hastily. "Especially given what she assumed I meant."

"Nice trick," Sophia said.

"I have them," he said. He'd learned a lot of tricks over the years, to get the information he needed out of sometimes less-than-cooperative people. Amazing what people sometimes gave away if you got them talking about something else.

"I know," Sophia said softly. Then, as if she regretted the words, or perhaps the memories they called up, she went on quickly, "Would you be all right with it if there was something going on between them?"

"I'd love it," he said bluntly, without looking at her. "We all would. We'd love to see her in a good, solid, happy relationship again. After all she's done, and everything she sacrificed for us, she's certainly earned it."

"And you'd be all right with Chief Lawson?"

"I would. I think we all would." He shifted his gaze to the picture wall. "I think he probably knows even more than we do about all the crap that happened. And he also knows, and has made it a point that my mother know, how utterly innocent of it all she was. He's the real deal, the kind of man we thought our father was."

"So you think she needs to move on?"

Then he did look at her. Straight on, letting her read whatever she wanted into his expression and his words. "Like the rest of us? Yes, she does. We all have to, at one time or another."

He saw pain flash in her eyes for a moment. He

truly hadn't intended his words to hurt her, but he couldn't deny he found it very interesting that they apparently did.

Chapter Twenty-Two

Sophia retreated outside after that painful exchange. And no amount of telling herself she didn't deserve anything better, that he'd probably been wise to remind her that last night hadn't meant a rekindling of a relationship between them, helped her feel better. They'd merely made the mistake of giving in to the tremendous chemistry between them. The chemistry that made them combustible with a glance, or the slightest touch.

It had been her mother who had told her that kind of thing inevitably burned out. That no matter how physically attractive you found someone, it would pale eventually. She'd wanted to ask her if that's what had happened with her and Sophia's father, why they were so…reserved with each other, but she hadn't had the nerve. Not after what had happened as a child when she'd asked why she and Father—which she was always required to call him—never hugged or kissed like her friends' parents did. The resultant banishment to her room for her impertinence had left a lasting impression. Not so much because of the punishment, but because it had been the first time she'd realized they might love her, because they felt as her parents they must, but they didn't like her much. At least, they seemed happiest when she was out of their way.

She heard the door open behind her. To her surprise, it was Isa, carrying her heavy jacket.

"It's chilly out here. You should have this on."

"I... Thank you."

"You should have Gideon take you for a walk around. It's lovely here, even this time of year. In another month it will be glorious, with spring coming."

"I'm so used to living in the city, I never realized how soothing a place like this could be."

"You want soothing, you need Gideon's place," Isa said with a smile. "But then, you probably know that."

"I haven't been there. And I doubt I will be." Sophia drew in a breath and turned to face her. "I don't want to hurt him again any more than you want him hurt. I've already done enough damage."

"Hmm," the older woman said. "What do you want, then?"

"What I can't have." The words were out before she could stop them. What was it about these Coltons that invited such foolish confidences? "What about you?" she asked abruptly, not caring at the moment if the evasion was obvious. "What do you want?"

"For my children to be happy, of course."

Happy. Such a simple wish. And one she doubted either of her parents had ever held for her. No, they wanted from her, not *for* her. Obedience, success and hopefully a little renown that would reflect favorably on them.

"And you?" She smiled, the encouraging smile she

sometimes gave patients. "You seemed quite happy when Chief Lawson was here."

"It's nice to have company," Isa said, not quite achieving the casual, breezy tone Sophia guessed she'd been trying for.

"He's a very handsome man."

Isa's cheeks turned pink, and Sophia was fairly sure it wasn't the chill or the very slight breeze. Then the door opened behind them.

"Oh, good, Gideon, you can take Sophia for a tour around the property. Get a little exercise while I go finish up some things."

She was gone before either of them could respond.

"Interesting talk?" Gideon asked, sounding wary.

"Your ears shouldn't have been burning too much," Sophia said. "We talked about having space like this," she said, gesturing to the expanse before them.

"It was a great place to grow up, most of the time. But it's a lot of work for her." He looked back toward the house. "Sometimes I worry she's only keeping it for us. Like it's some sort of shrine to better days or something."

How like him, to worry about that. She decided to plunge ahead. "We also talked about the chief's visit. You know, she does really like him. I think with a little of the right kind of encouragement…"

"We've all told her we'd be all right with her…moving on."

"Maybe she needs more than just knowing you'd be all right with it. Maybe she needs to know you'd actually like it, that you want her to."

"Counseling now, are you?"

She sucked in a breath and said as steadily as she could, "Just because I made a mess of my own life doesn't mean I can't help others not make the same mistakes I did."

He just looked at her, and for once she couldn't tell what he was thinking. He'd definitely learned to hide his thoughts, and the idea that she'd forced that on him made her stomach churn.

"Let's go for that tour," he said abruptly.

They walked in silence for the most part, except when he would point something out, like the high spot on the property where they could see anyone coming, and the low spot where in the spring a pond usually developed. There was even a point where the house was out of sight, and if you didn't know you could think you were all alone, with no one else around for miles. She wasn't sure how she felt about that—it was such a strange feeling for her.

"It's beautiful," she finally said. "So peaceful."

"Mmm" was all he said.

They reached what he said was the property line. She stood for a moment looking up at the mountains not too far in the distance. And thought that she'd missed more than she'd ever realized by always living in the city, amid the crowd.

"I WANT TO go see Mrs. Webber."

Gideon looked up from his meal, a plate full of various dishes from the most popular Italian restaurant in town. His mother had gone to pick it up—saying with a charming laugh that they'd all be better off than if she tried to cook dinner for them.

"Now?" he asked, sounding a bit like one of her young patients about to get a shot.

She did want to go now. She also wanted to go home. She needed to be away from him, so she could get a grip on these thoughts she was having. She thought she had relegated her feelings about Gideon to a "might have been" space in her mind, but clearly her heart— and her body—had other ideas.

But realistically she knew none of that was going to happen. Especially the dealing with her emotions for the man sitting across from her.

"In the morning will be fine," she said neutrally. "And since my car is still at the hospital, I can see her and then pick it up."

He went back to eating, but with a thoughtful expression. After he downed the big bite of lasagna, he nodded. "All right. We'll go there first, then I can follow you over to your office, where Caleb's approved security expert will be. I need to see Mrs. Webber anyway, to discuss Charlie." He gave her a sideways look. "Maybe you can vouch for me with her, since she doesn't know me."

Was he thinking she wouldn't? No matter what the situation between them, one thing she never doubted was his dedication to his work. And she'd seen it up close and personal now. She would vouch for him on that front to anyone, anytime.

"Of course," she said, and left it at that.

She watched—and, to be honest, envied—the ease between Gideon and his mother as together they cleaned up the dishes and debris from dinner. They chatted easily, with Isa asking him questions that indicated she was both knowledgeable about and interested in his life in general. She was filled with that odd wistfulness again. She knew there were parents like this, had known ever since she'd chosen pediatrics as her life's work. She'd just never realized it could continue into adulthood, that loving, caring kind of bond. And she felt an old, familiar ache, wondering if she would ever have the children she wanted so much, children she could have this kind of relationship with, for a lifetime.

Children she could only picture herself having with a man like Gideon.

No, *with* Gideon. An option she no longer had.

"You're very...comfortable together," she said after Isa had excused herself for the evening.

Gideon finished wiping his hands on the towel by the sink, then turned to look at her. "With Mom? Yes." His brow furrowed slightly. "Why wouldn't I be?"

She couldn't think of a way to explain that didn't sound pitiful, so she didn't answer at all. While she might deserve his pity for throwing away what they'd had, that didn't mean she liked it.

He walked around the kitchen counter, into the family room area. The room where they'd spent last night, naked in each other's arms, driving each other mad in that way she'd never experienced with anyone else. She remembered how she'd been so surprised by that, not only that the kind, gentle social worker was capable of wild, but how she herself responded in kind, in a way she would never have thought herself capable of.

And had only ever been with this man.

She stood staring at the couch, remembering. Envisioning.

Wanting.

It could not happen again. Not because she didn't want it to—she wanted that more than anything in this moment.

But because she didn't think she could deal with the aftermath. Because she knew what it would be.

This time he would walk away from her. And she would deserve it.

Chapter Twenty-Three

"Good night," Sophia said abruptly, and, without looking at him, she headed for the guest room.

He watched her go. Silently. Because he couldn't think of anything to say that didn't hearken back to the last time she'd walked away.

He'd thought, a couple of times since he'd walked into Charlie's hospital room, that she regretted that last time. She'd never said it in so many words, but…

And there you go again, idiot. Stop looking for signs that aren't there and read the ones that are.

First and foremost, clearly she thought last night had been a mistake. And maybe she was right. It was difficult for him to classify such a…transcendent experience as a mistake, but in the bigger picture, that of moving on, he supposed it was.

Obviously she hadn't changed her mind about them.

He felt a sudden, harsh jolt. Had he been hoping she would? Had he, down deep, wanted her to? And if so…why? Because he wanted her back? So she could dump him all over again when she decided once more they wouldn't work together? That she didn't want him?

Now, if he wanted her back so he could dump her

in turn, that he could understand. He could even picture it, using the same words she'd used, maybe. Just to drive the point home.

But even as the image formed in his mind he discarded it. It just wasn't in his playbook, to intentionally hurt someone, even as payback. Oh, he'd punch back if someone threw one—depending on who and why—but hurt in the emotionally, heart-wrenching way she had hurt him? No. He didn't want that on his conscience.

That damned conscience they had all inherited. Probably, their brother Gavin had once observed, they all got their father's, since he hadn't been using it.

Disgusted with the whole thing, and the churning thoughts it brought on, he snapped off the family room lights with more vigor than required for one little switch. And he headed down the hall to the room, his childhood bedroom, he'd intended to use last night but had never reached.

He didn't bother to turn on the lights once inside with the door closed. The last thing he wanted to do was see himself reflected in the dresser mirror. Not considering how many times after she'd ended it that he'd stood in front of a mirror staring at the idiot looking back at him and called him every synonym for stupid he could think of. Hell, he'd moved out of that damned apartment half to get away from that mirror. And all the memories tied to that place, of the first time he'd brought her there. The first time they'd spent an evening there, doing something as simple as watching a movie and snacking, and it had seemed so special because it was her.

The first time they'd made love in his bedroom.

Yeah, that's a good thing to be thinking about now.

Veering away from the thought that he feared would bring on dreams he didn't want to deal with, he instead focused on what needed to be done tomorrow, after he was free of Sophia's presence. He'd check up on Charlie—he needed to pick up some treats for Milo first—and see how he was settling in. Then he'd go to the office and catch up on the paperwork. And depending on when he got word—hopefully maybe even in the morning—that Rick Webber was again in custody, he would have Caleb call off his very discreet and inconspicuous guard. After that expert told Sophia she could resume life as usual. Not like Gideon needed to tell her himself. In fact, he'd be better off if he didn't lay eyes on her again, maybe even until whatever hearing there might be on Charlie's situation.

And after that?

After that, if he was lucky, he'd never cross paths with her again.

"It's all right, Mrs. Webber," Sophia said gently to the woman, who was looking at Gideon warily. "This is Gideon Colton, the man who's seeing to Charlie's welfare and safety." She glanced at Gideon, then went back to the woman as she added, with as much sincerity as she could pump into her voice, "You can trust him. He'll do whatever it takes to keep your son safe."

Ellen's expression changed—at least, it appeared to under the bruises and swelling. She shifted her gaze to Gideon. "You're the one who kept him away from Charlie?"

Sophia wondered how she'd heard. One of the staff

must have been talking. She'd noticed the sideways looks Gideon had gotten when they'd arrived—some curious, some smiling, some downright admiring.

And a few speculative, as if they were wondering if he was single.

That stabbed at her much deeper than it should have.

Gideon had looked surprised at the woman's question, but after a moment he nodded. Ellen studied him for a moment longer before saying assessingly, "You look like you could."

"He did," Sophia said, unable to stop the note of pride that crept into her voice. "It was as smooth as silk. And he would do the same for you, if necessary." As she said it, she knew it was completely true. Gideon would stand for this woman as he'd stood for her son. Her own words came back to her. *Strong enough to fight, yet cool enough to only do it to protect.*

Gideon never even looked at her, but kept his gaze on Charlie's mother. "He's safe now, Mrs. Webber. He's with some friends of mine who have dealt with men like your husband before. They'll protect Charlie."

She grimaced, then winced when it clearly hurt her bruised face. "He's got ways, friends… We've tried to leave before, a couple of times, to go to the city shelter, but he always found out." She hesitated.

"Go ahead, Ellen," he said gently, somehow knowing when to shift to her first name.

"He's got a friend who works…somewhere official. I don't know who, but somebody he grew up with, went to school with. I think maybe that's how he knows those things."

Sophia saw Gideon draw back, just slightly. "I'll

look into that," he promised. "But for now, you're safe here and Charlie's safe with my friends. They're not part of the city system." He smiled at the woman, that kind, genuine smile Sophia remembered so well. "Let me tell you about Milo."

Sophia listened as he told the woman about the affable, loving yet protective dog, and how Charlie had reacted to him. He did it in a chatty, normal way that had what she was certain was the desired effect: calming Charlie's mother to the point where she even smiled a little, despite the obvious pain it caused her. There was no doubt she loved her little boy—not given the beating she'd taken trying to protect him.

And then he pulled out his phone and showed her a short video, obviously taken by one of the Knights, showing Charlie playing with Milo. Smiling. And laughing. And Ellen Webber cried at the sight of her happy child.

"Charlie is safe," Gideon repeated. "But you need to think about that for yourself, too."

"I…" The woman's voice faded away, and it was the saddest, most weary thing Sophia had heard in a long time.

"I know it's hard," Gideon said, just as gently as he had to her child, "but whatever your husband has told you, whether it's you owe him, or you wouldn't get by without him because you're not smart enough, not pretty enough—" Ellen's reaction to his words showed he'd hit a strong chord, and Sophia realized he knew exactly what methods abusers like Rick Webber used "—whatever trick he used to keep you with him is just to control you, keep you beaten down, probably emotionally at first, but now physically, too."

"He... But he's right."

Sophia's throat tightened at the broken words.

"He's wrong," Gideon said firmly. "It's a lie, Ellen. A lie he likely tells because that's how *he* feels, not smart enough, not good-looking enough. And controlling you and Charlie is how he makes himself feel better."

Something flickered in Ellen's eyes then, as if that idea had registered. It didn't last, but it had been there. And clearly Gideon saw it, too, because he homed in.

"When you've had enough, Ellen, which I hope is now, for your sake and Charlie's, there's help. I'll get it for you, but you have to decide that you've had enough, that you deserve better. That your son deserves better."

"I'm not strong enough," she whispered.

"Then let someone else be strong for you until you are," Gideon said quietly, putting a gentle hand over hers. "I'll get you started. You only have to ask."

The flicker that came and went in Ellen Webber's eyes then was hope. And Sophia had to swallow past the knot that tightened her throat at the wonder this man was.

"You will look into what she said, about him having a friend who works somewhere official?" Sophia asked a little anxiously as they left, nodding in thanks to the uniformed officer stationed outside the hospital room door.

"Yes. And if it's true, if someone's knowingly been giving out confidential information from the women's shelter, they will regret it."

She heard the ring of steel in his voice, and it gave her an odd sort of shiver, half appreciation and admiration for his strength and determination, and half a longing for those things she no longer had a right to.

"They're lucky to have you on their side," she said, meaning it with all her heart. The heart that had shied away when she'd had the chance to have that steady, unwavering strength as part of her life. He would have been just as solidly there for her, whatever the situation. She knew that now. Now, when it was too late.

She tried to steady herself by thinking about the day's work ahead as they walked out to where she had parked her car yesterday, and Gideon had parked his when they'd arrived this morning. She was glad it was crisp and cold out—she needed it to keep from yawning after her sleepless night. Well, not entirely sleepless, but what sleep she'd gotten certainly hadn't been restful. Not when it was so colorfully painted with images from the time she'd spent in such an amazing, incredible way with the man walking silently beside her.

Oddly, it wasn't any easier when she was in her car alone, driving the short distance to her office. And it wasn't just because every time she looked in her rearview mirror and saw him, clearly recognizable behind the wheel of his blue SUV, her pulse kicked up all over again.

Again she tried to focus, thinking about her first appointment of the day. A follow-up on a thirteen-year-old girl who, coincidentally, had had a case of strep throat, one worse than Charlie's. Gideon pulled in beside her, and as he'd instructed her—there was no other way to describe it—she stayed in her vehicle until he was there, opening the door for her.

"Caleb said the guy he sent over, Steve Renquist, is ex-military. Served with our brother Ezra for a while."

"Okay." She didn't know what else to say. And felt ridiculous when her true response would have been *I'd rather have you.*

"You'll have somebody with you all the time until Webber's back in custody." One corner of her mouth tightened, but she only nodded.

Oh, she could live with an unknown guard. She could even live with it until this case was finally resolved, if she had to.

Next to living without Gideon, that should be easy.

Chapter Twenty-Four

Gideon leaned back in his chair, tapping a finger idly on his desk. He stared at the computer screen, knowing he should be finishing this update on the Webber case. The office was quiet this early Monday morning, but he knew that wouldn't last for long. The usual hustle and bustle would start any minute now, making it harder to focus.

That's it, blame it on the office. That's why you can't keep your silly brain on track.

His computer chimed the arrival of an email. Glad of the distraction, he went for it immediately. And sat forward when he saw it was from the police department, the records he'd requested on Rick Webber. He was a little surprised they'd arrived this quickly and wondered if perhaps Chief Lawson had put in a word.

That question was answered when he opened the email and saw the chief had been copied on it. He suppressed a smile—barely—at the memory of his usually unflappable mother getting so flustered when she realized who was at their door yesterday. Could there really be something going on there? Something with potential? He hoped so. He'd meant what he'd said, that he and all his siblings would be delighted to see Isa not just content, but happy again.

But right now he focused on this new information. Scanned Webber's record, which consisted of a couple of drunk-in-public charges and one minor assault charge stemming from a bar brawl a couple of years ago at the Corner Pocket. Nothing surprising or unexpected there; he apparently ran true to type. And it was interesting that when he'd made a stop at a convenience store, it had been the one near the billiard hall. Familiar territory? Stomping grounds? He looked back at the drunk arrests and found one of them had also taken place in that vicinity.

Once is happenstance, twice is coincidence, three times is enemy action.

The old saying Ezra had quoted to him once popped into his mind. He'd have to make sure that got checked out. Who knew who might know the guy—and where he might go to lie low—around there?

He kept going through the record, further back.

A friend who works somewhere official. Somebody he grew up with, went to school with.

That implied a relationship that had started precollege, didn't it? So he went further back, saw that Rick Webber had graduated from Blue Larkspur High School and made note of the year. Then he made a call to Detective Benitez.

"No sign of Webber yet," the man opened with.

"I figured, or I would have heard."

"I'm about to head out to talk to some people, find out if anyone has seen him."

"Around the Corner Pocket, maybe?"

"Absolutely." He could almost see Benitez grin. He should have known the detective would be on top of it. "I saw the same record you did. Everybody safe?"

"So far. Listen, Mrs. Webber mentioned something this morning that might be useful." He barely stopped himself from saying he and Sophia had gone to see her together.

"I was about to go interview her. She still pretty scared?"

"Yes, but more worried about Charlie."

"Good. What did she say?"

Gideon relayed the information. "It's only a suspicion on her part, but it would explain how he knew when she went to one of the women's shelters twice before."

"That," Benitez said with barely disguised anger, "should land whoever it was in jail for a long, long time."

"Indeed it should."

"I suppose she has no idea who?"

"None. But he graduated from Blue Larkspur High School over a decade ago. I was wondering if you could run a name check, student names from that class, against city and county employees."

"Good idea, Colton. Ever thought of being a cop?" Humor echoed in the man's voice, but it vanished in the next moment when he said, clearly away from the phone, "Morning, Chief."

He could hear the deep voice that was fresh in his mind from yesterday. "That Gideon Colton? On the Webber case?"

"Yes, sir," Benitez said politely. All the force had

tremendous respect for the man, Gideon knew, because he wasn't afraid to get out in the field with his officers—in fact, he made a point of it.

"Give him whatever he needs."

"Yes, sir," Benitez repeated.

"In fact, let me talk to him."

Gideon barely had time to brace himself before that big voice boomed in his ear. Interesting, how different he sounded now, on the job, than he had yesterday, in Mom's home.

"Mrs. Webber all right?"

"Yes, sir," he echoed Benitez.

"And the doctor?"

He took a quick breath and got out evenly enough, "Fine. I dropped her off at her office about an hour ago, and my brother's man was there."

"She seems a lovely woman."

I can't argue with that. "Yes, sir."

The man chuckled, and Gideon had no idea if it was his continued sir-ing or the inadequate response to Sophia's obvious beauty.

"Speaking of lovely women, how is your mother?"

After what he—and Sophia—had seen yesterday, Gideon wondered if this was more than just a casual inquiry. The tone of his voice was certainly different than when he'd been talking about the Webber case.

Gideon answered carefully, hoping he didn't somehow say the wrong thing. "As lovely on the inside as the outside."

"I've noticed that," the chief said, and there was a new softness in his voice that was unmistakable.

"She was very happy to see you yesterday," Gideon

said, still feeling his way warily; he didn't want to be the one to ruin this by saying something stupid. Whatever "this" might be or had the potential to be.

"I'm glad to hear that." More of that softness, and warmth.

What the hell, Gideon thought, and went for it. "You should stop by now and then. She'd love to see you."

"I might just do that. Maybe this evening. Thanks." Then, clearly to Benitez, he added, "Keep me posted on the case."

"Of course, sir," Benitez said amid the rustling as he took the phone back. "What was all that about?" he asked after a moment, when Gideon guessed he was making sure the chief couldn't hear.

"I'm not sure," Gideon said, and it was the honest truth.

"Strange," Benitez said. "I'll get back to you if I find anything on those names."

"Thanks," Gideon said, and when the call ended, he sat silently, facing his computer screen but not really seeing it because he was focused inward, wondering how he'd really feel if his mother and the chief…

He gave a sharp shake of his head, made a mental note to give his siblings a heads-up—maybe between them all, they could encourage this—then grimaced at the next thought that popped into his head. He wished Sophia had had a passel of siblings to do the same back when they'd been together. If she had, maybe she would have hung on, and both their lives would be very different today.

If, if, if… Better you should be remembering she didn't even try.

Chapter Twenty-Five

Except for the presence of the gruff, laconic body-guard in the office, it felt almost like a normal day. Better yet, Sophia thought, all her patients were normal cases, children with loving parents concerned about their well-being. Two were brought in by their fathers, both of whom obviously doted on their little ones. That did a lot to restore the faith that had been sadly rattled by the encounter with Charlie's father. One of them was particularly good at calming his understandably cranky little girl, in a way that reminded her of Gideon.

And there he was again, invading her thoughts as he had been all day long. It was beyond foolish to imagine that the night they'd spent together could have changed anything. Spectacular though it had been, it didn't change the simple fact that she had hurt him, badly.

I don't want him hurt like that ever again.

Isa Colton's words echoed in her head, as they had been doing ever since she'd heard them. They caused such a tangle of emotions, from wonder at a mother who so genuinely felt that way, protective of her son's feelings—her own mother had barely acknowledged Sophia had feelings, and had usually confined her to her room with the admonition to learn how to control them—and a deep, painful regret that she had been the cause of that hurt.

She had a break in the schedule midday, and since she seemed to have no appetite for lunch, she thought she might go back to the hospital and check on Mrs. Webber. She wished she could visit Charlie, see how he was doing. And that brought Gideon back into her mind, not that he was ever gone for long. But perhaps he could arrange for her to meet with the boy. Obviously keeping the child's location secret from his father was paramount, but there had to be a way.

She walked out of her office to the reception area and was startled back to reality when Steve Renquist, the muscular security expert with the reddish hair and neatly trimmed beard, was immediately at her side. She nearly laughed out loud; she'd pictured herself strolling the short distance to the hospital alone, enjoying the crisp air. As if somehow during her time at the Colton house, she'd been infected with the desire to be outside more. She'd completely forgotten her bodyguard.

"So how does this work if I need to, say, go to the market?"

"I go with you, Doctor," he said politely.

"And when I go home?"

"I follow you and maintain watch." One corner of his mouth twitched. "I won't be moving in, if that's what you're worried about."

"Not worried, just wondering."

"He'll have to come from outside, so outside I'll be."

She couldn't help smiling. "That was almost poetic."

She could see she'd startled him, because she got

a smile back. "No wonder," he said, almost under his breath.

"No wonder what?"

"Nothing," he said quickly. "Where do you need to go now?"

She smothered a sigh. "Nowhere, really. I was just… restless."

"Time for lunch?" her receptionist asked from behind her. The young woman gave Renquist a sideways glance. Of interest? Sophia didn't know—she didn't trust her own judgment in that arena anymore. Although it had been pretty clear with Gideon's mother and the chief yesterday.

"If you don't mind, Alicia, let's lock up and order in," she said. "I've got work I can do."

"I don't mind at all," the woman said quickly with another look at the guard, whose presence she had quickly accepted—welcomed?—once Sophia had explained what was going on, and Sophia thought maybe her judgment wasn't as bad as she'd assumed.

Except about yourself.

She went back to her office, closed the door quietly, sat down and rested her elbows on her desk. Then she let her head drop into her hands. She felt more exhausted than she had in recent memory, and she didn't try to kid herself that it was solely Charlie's situation, or the encounter with his father. No, it was the man who had kept that encounter from becoming a disaster.

You're so patient about everything; how do you do that?

I leave it all in the gym.

The fragment of a longer discussion came back to

her now. It had given rise to the realization that his workouts were for more than just staying in that amazing shape, more than maintaining that ability to intimidate by power alone. They were to take the edge off, to maintain that calm that had initially seemed effortless to her. She had grown up with a man who never bothered to sublimate his irritation with anyone or anything. In fact, Harold Jones had seemed to think it his duty to let everyone know where they'd gone wrong.

Her father didn't have to get physical to be the most daunting human being she had ever known. His scowl was generally enough to cow the most recalcitrant opponent. Gideon, on the other hand, was bigger, physically more imposing, yet had that gentle manner about him that made children trust him, despite his size.

The gentle manner that would make her father think he would be easily intimidated. But she knew Gideon had a solid, steady core, and while he would give where it would help, he would not be pushed around. And not for the first time she wondered how an encounter between the two of them would come out. Gideon had more spine beneath that quiet exterior than any man she'd ever met. The very thought of anyone staring down her father had always seemed preposterous, but Gideon might just outlast him.

She smothered a sigh and rubbed at weary eyes. That encounter would never happen.

An image from this morning formed in her mind, of Gideon with Ellen Webber. His approach had been different than with Charlie. With the scared little boy, he'd been gentle and protective. With the woman, scared but an adult, he'd been supportive, encouraging and, most importantly, he had reached her. And she knew that if Ellen found the courage to try, Gideon would be there for her. More importantly, Ellen knew it.

You only have to ask.

GIDEON HADN'T MET Steve Renquist before, but apparently the man had heard about him, from Ezra and then Caleb.

"You're Gideon, the do-gooder," he said when Gideon arrived at Sophia's office midafternoon, unable to find any more busywork to distract him. Renquist added with a slight smile, "And that's meant in the best, most literal way. According to Ezra."

Gideon blinked. "Ezra said that?"

"He said of all of you, you're the one who's probably done the most direct and hands-on good to balance out your father."

"I... Wow. I never knew he thought that."

He felt oddly embarrassed. Not because of the mention of Ben Colton and the reminder that what he'd done was common knowledge. They'd all had nearly twenty years to get past that, or maybe just grow tougher skin over the wound.

He intentionally summoned up the memory of the day their mother had announced, around the huge table where she'd called a family meeting the last time they'd all been home at the same time, how proud she was of them. Because that day while in town, she'd met with a client who had come to her graphics firm because of the Truth Foundation, not in spite of what their father had done.

So it wasn't that he was embarrassed about. Maybe

it was at getting this compliment secondhand, knowing he'd been a topic of discussion. When Ezra got home, he might just have to have a little talk with his big brother.

"Doesn't surprise me you didn't," Renquist said. "He's not the most talkative guy around."

Gideon smiled at that. "I've noticed."

The young receptionist approached them tentatively. They both turned to look at her, and her cheeks colored. She glanced at Renquist, then focused on Gideon. "I've let her know you're here, Mr. Colton. She should be done in just a couple of minutes."

"Thank you." He'd confirmed Sophia's last appointment was at 2:00 p.m., figured a half hour for that and then an hour for her to wind things up, so he had walked in at three thirty. Seemed his timing was good.

The woman stole another glance at Renquist, the sort of up-from-under-lowered-lashes thing that Rachel had once told him meant interest. Renquist smiled back. Gideon couldn't tell if there was any returned interest there, but then the guy was a pro. Still...

When Sophia emerged, she appeared ready to go. She smiled at Renquist, but not at him, Gideon noticed. Then she turned to the receptionist. "You'll lock up for me?"

"Of course."

"Thank you. And why don't you take off as soon as the day's entries are done?"

"Thank you, Doctor," the young woman said brightly. With another glance at Renquist, Gideon noticed.

Sophia shifted her gaze back to Gideon. Her expression was unreadable, and her voice carefully neutral when she spoke. "Would it be possible for me to see Charlie now?"

Gideon frowned. He wasn't surprised she wanted to see the boy. He knew she was dedicated to her work.

"If it's not possible—"

"It's not that," he said, "I'm just figuring logistics. I don't think we should go to my mom's house. We've worked too hard to keep that location a secret. But maybe a neutral, secure location. Maybe Tim or Stephanie could bring him someplace safe where you could meet."

"Not out in public," Renquist recommended. "Not with Webber on the loose."

"Agreed," Gideon said. "Not as long as there's even a chance he might be close enough to follow us." He thought a moment. "I wonder..."

He took out his phone and made a call to Detective Benitez. He explained what he needed, and the man immediately suggested they come to the station, where they could use the chief's meeting room. "I know the chief will okay it. He's pretty clear about you getting free rein."

Well, that was interesting. "Thank him for me."

He then called the Knights. They agreed to bring Charlie to the station in half an hour. When he hung up, he looked at Renquist, who nodded approvingly.

"Good idea," he said.

"I've got it from here," he told the bodyguard then. "After this meeting at the police department, we'll be heading out to my place," Gideon went on, ignoring for the moment that he sensed Sophia stiffen, "since we're fairly certain Webber doesn't know who I am or where I live."

Renquist shook his head. "I'll still be around."

"You know where?"

"Yes," Renquist said. "Caleb gave me the location when he gave me the case."

"Then why don't you at least take a break—" he managed not to glance at the receptionist, but barely "—and then head out there later." *Somebody might as well get something good out of this mess.*

Renquist looked doubtful for a moment. "I'm supposed to be on the doctor 24/7 until Webber's in custody."

"We'll be at the police station," Gideon pointed out. "I doubt he'll risk that. Give you time to eat, at least. A nice long dinner somewhere."

"I'll have to verify with Caleb, but all right," Renquist finally agreed, and when he gave Alicia a glance, Gideon thought he was right that there was something there.

Too bad you were wrong thinking you saw something more than just a spark with Sophia.

Chapter Twenty-Six

Charlie already looked much improved. Not just because the swelling on his face, which Sophia inspected and assessed carefully, had receded, but because he seemed happier. Relaxed, even. Clearly he already felt safe with the Knights.

But he was still worried, made clear by the first thing he asked her. "Is my mom okay?"

"She's better," Sophia said. "We saw her this morning, and she's awake and of course worried about you."

The little boy sighed deeply. "It's my fault. I made him mad. I shouldn'ta got sick."

Sophia felt a little clench of pain in her chest at his woebegone tone. "It is not your fault. None of this is."

"He told me it was. That I was bad."

She had no idea what to say except to deny it again. For all his coldness, her father had never gone that far. Of course, to say she was inherently bad might reflect on him. She hated that her mind had even gone there when she should be focused on Charlie. But then Gideon was there, again crouching down to be at the boy's eye level.

"I know it's very hard to believe your father is

wrong," he said, and it struck Sophia that that was much truer than Charlie knew, for Gideon. "But tell me about Milo."

At the mention of the dog, the boy brightened considerably. "He's out in the car, with Amy," the boy said, mentioning the Knights' daughter. "I got to ride here in the back seat with him. He even has his own seat belt fastened to his harness."

In the back, Sophia thought, recalling the SUV she'd seen pull up. With the tinted windows making it nearly impossible to see someone in that back seat area. And Gideon had told her the police would be watching the area around the station closely for the next hour. Obviously the Knights, and Gideon, were both experienced at this kind of situation.

"You like Milo, right?" Charlie nodded fiercely. "And he likes you."

"I think so," the boy said, with a glance at Mrs. Knight.

"Oh, he does," she assured him. "A lot."

"Then there you are," Gideon said cheerfully. "You see, Milo only likes good people."

That simply, the boy's expression cleared. And Sophia's vision blurred slightly as moisture pooled in her eyes. Gideon Colton was indeed an incredible man. And Charlie seemed to know it, too, because a while later he gave him a fierce hug before he and the Knights, escorted by Detective Benitez, left to go back to their vehicle. No doubt with Charlie safely out of sight in the back, with the loving Milo.

"You are a truly amazing man, Gideon Colton," Sophia said quietly when they'd gone.

He only shrugged. She guessed her praise didn't mean much to him anymore. And she fought against her own inner protests that the incredible night they'd spent together had to mean something.

"So amazing you scared me," she said softly, surprised at herself.

That got his attention. "Scared you?"

"You were different. From any man I'd ever dated, or even met. You just…gave." She'd never really told him this, perhaps because she hadn't really realized it until after she'd lost him, but he'd certainly earned it now. "I've always had to…earn love or affection from the men in my life. Accept that all I would ever get were tiny bits here and there. Especially with my father, who doles out praise as if it were costing him millions. And love…well, pretty much not at all."

He studied her for a long, silent moment. "Maybe," he said, his voice almost inflectionless, "you should think about why you kept dating men like your father."

That silenced her. Her mind had skittered around that idea for some time now, as if she knew it was accurate but didn't want to face that fact. She was deep into pondering that as they walked back out to his car. So deep she'd almost forgotten the startling thing he'd said about where they were going. His place? But before she could bring up the rather peremptory assumption, he spoke again, with a tone of simple curiosity in his voice.

"Did your father even want kids?"

"I…" She stopped, then plunged ahead with something she'd never voiced, even to herself. "I'm not sure, but maybe only if they reflected well on him. I didn't, so they stopped with me."

He stopped in his tracks, staring at her. "He doesn't think you reflect well on him? I know he's a hard... case, but is he blind?"

She noted the change from the crudity he'd probably been going to say and thought it probably would have applied better. But she wasn't, and probably never would be, to the point where she could accept that about her father. So she resorted to the gesture that seemingly had become frequent on his part—a shrug.

"So he wants perfection?"

"At the least," she said.

"A human impossibility."

She sighed. "Tell that to a child Charlie's age, who only ever wanted to please her father."

He looked at her for a long moment. "I have."

Of course he had. For all his big heart and loving soul, Gideon was utterly grounded in reality. He'd had no choice in that—the disgrace his father had brought down on them had guaranteed it. Perhaps it was that that gave him that enviable knack of connecting with the victims he dealt with so quickly. He'd been so young himself when it had all caved in on them.

She thought of the boy she'd seen in that photograph on his mother's wall. It hadn't been very long after that was taken that it had all come out, the saga of Ben Colton's corruption. In school at the time, she remembered that the gossip had been rampant, especially about the Colton kids, who were scattered through just about every level of the school district. None of the twelve were in her year, but she'd still heard it all.

Her father had been convinced Ben Colton had committed suicide, despite the evidence that it had been an accident on an icy road. Because, she had realized, to her father nothing could be worse than public humiliation. Not even leaving children fatherless. She herself had eventually decided it had probably at least contributed to the distraction that the police said had caused the crash, but that he hadn't intended to die. A small difference to Harold Jones, but a huge one to her.

And never the twain shall meet.

She had the feeling she was lucky to have never really known her grandfather. And vowed again that this devastating drive for perfection would end.

They had just gotten into Gideon's SUV when his phone rang. He pulled it out, looked at the screen and frowned, glancing back at the police station they'd just left.

"Detective Benitez," he said. "Must have forgotten something."

He answered, listened for a moment, and Sophia saw his expression change, turn a little grim. "Yes," he said after another moment. "Definitely. Meet you there."

He ended the call, slipped the phone back in his pocket, let out a compressed breath, then finally looked at her.

"He found a match on that name check I asked for."

"You mean what Ellen Webber said? About someone Webber went to high school with?"

He nodded. "Turns out he went to school with a woman who now works in the adult protection division of county social services."

She stared at him. "Surely not," she said. To her own

ears, she sounded as shocked as she felt at the idea that someone—especially another woman—who worked to help people like Ellen Webber would betray her.

"Maybe. But I think it's worth looking into, don't you?" He glanced at the clock on the dash. "Benitez is heading over to the county offices now. She's supposed to work until five."

Meet you there, he'd said. "You're going, too?"

"He thought I'd want to be there."

She studied him for a moment. Remembered the rather slight and obviously dedicated and smart detective. "If I were him, I'd want you there, too." He gave her a look she couldn't interpret, and she hastily added, "Let's go."

"I can drop you off—"

"No," she said firmly. "I want to be there."

"I'm not sure—"

"I am. I want to see the woman who was instrumental in putting my patient in the hospital."

"We don't know that for sure," he said.

"I don't believe in that much coincidence," she said. "But if you're worried, I'll restrain myself."

"This is a police investigation. You'll have to. Unless you want to end up in a cell next to Webber."

He said it flatly, but she caught a slight twitch at one corner of his mouth. Back then, that had warned her he was amused about something. She wasn't sure what it meant now, because she wasn't sure how he felt about anything.

Especially her.

Chapter Twenty-Seven

"Yes, I know Rick."

The blonde looked at Benitez warily, and Gideon even more warily as he stood there, a step back. The detective hadn't introduced him but had let the woman he'd confirmed was Courtney Miller think whatever she was going to think. Gideon just made sure he was standing as tall as he could and that his expression was a bit grim.

The woman glanced curiously at Sophia, who was standing beside Gideon. She hadn't said a word, either, but the woman's posture changed, became more rigid. It was all Gideon could do not to turn and look at Sophia. But he didn't really have to; he could imagine the expression she wore—when one of her patients was threatened, in any way, she became absolutely fierce.

"When was the last time you spoke to Webber?" Benitez asked.

"Why?" she asked, sounding as wary as she now looked.

"Please, just answer the question, Ms. Miller. Then we can be on our way and you can go about your business."

She looked a little less wary at those words. But she

looked worried, too. It showed in her eyes; she looked as if she hadn't slept well for a few days.

"I haven't spoken to Rick in nearly a month," she said suddenly, almost determinedly. And Gideon knew, with a gut-deep certainty, that she was lying. He sensed Sophia knew it as well, because she went very still.

"Fine," Benitez said, as if he was accepting her answer. "Thank you. That tells me how far back we need to go in your phone records."

She paled. "What?"

"To confirm your statement," Benitez said, his tone just a bit overly kind, as if he was explaining to someone who was having trouble understanding.

"You can't do that!"

Benitez just looked at her with raised eyebrows. And Gideon had to stifle a grin; the man was good. Very good.

"What is this about?" she demanded, clearly rattled now.

"I think you already know that," Benitez said.

"Whatever she told you, it's a lie," Miller said sharply. "Rick would never hurt anyone."

Gideon tensed at this blatant proof this woman knew exactly what this was about. And his jaw tightened at her declaration. Gideon had lost count of how many times he'd heard that justification in his career. In fact, the last time had been on a case Benitez had also been involved in. He must have made a sound, because Benitez turned his head. He gave Gideon a pointed look and a subtle nod. Gideon got it. So drawing on that experience, he gave the detective a knowing look, making sure Miller could see it.

"Well, that explains it. I told you that's what probably happened." The woman shifted her gaze to Gideon,
while he heard Sophia take in a breath. He made a
quick gesture to forestall her speaking, then, making
his voice as full of understanding and acceptance as
possible, he said to Miller, "That's why you told him
when she asked for help through this office, right?
Because you knew she was lying? I mean, what else
could you do?"

"Exactly!" Miller exclaimed with relief.

An epithet Gideon guessed rarely if ever crossed Sophia's lips exploded from her now. The blonde's head
snapped around to stare at her. "You utter fool!" Sophia exclaimed. "That pitiful excuse for a man you're
covering for put his son, a five-year-old too-little boy,
in the hospital!"

"Who are you?" the woman asked, and for the first
time there was actual fear in her voice. Benitez apparently decided to let Sophia run with it and stayed
silent.

"I am Dr. Sophia Gray-Jones," Sophia said in a tone
of pride Gideon had rarely heard from her. "And that
boy is my patient. I stitched up his wound, bandaged
him and held him while he cried in fear over whether
his father would come back and hurt him or his mother
again."

"But Rick wouldn't—"

"But he *did*! He showed up in that terrified child's
hospital room and threatened him, tried to grab him. If
not for this man—" she gestured at Gideon "—a *real*
man, he would have taken him right out of his hospital
bed. But Gideon stopped him. He stood for that child,

protected him, above and beyond what his job calls for. Stood against the man who *should* have been protecting him, but instead betrayed that trust."

"Gideon," the woman muttered, frowning as she looked at him. But then she seemed to shake off whatever it was and looked back at Sophia. "Did he—" she pointed at Gideon "—tell you that?"

"He didn't have to," Sophia said, her voice ice now. "I was there, in the room. I saw it all. And your precious Rick Webber threatened me as well. How dare you stand up for him and betray a battered woman, a woman you're supposed to be here to help!"

"I told you, she's a liar. She's always making up things about him. She—"

Sophia cut her off. "Don't be more of a fool than you've already been. If you think he won't turn on you as he did on his wife—whom he also put in that hospital, I might add—you're very sadly mistaken."

"Rick would never hurt me," the woman declared. "We—"

She broke off suddenly. Glanced at Benitez, who was watching with great interest.

"That's what I thought," he said with a nod. He shifted his gaze to Sophia. "Nicely done, Doctor."

Miller clammed up then, denying every-and anything, but they had an answer now; proving her part in it could wait.

Sophia looked puzzled as, at Benitez's nod, they left him to it. She shifted her gaze to Gideon. He smiled at her. She hadn't known this had been the plan all along, yet she had played it perfectly. Except Gideon knew she hadn't been playing at all; in fact, she'd meant every fiery, glorious bit of it.

"You want to explain what just happened in there?" she asked as they headed back out to his SUV. She pulled her coat closer around her as the chilly evening air hit them.

"She's obviously Webber's source," he said.

"Yes. It is so hard to believe a woman who is supposed to help people in Ellen's situation actually did that."

"It's going to cost her, one way or another," Gideon said.

"But she never really admitted anything—she caught herself. And now she's denying everything."

"A little too late. We know now." He hit the key fob for the car, and it obediently beeped as the doors unlocked. He pulled open the passenger door for her but carefully didn't touch her as she got in. He continued to assure her, "It may take him a while, and finding Webber is the first priority, but Benitez won't forget. He's a good guy."

"What if she warns him?"

He shrugged. "That the police are still looking for him? Pretty sure he already knows that."

He walked around and got in the driver's side, glad when the door cut off the wind that made it seem even colder. If it wasn't below freezing, it was darn close. Once the engine was running and started to show a little temperature, he turned on the heater. And Sophia spoke again.

"She's having an affair with Webber, I suspect."

He nodded. "That's my guess. And Benitez's, too."

"Lucky her," Sophia said dryly. "But what was that 'Nicely done' about? I wasn't doing anything except telling her the truth."

He took his hand off the gearshift he'd been about to put into Drive. "I'd guess she knows what she betrayed—everything her job is about. And your outrage prodded her into letting it slip. It was as nicely done as if it had been planned all along."

Her eyebrows, those beautiful arches, lowered slightly. "You mean, like your bit, playing along, pretending you understood why she did it, saying she had no choice?"

"Benitez and I had another case together where that worked," he said with a shrug.

"And you just did it on the fly like that?"

"He read her right. I just went with it."

"And then I butted in," she said, her mouth quirking as if she wasn't quite sure how she should feel about her part in it.

Gideon took a couple of seconds to decide, then turned to look at her. "In your magnificent, beautiful way. You dressed her down like a queen to a servant, and she deserved every bit of it."

She stared at him. Opened her mouth. Shut it again, as if she didn't know what to say. She looked utterly flummoxed. And that was unique enough that he savored it. It wasn't often he'd been able to do that, put her completely at a loss, and he couldn't deny he liked it. When he realized what he was feeling, he clamped down on it. He was already risking his heart, taking her to his place.

And he spent the rest of the drive hoping he didn't regret the decision for the rest of his life.

Chapter Twenty-Eight

Sophia had thought the Colton family home secluded, but Gideon's place was an entirely different matter. The driveway, if that's what you wanted to call the narrow gravel track, seemed to go on forever. The land was pretty, with a few small trees that looked as if they were starting to sprout spring leaves, and a lot of what looked like native plants, some even looking as if they were going to flower imminently. Often those were growing up against big, reddish-orange rocks, and she wondered if they'd been put there specifically for the contrast. It seemed like something Gideon would think of.

And then they rounded a curve and everything opened up to a big, flat expanse with a view that seemed to go on forever. In the middle of the flat sat a house, shaded by a few big trees and oriented to the view of the towering mesa beyond. It was maybe half the size of his mother's house and had a double garage at the end of the drive. It looked almost new, tidy and clean but plain. It was painted a slightly orangish color she thought an unusual choice until she realized it was a match for the hue of the mountains in the distance as they were being painted by the sun, now in the first stages of setting.

And suddenly it seemed perfect. Because that was exactly the kind of thing Gideon would notice and plan.

And belatedly it hit her that they were here, at his home, and she'd never addressed his presumptuous assumption that this was where they'd be going. It seemed a moot point now, but she wasn't sure she was capable of just letting go of it. She'd simply have to address it later, well after the fact.

There were what looked like other houses in the area, but to her they seemed quite distant. It must be so…quiet here. Peaceful. Peace giving. And she felt a sudden, unexpected yearning for just that. She'd always thought she thrived on hustle and bustle, on being in the city, but she was starting to wonder if she'd assumed that because it was what her father did.

When are you going to quit living to impress your father?

Gideon's words came back to her sharply. Just how much of her life was she letting her parent still run?

She didn't like what she guessed was the answer to that.

They pulled up to the garage, and she noticed a small travel trailer parked beside it. "Taken up camping?" she asked, nodding toward it, glad of the diversion.

"That," he said with a grin—that sweet, lovable grin, "is not camping. Camping is a sleeping bag and a campfire and a tent if you're lucky. That parked there is the height of luxury."

She couldn't stop her own smile. "If you say so."

"Actually, I lived in it when I was renovating."

She looked at the house again. "You renovated this place?"

He nodded. "It was practically falling down when I bought it."

How very like him. Fixing things. "I didn't know you went in for that."

For a moment he just looked at her. Then he said, "I didn't. Until I needed something all-consuming to do when I wasn't actually working."

It would have been impossible to miss his point, that he'd done this after their breakup. There was nothing she could say to that, so she stayed silent as they pulled into the garage.

Once inside, he paused at a panel just inside the door and keyed something into a keypad. An alarm, she guessed. That made her feel a little better. She supposed it was only smart; Rick Webber couldn't be the first unbalanced parent he'd encountered in his work.

They proceeded into the house. On her third step, she stopped, startled. The house that had looked rather simple and plain from the outside was sleek, modern and beautiful inside. But she barely had time to notice the interior, so overwhelming was the view straight ahead of her, toward the huge, high mesa through the wall of glass beyond. Almost involuntarily she walked that way, barely aware of the sound of her own footsteps on the floor.

She had no idea how long she'd been standing there, looking out raptly at the sunset-washed mountains, before she came back to herself and shifted her gaze to her immediate surroundings.

The glass sliding doors led out onto a covered patio. There was a small group of chairs around a fire pit to the right, and a table and more seating to the left, closer to a pretty intense-looking outdoor grill. A string of small lights was suspended along the edge of the roof extension, then went out to a row of tall posts that rose out of what looked like large flowerpots at the far edge of the stone patio. From there the lights came back to a corner of the house. It looked odd to her, and she wasn't sure what the point was—they certainly weren't big enough to help you see out there at night.

She turned back to look at the interior, really seeing it for the first time. This was essentially a great room. In the seating area of the big room, arranged in front of a huge fireplace, were two comfortable-looking couches in a rich green, with a large, low coffee table between. There was a tablet on it, next to a small stack of books; he always had been a reader. On the wood floor, which held the faintest wash of that same reddish, earth tint of the paint and the mountains, was a big rug in a geometric design of more green mixed with a sky blue.

She walked over to the kitchen off to the right, noting the gleaming stone countertops and clearly new, stainless appliances. The cabinets were an off-white, simple, but the fixtures and the hardware were a warm shade of copper that surprised her until she realized how well it blended with the paint color outside and the mountains in the distance.

He'd brought the outside inside, she realized. It all… fit. Perfectly. And was much more him than her home had ever been *her*. She'd told herself she didn't have time to personalize the place. But now, standing here, she knew it was more than that.

Admit it. You didn't have the heart. Not like it took to do this. Because you've smothered it in that need for perfection.

"It's wonderful, Gideon," she said softly.

He only shrugged. He hadn't done that so much when they'd been together. He'd talked to her, easily. And listened to her. Listened to her as no man ever had before. Or since.

What did you expect?

She looked around again, starting to feel desperate for something, anything, to say. She noticed a door half-open across the great room, leaving visible a part of what looked like some kind of odd machine. "What's in there?"

He glanced that way. "Gym."

Her brow furrowed. "Didn't you belong to the one over on Mesa Street?"

"I wanted one here, so I didn't have to go out."

It hit her then that the gym he'd always gone to was about midway between her office and her town house. Was that why he'd done it? To avoid even the slightest chance of running into her?

It's not always about you.

But here she thought it just might be. Then again, living this far out, maybe it was simply practical. She didn't know, didn't trust her own judgment, not about this. About him.

He turned away from her and walked over to the refrigerator. She smothered a sigh. For a moment she just stood there in the kitchen, slowly becoming aware of, oddly, her feet. Feet that had been chilled outside were warming. From beneath. She looked down at the floor. Lifted a foot and felt the difference.

He noticed the movement. "It's a radiant-heated floor," he said as he pulled open the fridge door. "I hated coming in here on a winter night for something and freezing my toes off."

The image of a tousled, barefoot Gideon made her heart ache. "You thought of everything." He always had.

He studied the interior of the refrigerator. "Not a lot of food options. There's some leftover spaghetti sauce, or Chinese takeout. Plenty of eggs, though, if you don't mind that for dinner."

"You don't have to—"

"I'm hungry. You will be, when things settle a bit more."

"Always the caretaker, aren't you?"

He closed the refrigerator door and looked at her, truly looked at her, for the first time since they'd left the county offices. "Each in our own way."

She supposed he was right about that. The difference was she took care of her patients. Gideon tried to take care of everyone.

They ended up making what had to be a unique concoction of scrambled eggs and some of the leftover shrimp of the Chinese, which she thought turned out to be surprisingly tasty. The glass of wine he poured her even more surprisingly tasted wonderful with the unusual meal. And she couldn't help wondering if he had wine on hand for other women he brought here. She didn't believe the other night would have happened if there was someone in particular, someone he was committed to, but that didn't mean there hadn't been others. In fact, there almost had to be, didn't there? He probably had a long line to pick and choose from. A man like Gideon wouldn't stay alone for long.

Unless he wanted to.

She slammed the door shut on the useless wonderings. There wasn't much conversation over the meal, probably because he didn't have much to say to her. Why would he? But the memory of that night at his mother's house hammered at her until she wanted to weep at the relentlessness of it. And at the ruin she'd made of what they'd had—in fact, of her life.

When he suggested they go out and watch the last of the sunset, she grabbed at the idea gratefully. Sitting quietly out on the patio, sipping at the glass of wine she'd brought out to finish, she watched the wispy clouds change color gloriously. They were taking on, she realized, the exact hue he'd painted the house. It somehow made her feel more a part of it, this striking part of the country with its stark beauty.

The light in the sky faded rapidly once the sun dropped behind the big mesa to the west. And as they were sitting there, suddenly the lights she had noticed earlier came on, clearly on a sensor. Her breath caught. They sparkled along the strand of wire, framing the view of the sky where the stars were becoming visible, as if a bunch of fireflies had gathered here in some kind of coordinated dance.

Another memory tugged at her, of her birthday a couple of months after they'd started dating. That evening, at about the same time, he'd driven her up to a spot that overlooked all of Blue Larkspur, and they'd sat there watching the lights come on across the city.

All those lights, Soph... Just think of how many represent people you've helped, children you've healed. You're an essential part of this place. And you're essential to me.

It was the best birthday gift she'd ever been given. On the day her father generally ignored and her mother acknowledged with a formal card at best, he had made her feel just that—essential.

It was also the night he'd scared her away. She hadn't earned that feeling from him, she hadn't proven herself to him, so how could he really feel that way? She was important to her patients, but there were other doctors, so she wasn't essential.

And she'd never been essential to a man in her life; why would he be different?

Because he's Gideon. And he is different.

And she had realized it too late.

A sudden urge swept over her. She wanted to pour out everything she'd learned, every bit of regret she'd felt since she'd ended things. She doubted it would make any difference, but she wanted him to at least know she knew what she'd lost, what she'd thrown away. He deserved that much, didn't he?

Then again, men didn't like that, those emotional eruptions, did they? And Gideon was all man. Nobody knew that better than she did. But he was also the kindest person she'd ever met, and he'd always listened before...

That was when he loved you.

Yet the weight of her own silence was growing unbearable, and she thought if she had to go through the rest of her life like this, without ever having told him how much she regretted what she'd done, it would crush her. After this incident with Charlie was over, it was entirely likely she wouldn't see him again, unless accidentally.

She might never have another chance. And as she sat there, looking at the sparkling lights that made her feel as if the stars were just an extension of this haven he'd created, she knew she couldn't let it get away.

She just had no idea how to even start.

Chapter Twenty-Nine

"This is a nice wine."

Gideon didn't look at her. He knew he didn't dare.

It was stupid, silly even, but there was something about the way she held a wineglass, the way her long, slender fingers held the stem and the bowl, even the way her wrist bent slightly. And staring at her fingers only got him thinking about the other things those hands could do. Had done.

Had it only been the night before last? It seemed an eon ago. Yet at the same time, it seemed as alive and crackling between them as if it had been only moments ago.

"It's nice," he finally agreed, when her continued silence made him realize an answer was expected.

"Did you pick it out?"

"Sort of. My brother Oliver once invested in this eco-friendly winery." His brow furrowed. "Why?"

"Just wondering who else has enjoyed a sunset here."

He nearly broke his own glass. His head snapped around, and he stared at her. She was looking up at the sky, as if she'd merely observed it was clear tonight. "And that's your business because...?"

"It's not." She set down her own glass and shifted in her chair to meet his gaze head-on. "It would have been, once. But I was a fool. No, worse than a fool. I was too blind to see, to believe in what I had. Because I didn't think I deserved it. Didn't think I deserved... you."

"How could you think that?" He sounded as incredulous as he felt. "You, you're brilliant, you're successful, you're..." He trailed off, shaking his head, because he'd been about to devolve into how she was beautiful. And sexy. *Oh, yes, don't forget that, Colton.*

He stayed silent for once. And for a while, so did she. He wondered if she regretted what she'd said, if she'd blurted it out in a moment of...he wasn't sure what.

Then, hesitantly, she said, "This is...very different from your mother's house."

Well, that surely changed the subject. "That house," he said flatly, "is still my father's house. Not something I want to live with every day."

"I can understand that." She hesitated, then said, "May I ask you something about that?"

"My father?"

She nodded. When he didn't say no, she went ahead. "In essence, what he did, he did for you, his family. To give you the kind of life he wanted you to have. Does that make it better...or worse?"

He didn't look at her. Felt muscles in his jaw tighten. "Better? Hell, no. Easier to understand...maybe." Then he turned on her. "What about yours? Does he care what he's done to you? Does he even realize?"

"He is who he is."

Nice cop-out.

"Right. He gets a pass. I forgot." She went still. Very still. And then, softly, he added, "Remember how angry you were at Courtney Miller?"

Her brow furrowed, as if she wasn't sure what that had to do with anything. "Yes?"

"You should hang on to that strength. Remember it the next time you're face-to-face with your father."

She was gaping at him. As if the idea of confronting her father that way, with the anger she'd felt at what that woman had done, was...astounding. "I... It would destroy our relationship."

"Relationship? Is that what you call it? Tell me, Doctor, just what do you get out of that? Besides constant criticism and that feeling of never measuring up?"

He saw her react to his use of the term *doctor* instead of her name, as if it had stung. But then she just looked sad. Almost unbearably sad. In the moment after he'd seen the moisture pooling in her eyes, she closed them, as if looking at anything was suddenly too much to bear.

He'd seen that expression before. That night, as she was closing the door on him, the night she'd thrown him out of her life.

You're a good, wonderful man. You can do better, Gideon.

Than you? Not a chance.

You deserve better. So go. Just go.

He'd stood there staring at the fancy chrome knocker on the door. Fighting the urge to hammer at the door with it until she had to come open it again just to get it to stop.

But he hadn't. There had been something in her voice, a flat, definite sort of certainty that had told him she wasn't going to change her mind. That she truly was throwing them away.

But he had never really realized until now that when she'd told him he could do better, she'd meant it. In so many words. It wasn't just a platitude, something to ease the pain of the breakup. She'd really meant it.

He nearly laughed. She gave him a sideways look, as if she'd sensed that. "Just thinking," he said, purposely letting some of that bitter amusement show, "of the night you ended it, told me I could do better. Me, a Colton, who spent half my life ostracized from polite society. I should have been the one saying that to you. That you could do better."

"I also said you shouldn't be blamed for what your father did." He at least had succeeded in distracting her, it seemed. And then, those hazel eyes clear now, she turned her head to look straight at him. "And you'd have been wrong, Gideon. I could never, ever do better than you. And that night was the biggest mistake I will ever make in my life. I had everything I ever wanted, everything I would ever need, right there. And I was too blind, too stupid—" she took a deep breath, as if her next words were going to need it "—too beaten down by my father's demands to do what I should have, which is hold on to it forever."

He stared at her. She had let down the last wall, shattered the last bit of the facade, and all her sheer, naked emotions were staring back at him. They were glowing in eyes that reflected the sparkling lights, and he knew those emotions were generated straight from her heart, mind and soul.

Regret.

Longing.

Hope.

Love.

It was almost overwhelming. When the memories of that night at his mother's swept over him again, it was truly too much. He couldn't speak, even if he had been able to find the words.

She let out a tiny breath. "I know it doesn't mean anything to you now, but I wanted you to know how much I regret what I did."

"It means something." He barely managed to get it out, and his voice sounded like a strange, sandpapery thing. He swallowed, tried again. "I just don't know what you expect. What you want."

"What I expect is you to tell me where I can put my confession of—" She broke off, shaking her head as she looked away. "No, that's not true. Of any other man, yes, I'd expect that. But not you. You'd never be that cold or cruel. It's not in you. So what I expect is that you will politely accept and say it's okay, even though it isn't."

It took everything in him to say with any semblance of evenness, "And what you want?"

She met his gaze again. She took a deep breath, and he could see her straighten slightly. And when she looked at him, she wore the expression of someone about to jump into something they weren't sure they would survive.

"What I want? What I want is what we had. I want

to take that and build even more on that foundation. A future. I want to be there for you in the same way I know you would always be there for me. I want us to be real in all the ways neither of our parents' relationships ever were." Her voice changed, went husky in that way that drove him mad. "I want an endless string of nights like we just had on that couch. Anywhere. Everywhere."

Gideon's gaze was locked on her. He couldn't look away. His body was responding fiercely to those last words she'd said, but his mind was grappling with the rest of it. The building-a-future part.

The part of him that had been so battered when she ended their relationship was screaming a warning. But the part of him that somehow still believed in the good in life, in people, was yelling in triumph. And at the moment he wasn't sure which voice would win.

Silence spun out between them, taut, making the air almost quiver. And when his phone rang, he wasn't sure if he should be irritated or glad.

He glanced at it, saw it was Caleb. That, at this hour, was unusual enough that he felt a small kick of urgency and answered. His eldest brother didn't waste any time with niceties.

"We've got a situation. We can't reach Renquist."

Gideon went still. "What?"

"He missed a check-in, so we called him. No answer."

"Can you track his phone?"

"Doing it now, but I wanted you to have a heads-up. She's with you?"

"Yes."

"Keep your guard up, then," Caleb said.

If you only knew...

"Let me know when you find out anything."

"Of course."

He ended the call and sat tapping the phone against his knee, staring out at the night sky. Was suddenly aware of what he hadn't noticed until now—that it was beyond chilly out here. Ordinarily, if it was just him and since it was a beautiful night, he would have simply turned on the gas fire pit. That made it warm enough for him.

Like she isn't already making it plenty warm enough?

But that wasn't an option now. Caleb's call had changed that.

"What's wrong?"

He didn't try to placate her. "That was Caleb. They can't reach the guy who's watching you."

She blinked. "Steve? But I thought he was off now, that…you were—"

"I am," he said flatly. "But he was still supposed to be around, just in case."

"Around here?"

"Yes." He was still tapping the phone. Stopped. Looked at it. "And we get a strong cell signal here."

"Do we need to go look for him?"

His head came up. He turned to her and saw in her eyes that she meant it. That if he said yes, she would probably be on her feet and ready in an instant. But that didn't matter to him as much as the other realization that hit him—how easily she'd said that "we."

As if she'd meant that, too.

He thought of everything she'd just said, before this interruption. The interruption he still wasn't sure if he resented or was grateful for. She'd truly bared her soul to him; that he couldn't deny. But what it meant to him, beyond the slight satisfaction of knowing she regretted ending it, he wasn't sure. He wasn't sure of how he felt about any of what she'd said. He needed time to process it all.

I want an endless string of nights like we just had on that couch.

Okay, he was in total agreement with that. He was sure of that much.

But the other thing he was sure of was that right now this situation with Webber had to take precedence. And that Renquist had apparently dropped off the grid was beyond concerning.

Every protective instinct he had was firing, telling him that it wouldn't matter how he felt about what she'd confessed if he didn't protect her.

And so he would protect her. No matter what.

Chapter Thirty

"You," Gideon said, "aren't going anywhere." He gestured toward the outside of the house. "Especially out there, now."

"But—"

"The whole reason we're here is to keep you safe."

Sophia felt a tightening in her midsection at those words. Not because she felt endangered, but because she didn't want that to be the whole reason they were here, together. And suddenly his decision to come here without even consulting her didn't matter anymore.

"What about you? Maybe Rick Webber doesn't know who you are now, but he might find out your name and where you live eventually. Then what?"

His mouth—that wonderful, tempting mouth—quirked. "Think I can't handle him?"

That idea made her let out a compressed breath, and she shook her head. "You proved you can, in the hospital."

"He's angry, and people who give in to their anger are usually sloppy." His mouth twisted slightly. "Like he was in Charlie's room."

"And you were the polar opposite of sloppy. Smooth

and strong and—" She cut herself off before she launched into a string of his attributes that would likely embarrass her. And him—Gideon was everything she thought him, but he was also amazingly modest and would probably be uncomfortable with the plethora of compliments she could easily pay him. Especially right now, in this situation that might have just gotten worse.

Someday.

She made the silent vow with every intention of keeping it. Even if those compliments were the last thing she ever got to tell him before he walked out of her life forever. She smothered her sense of frustration that when she'd finally worked up the nerve to pour her heart out to him, this had happened to interrupt, before he'd given her any kind of response.

And if something really happened to Steve Renquist, you're going to feel hideously selfish, and rightfully so.

Gideon was wearing a rather grimly thoughtful expression, and she made an effort to focus.

"What are you thinking?"

"How long it would take me to check my entire five acres." He tapped a finger on the arm of his chair, a familiar gesture that told her his agile mind was working. "The two close around the house are pretty clear, not much cover. But the rest has lots of trees and rocks and would take a while to check. And I'm not leaving you alone that long. He could get past me to the house."

She stifled a shiver at the idea of him out there in the dark alone with Webber on the loose.

"You're assuming Steve is…out of the picture."

"Since he's out of touch, wisest course temporarily. But even if he's not, if it's just a communication malfunction, it's a lot of ground to watch if you're not familiar with it."

"Do you know where, exactly, Renquist was supposed to be when he got here?"

He shook his head. "Just outside somewhere."

"'He'll have to come from outside, so outside I'll be,'" she quoted. "That's what he said today, when I asked where he'd be."

Gideon smiled then and nodded. "He's a pro." The smile faded. "Which makes this even more worrisome."

"But... Webber doesn't know who you are, so he shouldn't be able to find this place, could he?"

He grimaced. "He shouldn't have been out on bail, either." He got to his feet. "I think we'd better head inside."

She glanced around, suddenly a little nervous about the darkness beyond the sparkling strand of lights.

But that would only matter if you were alone. Helpless. You're not. Gideon is here, and he's far from helpless.

Just the way he'd spoken about this place after that phone call, in that very tactical sort of way, proved that. He might be too bighearted for his own good, but he was far, far from a fool. And she had to quash the old pain she carried, the result of knowing that she had, in part, forced him to build whatever barriers he had now around that too-big heart.

She had a little more trouble quashing the hope that those barriers weren't insurmountable. And the fear that they would be, for her more than anyone, simply because they existed mostly because of her.

They went inside and, feeling restless—okay, nervous—she walked around the great room and took a closer look. She was aware he was going from door to window to door, and she knew he was checking that they were locked, which made her more nervous. She tried to focus on the room, on seeing what he chose to live with in plain sight. Somehow she doubted his taste bore any resemblance to that of the designer she'd hired to do her town house because she had been totally focused on her practice. The designer had taken her vagueness about what she wanted as permission to instead produce something he himself liked. She had learned to live with it, had thought about making changes, but it seemed both wasteful and time-consuming.

Gideon would probably never face that. In fact, she would be willing to bet he'd done all this himself.

I needed something all-consuming to do.

She smothered a sigh. She didn't usually have this much trouble. But then, around Gideon she always had had trouble. He'd been all-consuming himself. Which had both thrilled her and scared her.

Again she tried to focus.

The far wall was one big bookcase, low in the middle and floor to ceiling on either side. It was what was in the wall space that drew her attention. The copper metal sculpture fit the rest of the room, the entire house so well, and she found the representation of the raccoon face peering out from the Y of a tree both whimsical and cute. Interesting, that he'd chosen this piece.

The shelves on the left side of the raccoon's space were full of books, of every kind, from child psychology to physics, and fiction from classics to thrillers. And they all looked read; there were no books that were here just because they looked good or their covers were the right color.

Her gaze shifted to the right of the sculpture, where there was what appeared to be a collection of mementos on several shelves, apparently from kids, judging by the type of item, from a toy action figure of a superhero to what appeared to be a dried rose and a childish drawing of that same superhero with Gideon's name scrawled beneath the slightly lopsided image. She wasn't surprised. He surely must be a superhero to the kids he helped, as he had been to Charlie.

Her eyes blurred a little, and she had to look away. Back to the amusing metal raccoon.

"His name's Baba." She blinked. He shrugged, but he was smiling. "Iris named him. Sort of. It's what she babbles every time she sees him."

"She's here a lot?"

"Whenever I can manage it, or if Rach needs someone to take her for a while, if she's on a big case."

An image instantly formed in her mind, of Gideon at his most gentle and caring, cuddling and delighting his baby goddaughter and niece, bringing on that happy babbling. Followed by an image of him with kids of his own, cuddling, playing... It was such a powerful image she almost had to turn away.

It was a moment before she could speak. "He's very cute."

"He cheers things up a bit."

No matter how much she told herself it wasn't all

about her, she couldn't help wondering if she was the reason he'd felt he needed to cheer the place up.

"That face would," she agreed neutrally. Then, because she couldn't seem to help herself, she pointed at the other shelves. "That's…quite a collection."

He looked at the shelves for a long, quiet moment before saying, in a joking tone she didn't believe, "Place ever catches fire, that's what I go for first."

How like Gideon to say it like that, so lightly, while at the same time expressing so beautifully the truth of what mattered to him, what he valued. She thought again of that night he'd driven her to the overlook and correlated the number of lights below to how many children she'd helped. But looking at this collection, she'd stack his record of helping up against hers any day.

He didn't seem any more able to settle than she was; that phone call had truly disrupted everything. Including what she'd dared hope might be a reconciliation of sorts. No matter how much she lectured herself that the other night had been merely physical, which was the one place where nothing had changed at all, she'd still dared to hope it might mean more. And she'd bared her soul to him in that hope, but the reality of their immediate situation had derailed that thoroughly.

Even as she thought it, a sudden, loud whooping noise startled her into letting out a gasp. A split second later she realized what it was.

The alarm.

Chapter Thirty-One

Gideon spun around at the sound. A glance at the alarm panel on the wall told him it was sector three, the northeast corner, where the spare bedroom and his office were. Exactly where he would have expected the problem to come from, out there where there were a couple of big trees and the fence around the trailer enclosure to hide behind.

The question was, now that the intruder had triggered the alarm, would they run?

A thump and the sound of something breaking answered that question. He'd say the bedroom, because of the proximity of the fence, which could give someone a leg up to the window level.

It didn't matter right now how Webber—and he had no doubt that's who it was—had found them. What mattered was stopping him.

"I'll call 911," Sophia whispered. He looked at her. She was frightened, but determination came off her in waves. No fragile flower, not her.

"The alarm goes to them, so they'll already have the address," he whispered back as she took out her phone. "But let them know it's real. Then get out of the house."

He swiped up his keys from where he'd dropped them on the coffee table and tossed them to her. "Take these and get in the car so you can get away if you have to."

She caught the keys easily but said, "I'm not leaving you— What are you doing?"

She almost yelped it, although still quietly, as he turned and started toward the back of the house. He wondered what the rest of that interrupted sentence would have been if he hadn't moved, but there was no time to dwell on it now.

"Trying to end this before it starts."

That had always been his motto since he'd begun this work that so often involved dealing with angry people. Failing that, de-escalation was his second step. And he wasn't above pleading, his third step.

But he also subscribed to a three-strikes-and-you're-out rule. Especially if someone else was in danger. But he'd never felt anything like what he felt now, when this time it could be Sophia who would be in danger. Sophia, who wasn't heading for cover.

He couldn't argue with her; he had to move before Webber got too far.

"At least be ready to run." Even as he said it, he kept moving. Sophia stayed right there, talking into her phone now in a hushed but tense voice. And he heard the sound of the door opening down at the end of the hall.

Good. The hallway is good. Narrow. Less chance for him to get past me.

Three things happened almost simultaneously. He reached for the light switch, hoping the sudden flare of light would slow Webber for a precious second or two. As he did so, he heard the light steps behind him that told him Sophia had not retreated at all. And then the ceiling fixtures lit up, changing what had been a darkened hallway into a well-lit space.

Webber reacted, throwing his hand up to shade his eyes. But his movements seemed a little odd, almost exaggerated; when he put his hand up it went past his brow, as if he'd misjudged the distance, and he'd had to move it back down. Then he gave up the motion, instead just rapidly blinking. Gideon registered that he was wearing the same clothes he'd had on at the hospital and in the store footage, and they looked as if he'd been wearing them the entire time.

And that gave him his opening. He spoke, making his voice as light as he could, as if he were speaking to an old friend.

"Whew, dude, you need a shower. Getting a little rank there."

For an instant Webber froze. Stared at Gideon uncomprehendingly. Then two more things happened, this time truly simultaneously.

Sophia whispered behind him, "He's on something. Look at his pupils, the way he's sweating and breathing fast."

Great. A drugged man who beats his kid and wife.

And second, Gideon saw a glint along Webber's right thigh. Metallic. But dark. He registered the shape, the way he was holding his hand.

A gun.

Internally Gideon kicked up his adrenaline to the highest level. Externally he kept his voice and expression the same—casual, friendly. As if he hadn't seen the weapon at all. As if this hadn't moved instantly into all-bets-are-off territory.

"Back up, Doctor," he said under his breath to Sophia, rather harshly; this was not the time to argue. Gratitude rushed through him when she did, and he was able to resume his genial tone when he turned back to Webber, who hadn't even seemed to realize Sophia was there, he was so focused on his target. Which was Gideon himself. Exactly what he wanted. "Come on, Rick, let's get you that shower. And some clean clothes. You'll feel better, then we can talk."

Webber was still staring at him. As if he understood the words but what Gideon was saying made no sense to him. The hand that held the gun seemed to be twitching. He was shifting his weight on his feet, as if restless, and his eyes began to dart around.

"Maybe after that have something to eat?" He continued to talk as if Webber was an old friend who had unexpectedly dropped in, in need of help.

Finally Webber reacted. Gideon could almost see the jolt as his brain—he knew now Sophia was right and Webber was on something, something that made focusing on only one thing difficult—steered him back to why he was here.

And the gun came up. A revolver, Gideon could see now. Blue steel. Maybe a four-inch barrel. And he could see the cylinder was fully loaded. "Shut up," Webber snarled. "Tell me where my boy is."

Gideon didn't react, at least not openly, to the threat of the weapon. He gave the man a smile, as if he'd told a good joke. "I can do one or the other, but not both."

Webber's brow furrowed, as if he was trying to figure it out. He was shaky enough that Gideon wondered what the odds were that he might pull the trigger without meaning to.

Gideon kept talking, as if the small—but likely still lethal at this close range—pistol wasn't aimed at him. "Come on," he urged. "You get that shower, then we'll sit down and talk about how we're going to get Charlie back to you."

It was a lie. He would do whatever he could to see Webber never got a chance to put his hands on Charlie again. But Webber showing up at his home—however he'd managed it—with a gun negated any small need Gideon would normally feel to be honest with a child abuser. Especially a drugged one, whose judgment was likely even more severely impaired than ever.

But Webber's brow furrowed again, as if he was having trouble processing the words, or more likely was slowly trying to decide whether to believe them. And the eyes darting around as fast as a rabbit's nose twitched when a coyote was around told Gideon whatever he'd taken—cocaine, at a guess—had him revved up and ready.

Gideon calculated whether he could move closer, in a jovial sort of way, clap Webber on the back like that old friend. Once he was that close, it would be simple to wrest the handgun from him. Easy, but not necessarily safe. Still, if it was only him, he'd probably try it.

But it wasn't. Sophia was here, and she was still in the hallway behind him. She could end up in the line of fire if things soured. And that was something he wasn't willing to risk.

Even as he thought it, Webber finally seemed to

realize that same fact that held Gideon back, that Sophia was here. And in the next moment he saw Webber recognize her.

"You," he spat out, followed by a string of obscenities. "You're that doctor who claimed I hurt my boy!"

"Actually," Sophia said before Gideon could tell her not to speak and just get out of the hallway, "that was determined before I arrived at the hospital. If I'd been there, that might not have happened. You are his father, after all."

She didn't react at all to the swearing and the crude names he'd called her. If not for the faintest of tense undertones, she would have sounded as if she was speaking casually to a worried parent. She'd followed Gideon's lead, implying she was on Webber's side, and between them—and whatever drug he was on—Webber was off balance.

"I should have known you'd be here, too. You're in on this together, aren't you? Both of you, conspiring to take my son away." The man shifted his gaze back to Gideon. "Where is he?" he demanded again. "I've had enough of your crap, you pretending to be a cop to try and scare me. Well, I'm not afraid of you, and you're going to tell me where my son is or I'll blow your damned brains out."

It was all coming out in a rapid, staccato rush now, without even a breath taken. The drugs were going to mess this up, Gideon realized. Still, he tried once more, although he inched forward a little, gesturing to Sophia to stay where she was; he wanted some distance between them.

"He's with friends, temporarily, until we can get him

back to you." He used that calm tone again, but apparently Webber had hit his tipping point. Or whatever he'd taken had kicked in fully. He was sweating even more, and his breathing had escalated, becoming faster and even more audible. The weapon came up, and suddenly Gideon was looking right down the barrel.

"You're going to take me to him *now*. Or you're going to die, right here, right now. No more crap. I want my son back and you're going to do it."

In that moment Gideon knew no effort at reason was going to work. Even if Webber had been halfway rational, the drug's effects had evidently destroyed any governor he might have had.

"Okay," Gideon said simply.

Webber blinked. Then again, three times in quick succession.

"Doctor, please toss me my keys," he said to Sophia, putting a little emphasis on the verb and hoping she'd catch it. She did. And just as he had to her earlier, she tossed the ring of several keys across the few feet between them.

And as he'd hoped, Webber's gaze naturally shifted to the small, moving object.

In that instant, Gideon launched.

Chapter Thirty-Two

Sophia stifled a tiny scream. What Gideon had done in Charlie's hospital room had been one thing, but Rick Webber had a gun now. And the thought of Gideon being shot, even killed, struck such a terror in her she forgot how to breathe. But she barely had time to think.

Gideon went in low. In an instant he was past the gun in Webber's outstretched hand, but at the same time he grabbed that wrist. Twisted it and pulled hard as he slammed his shoulder into Webber's chest, just below that shoulder. Webber screamed. The weapon hit the floor as he tried to pull away. His other hand clawed at Gideon's face. Drew blood. Gideon never stopped moving. He bent slightly, using his momentum and strength to practically pull the man over his back. Webber hit the floor, flat on his back. And Gideon was on top of him, his knee pressing down on his abdomen, just below the ribs.

Sophia stared in shock. It had happened so fast, in the space of one breath, if she could remember how to breathe at all. But in the next moment she realized the gun on the floor was still within Webber's reach, and she quickly went over and kicked it safely away. Gideon glanced at her and nodded approvingly. And that simple nod warmed her more than any hard-won praise from her father or any other man ever had in her life.

Webber flailed with his left hand—his right didn't seem to be working anymore—and Gideon caught it and held it still. "I suggest," Gideon said coldly, "that you just relax. Unless you want a full hundred and ninety pounds shoved into your gut."

Inanely, the only thing she could think of was that Gideon truly had to be ninety percent muscle, if he weighed 190 at his height. And to wonder again, as she had when he'd first done it, why she had suddenly become "Doctor" to him.

"In the garage, in the tall tool cabinet, third drawer, there are some flex ties."

He said it with barely a glance at her, his attention obviously focused on Webber, who was still struggling, albeit helplessly. Belatedly she realized that was a request—or an order—and she turned and went. She wasn't about to argue with a man who had just taken down an armed, drugged-up abuser.

Out in the garage, she found the cabinet and pulled open the drawer. Saw the plastic strips, looked at the various sizes, and grabbed one of each of the two largest. For an instant she wanted nothing more than to simply stand there in the quiet and pretend none of this had happened. But Gideon was in there with a clearly unbalanced man. So she slammed the drawer shut and hurried back inside.

Gideon took the smaller of the two ties she'd brought and started to loop it around Webber's wrists. The man swore in a long streak, clearly in pain. Yelped something about his shoulder—Sophia was guessing that smooth move by Gideon had dislocated it—and sounded utterly cowed now. He begged Gideon to stop.

"Like you stopped when you were hurting Charlie? And your wife?" Gideon said coldly, pulling the tie through the latch with a yank.

And in the distance Sophia heard the sound of sirens. From the way he tilted his head slightly, she knew Gideon had heard it, too.

"I just lost my temper," Webber said, starting to whimper now.

"If you don't want me to lose mine, shut up."

"You don't understand, the kid is disobedient all the time…"

Sophia didn't know what Webber had seen in Gideon's face that had made his voice trail away and fear flash in his eyes. Perhaps something like what she was feeling, as the pitiful excuse for a human being blamed a little boy, his own son, for his own cruel actions. Then Gideon took the second, larger tie, which she'd thought he wouldn't use, and used it to fasten Webber's ankles together.

The sirens had stopped. She hoped that was a good sign.

"Need another one, so I can loop them together and hog-tie him good and proper," Gideon said.

"No, my shoulder!" Webber yelped.

"Poor baby," Gideon said sweetly.

Sophia saw a flash of lights hitting the hallway wall, coming from the front of the house. Red and blue lights.

The police were definitely here.

But Gideon had already done what had to be done. As he always had. As she knew he always would.

There were a few minutes of chaos as first they de-escalated the emergency response, telling them Webber was restrained. Then, standing out in the great room while blotting at his bloody face with a paper towel, Gideon explained to the police what had happened. One of the first officers to arrive took notes while the other loaded Webber into the back of a police unit. A second police car with only one officer was farther up the driveway where it curved almost out of sight, where they'd found Webber's vehicle.

"We'll get that towed out of here shortly," the one taking the report, whose name tag read Nguyen, said. "It appears it's been in an accident recently. Sideswipe sort of damage. Was that you?"

"No," Gideon answered. "But I know who it might have been."

He explained about Renquist and told Nguyen the bodyguard had been planning to head here to check the grounds. Sophia stifled a gasp as she realized the implication of the obviously competent Renquist apparently not seeing or being able to stop Webber; he might have never had the chance.

"You need to find him," she said anxiously. "He could be hurt."

The officer nodded. "I'll have them start searching. Speaking of hurt, you want me to call medics out?" he asked as he looked at Gideon's bloodied face.

"No. They might feel compelled to put Webber out of his pain."

Nguyen smiled. "Good point. You should clean that up, then. And still get those claw marks checked."

"I'll see to him," Sophia said briskly.

The man gave her a smile as well. "So there really is a doctor in the house?"

She smiled back, but only briefly. Then with a nod toward the police car, she added, "I think his right shoulder is probably dislocated." The officer looked at Gideon as if impressed. "That's probably the only reason he was never able to fire that gun," Sophia added, just to pound home Gideon's heroics.

"Nice job," he said to Gideon. "Guess what I've heard about you is true." Sophia saw something flash in Gideon's eyes, as if he'd just realized something. But he said nothing as the officer went on, rather apologetically, "The crime scene folks will be here soon, but this is still going to take a while."

"As long as they're thorough. This needs to hold up in court," Gideon said. Sophia marveled at him; she hadn't gotten that far in her thoughts.

"It does," Nguyen agreed. "And he won't be getting out on bail anytime soon, that's for sure."

"He never got past the hallway," Sophia said, "so I presume we can stay out here while I tend to those scratches? Rat claws can carry some nasty germs."

The man chuckled and nodded, then went out to check on the ETA of the forensics team. Gideon smiled but didn't say anything. She went and got the small first aid kit she always carried out of her bag. He bore it stoically, as she'd expected, as she cleaned him up enough to see the scratches weren't as deep as she'd feared.

"No stitches necessary," she said in relief.

"Darn," Gideon said. "I was hoping for some dashing scar."

She stopped in the act of applying a couple of butterfly bandages, took a step back and looked into his eyes. "You already have an unfair advantage. Women would be swooning all around you."

"Right," he said dryly.

"At least one would," she said. And then, because she couldn't seem to stop herself, she asked him, "Why did you keep calling me 'Doctor' in front of him?"

He went very still. And she knew that her instinct that this was important had been right.

"Because," he finally said, "I didn't want him to think you could be a weapon."

She had to tamp down the hope that leaped inside her. He'd only said he hadn't wanted Webber to think she could be used against him, not that she could be. But something in his voice, in the way he said it…

"He's clearly not above using women to—" He stopped, and she saw that look in his eyes again, which had been there when Officer Nguyen had mentioned he'd heard about him.

"What?" she asked.

"Damn. I think I know," he said slowly, his gaze slightly unfocused in that way that she remembered meant his brain was racing.

"Know what?"

"How he found us."

"How?"

"Courtney Miller. I think she recognized my name when you said it. It probably goes through her office on occasion, in situations like this with child and adult victims."

Sophia gasped. "The way she looked at you. I thought she was just...appreciative." And then the full import of what he'd said hit her. "My God, it was my fault. If I hadn't said your name—"

He moved so quickly it startled her into silence. His arms came around her. "Stop it. It's not your fault."

"But she never would have—"

"Might as well blame my mother."

That derailed the rush of self-blame. "Your mother?"

"She picked out the name. It could have been something innocuous like Sam or Bill or John, but no, she had to choose something that stood out a mile."

For a moment she just stood there, looking up at him. "Your talent for de-escalation is epic, Mr. Colton."

He smiled at that. "I work harder at that than anything."

"Because you don't want to fight. Reasoning is always your first choice."

"Always."

She stood there, savoring his arms around her. The arms of the man who had gone from gentle caretaker of fragile little Charlie, to firm supporter of his battered mother, to fierce protector risking himself...for her, all in the space of a few days. No matter how he felt about her, he'd done what had to be done, used the force necessary and only the force necessary.

"And that's what makes you a true hero, Gideon. Because force really is your last resort." She took a deep breath and took the plunge. "And that's why I love you. I never stopped loving you. And I will always love you, whether you can forgive me or not. Whether you can love me back again or not."

She felt an almost staggering sense of relief as the words were finally spoken. She'd put it all on the table, and now it was out of her hands. What the rest of her life would be was now in his hands. And his big, open, generous heart.

She could only hope that heart would let her back in.

Chapter Thirty-Three

One thing you could always say about Sophia Gray-Jones—she picked her moments. Like now, in the aftermath of a life-threatening situation. But now that he thought about it, what better time? Wasn't that when many people thought of things they needed to say?

Needed to say.

Had it been reaction that had spurred her to say it? The adrenaline rush of facing an armed assailant making demands? Would she later, when everything calmed down, be sorry she had?

He didn't know. He only knew he couldn't take another rejection from her, if she changed her mind. Again.

"I don't blame you at all for doubting me," she said softly. "But I learn from my mistakes, Gideon. And I learned the most from the biggest one I ever made."

He didn't know what to say. Didn't know what he was feeling. Or thinking. And for the second time tonight, he was glad when his phone rang. When he saw it was Caleb, he grabbed it quickly.

"Caleb, your guy—"

"He's all right, relatively speaking. Webber ran him

off the road about a mile from your place, trashed his car. He was banged up a bit, but not bad. He couldn't get a cell signal, so he had to hike to where he could."

After assuring his brother that Webber was in custody and would definitely remain that way now, and thanking him for the help, they ended the call. Gideon remembered Sophia's worry when they'd deduced something like that had happened, so he quickly relayed what Caleb had said.

She breathed a sigh of relief. It was like her, to be so worried about a guy who'd only sat in her office a few hours.

But she didn't worry about you when she threw you out of her life.

The old pain jabbed, but it wasn't as powerful as it had once been. Was it the adrenaline? Did it just not matter right now, after facing down a man with a gun? Or had her declarations tonight soothed it?

But most importantly, did he want more than that old pain eased? She couldn't have made it more clear how she felt—he just didn't know how he felt. Which didn't make sense, when he thought about it. All those nights when he'd been unable to stop thinking about her, when all he'd wished was to have her back, to undo whatever he'd done to drive her away, to find a way to convince her they were meant to be together.

He'd progressed to nights spent lying in the dark tearing himself apart for being a fool. Vowing to toughen up, to never let it happen again. It had been Rachel who had put a halt to that one day when he'd told her that his new goal in life, besides renovating the run-down house he'd just bought, was to stop being such a softhearted fool.

"Don't wish for that, Gid," she'd said. "It's the very thing that makes you so incredibly good at what you do. The reason children trust you instinctively now is they can sense your goodness. If you harden your heart, the kids will know it. Especially the kids you so often deal with. They know a hard heart when they see one."

The words had truly resonated with him. He remembered looking at her and smiling wryly as he'd told her, "You know, sis, it's really not fair that you're only two years older than me but ten times smarter."

He would never forget the way her expression had changed. "Not always," she'd said dryly.

He knew what she had meant—whatever brief liaison it had been that had resulted in his goddaughter. None of them knew who baby Iris's father was, because Rachel refused to talk about it, even to him. And since he didn't want to talk about Sophia, they had reached a tacit agreement that they wouldn't push. And they'd kept to it.

He wondered what his smart, no-nonsense sister would have to say about this. Probably tell him to run and keep running. He wasn't sure she wouldn't be right. It would kind of be like him gutting this house and then trying to rebuild it exactly the way it had been before, wouldn't it?

Well, the gutting analogy certainly works. Because that's how you felt when you realized she really meant it. So why should you believe she's done a 180 now? Because of one night of sex?

Spectacular sex, yes, but then it always had been. There'd never been a doubt that they were explosive together.

He gave a sharp shake of his head. When it came to Sophia, he wasn't so good at compartmentalizing, but he needed to do it now. He shoved the mess aside and tried to simply focus on the next step. He went outside and found Officer Nguyen and told him what Caleb had said about where the crash had happened. Back inside, and not even looking at Sophia as she stood at the kitchen island, putting the small first aid kit she apparently carried everywhere back to rights, he called the Knights to tell them the immediate threat was over. Then called the shelter where Charlie's mother had been taken and told them the same.

Then he called Detective Benitez, intending to leave a message, but to his surprise at this hour, the man answered. He told him what had happened tonight and quickly relayed what he suspected about how Webber had found them.

"I think that warrants another visit to Ms. Miller," Benitez said, and Gideon heard the undertone of steely anger in his voice. "And I won't be waiting until morning."

That made him smile in satisfaction. And when Sophia approached him—almost hesitantly, he noticed—he told her whom he'd called and why, and what Benitez's reaction had been.

"Good," she said succinctly.

"Feeling a bit bloodthirsty?"

"In that particular case, yes."

"The security chief at the hospital could have warned her not to cross you."

She met his gaze for a moment, then said quietly, "I'm only a coward in my personal life, it seems."

You are a truly amazing man, Gideon Colton. So amazing you scared me.

What she'd said earlier that day at the police station after they'd met with Charlie and the Knights echoed in his head now.

Had that really been it? Had she just been afraid? Afraid of what? To believe? That he meant what he said? That *they* were real?

His head was whirling. Rachel had once told him that was what a woman's mind was like a lot of the time. He hadn't quite believed her at the time, because it seemed like it would be exhausting.

He'd been right. It was.

"You can go home now," he said abruptly. He regretted the brusqueness when he saw pain flash in her eyes for a moment, but he needed time to think. Time, and space.

"Yes," she said, her voice oddly lifeless, "I suppose I can."

SOPHIA STOOD IN her living room, looking around at the cool, modern furnishings that seemed sadly lacking now. She much preferred the warmth and whimsy of Gideon's home, in particular that silly, sweet raccoon.

Gideon.

It still stung, days later, that he hadn't even brought her back here himself. No, when the officer on the scene offered to drive her after he'd taken her statement, since he was heading to the station to file his report and it was practically on the way, Gideon had seemed to jump at the chance. To avoid a long drive alone in his car with her? To avoid an awkward scene at her door? She didn't know. It didn't really matter. All that mattered was that he couldn't wait to be rid of her. She knew that from the simple fact that she hadn't seen or heard from him since.

She supposed her emotional state right now was her own fault, for allowing herself to hope she could somehow make up for how badly she'd hurt him. But she had to get a grip. She'd maintained her focus on her patients this week, because she had to, but the rest of her life was a shambles. Just scanning the living room, she knew the debris was obvious; the chaos in her mind had been echoed in her life. Discarded shoes here, empty coffee cups there, takeout bags for the food she'd had to force herself to eat over there. She supposed to some this was normal, this mess that would probably take less than two minutes to clear out, but for her it was nearly shocking.

And she didn't care. That was the oddest part of all. She, who had always demanded perfection in her surroundings, didn't even care. She was beginning to realize that she had been nursing, in the back of her mind, a hope that someday she could patch it up with Gideon. And now she knew that was a futile hope. That she had to let go of that dream.

Had to let go of him.

She just didn't know how.

THREE AND A half days.

In just a few days, Sophia had blown his life to pieces.

He'd tried to go back to where he'd been, focused on work. He'd looked in on Charlie and found him a different child, in the best of ways. He'd also checked on Ellen, who seemed to be holding strong to her vow to never give her brutal husband another chance. He had promised Detective Benitez he would testify, if necessary, about Courtney Miller's actions, on top of doing anything he could to help make sure Rick Webber stayed safely away from his wife and son. From the outside, it appeared he'd had a successful week.

From the inside, not so much.

Gideon sighed as he pulled to a halt at his mother's house. She'd asked him to come by this Saturday morning, saying she was thinking about remodeling her bedroom and wanted his advice, since, she'd said almost gushingly, he'd done such a beautiful job on his own home. Gideon wanted to say he couldn't, but just the chance that she might really do it—change that room in particular—was a huge thing. Not just that she could afford it now, thanks to her own success, but that she was willing to make the change. Maybe that would spread into other areas.

And so here he was.

She met him at the door with a smile and a cup of coffee, which he carried back to look at the room. It was the bathroom she was most focused on, saying she'd always wanted a big spa soaking tub and wondering if there was a way to make room. He studied the space for a moment.

"Can you afford to lose that?" he asked, pointing to a tall cabinet that was next to the smaller, existing tub.

"If it will get me my tub, then yes."

"Should be doable then. And if we take it out, you'd also have a view to go with your new tub. I doubt you'll be able to match the flooring, so it'd have to have a surround to cover that."

"Actually, I'd like to replace that, too. I want a floor in here like you put in your kitchen. The heated one."

He smiled at her. "Liked that, huh?"

"It's brilliant," she declared. "So it's doable?"

"Sure you don't want to gut the whole thing and start over?"

"No, I just want my tub. And floor."

"Should be easy, then. Want me to do it?"

She blinked, looking surprised. "That's kind of you, Gideon, but I'm sure you have better things to do right now."

"Not a damned one," he said sourly.

She frowned. "But I thought you and Sophia…" Her voice trailed off.

He jammed his fingers through his hair. He needed a haircut but couldn't seem to find the energy. No, apparently he'd much rather sit and stare at a certain raccoon, practically unseeingly, for hours on end.

"I don't know, Mom. She…wants us to get back together, but…"

His mother studied him for a moment before saying quietly, "You're afraid to risk it?"

"She said all the right things. And more. She completely humbled herself and probably would have begged if things hadn't been so wild that night. But I don't know. I don't think I could take it if she changed her mind again."

"I don't blame you, after how badly she hurt you. But…"

"But what?"

She drew in an audible breath, shifted her gaze to the window that looked out over the open expanse of the backyard. Finally she spoke, rather unsteadily. "If you really, truly love her, Gideon, if there's a chance you can make it work…don't be like me. I've turned love away because I was afraid, after your father. Don't you do the same. Be careful, but if it's genuine, if it's real, it's too precious to throw away."

And then suddenly, abruptly, she was gone, leaving the room in a rush. Leaving Gideon standing there, staring out that same window but not really seeing it.

Did he have that much nerve?

Once he was back home, he tried to distract himself by planning what would be necessary to make the changes his mother wanted. But he always wound up back to what she'd said.

I've turned love away because I was afraid, after your father. Don't you do the same.

He spent the evening out on the patio again, trying to convince himself it wouldn't, couldn't be already full of unforgettable memories. Not after one evening with Sophia out there. But spring had lost the battle with winter tonight, and once the sun had set it was too cold to sit out there for long. And it was an effort not to believe it was simply cold because Sophia was gone.

He was in bed, staring into the darkness, before it belatedly hit him that in a way, he was feeling the same way Sophia had felt when she'd turned her back on what they had. She'd been afraid, just as he was now. And yet she'd been brave enough to try to fix it, to heal the damage.

Could he do any less?

When sleep finally came, it was restless. But in the morning, his hopes seemed to rise with the sun.

And somewhere down deep, he found the nerve.

Chapter Thirty-Four

When the heavy door knocker sounded, not loudly but insistently, Sophia wearily got out of the chair she was curled up in. She realized she looked like some ragamuffin, with her hair every which way and no makeup, wearing her oldest—and only—sweatpants and a T-shirt she usually only slept in, but she didn't really care. She was too exhausted to worry about it. It had taken everything in her to just get through the rest of the week, to see to the children who needed her. After that, there had been nothing left.

She was a bit groggy from lack of sleep and didn't even bother to check through the peephole, because she didn't have the energy to worry anymore. She figured it was probably the landscapers who maintained the row of townhomes, letting her know they'd be starting the spring cleanup soon; she'd seen their truck early this morning.

She pulled the door open. And stood there staring.

Gideon.

She didn't know how long she simply stood there, gaping, half wondering if she was imagining things. If she'd somehow wished him into being there, on her doorstep.

When she finally snapped out of it, she realized that, contrary to the weary image she'd confronted in the mirror this morning, he looked…wonderful. But then, he always had, to her.

"Going to let me in?" he finally asked, and she told herself not to read anything into his words.

Silently she stepped back to make way for him, mainly because she didn't know what else to do. She quashed the urge that suddenly seemed almost overwhelming, to go and tidy herself up; it didn't matter any longer what she looked like to him.

Belatedly a possible reason for his presence occurred to her. "Charlie? Is he all right?"

"Charlie is fine. He's doing great, in fact."

"And his mother?"

"She's holding fast. And before you ask, his father's been moved to the county jail."

She let out a breath of relief.

"And," he added, "Courtney Miller has been placed on administrative leave pending an investigation."

"Good," she said, unable to deny the satisfaction she felt at that.

"Now that we have that out of the way, I have a question for you and, depending on the answer, a request."

She stared at him. The brisk, businesslike tone seemed to exclude whatever the question was from the personal realm, and she couldn't imagine what request he could have for her. So she just waited.

And then he blasted her out of the water.

"Did you mean it?"

She blinked. "What?" she managed, barely, as she scrambled to keep hope from stirring.

"What you said. About us. That you—" for the first time, that businesslike tone wavered "—love me."

The jolt of those words nearly made her gasp. But then, in a tone as close as she could get to his, she said firmly, "Every word."

He let out a breath that sounded relieved. And that hope stirred despite her efforts.

"Good," he said. "It's important for kids to know their parents love each other."

Kids? Parents? Sophia stared at him, her pulse starting to race as that hope took off. Almost desperately, she strove for calm. And certainty. "What kids would those be?"

He held her gaze as if their eyes were truly locked together. "The ones we're going to give what you never had, and what I had taken away. The ones we're going to love with the intensity that we love each other." He waited a beat before he added, for the first time all the emotion she was feeling echoing in his voice, "Our kids."

That hope soared. He still hadn't even touched her, but there was no denying the meaning of what he'd said. She knew him well enough to know everything that came with the words he'd said. "Yes. Oh, yes, Gideon, I—"

She stopped as he held up a hand. "Now that request."

"Anything," she said, meaning it.

"Don't be too sure."

"Why? What's the request?"

He still held her gaze unflinchingly. "I want to meet your father."

THE HOUSE LOOKED pretty much as he'd expected it to. Big, formal and landscaped to within an inch of its life. He pulled into the long, curved driveway, wondering only half in jest if there would be a butler or at least a doorman.

Sophia had taken it better than he'd thought she would, in the end. Oh, at first she'd stared at him, tense, almost stunned. But he'd held her gaze, his jaw set, and after a moment he saw her tension shift to mere edginess. He guessed that was the best he was going to get when it came to Harold Jones.

"It's time," he'd told her. "I have my own piece to say, but so do you. It's long past due, Soph."

She'd started to scramble once she'd realized he meant right now, today. And he was proud of her when she called and said they'd be there by noon, not giving the man the option to say no. She'd spent the next hour in her bathroom, getting ready.

"For battle?" he'd asked.

"There are weapons and then there are weapons," she'd said, making him smile before she vanished.

He'd been so happy she was even able to joke about it that he'd been smiling the whole time, even as he resisted the urge to join her when he heard the shower start. No, this had to be settled first, before they could take their first steps on a new path.

She'd been quiet the entire drive, and he could tell her mind was working hard. Bracing herself for what was coming, he guessed, and he didn't interrupt the process.

But when they got there, before they got out of the

car, he turned, reached out, took her hands and said what he'd held back until now.

"You can do this, Sophia. You're one of the strongest women I've ever met. You've just never tried to be that here, in this house."

She didn't speak, and he saw her swallow. She lowered her gaze to their hands. Then he lifted one hand, reached out and tilted her chin up. Looked straight into the gorgeous hazel eyes that had haunted him for so long.

"I'll be right beside you all the way." And then he finally said what he'd once thought he would never say again. "I love you." He heard her breath catch and saw her eyes suddenly get moist. "I love you," he repeated. "I never really stopped."

She squeezed his other hand as if it were the only thing grounding her. And then, still without speaking, as if she had to save all her words for what was coming, she drew herself up straight and got out of the vehicle.

There was no butler, but there was a maid, who opened the door a little warily. "Doctor. Your mother is out, but your father's in his library," she said to Sophia.

"Does she always call you 'Doctor'?" he asked as they walked into the house that was no less elegant and perfect and spotless than he had guessed it would be.

"Yes. It's my father's preferred manner of address."

"Figures."

She led the way to the library, and it was as grand and impressive as he had expected as well. He wondered how many of the leather-bound volumes were there only for effect. Then again, perhaps the professor had read them all. But he spared it only an assessing glance, then focused on the man seated behind the expansive desk that could have graced some European palace.

Gideon had only seen pictures of Professor Harold Jones, and they had failed to capture the impressiveness of the man in person. His skin was nearly the same tone as Soph's, but his eyes were dark brown; that beautiful hazel had obviously come from elsewhere.

As they neared, he rose from behind his desk, looking rather imperious despite the fact that, at a guess, he was a couple of inches shorter than Gideon. His demeanor practically shouted he was above you, whoever you were, and you'd best know it.

Sophia introduced them nervously. She'd told him she'd never mentioned him to her father, knowing what his reaction would be to just the famous—and onetime infamous—name.

"Colton. Of *the* Colton family, I presume?"

"Correct."

"Your father put a friend of mine in prison, wrongly."

He heard Sophia make a little sound of surprise, but he didn't look at her. And he bit back the first words that rose to his lips. *You actually have friends?*

"My father put a lot of people in prison." He said it evenly, like one discussing ancient history. Which his father right now seemed to him—a small miracle in itself. "Including too many that didn't deserve to be there."

To his surprise, Professor Jones only nodded. "Your family's foundation also got him released."

"That's the goal. But I'm not here about anything to

do with that. I'm here about your daughter." He held the man's gaze, determined. "And about you."

Jones looked surprised. "Me?"

"Yes. I have some information for you."

The man frowned. "Such as?"

Gideon ticked off a rapid list. "One, I am in love with your daughter and am going to marry her. Two, you'd best get used to the idea, and if you can't be nice, we're going to do it anyway. And three, there will be no more impossible demands, or belittling when unfeasible perfection is not achieved."

Harold Jones stared at him silently, his eyes wide and his lips parted, as if he was speechless. Gideon guessed that did not happen often, so he counted it as a win. And he kept going.

"I would also recommend you wake up and realize what an amazing daughter you have. That you're not toweringly proud of her is a reflection on you, not her."

"How dare you?" Jones finally burst out.

"How dare I criticize you? Easy. You've earned it. Oh, and you'd better learn fast, too."

Sophia's father drew himself up rigidly. "Or what? You going to punch me?" he said sarcastically.

"Nope," Gideon said cheerfully. "I'm going to bring over the passel of kids we're going to have to play with their granddad. Oh, and probably a puppy or two, as well."

Professor Jones truly gaped at him then. Another win. But then the best win of all came.

Sophia burst out laughing.

"You mind your mouth," her father said, clearly furious.

She drew herself up straight. Gideon flashed her

a glance and a wink, and she smiled before turning back to her father.

"No more of this, Father. I'm an adult, and a very successful one, now on all fronts. So this will stop. I respect you. I admire many things about you. But love? You've never wanted nor invited that, so no, I can't say I do. I've discovered it doesn't appear—" she glanced at Gideon "—or disappear on command."

Gideon smiled at her, knowing what it had taken for her to confront this man who had overshadowed her entire life. She smiled back, and when she turned to face her father again, her tone was steady, strong and final.

"The bottom line here is that I won't subject another child to your demands for something impossible to achieve. You will have to earn the honor of knowing your grandchildren."

Shortly after she'd laid down her ultimatum, they left Jones standing there in silent shock. And with every step they took, Sophia's smile widened. And her step lightened until she was almost dancing. So much that by the time they reached the front door—where the maid opened the door for them with an unmistakably wide smile and a nod for Sophia—he couldn't resist any longer and pulled her into his arms for a long, deep, unbelievably sweet kiss.

"I love you, Gideon Colton," she said fiercely. "For so many reasons."

"I want a kiss for each one."

"Granted," she said, in a tone that matched her father's imperious voice so well he burst out laughing.

"We've got a lot to decide," he said as they got back in his car. "Starting with where we're going to live and how soon can we manage it." She went suddenly quiet. "Don't. Just say what you want, Sophia. No more hesitation or holding back."

"I never thought I'd say this, but I love the quiet and space of your place. And honestly, my place has never felt like a home any more than this—" she waved vaguely at the house vanishing behind them "—ever did. But your place, I think… I think I could even learn to relax there."

He remembered too well their many discussions about her apparent inability to do just that, relax. He'd hardly dared hope for this, that she'd want to live not just with him, but in the home he'd put so much heart and effort into.

"You're sure?" he asked, even as he called himself an idiot for giving her the chance to change her mind.

But she only smiled. "Sharing with Baba will be interesting. He looks like a bit of a troublemaker."

He cut loose every speck of happiness he'd been holding back. "Wait until you have to deal with the first puppy." He plunged forward. "And the first kid."

When she looked at him then, those hazel eyes were alight in a way he'd never seen before. And the excitement in her voice when she answered was undeniable.

"I can't. Wait, I mean. Right now I think I could do any-and everything else but wait."

"No more waiting, Sophia. For either of us."

They pulled out of the driveway and onto the road, heading away from an unhappy past and toward a future as bright as the Colorado sun.

* * * * *

COMING SOON!

We really hope you enjoyed reading this book.
If you're looking for more romance, be sure to
head to the shops when new books are
available on

Thursday 14th
April

To see which titles are coming soon, please visit

millsandboon.co.uk/nextmonth

LET'S TALK
Romance

For exclusive extracts, competitions
and special offers, find us online:

- facebook.com/millsandboon
- @MillsandBoon
- @MillsandBoonUK

Get in touch on 01413 063232

For all the latest titles coming soon, visit
millsandboon.co.uk/nextmonth

JOIN US ON SOCIAL MEDIA!

Stay up to date with our latest releases, author news and gossip, special offers and discounts, and all the behind-the-scenes action from Mills & Boon...

 millsandboon

 millsandboonuk

 millsandboon

might just be true love...

MILLS & BOON
MODERN
Power and Passion

Prepare to be swept off your feet by sophisticated, sexy and seductive heroes, in some of the world's most glamourous and romantic locations, where power and passion collide.

Julia James

PREGNANCY SCANDAL

MILLS & BOON
MODERN

Jennie Lucas

Chosen as the
SHEIKH'S ROYAL BRIDE

MILLS & BOON
MODERN

Kim Lawrence

A WEDDING
at the
ITALIAN'S DEMAND

MILLS

Sharon Kendrick

The
SHEIKH'S SECRET BABY

MILLS & BOON
MODERN

Eight Modern stories published every month, find them all

millsandboon.co.uk/Modern

MILLS & BOON
MEDICAL
Pulse-Racing Passion

Set your pulse racing with dedicated, delectable doctors in the high-pressure world of medicine, where emotions run high and passion, comfort and love are the best medicine.